THE AUDIBLE AMNESIAC

and other
LIZZIE BORDEN
GIRL DETECTIVE MYSTERIES

THE AUDIBLE AMNESIAC

and other
LIZZIE BORDEN
GIRL DETECTIVE MYSTERIES

Richard Behrens

NINE MUSES BOOKS

Nine Muses Books

New England, USA

LizzieBordenGirlDetective.com
NineMusesBooks.com

© 2018 Nine Muses Books
© 2018 Anna Brindisi Behrens

ISBN-13: 978-0-9912784-2-8

Cover art: Marc Reed, MarcReed.com
Interior Art pages xiv, 134, 258, 294, 304: Bob Askey, BobAskeyArt.com
Interior Art pages 76, 202, 230, 324, 334: Charles George, CharlesGeorge.net
Book design: Stefani Koorey, peartree-press.com

for Richard (1964-2017)

"...that has always been a mystery." —Lizzie A. Borden, 1892

Also by Richard Behrens

Lizzie Borden: Girl Detective
(2010, Pear Tree Press)

The Minuscule Monk
(2015, Nine Muses Books)

*The Audible Amnesiac and
Other Lizzie Borden, Girl Detective Stories*
(2018, Nine Muses Books)

Garden Bay Stories
(2018, Nine Muses Books)

Of Moons and Monoliths
(2018, Nine Muses Books)

Acknowledgments

Sincere gratitude to all those who contributed to Richard Behrens' GoFundMe page to make the posthumous publishing of his writing possible and fulfilling his wish to publish his completed Lizzie Borden, Girl Detective stories. A heartfelt thank you to Susan Behrens and Catherine Behrens, who masterfully edited Richard's stories. We also gratefully acknowledge talented interior illustrators Charles George and Bob Askey, and long-time friends Lorraine Gregoire for her kind introduction, Marc Reed for his beautiful cover design, and Stefani Koorey for her skillful book design and insightful prologue.

TABLE OF CONTENTS

FOREWORD

Richard Behrens came to me in 2008 with an idea. I had known him for about three years through the circle of historical interest in the Lizzie Borden story. He wanted to create a fictional character based on a real historic person and give her all the attributes of the great Nancy Drew. He said he wanted the person to be Lizzie Borden, before her infamy, while she was just a girl, and to endow her with the intelligence, cunning, and reasoning ability of Sherlock Holmes. She would be a crime-solving Victorian living in Fall River, Massachusetts. Instead of a Dr. Watson character to aid her in her mysteries, Lizzie would have as her sidekick one Homer Thesinger, boy inventor. And he decided to call this book *Lizzie Borden, Girl Detective*.

At the time, I was publishing an online/print journal called *The Hatchet: Journal of Lizzie Borden Studies* as well as running an online forum dedicated to the case, Fall River, and Victorian America. As a publisher, Richard asked me to produce his first book in what he envisioned as a series, possibly a grand collection of short stories—all with the same premise of Lizzie Borden fighting and solving crime in her community.

I was not only amused and delighted, I must admit I egged him on in his creative ideas, sharing ideas for future exploits. Soon we began a close working friendship that would last for the rest of his very young life.

You cannot read any story by Richard in his Lizzie Borden, Girl Detective genre without falling for her and rooting for her success. This Lizzie Borden is quite timeless. She is smarter than those around her, more sure of herself than her gender allows, fearless in her quest for the truth, and able to move about polite society with ease and abandon.

I suppose the very best thing about his creation is that we so wish that this was how Lizzie Borden actually was. We want her to be so eager to solve these crimes that when her own tragedy befalls, she is able to see beyond the hopelessness of her loss to determine the guilty party or parties. But, alas, that was not history.

These stories in this volume are most pleasing to read for they are like mini-time-travel machines—you are seriously transported to the years between 1868 and 1881, with all of the vernacular, historical accuracy, and atmosphere of a Victorian Fall River. But the very best part of every story is the plausibility that manifests in the tales. It could have been like this, as it feels right. A great feat for any writer, and a stunning achievement of one Richard Behrens.

Stefani Koorey
Fall River, Massachusetts
July 2018

INTRDUCTION

You hold in your hands the work of one of the most creative, humorous, loving, and descriptive writers that I have had the privilege of knowing.

Every book is an adventure and a mystery. Lizzie Borden, Girl Detective is a character who comes alive in every story. She is not afraid of anything if it helps her to solve the mystery that is put before her. The stories are so well written you can close your eyes and see, hear, and feel her surroundings.

I surely miss my dear friend. However, when I pick up his work I feel he is close at hand again with his smile, laughter, and sense of humor.

So reader, be prepared for an action-packed story, from chase scenes that land you in all kinds of locations, to grand finales with the solving of another mystery.

The first official fan,

Lorraine Gregoire

The Audible Amnesiac

The Caterpillar and Alice looked at each other for some time in silence: at last the Caterpillar took the hookah out of its mouth, and addressed her in a languid, sleepy voice.

'Who are You?' said the Caterpillar.

This was not an encouraging opening for a conversation. Alice replied, rather shyly, 'I-I hardly know, Sir, just at present— at least I know who I was when I got up this morning, but I think I must have been changed several times since then.'

—Lewis Carroll, *Alice's Adventures in Wonderland*

April, 1881. Fall River, Massachusetts.

The Thesinger Box

In an upper-floor bedroom of a staid Greek Revival house on Second Street in the heart of Fall River's downtown district, a dour-faced woman named Emma Borden stood by her dresser eyeing with great suspicion the fainting sofa against the western wall. Resting on its embroidered surface was a medium-sized wooden box whose ornate panels hosted embossed astrological symbols. The box's presence was proof that her sister Lizzie Borden had been using her room as a makeshift office for her consulting business, which in Emma's mind was little more than a passing fancy. In fact, the idea that a young woman in Fall River could be a criminal detective was a mad delusion.

Emma's hands curled into fists by the side of her dark muslin skirt; her cheeks puffed until they blushed. She strode toward her sister's bedroom door, which happened to be inside her own room, and listened intently at the silent wood paneling. From inside the smaller bedroom came mutterings which did not seem to be her sister's voice. In fact, it sounded like a man.

Outrage upon insult! Was Lizzie scandalously entertaining a suitor in her own father's house? In her own bedroom? In her own sister's bedroom? Emma leaned in closer. The voice was distinctly male but very strained, as if the speaker was shouting into a piece of piping that clipped his voice into a pitched squeal.

Emma rapped a knuckle against the door and the voice stopped in mid-speech.

"Lizzie!" she snapped. "Open this door!"

For a moment, there was silence, as if her sister had the audacity to pretend she wasn't there. Emma turned the knob and found that the bolt had been applied.

"This is my room," came a soft reply from inside. "As long as I stay behind this door I am in no violation of your privacy."

"Then what is this box thing doing on my sofa!" Emma shouted. "It looks like an organ grinder box from a medicine show."

After a great big hush, the bolt drew back and the door hissed open to reveal Lizzie Borden's squat form, her brown hair pulled back from her round face and large gray-blue eyes.

"What have you done with my box?" she asked quickly, betraying concern.

"I've done nothing with it. But it sits there in my private space. And I'm not even sure whether it's wholesome. You have some very peculiar friends who manufacture most peculiar things."

"It's a trick," Lizzie said, her face relaxing. "Homer Thesinger built a magic trick."

"Homer Thesinger," Emma wheezed. "He's the worst of them all. Remember he was the one who blew up that tree in his own backyard when he was distilling nitroglycerin. For all we know, that box could be an anarchist's bomb."

"Nonsense," Lizzie declared, then waltzed across the room and heaved the box up into her arms. She fiddled with the latches and opened the two flaps, one of which resided on the top and one which swung down from the side. She angled it towards Emma to show her its empty interior. "Nothing," was how she described it.

Emma peered into the box with a scrunched face then glowered at her sister with lingering suspicion. Lizzie snapped the two doors shut and patted the side with a thump of confidence.

"Why would he make an empty box?" Emma asked persistently. "It's not proper enough for anything I can think of. Jewelry, hats. It could be a cigar humidor but it would have to be refitted."

"It's a receptacle for anything you please," Lizzie said, swinging open the door on the top. She reached in, and with a single deft gesture, pulled out what seemed at first to be a handkerchief, but then expanded into a full-blown rose-pink wrapper. It was elaborate with fluffy laces and ruffles and bows, not the Puritan vestments that Emma was so accustomed to wearing. Lizzie's arm pulled upwards over her head to accommodate the size of the article.

Emma's hands reached for her mouth as she emitted an inarticulate scream. Her brand new wrapper was being drawn from what had moments before been an empty box. It was a betrayal of her senses.

"That's mine!" was all she could muster, and wrenched the clothing from Lizzie's hand with a savagery that surprised even herself. Her worst fear had been realized. Lizzie had violated her privacy to a most humiliating degree. It could not have been worse if her bloomers had been produced from the Thesinger Box.

Lizzie chuckled and folded up the box, pressing it down on the sofa and holding out comforting hands for Emma. "I apologize for the effect, but it was too good not to perform. The box is a trick, Emma. There's a mechanism inside that gives the illusion that it's empty. A slanted mirror. You can see if you wish."

Emma clutched her wrapper, pressing it to her trembling lips. "Get out! Remove yourself from my room." Lizzie slouched in defeat and started for the door. Emma gasped and pointed at the box. "And take that with you. I never want to see you again. Move out of this house immediately. Go to some monastery and remove yourself from the world, you beast! And the same goes for Homer Thesinger. I don't care how much research money he needs from Father, he is not welcome here. He is dangerous."

"A monastery," Lizzie remarked, relishing the word. "Not a bad suggestion. I will take this up with Father. I am certainly not appreciated here."

Emma's face slackened as she stroked her wrapper and the blood rushed from her cheeks. "Fine," she grunted. "You can stay here, but you are never to use this room again for your detective agency, or whatever you call it."

"I will set up shop in the guest room," Lizzie said. "It will no longer be any of your affair."

Emma nodded then glanced anxiously towards Lizzie's bedroom. "And you are not to have any visitors in there," she commanded.

"I never have, and I never will," Lizzie protested.

"Then why did I just hear a voice? Plainly it was a man. I heard it through the door."

Lizzie held out a palm towards the room, encouraging Emma to take a look. The dour-faced sister walked slowly towards the smaller room, clutching her wrapper and murmuring nervously. She peered into the small space, surveying the dresser, the full length mirror, the single bed and the nightstand, the small bookcase overstuffed with volumes. She dipped her knees and tilted her head to see under the bed draping.

"Nothing," Lizzie said, oddly echoing her earlier performance.

"You have turned your whole room into a Thesinger Box," Emma declared. "If you lift the roof a man will emerge, I have every faith."

"Nonsense," Lizzie declared. "Your imagination is hyperbolic! There is no man in my room."

"Get out," Emma said through strained lips. "Leave."

As Lizzie turned, failing to resist a silent wink to her strained sister, a harsh cry came from the hall stairs. The pained voice crossed the landing and snaked into the space between the two sisters. "Lizzie!" came the shrill alarm. The spell between them broke, and they bounded to the hall landing where they confronted a rather flustered Abby Borden, their stepmother. The hefty woman had climbed to the top stair in the time it had taken the sisters to react.

"Mother," Emma said plainly.

"Mrs. Borden," Lizzie followed.

"There are two visitors to see you," Abby announced. "One of them is that Homer fellow. He's brought someone with him, a most abnormal man! He took my hand and asked me who I was, and then he asked me who he was. Is this normal behavior, I ask you? What kind of diseased minds are you attracting here, Lizzie? You simply must—"

"Ah!" Lizzie said delightedly, pushing past her back into Emma's room. "I will receive them in the parlor. I need a moment to change my wrapper."

Abby Borden sighed. "Really Lizzie, this is a private home, not a police station. Tell Homer that he can't just—"

"Yes, Mrs. Borden," Lizzie said closing the door to her room with

a polite bang. Emma and Mrs. Borden assessed each other with struggling eyes and remained so until Lizzie returned, pressing her hair into
place and coughing into her fist. She had replaced her morning dress
with a rose-pink wrapper almost identical to the one that Emma was
supporting in her tense hands. This insult brought a grunt from Emma
who quickly hid her wrapper behind her in a flash.

"You didn't hear a word I said," Abby said flatly to her stepdaughter.

"No," Lizzie replied. "I didn't. Now excuse me as I have to see
my clients."

She made a deft waving motion to force Mrs. Borden against the
wall of the stairwell and pushed past her with a purposeful march down
into the first floor.

Abby and Emma climbed down the staircase after Lizzie to the
front hallway of the house where a tall thin man in a black frock coat,
holding an aged straw boater, his angular face sporting a trim jaw bristle
stood under the architrave of the parlor from where he had just emerged.
As they approached he closed the door behind him. His black beaded
eyes stared alarmingly at his new audience.

"Father!" Lizzie choked. "What have you done to my clients?"

"Is that what they are?" Andrew Borden asked almost in a whisper.
"I thought they were stunned patients from the nervous hospital. I don't
know which is worse: Rip van Winkle or that man without a name!"

"Get them out of here now!" Abby shouted over Lizzie's shoulder.
"We have no need for an escaped lunatic in our home."

"Lunatic?" Lizzie asked. "What basis do you have to consider him
a lunatic?"

"Go in and see for yourself," Andrew said, tapping the door. "But I
warn you, this man's missing a few yarn spindles."

Lizzie blinked and pouted, then turned to her sister. "You saw my
bedroom transform into a Thesinger Box. You predicted it would magi-
cally produce a man, and in fact it has. Not just any man, but the creator
of the box himself, Homer Thesinger. Let me see what this is all about."
She motioned her father aside and then pressed on the door. Turning
to her family she took in their anxious faces, their shaking hands and
spoke earnestly, "This is a private matter. Please retire to your rooms."

Mr. and Mrs. Borden, along with their daughter Emma, let out
with fresh gasps at Lizzie's remark as the young woman pushed open
the parlor room door and entered to greet her new client.

A MIND REMOVED

To Lizzie's surprise, Homer Thesinger was asleep on the couch, snoring sonorously, his bowler hat slumped over his brow. The young inventor who had joined Lizzie in many adventures looked weak and thin, his hands rubbed black with charcoal dust. Traces of the dust wove patterns on his lower sleeves. She could take in at a glance that he had been awake all night, judging largely from his exhaustion and from the deplorable condition of his wrinkled and creased clothing. She also deduced that he had been working on his iron-ore extraction project, simply because the stains on his hands could not have been caused by anything other than grinding charcoal to roast with iron pyrite to extract gold dust. In fact, it was plausible that he was employing arsenopyrite, a rock that gave off dangerous vapors when heated with coal. The poor boy was poisoning himself, which accounted for his inability to stay awake. As he snored, he would wheeze and twitch his nose, then rub it with his stained fingers before slumbering again.

But none of that was important for the present. Seated next to Homer on the couch was another man, thin and nervous, with a pointed face, a triangular chin, and a peaked brow that sported two bushy eyebrows that crawled towards each other with almost pained reluctance. Balanced on his nose was a pair of pince-nez spectacles while a trembling mustache almost obscured his small mouth. The man was swathed in a tweed jacket that had all the signs of domestic neglect as it was missing buttons on the sleeve, had threads frayed at the edges of the pockets and lapels, but which also whispered of an unusually penurious nature. He had not yet removed his gloves, one hand rested on a walking stick made from stained cherry wood with a polished ivory handle, and his congress boots looked as if he had just purchased them from a men's dressing shop. Other than the fact that he was a Freemason, had recently walked a dog that was covered in light brown fur, and was currently enduring a competition between his wife and his housemaid to keep up his appearance, Lizzie could tell nothing else about him.

The man's eyes twinkled when he first saw Lizzie, but then his face slackened into indolence as if his expectations, brightened by her entry, were now diminishing. "Hopeless," he muttered in a wheezy voice. "It will never work."

"What will never work, Mr.—" Lizzie waited for him to complete her sentence.

"That is the problem," he said. "I do not know my name. When you entered, I thought I knew you. But I think that of everyone I meet nowadays. Everything is so familiar and yet I cannot recognize anything."

His voice, despite its thinness, stirred Homer into awareness. The boy inventor shook his checks, grabbed at his tussled hair, and swallowed as if to remove a bitter taste from his mouth, no doubt some residue from his late night experiments. "Who?" he said as if his mind was starting to open its lids. "What?" he continued.

"Exactly," his companion lamented. "Not only am I plagued by the 'who'? But also the 'what'? What am I? I would forswear the 'who' if I could just ascertain the 'what'?"

"Oh," Homer said, realizing where he was. "Yes…Lizzie…allow me to introduce my new friend."

"What is his name?" Lizzie asked amusedly. "Surely you must—"

"I call him Policeman Lot for lack of a better term, because when I first met him he was babbling those words."

"Were you?" Lizzie asked, taking a seat just opposite their couch.

"I don't remember," the man said, rubbing his chin. "Does that mean I'm a law officer? I hardly know. I can't remember."

"When did you first meet him?" Lizzie asked Homer. "For if I am not mistaken, you have been spending all night in your barn laboratory working on your ore extractor, and this man you call Policeman Lot has been up since dawn getting shaved in a tonsorial parlor and buying a new pair of congress boots. Unless you have accompanied him on his shopping excursion, I would estimate that you met him almost two hours past."

Homer smiled wryly and tapped open his pocket watch. He nodded then muttered, "How did you know about the ore project? Oh, yes, the stains. And I suppose he has particular dust on his shoes that tell you he has been on North Main Street."

"On the contrary," she snipped. "It is the lack of dust on his shoes that tell me the story. That plus the advertisement in yesterday's Herald that there will be a shoe sale at Tyler's this very morning, doors opening at eight o'clock. Added to that is the left-handed style of his chin shave that could only have been produced by the barber on Columbia Street, which also gives me a good judge of the distances that he covered."

Lot tapped Homer's forearm and admitted, "You are right, she is uncanny. I couldn't even have told you that."

Homer smiled at Lizzie. "He seems to lose his memory every half hour. Soon you'll have to introduce yourself all over again."

"How singular," Lizzie said, staring at him with renewed interest.

"Yes," Mr. Lot said glumly. "My earliest memory is being in this room meeting Mr. Thesinger and hearing him describe your unique talents. I am delighted that such a remarkable mind will be dedicated to solving the problem of my identity."

"I have heard of such a condition," Lizzie said, tapping her temple. "There have been reports from Europe and a famous case in Philadelphia from earlier in the century. I consider this to be the ultimate challenge, and a mystery refreshingly devoid of any criminal activity."

"That we can't say." Mr. Lot shifted uncomfortably on the couch. "I am also filled with a tremendous dread, an anxiety of drastic urgency. My instincts tell me that I am in danger, that someone I am hiding from will find me and damage me. I cannot see the face of the person pursuing me, but I can see a shadow coming up a staircase. I am filled with the most awful feeling, that my most intimate secrets will be exposed and I will be destroyed."

"Are these the only impressions that survive your recurring amnesia?"

"No. Well, excepting one. I can clearly see the face of a monkey, some sort of howler creature from the jungles of South America. It is laughing at me, as if I am an object of great ridicule."

"You have been laughed at by a monkey?" Homer said, surprised.

"But it is not just a monkey. It is wearing a tricorn hat."

"Tricorn?" Lizzie gasped. From the wide grin appearing on her lips, Homer could tell she was taking the bait. This was a mystery that she could relish.

"Like in the war of independence," Mr. Lot explained. "And he has on a printed silk jacket and is holding a lace handkerchief."

"Not like any monkey I've seen," Homer quipped. "Perhaps he is conflating two exhibits he saw at the menagerie."

"No," Lizzie said. "I sense that there is an even more meaningful explanation. But enough of that, we are poised at the beginning of a strange journey. We have a man who clearly is married, lives in comfortable middle class conditions, doted on by his wife, harassed by his housemaid, and sports a rather expensive cherry and ivory walking stick. He can afford the finest of clothing, clear enough from his habit of buying a new pair of boots when the old ones get dirty, and yet wears his jackets until they fray. There are odd contradictions here."

Mr. Lot looked at his stick as if seeing it for the first time, and then pulled at the threads wafting from his jacket. "Oh," he said. "So I do! Perhaps I should go buy a new jacket." He gingerly patted his pockets. "I don't suppose anyone here can lend me some money. I fear I have come *sans sous.*"

"And with a knowledge of French customs," Lizzie added.

"You know so much about me," Mr. Lot said hopefully. "Can you tell my identity?"

"Nothing other than you are a member of a Masonic lodge or so the ring on your left hand informs me, and at some point this morning, after putting on your jacket but before buying your congress boots, you took a small dog, perhaps a Pomeranian, for a walk."

The man checked the ring and the hairs on his overcoat with great interest then turned his attention back to Lizzie as if he were profoundly engaged by a doctor's diagnosis.

"Perhaps it was on this sojourn that you had your morning shave on Columbia Street by a left-handed barber, I would say Samuel Borden who is just this afternoon taking off on a vacation to the wilds of Maine. Hence the haste with which he missed some patches of growth on your right chin."

Mr. Lot turned to Homer and grinned. "She's very good! What did you say her name was?"

Before Homer could reply, Lizzie resumed. "Now if we confine our search to this city, we can use various techniques of a mental nature to distill from these clues, as Homer distills gold dust from pyrites, where you would live, who you would have as associates, and make the rounds to ascertain an identification. Your Masonic lodge is a good place to start, or Sammy Borden himself, whom you may have employed on a regular basis at a time when you knew your real identity. I don't see this case as particularly complicated, nor do I expect it to take very long, and since it is Homer who has brought you to me and he is a dear friend of mine, I will even perform this investigation gratis, expecting nothing in return but a good evening's banter over a delightful home cooked meal, good company, and a mug of medicinal syrup water. Eh, Homer? Doesn't that sound grand?"

"Not complicated?" Homer asked. "Lizzie, I don't think you understand what's going on here."

"Don't I?" Lizzie's smile had turned sour.

"I met this man outside the police station. He was part of a crowd that was gathering to get news of the murder."

"Murder?" Lizzie recoiled.

"Yes, the murder of Sam Borden. He was found dead in his barber shop not two hours ago. His throat was slashed with his own razor."

The room fell into a painful silence as Lizzie lost her sense of direction. She was swooning, watching the walls turn about the ceiling. Homer raced to her side and held her in position as she slowly regained her senses.

When she had found her balance, she stared at the man seated on the couch opposite her, assessing him with a fresh set of eyes. Now his ordinary face seemed sharpened to the point of treachery. His gaze, once blank and neutral, now seemed coarse and cruel. Perhaps the sinister shadow in his memory was himself, and he was on the verge of confronting his own guilt, his own sins. Lizzie's instinct was to call out to her father, charging it to him that he would confront this beast and save her from this unpleasant feeling of danger.

"Mr. Lot," Lizzie said shakily. "Do you have any idea what happened to the barber Mr. Borden?"

"Who?" Mr. Lot responded. "I'm sorry but have we met before?"

"We have been in discourse for about ten minutes," Lizzie assured him.

"Have we?" the man said alarmingly. He turned to Homer and gasped at his face. "Oh dear," he said. "It's happened again."

"What has happened again?" Homer asked desperately.

The man thought for a moment, blinked, and then said with all sincerity, "I don't know."

Lizzie's palpated breathing had reached a zenith, but she summoned enough energy to blurt out the only words that she could articulate:

"Father! Call Dr. Bowen!"

THE DOCTOR'S DILEMMA

Dr. Seabury Bowen performed a thorough examination on the man who had been introduced to him as Mr. Policeman Lot. The exam was conducted privately in the doctor's consulting room in his house on Second Street, just across from the Bordens. That peculiar family had appeared *en masse* on his doorstep at eleven o'clock in the morning with a jittery and obscure stranger buried under a frock jacket to disguise his features. On his doorstep, they huddled about him as if shielding him from the gaze of any passersby, creating the effect of mystery that always seemed to be associated with the daughter Lizzie.

The stranger was in perfect health, and other than the fact that his mind was almost completely erased and that he suffered tremendous anxiety, and that the Bordens had told Dr. Bowen in secret that the man may have murdered a Fall River tradesman that very morning, the patient was in good spirits and wanted to drink a glass of water because his throat was dry.

"Thank you," Mr. Lot said as Dr. Bowen handed him the glass. "I appreciate all you have done, Dr.—" The man paused and stared into space. "What was your name? Have we met?" Then he looked down at the glass. "Is this yours? Where am I?"

Dr. Bowen left the patient in his examination room and rejoined the Bordens in the parlor where his wife was entertaining them with accounts of their recent trip to the wilds of Maine. In fact, it had been in casual conversation with Dr. and Mrs. Bowen that Lizzie knew of the Barber Borden's plans to explore Mount Desert Island.

"We brought back spectacular views of the sea," she was saying joyfully. "I am having them put into an album but I can show you them in their unorganized state."

"Yes," Dr. Bowen said nervously, placing his hands on her shoulders, effectively silencing her. "The views can wait. I believe we have a serious dilemma on our hands."

"You mean the murderer in the other room?" Mrs. Bowen said with a dismissive wave. "Call the police and hand him over. We can't have odd men who don't know their names murdering our barbers. We've carved a civilization here in Fall River and we have to abide by the rules. Without the rules we'd have anarchy and we can't have that. Wouldn't want bombs going off in carriages and women demanding the vote, would we?" She waved a hand about at the potted plants, the decorative stained glass lamps, the ornate walnut furniture, the ormolu clock on the mantelpiece. "Civilization," she said. "And my dear honey of a husband eliminating all diseases which we all know come from the Red Man. Such savages."

"Perhaps this is a discussion for another day," Dr. Bowen winced. "Please my darling, there must be a gin game you can sit in on."

She arose and bowed to the Bordens who stared at her with blank faces. "Thank you for your company. I'll have those views for you next week. We must have supper together."

When she had gone, Andrew Borden let out with a prolonged "Bah!" and then shouted, "Bowen, I can't be paying for this exam. I didn't approve of this man's entry into my own house, far less of this senseless visit. I say we follow your wife's advice and hand him over to the police."

"Yes," Dr. Bowen said. "I do believe that would be the correct course of action. But I'm haunted by the thought that he may be guiltless and that his extraordinary condition, one that I have never before seen in my professional career, would prejudice the investigators against him and he would have no defense. After all, the only evidence we have that he had anything to do with barber Borden was Lizzie's observation of the bad shave on the right side of his chin. That is hardly enough to get a man arrested."

"Don't forget he was at the police station trying to get information about the murder," Homer said pointedly. "When I first saw him he was at the back of the crowd outside the station and was agitated and quite determined to speak to the police."

"Perhaps he knew something, or had witnessed the tragedy," Dr. Bowen suggested.

"That's what I assumed," Homer confessed. "But when I pressed him to tell me what he knew, he could only mutter words that to me sounded like 'Policeman' and 'Lot'. On further examination I discovered that he didn't even know who he was, or why he was at the station. I believe at that very moment, he went through the amnesia transition, his first since the murder, and all his knowledge was lost. His mind is a bit of a *tabula rasa*, a slate wiped clean waiting for the next set of instructions."

"He clearly knows something," Andrew Borden said. "I don't know why we are wasting our time. If we're not going to get him arrested, let's at least dump him on the City Marshal and go about our business."

"Yes," Mrs. Borden said. "This *is* none of our business. Homer has done us a great disservice by getting us involved."

"Homer does us nothing but disservice," Emma sneered. "He's a horrid young man!" She stamped her boot against the rugged floor as if trying to eliminate an insect.

"Steady on," Homer said, putting up his palms. "I don't want to be involved in this any more than all of you combined. I was in the middle of tinkering with my ore extractor and now my concentration is all in pieces."

"Imagine our position," Abby Borden countered. "I had plans with my family and shopping to do. We may not be trying to invent new-fangled machinery but our chores are important."

"I don't invent things!" Homer said, shaking a fist. "I'm an electro-machinician and a general engineer. I tinker with existing inventions to improve them, to optimize their efficiency."

"Ore extracting," Andrew puzzled. "How is that useful to us, in this day and age?"

"I'm using electromagnets! It will revolutionize the industry, save thousands of dollars per load."

"What difference does it make," Dr. Bowen interrupted. "We have only a brief amount of time to fit these puzzle pieces together and make a decision. Do we or do we not hand the man over to the police."

"Why is this even a debate?" Andrew scowled. "The man is not our charge."

"What man?" came a voice from the parlor door. Policeman Lot was standing fully swathed in his overcoat and bowler and was twirling the handle of his cane, examining it meticulously as if it contained a great mystery.

"You," Lizzie said bluntly. "We are trying to solve the puzzle of you."

"I am glad of it," the man said and tipped his hat as if following a protocol that was so embedded in his habits that he could not feign to do otherwise. As he placed his hat back on his head, he stared at his hand, extended the thumb and gazed at it perplexedly. To everyone's surprise he hopped into a strange position, placing his feet at right angles to each other and then stepped forward awkwardly while fanning the fingers of his hand before him at chest level.

"Yes," he was saying. "I believe this is the correct form. Is that not true, Brothers?"

"What is this tomfoolery?" Andrew asked hastily. "Is he from a music hall act?"

"No," Lizzie said, staring fixedly at his gestures. She stepped forward before him and made some hand gestures of her own. He watched them with mounting excitement and then performed a few more hand gestures.

"What is the password?" Lizzie asked in a hushed mannish tone.

Mr. Lot's face brightened as if a great calm was coming over it. He was about to speak when Lizzie pressed her fingers against his lips. "Silence," she said. "No need for now, we can always sign later."

"What is the meaning of this?" Dr. Bowen asked. "Lizzie, what do you know about these steps and signs?"

"Clearly, Dr. Bowen," Lizzie chuckled, "you are not a member of the Fall River Lodge of the Ancient Order of the Masonic Odd Men."

"Almighty!" came the cry from Abby Borden. "The Odd Men! I have had enough! Cast him into the street, he is not worth the dust on our boots."

"The Odd Men," Dr. Bowen repeated, then displayed understanding. "The Odd Men! The Ancient Order! They are not recognized as regular Masons but they do have a Lodge on Ferry Street. They are odd indeed. Believe in a golden egg that will heal all maladies. Yes, this is starting to make sense. He is remembering the signs and steps of his degree in the Ancient Order of the Masonic Odd Men."

"Am I?" Mr. Lot said, flexing his hand. "It seems as if my hands and feet are doing all the remembering for me. By the way, have we met? Do you know who I am?"

"Later," Lizzie promised, then pondered deeply with her fingertips to her temples. "When I first met this man I had made several deductions about his home situation based upon his clothes and his grooming. The addition of a secret brotherhood may change some of those observations. For instance, the ring on his finger. It is distinctly Masonic."

Dr. Bowen lifted Mr. Lot's hand by the wrist and examined the jewelry. "The Odd Men adapt many Masonic symbols. This ring bears the Masonic square and compass, a pictograph that is allegorical for their morality. But the Masonic pictograph has at its center the letter G presumably for God. This ring depicts the letter A."

"And what does A stand for?" Lizzie asked, gazing at Mr. Lot.

"How the blazes do I know!" he rattled. "By the way, who are you people? Where am I?"

"You've had another one of your *tabulae rasae*," Lizzie explained. "If we have to explain everything that has happened today every time you make that transition we shall waste your time and ours."

"But I am clearly in a bind," he said, gazing wearily at the ceiling "I fear a shadow moving over my being, ready to pounce and devour me."

"Yes, we know," Andrew Borden sighed. "Confound it; this man belongs either in a jail or an asylum. I say we hand him over to the Marshal and be done with it."

"The Marshal," the man said, gripping his fist upwards. "I must tell the Marshal! Yes, that's right." He turned to his silently staring audience and asked meekly, "Who is the Marshal? I seem to have forgotten that one."

"Interesting," Lizzie said. "His *tabulae rasae* are getting closer and closer, but a curious inverse ratio is also occurring. He is starting to retain more and more detail. First the signs and steps of his Odd Men degree, now the City Marshal. Perhaps after a few more *tabulae rasae* he will remember more information that can help us solve this mystery."

"One moment," Mr. Lot said, stiffening his spine. "I'm standing here, and I'm a person. You are talking about me as if I were a specimen on a slide for a scientist to observe patterns of behavior! I resent being reduced to an object of observation. I am a person! A person!" Just then a curious shade glided across his face as he stared blankly at Dr. Bowen. "Excuse me," he said. "But can you tell me who I am? I seem to have forgotten!"

"Oh I have had enough of this!" Emma Borden shouted, and wagged a finger in her sister's face. "Your delusion that you are some sort of detective has hurt this family enough. This man is not our responsibility. Father is correct: we should hand him over to the Marshal as soon as possible and wipe our hands clean. I'm sorry the local barber has been murdered, but I'm sure the proper law enforcement officials will discover the killer and bring him to justice. It's none of our affair."

"I feel the same way," Abby Borden thundered. "I've heard of these Odd Men and they are a breeding ground for vice. The men who inhabit their ranks drink alcohol to excess and beat their families. They frequent houses of assignation. They wassail to all hours of the night."

"And they conspire to rule the city!" Andrew Borden added. "They infiltrate City Hall and bring their cronies into power. Lizzie, you don't know the stories I've heard at the club, how these devils with their secret handshakes and their hooded meetings declare their allegiance to chaos!"

"It's all speculative," Lizzie insisted. "There is no proof that they are anything but fraternal brothers looking for an evening at the Lodge to trade some stock tips and argue over elections. What harm do they cause?"

"Ask Samuel Borden," Abby Borden snarled. "Ask the man who has been murdered how benign the Odd Men are!"

Lizzie froze, not being able to produce a response to her stepmother's rhetoric. Before she could recover herself, there was a heavy pounding at the front door. Dr. Bowen ran for the hallway just as the sound of his wife's voice welcoming a visitor was heard from where they stood in the parlor. The Doctor returned ashen-faced.

"It's the Marshal!" he announced. "Quick! We must hide this man!"

Mr. Lot grinned and stepped forward extending his hand. "The Marshal! I have to tell him something!"

"What?!" Dr. Bowen asked desperately. "What do you have to tell the Marshal?"

The man grimaced and huffed his cheeks. "I don't know."

"Then get out of sight and be silent!" Dr. Bowen pushed Mr. Lot toward Homer who led him impatiently into the doctor's surgery. All was silent just as Mrs. Bowen ushered the Marshal into the house. The police official was broad and barrel-chested, mustached, with a red beefy face and gray eyebrows. He was dressed in his official tunic and white gloves. Trailing behind him was a thin whispery policeman holding his helmet in his hands. His face was clean-shaven and crooked and Lizzie could tell that he was feeling out of place, shuffling in his place, nervous about being in a prominent man's household.

"Seabury," the doctor's wife said delightedly. "Look who has come to pay us a visit! Shall I bring out the Calabrian tea service?"

"Not now, dear." Dr. Bowen had composed himself and was standing by the mantle as if he had been there all along. "Go back to your chores." And the woman, smiling broadly, withdrew from the room.

"Mr. Borden!" the Marshal remarked upon seeing Andrew with more than a hint of surprise. "And Lizzie! Just the ticket! Officer Periwinkle here came round to find you and was told by a street vendor that you had come here to see the Doctor."

"A vendor?" Lizzie asked.

"Yes, a fruit cart just in front of your house. He spoke in a Polish accent, isn't that right Officer Periwinkle."

"Correct!" the officer said, snapping to attention. "I inquired upon the first instance the nature of his business and he told me that he bought imported fruit for resale for the benefit of his trade."

"That is not relevant," the Marshal said through strained teeth. "The important information is that he saw the Bordens crossing Second Street and entering *en masse* into the home of Dr. Seabury Bowen. And why was that suspicious, Officer Periwinkle?"

The officer tilted his head as if encouraging something in his mind to roll into its proper place. "The action was suspicious because they were accompanied by an unidentified man who held his coat over his head so as not to be seen by passersby. Although the Pole was not a passerby but a man on a cart, and the cart was at the time decidedly stationary."

"Is that right Andrew?" the Marshal asked. "Were you escorting a man with a coat drawn over his head?"

"What are you asking me for?" Andrew hissed. "I'm Bowen's neighbor. I can come see him any time I want. And what business is it of yours to come marching in here treating us so suspiciously as soon as we cross the street to visit a friend?"

"It is my business," the Marshal announced, "because the man with the coat over his head was not an ordinary man with a coat over his head. The Pole on the cart did not just observe a man with a coat over his head. He observed...well, tell them Officer Periwinkle what the man observed."

The officer cleared his throat. "He observed a man hiding his face in a coat, but there was occasion for the man's face to slip from the coat and reveal its true appearance. That appearance was clearly identical to the description of a man seen leaving the tonsorial parlor of one Samuel Borden not two and a half hours ago."

"And why is that face having left the tonsorial parlor so important on this particular day?" The Marshal rocked on his heels.

"On this particular day the proprietor of that tonsorial parlor has been murdered and that man seen hiding his face under his coat in the protective custody of the Borden family was the last man seen entering the tonsorial parlor before the murder. We have witnesses to that effect. Particularly the proprietor of the compounding pharmacy across the street; Mr. Buffington who was getting his hat blocked at—"

"That's enough Officer Periwinkle. Now tell them why you have summoned me, your Superior Officer, to 92 Second Street after interviewing the Polish fruit vendor and discovering the alleged protection of the suspect in the Borden murder by the Borden family?"

"Because we have reason to believe that the Borden family knows something about this affair that they are hiding from us law officers."

"Hang you Lizzie!" Andrew bleated. "Do you see what you've gotten us into?"

The Marshal frowned. "Andrew, is that a confession? Do you admit that you've harbored this fugitive from the law?"

"I confess nothing!" Andrew said, slumping into a sofa and running his fingers through his hair. "I am done with this."

Lizzie coughed uncomfortably. "Mr. Marshal, as you know I have been helping the Fall River police in many singular affairs and I feel that I have gained a good deal of trust with your department. I ask you to give me the benefit of the doubt in this affair as well."

"It is true," the Marshal admitted. "You have gained my trust over these past few years and there is many a guilty rogue in prison because of your dedication to the law. But this is a serious offense, Lizzie."

"I agree. And therefore I ask you to listen to me very carefully. There are circumstances here that have to be considered."

"What circumstances? I can't imagine what..."

Before the Marshal could finish, the door to the exam room creaked open and a very strange spectacle emerged, one that startled everyone, especially Lizzie. A man was standing in the door frame dressed in the exact clothing, bowler hat and overcoat as those worn by Mr. Lot. But it was not Mr. Lot. Beneath a dangling strip of velvet ribbon that had been sheared and pasted upon his upper lip, was the countenance of a very confused looking Homer Thesinger. The young man was staggering, his arms delicately outstretched and floating before him. He kicked the door shut behind him and walked as if in a somnambulist haze towards the Marshal.

"Who am I?" he muttered. "Where am I? I don't remember a thing. Perhaps I was in a barber shop. I don't recall what I did there, but I do know I went to the Bordens! Ah, here they are! Thank you for bringing me to the doctor but I feel fine now. I don't know what I would have done without Dr. Bowen's help."

"Homer Thesinger," the Marshal said, half with contempt.

"Yes, that's my name. When I awoke this morning, I went strange in the head. I cut up this ribbon and pasted it to my lip, and I tried to get it shaved at the barber shop."

The Marshal reached for the dangling silk and ripped it from Homer's mouth. The boy inventor grimaced and held his face with both his hands.

"You are trying to make me believe that Homer Thesinger was at the barber shop at the time of the murder," the Marshal asked, "and that he was the man that the Polish fruit vendor described to Officer Periwinkle?"

"I don't know," Homer said. "I don't remember what I did this morning."

The Marshal gazed down at the ragged strip in his hand, and then examined the overcoat that dangled about Homer, obviously one or two sizes too large. He heaved a sigh and stared at the ground.

"Lizzie," he said, breaking his silence. "I must talk to you in private about this nonsense. I can't believe for a moment this buffoon would be capable of slashing a man's throat in broad daylight, so I am willing to treat this sad display as a lighthearted farce. So can we proceed with a proper investigation of the murder of Samuel Borden?"

"With pleasure," Lizzie said, relieved and renewed. "Let us retire to 92 Second Street and I will be at your disposal for a consultation. My good thanks to Dr. Bowen for helping Homer with his bafflement."

"You're welcome," Dr. Bowen said listlessly.

"And my thanks to my own family for taking concern for him in his mania. Now that we are done here, I would like to thank Mrs. Bowen for her hospitality. Will you please convey my sincere sentiments, Doctor?"

"I shall," Dr. Bowen said, shifting his balance nervously.

"Now, Marshal, I am ready." Lizzie performed a slight curtsey, and as she arose there was a creak of a hinge and the door to the exam room opened once again. This time Mr. Lot, stuffed inside of Homer Thesinger's vest and overcoat, bareheaded and gloveless, wobbling without the aid of his cane, appeared in the door frame and motioned for the Marshal.

"Mr. Marshal," he said, his mustache trembling. "You are Mr. Marshal! Yes, I have something to tell you!"

The Marshal peered at Lizzie, his eyes narrowing. He marched up to Mr. Lot and pulled at his mustache, causing the man to yelp and rub his sore whiskers.

"Who are you?" the Marshal practically screamed.

"Ah!" Mr. Lot replied. "That's a very good question. Can you kindly tell me who I am? I'm afraid I have forgotten."

"Not another one," the Marshal said, his eyes steaming. "Alright, Mr. Nobody, what do you have to tell me that's so important."

Mr. Lot opened his mouth exuberantly, raised a hand with a pointed finger, flinched and then chomped his jaw shut.

"I'm afraid I have forgotten. Dear me, this is getting quite alarming."

FEET IN THE DUST

Without the body that had been removed an hour earlier, the

interior of the barber shop was a haunted landscape of scuffles, smeared footprints, scattered combs and scissors, clients' chairs turned in random directions, one liberally stained with drying blood. The mild odor of Macassar oil laced the air along with coconut and other flower oils. Several jars of the unguent were lined on a long shelf before the tall framed mirrors. Two reclining barber chairs, upholstered with leather and equipped with the new elevation levers, were regimented before the mirrors, empty vessels facing empty versions of themselves.

Samuel Borden had been of unusual height, earning him the nickname of Uncle Sam in the upstreet area. His corpse had been found reclined in one of his own chairs; bruising on his arms revealed that two assailants had held him down while a third methodically cut his neck. Spidery cracks in the glass casements in front of the chair indicated where his feet had kicked violently from the end of his long legs in an attempt to save his own life. The other two assailants had put up a fight, wrestling against Uncle Sam's ferocious stamina. The victim had nearly overtaken his attackers, as evidenced by indications that he had bolted to the front door and had been dragged back kicking to the barber chair.

All this Lizzie had read in the floor dust, from the drags and stamps that were so dramatic they were highlighted even in the presence of the policemen and coroners' prints that were almost as copious. Lizzie would have preferred a cleaner crime scene and a better floor from which to read the past scene, but fortunately the officials who had compromised the floorboards had unique booting of their own that could easily be distinguished.

As she studied the dust in the presence of the Marshal and Officer Periwinkle, two other officers were just outside the shop's front entrance, holding at bay a galvanized crowd of pedestrians and newspaper reporters. They begged for information, asked to be let into the shop, cursed, and eventually one threw a rock which failed to shatter the glass fronting, before the Marshal chased them off the stoop and back across the street where his men held them in check.

"My apologies, Miss Lizzie," the Marshal said, touching his helmet. "Whenever a murder occurs, the crowds are sure to follow."

She shuddered, thinking of such a mob outside her own home on Second Street. Father would not like that, regardless of who had been killed. She shook off the terrible thought and returned to the problem of the feet in the dust. As she worked her way through the thorny scenario that had emerged, she began to see signs of another character, neither the dead man, nor the three attackers, nor the law enforcement and medical officials who had left their marks: a man sporting square-toed congress boots. While the other paths were erratic, the result of violent fights and dance-like engagements, the congress feet remained steady in one position at the front counter, tapping their toes as if tearfully bored, then walked straight for the front exit where they disappeared into the busy street. A careful examination of the prints showed that they crossed behind the barber chairs, straight through a patch of blood. Most significantly, none of the prints, neither the killers' nor the mysterious witness's, indicated the sharp-toed boots worn earlier by Policeman Lot. It was still pure speculation that Lot had witnessed the slaughter. And yet Lot was wearing brand new boots that had no dust or barber shop residue on them at all; they were of shiny and clean leather.

A bowl of slop water was discarded casually before a tall shaving mirror showing evidence of cut facial hairs floating in soapy liquid. Was this Lot's shaving residue? A cursory examination of the follicles showed that it could very well be. Yes, the man had been here and had witnessed the murder. He must have removed himself from the scene, suffered a tabula rasa, emerging from the memory loss clueless as to how blood came to be clotted on his boots and headed for the nearest store on North Main where he could buy a brand new pair.

Lizzie was now faced with another decision. The Marshal had been generous enough to ignore her subterfuge in the affair of the amnesiac who was now the prime suspect in the murders. He had allowed Homer Thesinger to go home rather than face charges of lying to a police official and becoming a suspect himself. But would he hold his convictions in the light of the evidence Lizzie had drawn from the very dust of the crime scene?

"What is it?" the Marshal asked, recognizing a peculiar lop-sided grin that Lizzie made when she was experiencing epiphanies.

"I can give you a scenario," she said, holding out her hands and spreading her palms over the scene. "There is no doubt in my mind that Uncle Sam was attacked by three men who entered the barber shop without weapons. They commandeered Uncle Sam with the razor that you find discarded at the base of the murder chair, dropped where it had last been used. The victim was murdered here, in this chair where his body was found. Borden's height necessitated that he be lowered into a chair before his throat was slashed. Based on these crude statistics and measurements of the victim's height, I can say that the killers averaged between five foot six and five foot eight. Three wore pointed-toed boots suggesting a dandified nature, or at the least a fastidious one. A fourth was square-toed. He stood by the register and waited out the murder then escaped through the front door while the three murderers absconded through the rear entrance. The duration of the struggle may have been a matter of minutes, but it is also clear from the dust that the men, all five of them, stood around the store as if conversing before the attack."

Lizzie peered down on the surface of the table as if seeing it for the first time.

"There was an object set on this table which has recently been removed. It was rectangular in nature, I would assume."

The Marshal harrumphed, staring down onto the table top. "I do see a faint trace of where such an object may have rested. Do you think the barber was having his photograph taken?"

"Unlikely," Lizzie said. "But the box, of whatever it was, seems to have been the focus of attention. This alignment of box, victim, and murder is most peculiar."

The Marshal shrugged. "Either way, if this Lot character was here to get his face shaved, was he here before or after the murder?"

"It is likely that he has witnessed the murder but his tabula rasa excludes him from giving any credible testimony. He simply won't remember."

"Then what was he doing at the police station demanding to see me?"

"That has always been a puzzle. I don't think anyone knows enough about amnesia to explain how some details can come through and others vanish into nothingness. Well, we must think upon that. Suffice it to say that after witnessing the murder, he left the shop and promptly forgot everything he had seen. Then, upon noticing that there was blood upon his square-toed boots, he ran straight for the nearest clothing store and purchased a brand new pair. Perhaps he believed himself to have murdered someone and was at the police station intending to turn himself in, or perhaps he had some vague memory of the murder and wanted to surrender what he could."

The Marshal walked carefully around the chairs to the counter. He stood staring quizzically at the square-toed footprints. "Could he have been this man?"

"I'm convinced of it. After getting a shave, he stood by and had a front-row seat for a massacre." Lizzie tapped her chin with a gloved finger. "But why would he stand there and watch, tapping his toes, and then walk right past the murderers into the back room?"

The Marshal snapped his fingers. "He was the head of the gang. The murderers were doing his bidding!"

"But there is other evidence which I have not yet summarized. You may notice that there is at present no discernible presence of human hair on the floor, and yet there is a profound amount of dust. As you can see, these two brooms, the only ones found in the store, have been cleaned and are void of any hair residue."

"Borden had not yet broom swept," the Marshal nodded. "The shop opened at eight o'clock and took in Mr. Lot as its first customer. The alarm was raised at 8:15 by a random passerby who witnessed Lot emerging from the shop in an agitated condition and then saw through the front glass that the proprietor was reclining with his throat slashed on the barber chair. I can imagine the murder being closer to 8 than 8:15."

"I would say that it occurred earlier than eight o'clock, performed behind a locked door with the blinds drawn."

A light was dawning on the Marshal's face. "This means that Lot arrived before the shop even opened. It must have been by invitation. He was not just a random customer."

Lizzie grabbed one of the brooms and made a small excursion in a corner of the floor to flick at the floorboards with the swatches. "The dust comes up easily. Uncle Sam retired from business last night without fully sweeping the floor, leaving it for the morning, but he never had the chance to do so."

Officer Periwinkle, who had been standing like a statue by the front door, made a curious wheezing noise, as if an attempt to get the Marshal's attention had turned rapidly into an inarticulate nervous twitch.

The Marshal sighed. "Yes, Periwinkle?"

"Sir, I would be remiss if I did not tell you what I know about the nocturnal habits of Mr. Samuel Borden. As it was my duty to patrol this street at nights until recently, I was privy to the information that Mr. Borden was rehearsing singers for his harmony quartet, one that intended to perform novelty songs and standard ballads of the day to a pleasing audience."

"A harmony quartet!" Lizzie exhaled. "That would add some dimension to this mystery. Particularly the line-up in front of the mirrors."

The Marshal sputtered. "Do you mean to tell me that the murderers sang to their victim before they butchered him?"

"I would say," Lizzie offered, "that Samuel Borden sang with his killer before they butchered him. And Policeman Lot was the audience."

The Marshal barely blinked. "I'm going to keep that in mind, although it seems utter rubbish. Go on, Officer."

"He held rehearsals at night," Officer Periwinkle continued, "often neglecting his custodial duties. And sometimes he rehearsed in the morning before opening doors for business so as not to interfere with professional duties to the public."

"We must obtain a list of his singers!" the Marshal remarked sharply. "They are the murderers!"

The Officer frowned. "I believe that in recent weeks he was auditioning for new singers since the old ones have retired to other hobbies. Signs in the window of the shop indicated that Mr. Borden was fielding for a tenor, a baritone, and a lead for the accompanying vocal parts of his harmonic quartet."

"The killers may have come disguised as candidates," the Marshal relented. "And that rectangular box on the table could have been a music box to set pitch and harmony for the singing."

"Doubtful," Lizzie said. "A harmony quartet is a Capella."

"It's what?" the Marshal frowned.

"Without music."

"Hmm," the Marshal said, holding his chin. "You see no scenario in which music flowed from this box?"

"Not quite," Lizzie remarked. "But I do see a scenario in which music could flow into the box."

Officer Periwinkle snorted nervously, then composed himself by straightening his helmet. The Marshal peered at Lizzie with a squinted left eye. "You often have said peculiar things that usually made sense in the end, but I'm afraid you'll have to explain that one."

"And I shall in time," Lizzie agreed. "But we are focusing too hard on the box, if indeed it was a box. I am meditating upon the role of Mr. Lot, which is still a deep mystery. If only his memory would revive. He may give us the identity of the killers."

"Even if it's himself," the Marshal steamed.

Lizzie paced the floor, taking a last look at the traces in the dust, and then said wistfully, "The crime scene has revealed all that it can. My next move would be to gain access to the Ancient Order of the Masonic Odd Men and see what I can find out in their ranks. Mr. Lot is a member, as his ring testifies. Attending one of their meetings may illuminate his identity."

"Attend?" the Marshal asked. "What the devil do you mean? They allow only men into their meetings. And even if you were a man you'd have to be an initiate."

"I will take care of those matters," Lizzie chuckled, and then turned to Officer Periwinkle. "I need access to Mr. Lot in the jail."

"For what purpose?" the Marshal asked hastily.

"I need to ask him about his steps and handshakes," Lizzie announced. She turned and mused for a moment, a bright cast of startled possibility on her brow.

"Oh yes," she added. "And I need to borrow his mustache."

She then waltzed from the barber shop leaving behind two baffled law officials.

Non Omnis Moriar

The doors to the Inner Temple Hall turned on their great hinges, pushing forward the oaken panels with an almost silent hiss. Three men strode into the room, each holding his white-gloved left hand onto the right shoulder of the Brother before him, and holding his right hand forward with outstretched fingers. They were appareled in black cloth frocks and striped trousers, each sporting a ribbon-less bowler. Highly decorated sashes glowing with saturated colors were crossed diagonally across their chests.

"Into the light!" they chanted in unison. "Out of the darkness! Into the light!"

Behind them, standing at attention outside the temple door, a congregation of men dressed similarly, waited patiently. A door keeper with a black mask over his face held out before them, barring their entry, a crude birch club with one tiny green leaf spouting from its tip.

The three men turned and saluted each other in various combinations of arm gestures and hand shapes, then formed a circle by linking their arms. About them were three waist-level candle holders, each with a brightly burning flame that cast an eerie light on their circle.

"Three in one! One in three!" they chanted, then shook each other's hands in casual fellowship. "I in you, and you in me!"

"Master Warden of the East," spoke the tallest man of the three, solemnity defining his entire face. "What is your duty?"

"To see that the Temple of Verified Wisdom is inviolate," the stout-
est of the trio explained, "free from contamination, safely guarded
against the force of Darkness."

"See that it is so!"

The Warden of the East walked in a brisk circle about the Temple,
thudding his feet on the floor under him, then took his place back at the
Eastern candle.

"The Temple is inviolate, O Holy Hierophant."

The leader nodded then spoke. "Master Warden of the West, what
is your duty?"

The doddering fellow before the western candle looked ancient, as if
he had personally seen the first cloth manufactory built over the stream
of the Quequechan back in the days when Fall River was only a village
of twelve dwellings and a saw mill. His creased face and withered white
hair framed his toothless mouth and a hawkish profile. When he spoke,
the words were rounded as if by decades of exposure to the winds. Added to this was an incessant twitch that forced several rapid eye blinks
every minute or so.

"To see that all Odd Men coming into the Sanctuary of Verified Wisdom are properly instructed and initiated," he said, almost in
a whisper.

"Shall we admit the Master Odd Men into the Temple of Verified
Wisdom," the Hierophant asked, "that they may partake of our wisdom
and secrets and live perpetually in the light?"

Before the Warden could answer, a nasty wheezy hoot broke from
outside the door. Someone had sneezed noisily into a handkerchief. The
report startled the Hierophant who paused momentarily, then waggled
his face to regroup his thought.

"Shall we?" he repeated.

"I shall, Master Hierophant," the elder Warden affirmed. He gestured to the gatekeeper who seemed to have trouble seeing through the
eye-holes of his mask. He stumbled back to the congregated Brothers
and waved a black gloved hand in the direction of a seemingly random
member.

The congregate stepped before the nearly barren tree branch.

"Whisper in my ear the password that you may enter the Holy
Sanctuary!" the gatekeeper barked, then he stooped to hear the word in
his ear. The club sprang upward and the Brother stepped into the room,

strolling eagerly to a place before the font. The three men stood in a row on the other side of that demarcation.

"Brother Buffington," the Warden of the West said shrilly. "You have been granted the privilege to enter our most Holy Temple. Can you give us the step and sign of our most solemn degree of Most Excellent and Most Enlightened Odd Man, Knight of Antioch and Scholar of Alexandria?"

"Sure," Brother Buffington gulped and then contorted his legs and feet into a twist of angles while drawing his hand to his chest, alternatively extending and then withdrawing certain combinations of fingers.

"Accepted!" said the Warden.

"Master Warden of the West," the Hierophant declared, "you have observed this man's fidelity and his strict observance of our rules."

"I have," the Warden said, twitching twice in one moment.

"You will observe the fidelity of all the Brothers as we admit them into the Holy Temple."

"I shall!" the Warden of the West declared. "It is my duty to see all and to affirm that all is correct in the Sanctuary of the Verified Wisdom."

The Hierophant motioned for Brother Buffington to kneel upon the ground and bow his head before the three. "So shall it be in the Temple of Verified Wisdom."

One by one, the congregants were admitted, all being subjected to the pomp of entry and password verification. When all twenty had been so admitted and were in their places on the benches along the northern wall, the Hierophant motioned for the Gatekeeper to close the doors.

"Brothers and Warders of the Temple of Verified Wisdom," the Hierophant said solemnly. "It is my intention to open this Temple at the Grade of the Axiomatic Profundity. Is there any Brother present who stands forth with an objection to this most sacred opening?"

Once again, a member of the congregation sneezed into a handkerchief, causing a few of the Brothers to rattle in their seats. The Hierophant stared pop-eyed at his flock. "I put into the record that none of the Brethren have objected to the opening of this Temple of Verified Wisdom in the Grade of the Axiomatic Profundity."

After an awkward silence, the Hierophant performed a series of hand gestures and facial gestures, accompanied by a few utterances in a language that was decidedly uncommon and inscrutable. When he finished, the Wardens of the East and West did a few of the same gestures, uttered a few of the same syllables, and then walked towards each other to lock hands, swaying to the chant of "Three in one! One in Three!"

"I declare this Temple of Verified Wisdom to be open in the Grade of Axiomatic Profundity!" the Hierophant bellowed. "Master Warden of the East, is there any business to which you must attend?"

The stout warden coughed into his fist and pulled some notes from his vest pocket. "We are all aware of the tragedy that has befallen Brother Samuel Borden. To many he was an uncle; to us he was a brother. His loss is incalculable. His skills as a Master of the Prismatic Theorems will be sorely missed. We will also miss his tonsorial skills which are unparalleled in our city. Many a Brother has shaved and trimmed their face at our Brother's parlor. He should be receiving a statesman's funeral, but sadly, his family has been rendered insolvent even with the sale of the barber shop. I will take charge of a relief fund. Each and every one of you must contribute and meditate upon the day that your own insolvency shall come, and your family shall be in need of the Brotherhood to sustain itself."

The congregation grumbled in agreement.

"Any word as to the culprit of this deed?" the Hierophant asked eagerly.

"The City Marshal has informed me that there are presently no suspects. Brother Borden was attacked by three men, all of whom have escaped detection. There are investigations under way."

"Tragic," the Warden of the West said, clucking his tongue and blinking spasmodically.

"Very tragic," the Hierophant declared, then crossed his arms in a semblance of a wrapped mummy. The entire congregation followed suit. "And very incongruent," he added. "But such is life and death, two sides of the same coinage, the beginning and the end of a process that has no beginning and end. After a brief period of sleep in which there is no self to perceive the world, he shall awaken to a new life, forgetful of his previous sojourn on this ball of dust, and start a new cycle of life. Such is the turning of the universe's wheel."

After a mournful pause, he began: "My understanding is that we have a new initiate into the Grade, a Brother St. Clair from Muskegon, Michigan, who has been seeking the light in the Holy Ways of the Masonic Odd Men. Brother St. Clair has moved to Fall River to take employment with Jonah Ford's law firm, and comes with recommendations and reports of good behavior within the congregations of his Temple Valley."

"It is good that he has come among us," the Warden of the West said creakily. "With the death of Brother Borden we have need of a Brother who will walk on the Path towards the Prismatic Theorems."

"Then let the Brother be admitted to the Temple," the Hierophant announced, clapping his hands.

The Gatekeeper swung open the door and disappeared into the outer hall. After a pause, he returned leading a Brethren behind by a slack rope tied into a semblance of a noose and slung casually around the candidate's neck. Further, the man's hands were tied and a blindfold wrapped around his eyes. He stumbled forward as best he could until he had been led before the Three Masters.

"Stand right there," the Gatekeeper growled, then slunk back into the shadows.

"Stranger," the Hierophant said. "It is not often that one unknown to us approaches the Temple of the Verified Wisdom. Before we remove your ties, bonds, and blinds, we must be satisfied that you are indeed an initiate of the Degree of the Axiomatic Profundity and are duly prepared to enter the Paths of the Prismatic Theorems. Are you willing to undergo this ordeal?"

"I am," the candidate said, almost smugly, wiggling his mustache that drooped below the blindfold.

"Let it be so," the Hierophant said. The Warden of the West, at the silent command of the leader, removed the bonds about the candidate's wrists. "With your hands now liberated, give us the sign of the Congruent Trio."

The candidate performed thus.

"Now give us the sign of the Trinomial Terminus."

The candidate performed thus, as well as the sign of the Polysyllabic Logos and the Compressed Arcanum.

"Right glad we are to receive your signs," the Hierophant said, encouraging the congregation to clap by demonstrating with his own hands. He then gestured to the Wardens to remove the blindfold from the candidate's face. "We retain the noose until you have shown us the Step of the Portal of Axiomatic Profundity."

The candidate scanned the trio as if photographing their faces, then stepped forward, propelled on an imaginary line, advancing like a wire walker from a circus. After a complex configuration of foot placements, there was another acknowledgement from the Hierophant and the noose was removed.

The man who stood before the Trio was on the short side, and had a slightly pear shaped appearance. He wore the same striped trousers and vested jacket as the Brethren. His slightly pudgy face sported a languid mustache and some dark straight eyebrows that were a shade darker than the tufts of hair that stuck out of his bowler.

"What is your name in the Christian world," the Hierophant asked. "The name given to your temporal body by your biologic agents."

The man spoke in a tempered voice. "August Hannibal St. Clair."

"And in which zone of the mundane sphere were you incarnated?"

"Cleveland, Ohio."

"And your age?"

"Twenty-one," the man said, holding up a single white gloved finger. "This past April."

"Right glad we are to welcome you into our degree. We will now bestow upon you the papers, documents, labels, seals, apron regalia, signs, steps, and passwords of the Path of the Axiomatic Profundity."

One by one, the Master and Wardens instructed Brother St. Clair in the Arcanum of the degree, walking him about in the Temple, showing him diverse implements and manuscripts. The young man was pleasant enough about the whole business and listened intently, especially when the Trio read the charge of the degree, a lengthy text that included amongst its corollaries:

"We pronounce the abundancy of the Holy Triad. Our culture and religious beliefs are rife with reference to the Holy Triad. Be it known as the Father, Son, and Holy Ghost; be it known as the Three Wise Women; the Three Pitches of the Harmonic Chord; the Trio of the Earth, Moon, and Sun. There is nothing which does not harmonize as the Mystery of the Third on any plane of existence."

Brother St. Clair stared blankly, then retorted, "It seems like the number three is a big deal in this neck of the woods."

The Master Hierophant seemed a bit displaced by the Brother's comment, but soldiered on. "The Brother shall not reveal any of the secrets bestowed upon him to the Mundane World nor shall he even hint that such secrets exist. Nor shall he reveal that in the oath he will take that he will not reveal such secrets even exist. He will swear such an oath binding him to total silence and to live under the penalty that should he break such oath in any way, he shall have the air of his lungs removed from his body and the blood within his veins drained until he is a lifeless corpse that will subsequently be unceremoniously dumped in such an area that the beasts of the fields shall devour it."

At this Brother St. Clair blinked, and the sickly congregant with the chronic cough whooped once more, muttering an apology to create a distraction at such a solemn moment.

Brother St. Clair nodded and agreed to take such an oath, after which his hands were placed upon a large leather-bound volume which he took to be the Holy Scriptures, and repeated the barbarous words after the Hierophant.

Once more, a complex series of steps, signs and handshakes were orchestrated and Brother St. Clair was declared a fully admitted members of the Path Seekers of the Axiomatic Profundity.

"Congratulations, Brother St. Clair," the Hierophant announced. "You may speak freely. Do you have any questions of us, your Holy Hierophant and Wardens of the East and West?"

"Why yes," the young man said, chuckling. "I notice that there are three officers presiding over the Temple? They correspond to the directions of the compass: North, West, and East. Would it be impolite to ask what happened to the officer presiding over the South?"

A murmur spread through the ranks of the congregation and the Hierophant, his own brows growing stormy, shook an index finger in the young man's direction. "There has never been a Southern officer in this Temple. We are a Trinity-based order. You should know that from your studies in the Arcanum."

"Why, yes," St. Clair said, coughing slightly into a fist. "I was merely referring to the apocryphal rumor that at one point in the history of the order, there had been a fourth officer."

"Many years ago," the Hierophant explained. He breathed deep and stared downwards, then added, "The absence of the Warden of the South is a deep mystery. One that shall be revealed in the secret teachings of the Sanctuary of the Profound Absence. More than this, I cannot reveal, bound as I am to my oaths."

St. Clair beamed. "When I left Ohio, I had no foreknowledge of the honors that would be bestowed upon me. And in Fall River, no less! I mean, for God's sake!" The congregation laughed heartily at his humor, then fell into a scattered mumbling as they began to suspect that it was an insult.

Brother St. Clair resumed: "I have absorbed the secrets, internalized the Arcanum, and grasped the profundities of your doctrines. Armed with these mystic tools I shall go forth into the world as a man of Enlightenment and Wisdom. I shall strive to uphold the Sacred Morality, practice the craft of Scientific Realism sprinkled with tinges of Mythic Poetic Allegory. With these weapons, I shall be a beacon of hope and light to all my fellow man. Thus swear I!"

The congregation broke into a chorus of huzzahs and then broke ranks to lift Brother St. Clair on their shoulders and parade him out of the Holy Temple into the reception lounge. Everything had devolved into casual celebration and before long the carts of spirits were wheeled out, corks were popped, and the air was rank with the dense cloud of cigar smoke.

Everyone sought to congratulate the new brother, but St. Clair now seemed unduly distracted, casting about the festive crowd for the source of the persistent coughing that had been so audible during the Holy Proceedings. After a few forays into the ranks of drinking and smoking men, St. Clair discovered his prey by the drink bar trying to soothe his cough with a glass of water. When the brother gazed up at St. Clair he went into a coughing fit. The newly sworn Brother patted him on the back.

"Thanks, Brother," the coughing Odd Man said gratefully.

"I am merely coming to the aid of my Brother," St. Clair announced, breaking into a smile. "Working on your ore extraction methods must have caused some sort of upper respiratory ailment."

"What?!" the Brother said startled. He backed off a foot, then leaned forward. "Who are you?"

"Ah," St. Clair said cheerfully. "Who are you seems to be the question of the day. I suppose answering the problem of 'Who am I' can be devastating if you suffer from amnesia."

The Brother's eyes twinkled with a faint hint of recognition. Finally he blurted out, "Lizzie?"

"Not so loud," Lizzie Borden said, peeling back a slight portion of her mustache to reveal the glistening of theatrical glue beneath, then pressing it back into position. "Or I may require you to take an oath of silence."

Homer Thesinger blinked and then stared incessantly at his companion. "How? Why?" He coughed again, a mighty whoop that almost dislodged his bowler.

"The same way you did," Lizzie explained. "A few moments alone with a man who can't remember anything about his existence except his passwords, his steps and signs, and a laughing monkey face. But we talk in a manner that may betray us. For now we must fraternize as Brother St. Clair and Brother...uh..."

Homer bashfully announced, "Brother Leonardo Copernicus Edison."

After a hearty laugh, St. Clair turned to the bartender and ordered a lime water. "I see we are fellow seekers after knowledge. This organization may be a bit long winded about things, but I do believe they are barking up the right tree. Their precepts are serviceable."

"I agree," Homer said. "They are perfectly compatible with the natural sciences although they would not please any Logical Positivists."

"Only if you allow for thin layers of Kantian Idealism or Lockian Human Rights and Voltarian Enlightenment to ice your cake."

"They would definitely strike the dialectic materialists as borderline anti-socialistic."

"Only if you insist on the absolute priority of social injustice and interpretation of emerging industries."

"Which they seem to discard, leading one to believe they may be bourgeois."

The two chuckled together at their merry philosophical banter. Then Lizzie observed, "They are at least an egalitarian bunch. I count at least eight textile investors in this room as opposed to only four tradesmen."

"Nonsense, I count seven textile, one print mill investor seeking new markets, a Masonic defector, one butcher and a post office clerk."

Homer gave the crowd another scan and then conceded. "Brother St. Clair you have keener eyes. Not only do they see more but they observe more."

"What did you miss?" Lizzie asked.

"The butcher. His odor must have wafted directly to your olfactory but bypassed my own. Your other observations need some explaining since I find some of them uncanny."

"The post office clerk was easier since I recognize him from my visits there."

Homer grunted. "Well, that one was...yes...you knew him already."

"On the contrary. I recognized only his face. I know nothing about him, outside of the fact that he is a member of the Masonic Odd Men and that his father died of alcoholism and his sister ran off with the circus."

"Yes, that would follow from circumstance, not recognition."

"Or that he has recently lost his only child and is resisting all of his friend's persuasion to produce another one."

"That could be post office gossip. I suppose you are going to tell me that he has strained relations with his wife."

"Nonsense, Brother Leonardo. It is plain as day that his difficulties are with his brother-in-law."

"Plain as day," Homer repeated. "And that man over there, the Hierophant. For all his pomp and circumstance, is he also troubled at home? An unpaid debt? A disagreeable man servant?"

"Nothing to do with domestics," Lizzie answered. "He doesn't seem to be married at all. And he washes his own plates. Either that or works with his hands in a restaurant."

"The Most Holy and Sublime Hierophant of the Masonic Odd Men," Homer said baffled, "a dishwasher."

Lizzie peered closely at the Hierophant, engaged in conversation with the print mill investor seeking new markets, waving his hands about rapidly. She even tilted her head before announcing, "Omnibus boy," she concluded. "With occasional duty at the grilling rack."

"Of course," Homer acquiesced. "Now Brother St. Clair, if we are done here, may we commence with our investigation? Your client has lost his liberty, a Brother of the Odd Men has been murdered, and we have made little progress in solving the mystery"

"On the contrary," Lizzie said. "I have already solved much of it. But I need more data. And there are one or two points that still evade me, especially those touching our client's knowledge of wax cylinder manufactory and whether his wife has access still to his collection of French automata."

Homer grinned. "I always know you are getting close to the truth when you begin to make no sense whatsoever."

"Why Brother Leonardo," Lizzie said charmingly, patting her Lodge mate on the back. "What a very nice compliment, indeed."

THE PRISON BOX

On a typical afternoon in the Borden household, the family members reveled in the absence of Lizzie Borden. She often exasperated and irritated them with her sharp wit, her coy games to showcase her genius, her insistence that she was a professional crime investigator, when clearly she was recklessly play-acting some delusional fantasy. Mrs. Borden often lamented how she had failed her stepdaughter in her upbringing, ascribing the mania to the loss of her biological mother at age two, whereas Mr. Borden declared her a victim of moods and melancholic phases, as the nervous doctors described it. At best she was flexing her powers, putting on airs, playing different roles to see which best suited her. Before long, Andrew Borden was hopeful, some man would come along and tame her. She would be wooed rigorously in the Padua of the imagination, tamed into servile domesticity. And so they tolerated her eccentricities.

This particular morning was different. A man had bled to death in his own place of business, a man without a mind had become inexorably linked to the Bordens' affairs, and the entire family had become associated with the brutal murder: harboring a criminal, as well as lying to the police, withholding evidence. Andrew Borden, a practical man who carefully cultivated his reputation in the town, was as nervous as the rest of them, but stoically hid his concerns.

"She hasn't been seen for hours!" Emma said woefully. "Aren't you the least bit worried?"

Andrew, ensconced in his sitting room chair and ruffling his newspaper, shaking his shoulders, replied. "I have long since given up tracking that girl. She has an agenda all her own."

"I assumed she was all clear of that nonsense with the barber shop, but there are very suspicious things going on."

"Things?" Andrew repeated, twisting up his brow.

"I can't explain it, but there is a man living in Lizzie's bedroom, and I can't prove his existence."

Andrew pulled himself up to a seated position, pushed aside his newspaper and stared at his daughter. "I've heard talk like that before," Andrew said. "And it never ends well."

"I'm being serious, Father. For the past several days voices have been coming from Lizzie's room. A single voice in fact. A man's voice."

"In this house!" Andrew said, startled. "Lizzie is keeping a man in her room?"

"Not exactly," Emma said exhausted. "I hear the voice through her door, but when I enter the room he is nowhere to be seen."

"Then how can you claim he exists?"

"That's what is bothering me. I know he's there because I hear him, but every time I enter, Lizzie is alone."

"Well," Andrew said, drawing himself upwards. "There's only one way to resolve this mystery. We'll just have to become detectives ourselves for a little bit."

Abby Borden, who had wandered in on the conversation, wagged a finger. "That girl is hiding something. Best to have it out now."

"Right!" Andrew said, pulling at his vest and rising on his lanky legs. "Time to assert our privileges! We are only protecting her from herself!"

The family marched together into the hallway and single file up the front staircase. As they approached the door to Emma's bedroom, they halted and stared at each other.

"She is gone, is she not?" Andrew asked.

"Most decidedly," Emma nodded. "I was reading in my fainting sofa just ten minutes ago and her bedroom was empty."

Andrew shuddered and marched into the room, his family behind him. Lizzie's door was closed and Emma announced her concern that it would be locked. "She prefers her privacy," Emma said, then grinned. "But she doesn't know I have the key!" She opened a desk drawer and rifled through some papers before producing a copper key. After a communal huzzah, Emma inserted it into the lock and opened the door to Lizzie's room.

It was dark and quiet, the bed properly made and the dresser tidy, the articles of Lizzie's toilet neatly aligned on its top. Andrew sniffed about, pulling back the sheets, peering under the mattress, while Emma and Abby opened drawers and pushed aside discarded dresses. Finally, Andrew buckled his legs and inspected under the bed-frame.

"Ah ha!" he announced, before sliding out a curious object which he lifted and placed on the small desk by the side of the bed.

"What is it?" Abby asked, daring to reach out and touch it with a fingertip. "It looks like a carding machine."

"More like a telegraph device," Andrew said, running his hands over its various armatures and shafts. A large piece of metal, shaped like an ear trumpet for a deaf uncle, jutted at a diagonal angle from the central mechanism, and there were two distinct shafts that looked rotatable, one of which was sheathed with a waxen-coated cylinder. "There's a crank, this must power its engine." He turned the crank several times as if he were winding a large clock, then let go of the mechanism. As soon as he did so, the main shaft began rotating and the room was filled with a very unusual sound, quite unlike anything they had ever heard before.

After first it was just cracklings, as if two cloths charged with electricity were being violently pulled apart. Then there was a loud outburst of what seemed to be an explosion moving very slowly, but settled into their ears as a simulation of a large crowd of people applauding.

Then, abruptly, so sharp that the hairs on the back of their necks pickled with static electricity of their own, they heard a man's voice speaking plainly and clearly. "*Thank you!*" he said. "*I thank you!*"

"There's a man inside the machine!" Andrew barked and took a step backwards.

"*It is an honor to speak before you today,*" the man said. The pitch of his voice, surrounded by the crackling, made him seem small, as if he were reduced to the size of a house cat and stuffed inside the rotating machine.

"That's the man!" Emma cried, nearly fainting onto the bed.

"*There is much to discuss so I will be brief,*" the man continued.

"Magic!" Abby Borden thundered. "The girl has created an homunculus!" She reached forward and seized the machine, lifting it upward with a painful grunt. "We must destroy it!" she screamed. Just then, the crackling stopped.

"Wait!" Emma said, seizing her step-mother by the arm and preventing her from hurtling the machine. "Now I recognize that voice! I know who it is!"

Abby continued to hold the device upwards but cocked an eye towards Emma as if intensely interested in her disclosure.

"*I have determined that the extraction of gold from the pyrite can be accomplished through a combination of granulation and ferromagnetic options. What I cannot accomplish is adjusting the height of the descent of the pyrite granules so that the magnets will extract at a rate commensurable with...*"

"If that's not Homer Thesinger," Emma groaned, "then I'm Emily Brontë!"

"Homer?" Andrew said puzzled. "Homer Thesinger has shrunk himself and climbed inside that machine?"

"I don't know how it's possible, but there you have it. Now, Mother, can you please put that down before you hurt Mr. Thesinger."

"No!" Abby said definitely. "It's unnatural and evil!"

"Not to mention that it belongs to me!" came Lizzie's voice, harsh and bold.

At first the Borden family remained frozen, startled to hear their Lizzie's voice emerging from the same infernal box that had trapped a minuscule Homer Thesinger. In fact, it was Lizzie herself, standing in the doorway, still garbed in her masculine costume, having just removed the mustache and side burns.

"Lizzie?" Emma said with a twisted face. "Why are you dressed like a man?"

"Am I?" Lizzie said, smiling. "I almost forgot." The mustache slipped from her fingers and fell to the floor. She absentmindedly ignored it.

"You haven't joined...." Emma's voice went faint as if the possibility she was suggesting was unthinkable, "...one of those clubs, have you?"

Abby, who had placed the voice box with a thud on the desk top, clicked her tongue. "You have finally crossed the borderline into madness. But do not despair, Lizzie, there may be a cure. Dr. Popcorn in Tiverton has the most optimistic literature about his lunatics and I believe—"

"I am as sane as any man," Lizzie announced, removing her bowler and rubbing her upper lip for extraneous glue residue. "I was out on an investigation and did not expect my own family to snoop into my private affairs while I was gone."

"You have a lot to answer for, Lizzie," Andrew chastised her. "For one thing, what is this machine? It seemed to us that it shrunk Homer Thesinger down to size and swallowed him into it. And now he's announcing some sort of congregation of fellow prisoners who have also been trapped inside."

"That's Homer's Phemegraphic Speech Writer."

"Oh," Andrew hissed. "Well, I'm certain no good can come of that!"

"Seriously, Father. It's an invention that captures sound and recreates it for transmission. That particular cylinder has encoded within its wax a speech that Homer Thesinger made to the Edison Society of Bristol County last month. Imagine, my dearest family, a speech made a month ago, played back in this very room without any of the participants present. I have been listening to it for days, wondering at its almost mystical properties."

"It's a trick!" Emma announced. "Just like that Thesinger box!" She bent over and peered around the mechanism which sat motionless before her. "There's some sort of mirror, like you said. Parlor games!"

"Of course there's a trick!" Lizzie said freely, loosening her tie. "But it's not a magic trick. It runs purely on scientific principles. Homer can explain better than myself. Come downstairs and hear it from his own lips."

"Homer is here?!" Abby said, hopping about nervously.

"In the parlor," Lizzie said. "If you would go keep him company, perhaps serve him some coffee, I'll get back into the attire appropriate to my sex, and join you."

As Abby withdrew from the room along with her family, she jabbed a finger towards the Phemegraph and said hastily, "Destroy that thing! If I want to hear a man speak, I will listen to him directly!"

The last to leave was Emma who paused in the doorway to say, "I can't say that I am not impressed with the ingenuity of the device, but please do not leave it about my room. It gives me the creeping willies."

"Fairly spoken," Lizzie said. "But please remove your foot. You're stepping on my mustache."

Emma glanced down, growled with frustration, and darted away hastily.

Caged Voices

When the Bordens entered the sitting room, Homer Thesinger was seated in the parlor between two globe lamps chatting nattily with the Irish maid who was standing with a service tray full of coffee cups.

"Obviously," Homer was in the midst of saying, "the potato crisis in your country could have been resolved using the principles of progressive agriculture. Yet the various governments don't seem to be—"

"Maggie!" Abby shouted. "Are there not dishes to be washed, and potatoes to boil for supper?"

"I was only answering Mr. Homer's questions, Mrs. Borden," the thin young girl said, dunking her face. "I meant no harm." She slinked from the room with a sniffle.

"She meant no harm, Mrs. Borden," Homer pleaded, pouring his coffee from the pot and then sneezing liberally. "Now," he shrugged, crossing his legs and settling into the couch. "From what I heard, the four of you have discovered the Phemegraph. Quite remarkable, isn't it?"

"Is that one of your tinkered toys?" Andrew snapped. "I have to say, with all my contempt for you, despite your blistering arrogance and your reckless behavior with dangerous chemicals and madcap mechanisms, I was impressed with the reproduction of the human voice."

"Thank you," Homer said, mulling over the compliment in his mind. "But it is yet to be seen whether it is a reproduction or the actual voice itself trapped in wax. It's a matter of encoding as opposed to imprisonment."

"Such distinctions elude me," Andrew said. "I sense only merriment at the novelty. Perhaps you can make quite a bit of money off of it, especially with some minor investment for its manufacturing."

"Father!" Emma erupted. "You can't possibly be considering putting your money into this. This man has gotten us involved in a very dangerous murder."

"The Phemegraph has nothing to do with the murder," Homer said. "Well, not this particular Phemegraph."

"What do you mean by that?" Andrew said astonished. He turned to his daughter abruptly, "Lizzie, what do you mean by that?"

Lizzie smiled and lowered outstretched palms. "Why don't we all sit down and enjoy some coffee. Then I can explain all that Homer and I have been able to deduce from this most singular affair."

Begrudgingly, the Bordens settled into the parlor's chairs and prepared their individual cups of coffee. The Irish domestic returned with some cream and cubes of sugar all of which vanished within a minute. Homer was the only one present whose coffee was black and unsullied.

"To begin," Lizzie said, placing the Phemegraph onto the table before them, "I need to explain this mechanism so there is no accusation of mysticism. We have before us a product of science, one that captured the vibrations of our voice and reproduced them for playback. A most remarkable invention and one that is by no means unique in the world."

"Edison beat me to it," Homer said with a bemused and crooked smile. "I couldn't file the patents but I can make improvements. I have already filed a caveat."

"A what?" Andrew asked, annoyed.

"That's a legal document filed with the US Patent Office. It prevents another technician from copying my design for one year while I tinker with this one."

"But how does it work?" Andrew said, tugging at his jaw bristle. "I'll be darned if I can puzzle it out."

"The simplicity of it," Homer laughed, "is patently absurd. Here's the shaft that controls the recording. You speak into the horn, the vibrations of your voice move this needle which literally writes your words onto the wax surface."

"Writes? Like an amanuensis?"

"Precisely. And when you flip this switch, the same horn provides playback. The vibrations are reversed. Your words are encoded upon the surface of the wax, waiting to be resurrected."

"It can't be that simple," Abby said suspiciously. "There must be magic afoot."

"Nonsense," Lizzie said, glaring sternly at her stepmother. "We can demonstrate. Now Father, if you would be so kind as to speak into the horn."

"What do I say?"

"The first words that come into your mind." With that she toggled the switch and the clean waxen cylinder began to rotate.

Andrew screwed up his eyes as if attempting to draw words from his head, then raised a finger in a revelatory manner. "Four score and seven years ago, our forefathers…ah…yes, well how does that foolish speech go. They say it was short and sweet but I could never memorize it."

Lizzie toggled the switch once more bringing the cylinder to a halt. "I would like a clean recording. I can supply the words. Maggie, will you please go to my room and retrieve the volume of Mr. Lincoln's war time speeches. It is on the dresser underneath my translations of Plutarch."

The girl nodded and raced from the room. While she was gone, Lizzie had slipped the waxen cylinder from the machine and had replaced it with another one that Homer had retrieved from his kit bag. Within a minute, the Maggie had bounded back down the stairs and handed the book to Andrew at Lizzie's request. He thumbed through it and found the text of the Gettysburg Address.

"A tragic affair," he muttered. "Quite a large amount of death."

"The words," Lizzie said pointing, then flipped the recording switch.

"Four score and seven years ago," Andrew read, holding one hand on the book, the other on his lapel. It took only a few moments, and he was done before the wax cylinder had exhausted its capacity. When he had finished, Lizzie and Homer broke into a wild applause and hooting that caused Emma and Abby to shudder.

"Well, done!" Lizzie acknowledged, then motioned for them all to pay careful attention. She moved an armature, adjusted a switch, and then began the rotation of the disk. They were all chilled to hear Andrew's voice emerge thin and scratchy from the horn.

"I am sitting here," Andrew said over his own performance, "and I am inside that box at the same time! Extraordinary!"

"It is remarkable," Abby said, warming to the occasion. "But what does it have to do with the murder at the barber shop?"

Lizzie lifted the playback armature and sat upright on the edge of the couch. "When I examined the crime scene I noticed that a small table had been dragged to the center of the room, just behind the tonsures' chairs. On this table, there was a layer of dust disturbed by a rectangular area bounded by a larger rectangular area and as you can see," she lifted the machine and turned it at an angle so the Bordens could see the bottom surface. "This Phemegraph has such a pattern at its base."

"You are saying that this invention of Thesinger's," Andrew said, "was in the shop at the time of the murder."

"Not this one," Lizzie said pointedly. "There were two more manufactured in Homer's machine shop and one was sold at a private auction just one week ago. Homer is the only source of such a machine in Fall River, as well as the only manufacturer of the recording cylinders, without which the machine is as useless as a stone."

"Then who purchased those machines?" Andrew bleated. "Surely that must be the murderer."

Lizzie glanced at Homer who gave her a subtle nod of approval. "This device was the prototype and the first model off the workbench," Lizzie explained, resting it back down on the table. "The second model was sold to a Mrs. Fenchurch of Franklin Street."

"Fenchurch," Andrew muttered. "God abounds. What does this all mean?"

"It can have several meanings. One of the most obvious is the alignment of the Phemegraph to the tonsure chairs and the row of men standing before them. Remember that Mr. Lot was the only one standing behind the Phemegraph, meaning he may have been the one controlling the recording."

"Recording?" Andrew blinked. "Of what?"

"Of a rehearsal of the Uncle Sam Harmony Quartet. The barber was auditioning singers for a quartet. Four Men and True, as he put it in his advertisement. The audition was conducted in the barber shop before its posted hour of opening. The door was locked and the blinds were drawn."

"So the man was murdered while they were singing?" Emma asked bleakly. "Is that all that your supposed genius can come up with?"

"Not while they were singing," Lizzie corrected her. "After the song was over."

"What song?"

"I'll let you hear with your own ears." Lizzie turned to Homer who had produced another waxen cylinder from his kit bag.

"Where did you get that?" Andrew barked, jabbing a finger at the wax.

"It was found in Policeman Lot's trousers," Lizzie explained. "He was thoroughly searched at the Central Station and the Marshal has given us this evidence as a personal loan. The man has great trust in our careful guardianship of such important evidence."

"Evidence?" Abby said thinly.

Homer handed the cylinder over to Lizzie who fitted it onto the device and began the playback. Within a moment, they could hear a voice, sharp and clear, shouting.

"Gentlemen, begin!"

It was the voice of Policeman Lot, unambiguously him. Andrew, Abby and Emma gasped audibly and craned their necks to listen more closely.

Four voices began to curl in the air from out of the horn. They were sweet and melodious, each hitting his own pitch parts with deadly accuracy.

> *When a felon's not engaged in his employment*
> Then the bass part, deep and bellowing despite the tinny rasp of the recording, rang out with a melancholy: *(his employment!)*
> *Or maturing his felonious little plans (little plans)*
> *His capacity for innocent enjoyment (-cent enjoyment)*
> *Is just as great as any honest man's (honest man's)*
> *Our feelings we with difficulty smother (-culty smother)*
> *When Constabulary duty's to be done (to be done)*
> *Ah! Take one consideration with another (with another)*
> *A policeman's lot is not a happy one!*
> *AHHH!*
> *When Constabulary duty's to be done (to be done)*
> *A policeman's lot is not a happy one!*

"The bass," Emma said. "That is Uncle Sam?"

"Without doubt," Lizzie said. "And three others were assailants."

She snapped off the recording and the waxen cylinder came to an immediate halt, echoing a silence into the room.

"And more importantly, one of the three parts—the tenor, baritone, or lead," she added, "is the murderer!"

The Forgotten Prisoner of Franklin Street

Mrs. Leonard Fenchurch had never heard of such a thing. Her husband, once so meek and mild a man, had been arrested for murder. And as if that wasn't weird enough, he had finally lost his mind and couldn't even recognize himself as he stared into a mirror.

The news had been broken to her by Lizzie Borden of Second Street, the daughter of that furniture man who had been in the papers a few years back for a corpse found in the basement of his sales room. She was accompanied by that Thesinger boy, the one who had blown up his backyard and was seen at several athenaeum events peddling his gadgets, most of which no one trusted to be incapable of killing its owner.

The young Miss Borden and the dangerous tinkerer had arrived shortly after four o'clock in the afternoon, just as Mrs. Fenchurch, a jittery chestnut-haired woman with touches of drab gray, was preparing a lonely supper for one. They told her of her husband's fate and promised that he was experiencing the best of care, despite his location in the tower cell of the central police station.

"We shall take you there momentarily," Lizzie assured her. "But first we must ascertain a few facts."

The three of them were seated in Mrs. Fenchurch's parlor and a rather diffident and cold looking butler was serving them tea and crumpets, honoring Mrs. Fenchurch's English heritage. From her position on the couch, Lizzie could make out that Leonard Fenchurch was an industrious man, practically an inventor himself. He wasn't a wizard of space and time as Homer Thesinger was turning out to be, but a clever tinkerer who had designed his own brand of cuckoo clock that spun its own second hand, fashioned a rather clever service tray for the tea that held the cups in the security of embossed ridges, and an odd assortment of fireplace pokers, each of which was tailor made to tackle a different size log of wood with appropriate grab handles and metallic alloys adjusting to all levels of temperature. Homer had inspected all these items with admiration and declared, "Mr. Fenchurch has a great mind waiting for him when he returns to his own sense. These are delightful and ingenious novelties."

Mrs. Fenchurch shrugged as she sipped her tea. "His mind may not be as brilliant as you suggest. He has large holes in it. Perhaps his memory of himself existing slipped into one of them when he leaned over too far one day. I wouldn't put it past him."

"I suspect his condition was caused by something a little less mundane," Lizzie suggested. "Mrs. Fenchurch, I have to ask why you did not report his disappearance to the police."

"Because disappearing for days at a time was not uncommon for Leonard. He only lived here four days a week, sometimes less. He had business out of town and his concern paid for his traveling and lodging expenses."

"What business is he in?"

"Historical research for a Professor Wilmarth at Brown University. They specialize in the War of Independence and Leonard often travels to remote battlefields and places where George Washington was known to bivouac. You know those signs you see all over New England? George Washington Bivouacked here!"

"Do you have reason to believe that your husband was telling you the truth about his travels?"

"What are you suggesting? He would never lie to me! No, he wouldn't dare." She stared into space as if transfixed on an invisible object. "I wonder if he is even capable of such a thing."

"Mrs. Fenchurch, this may come as a shock to you, but I have to ask you if your husband is in possession of a machine that records human voices."

"Yes, the Phemegraph," she nodded, visibly shaken by Lizzie's precognition. "But it vanished when he did. I assumed he took it with him to record his interviews."

"Have you heard any of these recordings?"

"No, in fact. I'm not very mechanically inclined and have kept my distance from his sound experiments."

"Then why did you buy the machine for him at Mr. Thesinger's auction?"

The woman frowned, then looked very confused. "I'm afraid there's been a mistake. I didn't buy the machine. It appeared one day and Leonard explained to me that he had borrowed it from a neighbor."

"Did he say which neighbor?"

"Not particularly."

"Would it surprise you that this man sitting right here, Mr. Homer Thesinger, is the inventor and manufacturer of the Phemegraph and the machine was sold to yourself at an auction?"

"I was never at an auction," she announced. "And I only know of Mr. Thesinger through gossip in town."

"Yes," Homer said, sighing. "The tree explosion. Well, I've done a lot of good for this community."

"Perhaps," Mrs. Fenchurch added. "But you are a menace nonetheless. This machine for example that you speak of, it is bewitched. It doesn't play back what you record but some infernal nonsense of its own devising."

"What do you mean?" Lizzie asked.

"I had Leonard recite "Charge of the Light Brigade" into it one evening, more to assure me that the machine was receptive to cultural voices as well as coarse and crude conversation. The machine recorded his recital perfectly, but a few nights later, I played it back and was shocked to hear Leonard reciting some mystical nonsense about Essential Theorems and Prismatic Truths. It shocked me that the machine decided that Tennyson was too vulgar and had replaced it with its own brand of hocus pocus."

"That is most mysterious," Homer said. "Perhaps it was a different cylinder."

"It heard what it wanted to hear and recorded that," she insisted. "Not what my Leonard spoke. The bard has been replaced with balderdash!"

"Had any other unusual contradictions occurred before his disappearance, Mrs. Fenchurch?" Lizzie asked.

"Several. Small items would vanish. A toothbrush, a piece of silverware. Sometimes books would vanish and then reappear a few weeks later but filed in the wrong place on the library shelf. The Phemegraph itself vanished one day before his disappearance and the murder of this unfortunate barber. I often interpreted these disappearances as resulting from Leonard randomly packing items for his trips. But their return several weeks later after several trips elsewhere was puzzling."

"Was your husband in possession of a rather peculiar item: the statue of a monkey dressed as a French aristocrat riding a bicycle?"

The woman's face went pale and she hurriedly sipped some more tea. "That is the most peculiar of all. Such a thing as you describe appeared in our home just one month ago. It was a horrid and loathsome thing. I asked him to remove it from our premises and he said it was a silly automaton, an antique in fact. I'm ashamed to say how much money he paid for it."

"How much?" Homer asked.

"More than a month's salary. We have been behind on our tax payments ever since."

"Where is the toy now?"

"Gone," Mrs. Fenchurch said, spreading her hands in the air. "Back to wherever it came from. I haven't seen it since. And the money he paid for it is still gone as well."

"I am sorry for that, but I have two more very important questions to ask you, Mrs. Fenchurch. If I may?"

The woman nodded almost imperceptibly, her thoughts clearly having drifted.

"When he went on his business trips, would you accompany him to the station?"

"No, Miss Borden, he always insisted on going by himself. Besides, it was always too late. He would leave after midnight, boasting that he could sleep on the train."

"So you never actually saw him depart?"

"Now that you mention it, no. I would say goodnight and goodbye, retiring to my room to put myself to sleep with a gripping Gothic novel. The last departure in question, I was reading *The Castle of Otranto*. Such atmosphere! Now what pray tell was your second inquiry?"

Lizzie blinked and visibly blushed. "I cannot phrase this question any other way. When your husband was prone to void his bowels, did he used an indoor privy or the outside one that I observed in your backyard?"

"My, that is a bold question. But Leonard was a difficult husband, no eccentric detail must go undocumented. Yes, my husband used the backyard privy. It was only appropriate since he would take reading matter with him and stay there for hours. If he had used the indoor privy I would have been denied my own chamber of solitude."

"Ah!" Lizzie said glowingly. "Your answers are most satisfactory. Now, we are losing time. The Marshal is waiting for us to reunite you to your husband."

"I cannot wait to see his face," Mrs. Fenchurch said listlessly.

The three were ushered to the street by the strangely silent butler who had called a taxi for them to ride to the police station. Guided by two strong horses and a very vocal cab-man who angled his whip ruthlessly on their backs, they arrived at their destination within a matter of minutes. The large-framed Marshal was waiting for them in the reception room.

"How is our guest?" Lizzie asked.

"His break moments are only a minute apart," the Marshal said sadly. "He only has time to learn your name and where he is before he loses it all and has to begin again."

"I'm sorry to hear so. Here is his wife, Mrs. Fenchurch, for that is his real name. Mr. Leonard Fenchurch. Perhaps her presence will startle his memory into sensibility."

"We'll see, this way," the Marshal said, smiling and helping the wife to alight onto the staircase to the tower.

The corridor snaked along the side of the building and was flooded with light from the outside. The cells were three in number and two were empty. The third was occupied by Fenchurch who sat with a vainly perplexed gaze on his face facing the iron gate that fenced him in. When he saw his wife standing behind it, casting a soulful and anguished gaze, he hardly blinked.

"Hello, Madam," he wheezed. "Can you possibly tell me who I am?"

Mrs. Fenchurch turned to Lizzie and pressed her face into her shoulder, sobs beginning to heave from her body. "Dear Lord, I did not know it was so bad," she said.

"No need for tears," Fenchurch said in a calm and kind voice. "I only need to know my name and I will be most gratified."

"Leonard Fenchurch," Lizzie said, enunciating clearly.

The man's face did not change one shade. "Is that my name? How extraordinary!" Suddenly, he blinked and twitched and a wave of turbulence filled his countenance. He was experiencing another *tabula rasa*. "What is this?" he asked. "You, Madam, can you please tell me who I am? I fear I have forgotten."

This sent Mrs. Fenchurch into a fresh spasm of sobs. "I love him, it's true," she said, choking on his words. "Despite the pain he has put me through. Please, Miss Borden, return my husband to me."

"I will do what I can," Lizzie said. "But you must tell me one singular fact."

"Anything," Mrs. Fenchurch said. "Just ask me and I will tell you."

Lizzie smirked at Homer and the Marshal, then said very carefully, "May I have the key to your backyard privy as well as permission to inspect it?"

The woman backed away from Lizzie with a cautious sneer. "I cannot fathom your method of discovery, but I can surely let you inspect our privy."

"Thank you," Lizzie said. "Now I have a few more charges to give to law enforcement to enact my final strategy in this affair. Officer Periwinkle, will you kindly go to the offices of the Ancient Order of the Masonic Odd Men and give this note to the presiding Master."

The officer's attention, placed firmly in the empty air before him, softened and he gazed googled-eyed at Lizzie. "Is that the crazy place on Belmont? What do they do in there?"

"Nothing that will cause you any harm," Lizzie proffered, handing him a folded note. "Now, Marshal, if you please. I have instructions that must be followed implicitly or else we may fail in our endeavor."

"After what I have just witnessed, I will trust that your instructions are not rooted in nonsense."

"Excellent. Now, I must insist that you take Officers Whatley and Baxter and go to 47 Franklin Street at precisely eight o'clock. You will also bring the Phemegraph that is in possession of Mr. Thesinger as well as a waxen cylinder. Mr. Thesinger will instruct you in the use of this device and how to mount and play the cylinder. At eight o'clock you will knock upon the door of 47 Franklin Street and wait until you hear my voice asking for the identity of the caller. Then you will play the cylinder. That is all you have to do, play the cylinder, holding it to the door so the occupant can clearly hear the sound that emerges from it. After the door is opened, all will be revealed."

"Iron and thunder!" the Marshal gasped. "You have solved the case! Lizzie Borden the Girl Detective strikes again!"

"Most decidedly!" Lizzie said proudly. "There is only one small matter that is still a mystery and that is the identity of the woman who lives in the house behind the Fenchurch residence."

"A very reclusive couple," Mrs. Fenchurch said smugly. "The husband is often away for days at a time. Just like my Leonard. Sometimes I wonder if they belong to the same fraternity or..." Her voice trailed into silence, then her body tightened and she gazed suspiciously at the man seated in the jail cell. "Are you telling me that Leonard is in some sort of conspiracy with that man? I was always told the Odd Men were harmless buffoons, a group of giggling fatheads who chanted their mumbo-jumbo and performed senseless pageantry to disguise how vapid they were in real life."

"I cannot say for now," Lizzie confided, "but I can assure you their rhetoric is mumbo-jumbo at best. Now Homer, be as kind to give instruction to the Marshal in the use of the device and meet me in front of 45 Barkley Street at precisely seven o'clock by the City Hall Tower. Precision timing is required in this affair, and we must all play our part." She turned to the cell and addressed the occupant. "You shall as well," she intoned.

"I most certainly will oblige you," Fenchurch said tearfully. "But can you first please tell me something most urgent."

"Yes, anything," Lizzie said.

His brows furrowed and tears appeared at the corner of his left eye.

"Who am I? I'll be deuced if I can remember!"

Mrs. Fenchurch burst out into a fresh set of tears.

The Aromatic Underworld

Homer Thesinger and Lizzie Borden strolled amidst the early evening horse traffic, passing pedestrians, and clattering vendor carts wheeling back to their warehouses for the night. The lamps had been lit and the sun was disappearing beyond the bay.

"Who does live in the house behind Fenchurch?" Homer asked bluntly.

"We will discover that in time. Suffice it now to say that life can often resemble that most prized novelty box of yours, the one with two compartments. At time, it can appear empty to the audience, but carefully concealed behind a slanted mirror is any object that you can stuff into it."

"My magic trick," Homer sighed. "What does that have to do with this case?"

"Nothing directly, but one day when I performed the trick to an astonished Alice Russell, I realized that I had held it upside down, and that she had witnessed the opposite effect. Rather than seeing an empty box, and then having a handkerchief mystically appear within it, she witnessed a disappearance. She saw the handkerchief first, and then saw it vanish."

"It's true, the box will work either way. Are you implying some sort of allegory behind my magic box and the mind of Leonard Fenchurch?"

"I will be able to state all in the plainest language within one hour," Lizzie said, then slapped Homer's shoulder and pointed toward the Fenchurch home. A two-story affair that, with its bland clapboard exterior and standard gable and pediment, resembled all the other houses that lined the unassuming street. A single lamp burned in the parlor window, adding a touch of gloom to its aura. It stood upon an elevated cellar as if trying to distance itself from the ground on which it was built.

Mrs. Fenchurch, still jittery and distracted, answered the door and after a few pleasantries ushered them into the parlor where she had prepared a tea service. They sat for a while, listening to the ormolu clock on the mantle strike the half hour before seven. Homer sipped anxiously at his china cup and stared largely at the ceiling as if admiring the engineering that goes into holding a roof over one's head.

"Would it be folly for me to ask what we are doing here?" Mrs. Fenchurch asked. "I don't see what this can possibly accomplish."

"I have insisted on precise timing," Lizzie stated. "In one quarter hour we shall inspect the backyard privy and if my deductions are correct, we shall be confronting the murderer of Samuel Borden by seven on the clock."

The woman shuddered. "There is a murderer hiding in my privy?"

"Not precisely," Lizzie said. "I don't believe the murderer ever went near your privy."

"Then what does the privy have to do with all this?"

"I don't want to reveal too much of my thinking, but when you told me that your husband would spend large amounts of time in the structure, often blaming the intervals on his tempestuous bowels, I developed a theory based on your disclosure that he never left on business trips while you were awake, that he always left by a midnight train after you had gone to sleep."

"What does the train schedule to Boston have to do with my backyard privy or the state of Leonard's bowels?"

"Everything," Lizzie said slyly, "including the disappearance of the French automaton and the reappearance of the tea cups that we are currently using for our refreshment."

Mrs. Fenchurch shrugged. "Either you are as full of nonsense as those Odd Men or I'm just going to trust that you'll make an arrest and restore my husband's memory."

"As to your husband's memory, I can't honestly say that the restoration will be successful, but we will give it a go." Lizzie glanced at Homer and reached over to nudge his knee. "What has seized your fascination, my magic boy?"

Homer pointed towards the plastered ceiling. "I may be lagging behind you by a lap, but I'm assuming you've noticed the accumulated stains from cigar ash."

"A filthy habit," Mrs. Fenchurch said dismayingly. "One I tried for years to get him to cease."

Lizzie did not raise her eyes. "Of course, I've noticed. The odor in this room: cheroots, I presume."

"Precisely," Mrs. Fenchurch nodded.

"The same brand of my father."

"What does this have to do with the murder?" the poor woman pleaded. "Was there cheroot ash-smoke at the scene of the crime?"

"No," Lizzie said. "But those stains and this odor will serve us well when we arrive at our destination."

"Oh, are we going somewhere? Perhaps I shall retrieve my hat."

"No need," Lizzie said, rising from the couch. "But it is time for our departure. Please follow me."

They made their way to the back kitchen and exited into the yard through the screen door. The privy was against the back wall, a small wooden structure that leaned wearily to one side. The door swung on an uneven pitch.

Lizzie was able to coax her companions into the confined space. The single seat was pressed against the far wall, leaving a fair amount of space for them to stand in. With the door closed they had to huddle in a circle facing each other.

"Now," Lizzie said. "We shall begin."

After a tense moment, Mrs. Fenchurch broke the silence. "How are we going to solve the murder of the barber and the identity of my husband by standing in this privy?"

"Patience," Lizzie insisted. "We start with the observation of how this privy smells."

"Smells?" Mrs. Fenchurch crinkled up her nose. "I smell only grass and verbena and…" She blinked a few times and stared about madly. "There is no smell, no scent of filth."

"Mrs. Fenchurch, when was the last time this privy was dipped?"

"Dipped? I left that to Leonard since this was his privy. But to be honest I've never known it to be dipped." She turned about searching the ground and the seat. "And I don't see any newspaper either."

"And for a privy that had been used for hours at a time for years at a stretch for a man to evacuate his bowels and to read his newspaper, this privy is blissfully free of any detritus from either activity."

Homer Thesinger gave out with a hearty chuckle. "Lizzie, you never fail to amaze me. Of course! Of course!" He reached down and lifted the seat, hardly surprised when the entire wooden plank lifted with it, revealing a gaping space. He reached into his vest and pulled out a long wooden match, striking the head against one of the posts. A glowing ball of orange light enveloped the area before Homer's nose.

"Careful!" Mrs. Fenchurch shouted. "The methane!"

"There is no methane," Homer assured her and then pointed to a makeshift ladder that lowered into the ground below the privy seat.

"A tunnel!" Mrs. Fenchurch gasped.

"Yes," Lizzie said. "I now have every reason to believe that all of our answers lie at the other end. I have solved the case!"

THE ORACLE

Madame Olonsky's sitting room was festooned with mechanical toys that promised a dynamo of motion: Arabian boys playing flutes; Chinese acrobats tumbling over each other in endless procession; lion tamers balancing hoops before savage jaws; a seven-veiled Salomé; gyrating belly dancers; antic clowns juggling pins; sea captains raging at the tidal winds; and the largest item of all, a turbaned and sallow cheeked Turk, rising from a table, his legs obscured, lifting cards and chess pieces, his face consumed by laughter. Yet, despite their joyous and life-affirming motions, they were all as still as rocks. No key had yet been turned to force their movements, no clockwork mechanisms whirled within to blindly parrot the actions of humans, mimicking not just happiness and joy, but human will. The scene was as formant as a bustling Arabian bazaar that had been frozen in place, a graveyard of silenced animation.

Madame Olonsky drew out a pack of cards and placed them referentially on the table before her, itself cluttered with globes, leather-bound tomes, and manuscripts. Her long slender fingers withdrew one card at a time and laid them down in the shape of a giant tetraskelion, after which she drew four more for each empty quadrant defined by the cross itself. Upon placing the last of the cards, she uttered a small gasp and gripped the remaining deck in her hands as if they had suddenly scalded her palms.

The final card depicted a young woman standing upon a steep boulder, dressed as one would in a Wagnerian epic with iron breast plates and a wild tartan battle skirt. She held a larger than life lance, sprouting abundantly with leaves and pointed downwards towards the wild vegetation that grew from the soil beneath her. A single green sprig grew from the lance's tip.

"The Daughter of Earth!" Madam Olonsky spoke chillingly.

The Gnostic Tarot of McAlastair Mundy never failed to produce deadly accurate results. Its eerie habit of revealing precisely the essence of whatever situation the querist found herself in always reinforced Madame Olonsky's belief in the sympathetic magic that underlined life itself. There was the Daughter of Earth, and such a person she had feared for two days and nights, ever since her informant in the police department had told her that Lizzie Andrew Borden of Second Street had been investigating the unfortunate affair at the barber shop. For the Daughter of Earth was clearly the Borden girl unveiled. Her damned lance was ready to rend the veil that the Society had drawn around itself for years. The meddlesome pest knew not the solemnity of that which she threatened to disturb.

"Lizzie Borden," she hissed, directing her venom at the lacquered card which lay innocently upon her drawing table.

"Precisely," came a voice from behind her. Madame Olonsky's body was seized with an involuntary fluctuation, one that hurled her from her chair, tossed her like a mindless doll upon her feet, and jerked her about to face her nemesis.

"The Devil!"

"If you wish," Lizzie said. The young detective stood in the door to the parlor in her dark Bedford cord with mutton sleeves and a flat slanted hat from which sprouted a few feathers that would have served the Daughter's lance quite well. Beside her was a curious man, one Madame Olonsky knew from the newspapers, in his double breasted Burberry and fashionable bowler. Not just the Daughter, but her cross-suited brother, the Son of Swords, as well. Here was an inventor, an acolyte of the natural sciences, a skeptic whose pestilent writings on the failure of occult metaphysics to achieve any coherence for practical application appalled the Society with its arrogance and lack of spirit.

"We apologize for the intrusion into your private home," Lizzie said. "I can understand your alarm, but we wish only to ask you why there is a tunnel connecting Mrs. Fenchurch's backyard privy with your cellar?"

After a moment's silence during which Madame Olonsky screwed her face up into a rictus of suspicion, Lizzie brushed some dirt from her breast and said, "I can repeat the question, and you will no doubt profess ignorance of the tunnel after which I will be obliged to accuse you of lying. My colleague and I have just explored the tunnel and found it to be quite serviceable. One can traverse the distance between the properties in a matter of two minutes. The engineering is rather eloquent and comfortable. There is a walkway made from planking, two kerosene lamps to illuminate the way, even a changing station with an armoire and wardrobe of men's clothing. I don't suppose you would be able to explain why such a set-up would be in a tunnel under your cellar?"

"That is a private affair!" Madame Olonsky stammered.

"Private for whom?" Lizzie added. "For yourself? For the man who used the suits in the armoire? For Mrs. Leonard Fenchurch who has lost her husband to that privacy? I'm very, very interested in learning more about this."

"I can have your arrested," the woman bleated. "You have broken into my house!"

"On the contrary," Homer said. "You have broken into the Fenchurch house. How long has it been since you first devised that your husband would disguise himself as Leonard Fenchurch and what possible purpose could it have served?"

The sallow-faced medium sulked for a moment, and then sat back at her table in defeat, glancing with cynical briefness at the cards before her which told her clearly of her own defeat. She motioned for Lizzie and Homer to enter the room and be seated at the table as well.

"It was not my doing," she admitted. "But I certainly exploited the situation for my own gain. But it was for a higher gain! You cannot imagine the delicate threads that you are disturbing!"

"I am familiar with the murky world of secret societies," Lizzie assured her. "And I'm very familiar with how the members of such societies always believe they are struggling for a higher goal, one that cannot be understood by the mundane masses."

Madame Olonsky scowled petulantly. "I'll ignore that insult for now. But I must at least pretend to be civil. A seat, if you will, and I will explain all." She gestured for them to join her in seats around her work table. As Homer sidled into an embroidered Queen Ann chair, he spied the Tarot cards, turning his head sideways to see the various arms of the fylfot cross. He ended his perusal with a dismissive grunt.

"The man you know as Leonard Fenchurch," Madame Olonsky began, "was injured very severely in the great war with the South. His brain was damaged and for a time he did not know who he was. He came to my booth at a county fair several years ago when I read the cards for pocket change. I was not able to discern his real name, but I was able to read his character. I gave him a permanent residence by welcoming him into my home and nursing his mental state back to a healthy one. He took to his new identity well and once upon a glorious Sunday which shall glow radiant in my memory as time advances, we exchanged vows in a private Gnostic ceremony with a Priest of my own denomination."

"Which one?" Lizzie asked. "The Gnostic Catholic Church of the Incarnated Word, or the Church of Ephemeral Transposition?"

"The latter," Madame Olonsky said proudly. "I am a student of the mysteries and I will no longer be bullied by Papal stooges."

"A rather tepid point," Lizzie said dismissively, "but pray continue."

"Frederic Olonsky, for that was now his name, enjoyed all the comforts that I could afford, but he was essentially a man off the ledger book, having no real place in the society of Fall River, and associated with a woman, myself, whose reputation amongst the pious Puritans of this hypocritical town had been a shabby one at best. For a few years he dallied in these rooms, absorbing the mysteries, learning the wisdom, and training himself in the Seven Arts of the Ancients."

"When was he initiated into the Ancient Order of the Masonic Odd Men?" Homer asked. "For I believe he joined under the name Leonard Fenchurch."

Madame Olonsky's face became tight and red. "That decrepit organization is composed of lousy meddling Dualists!" she hissed. "Third rate natural philosophers! Hypocritical worshippers of Emanation!"

"These metaphysical categories are a bit beyond me," Lizzie admitted. "You must realize that this internecine squabbling amongst the brotherhoods is laughable to outsiders."

"As is the internecine squabbling between the thinkers of your own shabby religions. Trinities versus Unities! Virgin Births versus Miracle Cures! Incarnationism versus Consubstantialism!"

"Actually," Homer was quick to point out, "Incarnationism never contradicted the Doctrine of Consubstantialism!"

Madame Olonsky's face grew stormier. "Pah! To spend your days prodding each other over such pettiness as to whether God is one with the Son in Essence or in Substance! Think twice before laughing at our debates over the Prelapsarian nature of Protomatter."

"Point taken," Lizzie conceded, thinking of the endless reams of theology she had absorbed during the summer after the Affair of the Lovelorn Minister. "But I endeavor to discover which of your husband's identities, Frederick Olonsky or Leonard Fenchurch, was the true brother of the Order, and which was the spy sent to determine their agendas and strategies."

"You put me into a very difficult position. You cannot comprehend the true scope of this problem, Miss Borden! After a few years, Frederic regained his memory and discovered he had been Leonard Fenchurch. With that memory came the knowledge that he was married to the woman whose backyard privy led you to the traversing tunnel. At first Leonard was filled with joy that he was truly an integrated member of the Fall River society, welcome into their ranks, and their Congregational life of staid and stagnant obedience to social order, their clubs, their money. But he quickly went into mental disarray, filled with guilt that he had abandoned his wife and left her to believe in his death for several years. He knew that his reappearance would be a shock and prepared thoroughly for the reunion.

"He built the tunnel, working day and night with his own hands, until he had reached the property line. He dared not go further in fear of being discovered. For the higher purpose, he left me to return to his lawfully wedded wife. I was despondent, losing the only man I had ever trusted, far less loved, but he swore he would keep in contact through the tunnel.

"I was not present when he returned to his wife, but it was by all accounts a joyful occasion. Mrs. Fenchurch reacted to her husband's appearance as Mary at the empty tomb responded to the risen Lord. She picked up life with him as it had been before he went to war. They re-established conjugal relations, as could be witnessed from the lamp that burned all night within their chamber which I could see from my position of woe on my back veranda. But I took it like a warrior of the Gnosis! Something told me that the man's soul belonged in conformity and with the legitimacy that he had established long before he met me."

"A noble sentiment," Lizzie said, seemingly pleased. "Now kindly tell me what went wrong?"

"His memory damage still had some life to it," Madam Olonsky said ruefully. "I found him in my bedroom one night, having prepared himself in sleep apparel from Frederic Olonsky's wardrobe. He was muddled, no longer capable of recognizing himself as Leonard Fenchurch. I was in a dilemma. My husband whom I loved very much was back, but he didn't believe me when I told him he was not really my husband and his life belonged in another house. It took days for me to persuade him to return to his wife."

"And was that successful?"

"Too successful. He vanished back into Leonard Fenchurch for months, passing me in the street without so much as a wink of recognition. And he would then reappear in my home with little memory of Fenchurch. And so the cycling went for days at a time. It eventually settled into a routine where he would be away for three and a half days and then present for three and a half. He would always make his exits in the middle of the night, after having explained that he was going to Boston on a business trip. I truly believe he wasn't even aware of these transitions and that after a time he was so jumbled that he was almost insane. I'm afraid rather than helping the poor man with his mental maladies, I had created an impossible situation that threatened the unity of his very mind."

"I can see the dilemma," Lizzie said. "It sounds as if you were attempting to handle things with an ethical sensibility."

"Thank you," their host said breathlessly. "I have never been so complimented before. But my altruism only lasted so long. I only gradually became aware of Leonard's association with the Odd Men and that is when I made my second fatal error, the first being the acceptance of his dual life."

"You created a Dual initiate," Homer said, a light of illumination flashing on his brow. "Leonard Fenchurch had advanced to the Third Degree of the Odd Men. He had reached the top of the ladder. It was now time for Frederic Olonsky to begin his ascent from the bottom of the ladder."

"It was not my idea, but I allowed it. Frederic was as incensed against the Order as I was, and was determined to penetrate its ranks and discover its secrets for my own Order."

"The Order for which you cannot name," Lizzie clarified.

"I am bound by oaths," Madame Olonsky flickered irritably. "Frederic was as well. But the Oaths he took in the chambers of the Odd Men did not seem like valid oaths. They were toys to be trifled with. After each meeting, and especially after each initiation ceremony, he would write everything down and hand the manuscript over to me. He had a photographic memory, you know." She twisted up her brow for a moment. "Hmm, photographic memory. There's a bit of an irony there, isn't there?"

"Certainly," Lizzie said, "but pray tell us how the members of the Odd Men failed to notice the physical resemblance between Brother Olonsky and Brother Fenchurch."

"That is simple enough. The ranking is such that a different body applies the degree and opens the Temples from one degree to the other.

Once a certain ranking of members are elevated, they see only the men of their rank. It is quite like being in school where the members of the first grade do not share a classroom with the third grade."

"And yet," Lizzie said, "the Hierophant and the Wardens are present at all ceremonies."

Madame Olonsky's silence now dominated the conversation. For a long moment, the significance of what Lizzie just said began to flood their thoughts.

"My God," Homer whispered. "That means—"

"I cannot say more," Madame Olonsky breathed. "I fear that I will have to answer for my indiscretion."

Before any further discussion could be had, there was suddenly a rapid and violent knock upon the front door. It startled all three, who had grown twitchy and apprehensive during the latter half of their discussion.

"I must see who it is," Madame Olonsky announced. "I am not accustomed to visitors at this hour of the night."

"One moment," Lizzie said, rising to her feet. "Let me answer."

"It is my house!"

"Then attend me," Lizzie said, hopping ahead of her reluctant host. Homer followed behind them and they found themselves at the front door, listening intently before Lizzie bellowed, "Who is there?" with perhaps a slight attempt to mimic Madame Olonsky's raspy voice.

After a brief moment, one that Lizzie felt was uncomfortably long, there was a loud rustling noise, as if fireworks were going off but lacking the fullness and richness of an actual crowd. Then came a voice, thin and tinny but audible enough to make out timbre, pitch, and color.

"Thank you gentlemen, unaccustomed as I am to public speaking..."

Madame Olonsky's face lit up as she scrambled for the lead bolt. "Frederic!" she bellowed and fidgeted with the locks, flinging the door open once she had mastered them.

Standing outside the doorway was the Marshal, all six-foot three of him, fully uniformed and topped with his shell hat and bristling mustache. He held in his white gloved hands the Phemegraph whose cylinder whirled rapidly, still producing the words of Leonard Fenchurch from its tiny horn.

"Good evening, Madam!" the Marshall said, lifting the armature and terminating the playback of the recording. He handed the machine over the threshold to Homer who took it greedily, examining it for damage. "It's a most damnable thing," the Marshal said, pointing at the box. "I played it a few times for amusement and I still can't believe there isn't a man trapped inside there."

"Perfectly sound principles!" Homer emphasized. "Pardon the pun."

"Where did you get that?" Madame Olonsky said, gesticulating at the Phemegraph. "That belongs properly with Frederic Olonsky the Rational Gnostic Spiritualist, not Leonard Fenchurch the Tinkerer of Novelties."

"If we may be permitted," the Marshal said, removing his helmet. They all withdrew to the parlor where the Phemegraph was placed delicately on the table. Madame Olonsky continued to eye it skeptically.

"Marshal," Lizzie explained, "in the past half hour we have learned a great deal about Leonard Fenchurch and his connection to both Madame Olonsky and the Masonic Order of Odd Men!"

"Good, I'm glad someone is able to puzzle this out. Please fill me in."

"Madame Olonsky just told us a story. Quite a remarkable one that seems more a fantasy than a reality. With her recognition of Fenchurch's voice through the door, I am more than satisfied that it is not fantasy at all."

She proceeded to fill the Marshal in on the story, and with emphasis on the personal tragedy of Fenchurch's mental malady. She graciously, and to Madame Olonsky's relief, excised any mention of the final revelation concerning the Master of the Inner Temple of Odd Men.

"Extraordinary," the Marshal said, twisting one end of his mustache. "I've never heard anything like it."

"Something out of the pages of Ann Radcliffe," Lizzie asserted, "Or the Brontë Sisters."

"To think that a man who has had two identities," the Marshal said astonished, "now has none."

"We may look upon it," Lizzie said, "that he currently has no identity and has two to discover."

"I'm not quite sure which is the more desirable," Homer said, glancing skeptically at his host.

"Enough of that for now," Lizzie interrupted. "We still have a murder to solve and precious little time to do it. I am awaiting the final piece of the puzzle. I freely admit that my strategy may not yield all the answers we crave, but it shall be illuminating nonetheless."

"And what strategy is that?" the Marshal inquired.

"When I first heard of the murder at the barber shop, I suspected that the motive was much greater than theft. After all, no money was stolen from the till, nor was the victim robbed of his belongings. In fact, the murdered man himself had thirty-two dollars in cash in his jacket. When Mr. Fenchurch appeared at Homer's workshop with his mind erased, we determined that he had been to the barber shop that very morning. But he was there before the store had opened, and he was not there primarily for a shave, although he seems to have relented to the offer made by Mr. Borden. The barber, however, was in a hurry, because his purpose of opening his shop to a private party was to use the remarkable Phemegraph machine of Homer Thesinger's to record his harmonic quartet onto the wax cylinder that you see before you.

"Yes, this humble cylinder contains the sound information needed to recreate the final moments in the barber shop before the crime. Three men joined them, four of the assembled positioned themselves before the tonsure chairs, and one of the assembled set up the Phemegraph in such a manner as to capture the sound of their voices in the most efficient manner.

"Leonard Fenchurch, acting as sound technician, recorded their Gilbert and Sullivan recital onto this waxen surface, preserving it for all to hear."

"How did this result in murder?" the Marshal asked. "Was Borden so painfully off-key to merit a horrible penalty?"

"On the contrary, his performance was quite harmonious that day. He had a lovely bass voice."

"Then why was he killed, and by whom?"

"I hope to reveal that in just a few moments," Lizzie said, glancing at the clock. "If my instructions are followed to the letter, then I shall be successful in determining precisely who, although I still fear the why may elude us. We must now but wait."

"Why was Leonard involved in this affair?" the Marshal asked desperately. "Was he brought there to aid in the murder? They couldn't have just invited him along to work the recording machine. He would walk away with the identities of the murderers and the details of the killing."

"Precisely the opposite!" Lizzie said. "He was the only person in Fall River who could witness the event and not walk away with either the identities or the details!"

"Ah!" Homer said, nodding. "A perfect witness, one whose memory is erased every ten minutes."

"But why bring him there in the first place?"

"Because Mr. Fenchurch wasn't only a man suffering from *tabulae rasae*. He also knew how to operate a Phemegraph, apparently in both identities. Where else in the city, far less the entire country, would you find such a combination: a recording engineer who would also lose all memory of the recording session?"

Homer stared blankly and then grinned liberally. "I'm starting to see the picture. Borden was baited and drawn into a trap. His own harmonic quartet murdered him and retained a mindless engineer so there would be no witnesses."

"Let me get this straight," the Marshal said, counting numbers in the air before him. "Fenchurch was only Fenchurch for a few days at a time, but then would turn into Olonsky for a few days at a time. After a while, those intervals were getting closer and closer, each time erasing his memory of the last interval. So he goes to the barber shop as Fenchurch and walks away as Olonsky."

"That was the plan," Lizzie explained. "However something went horribly wrong. When Fenchurch witnessed the crime, he had a traumatic seizure, the two halves of him collided with guilt and confusion, and he resolved into being no one at all. Except he still has his *tabulae rasae*."

Madame Olonsky clicked her tongue morosely. "What a horrible existence! Losing memory of being no one at all! It is the exact opposite of our spiritual mandate."

The Marshal was still puzzling out the details. "So whoever invited Fenchurch to the barber shop knew about his condition, and knew the properties of each identity. Who could that have been?" His eyebrows arched. "His fraternity!"

Almost as if an invisible spirit had descended upon the house, conjured by the Marshal's revelation, there was another ringing of the front bell. At first no one moved, until it became clear that Madame Olonsky had been expected to comply. She stirred uneasily and drooped along to the front door, her dress hem dragging behind her.

"Who is it?" she asked wheezily through the wooden panel.

A large heavy voice came from without. "Miles Standish," It bellowed.

The Marshall looked back and forth from Homer to Lizzie. "Miles Standish?" Lizzie motioned with her finger to her lips and the Marshal clamped a palm over his mouth.

"I'll be with you shortly," she said, grabbing Homer's kit bag and disappearing from the room.

Madame Olonsky reluctantly opened the door to reveal a large heavy-set man with a prodigious mustache. He waltzed into the house, whisking the door closed behind him, and practically danced on his tiptoes.

"Pumpkin!" he said, grabbing her hand and covering it with kisses. "I received your note! I am delighted that you want to dally with me! I have missed our dallying! I am most exhilarated!"

He paused, noticing her trembling pale cheeks. A subtle shift of her eyes towards the parlor produced an audible gasp from the newcomer. He dropped her hand, pulled at his hat, and groped about with hands in the empty air.

"Hide me," he said meekly, then turned to face the Marshal who had walked up behind him, accompanied by Officer Periwinkle who was fiddling with a set of hand irons.

"Mr. Jason Smedley," the Marshal said, recognizing the face behind the mustache. "I'm hoping that you can help us in a small affair. It seems as if a barber on Columbia Street was slashed to death this past Tuesday and we have reason to believe that you have information regarding this most singular affair."

The man's strong and confident voice had grown quizzical and breathy. "I get my shaves on North Main, at O'Hare's. He is a superior tonsure, quite reliable." With that he stroked his mustache.

A second later, a figure crossed into the room toward where they were standing. It was a small pear-shaped man with a trim mustache and a bowler hat, standing in pin- striped trousers and a bank clerk's jacket.

"Good evening, Holy Hierophant!" the young man said, lifting his bowler, which sent long curly hair tumbling down to his shoulders. "I trust that the Prismatic Theorems are fully concealed and the Temple is duly guarded!"

"You!" Smedley roared. "You're a woman!"

Lizzie removed the mustache and took a small bow. At that instant, the air about them was filled with the distinct strain of four men singing in harmony. Homer Thesinger was in the parlor, controlling the rotating disk on the Phemegraph.

"A policeman's lot is not a happy one!"
Then the bass voice let out with a sustained bellow.
"Happy one!"

Smedley spontaneously yelped and jumped into the air, landing again with a thud. Then with a jerk and a two-step, he raced towards the rear of the house. By the time the large man had disappeared around the corner into the kitchen, Lizzie had taken off her mustache and was smiling at her audience, holding up a hand. "Let him go for now. He's heading for the tunnel, hoping that we don't know about it. But I have arranged an evil surprise!"

The Marshal pulled furiously at his whiskers. "What the devil?"

"Officer Periwinkle should be positioned by now," Homer said, glancing at his watch fob. "And he has an honored guest with him."

The Marshal gulped, scratched his head, and then began to laugh heartily. The laugh turned into a guffaw and then a full belly howling. "By Jove," he roared, "that is most brilliant! Most brilliant! I shall be prepared to receive our prisoner with the appropriate hand shackles!"

Trapped!

Mr. Leonard Fenchurch, without blinking, had been led by the officer through his own house that he had owned since before the Great War. He recognized nothing, not even his doting wife who stared at him with teary eyes. When confronted with the backyard privy, he glared at it, then turned and said, "I am not yet ready for my toilet!"

The officer lifted the privy seat and held out a hand. "My orders are to proceed forthwith into the gaping maw of the privy box, secure in the knowledge that there will be no filth or foul residue. I extend that assurance to you, my charge."

Fenchurch grumbled and proceeded to climb down into the aperture. All through the length of the tunnel he patted the wooden supports as if nervous that the roof would collapse on him, reducing his wretchedly empty life to even less than what it was currently.

"My dear sir," he announced after pausing in his steps. "I realize that I do not know where I am, nor do I know your identity, although my mind still retains the concept of law official. However, I can only assume that you are leading me to my death. In which case, will you permit me a last cigar before I die?"

"Do you even smoke?" Officer Periwinkle shrugged.

Fenchurch tapped a forefinger against his chin. "Hmm, good question. I don't think I know."

"Then why don't you just sit in this chair," Officer Periwinkle offered, leading his charge to the chaise. Fenchurch inspected the chair, practically bowed over to sniff it, then dusted his pant seat and lowered himself into the furniture. He toyed with one of the books, flipping through its pages while the Officer checked his watch for some unknown reason.

Suddenly, he went through another transition and had to reorient himself. He was in an underground tunnel sitting in a chair reading a book while a police officer waited patiently. How extraordinary! He glanced at the title of the book that was splayed in his hands.

THE HISTORY OF MECHANICAL AUTOMATA IN THE FRENCH REVOLUTION AND BRITISH REGENCY
PROFESSOR JAMES OTTO
AUGUST 22-27, 1869

The pages revealed pictures of trombones and harps and cartoons of conductors from the waist up, dressed in tuxedos and waving their batons with clock-like motion.

How extraordinary!

He was lowering the book onto the nearby shelf and touching another one when there was a scuffle up ahead in the dank tunnel. A large man, practically filling the width of the walkway was barreling forwards, incoherent gibberish bellowing from his mouth.

Mr. Fenchurch took to his feet and stood in the walkway before the accelerating man. He tipped his hat. "Excuse me," he said to the agitated man in motion. "Can you be so kind as to explain to me where I am? And, if you are even more so inclined, to explain who I am?"

The large man froze, his feet practically bolting into the wooden planks below. After a brief moment scrutinizing Fenchurch's face, surrendering to the gravity of the situation, he let out with a prolonged scream that shook the tunnel, causing dirt to fall like heavy rain on all their heads.

This was followed by a series of bleats and jabs that did not make any sense outside of the general message of panic. He turned to face the direction from which he had emerged, started a manic sprint for the entry to the Olonsky house cellar, but froze again. Realizing that he was trapped, he reached for his face with his clutching hands, pulling at his tongue and poking his own eyes, his reason unhinged. His knees buckled and he collapsed downward, his large torso jamming both sides of the passage. From his position on the ground he let forth with a stream of words so nonsensical they didn't seem to have equivalence in any language.

Mr. Fenchurch watched all this with intense curiosity. He turned to Officer Periwinkle and asked, "Would you be so kind as to tell me who this man is?" The officer shrugged and Fenchurch chuckled, "I'm happy to know that I am not the only man alive whose name is undiscoverable!"

Periwinkle tried to lift the babbling Smedley to his feet. "Time to go, my friend," Officer Periwinkle said. "I may not know your name, but Miss Lizzie was very precise that anyone trying to escape through this tunnel should be arrested for murder."

"Murder!" Mr. Fenchurch said anxiously. "Is he safe? Did he escape from a nervous hospital?"

"Just come!" Officer Periwinkle motioned for Fenchurch to follow them. It was only a few yards before another ladder ascending into the cellar of the Olonsky house. He coaxed the barely conscious Smedley up its rungs and helped Fenchurch ascend as well. The trio walked through the dark murky basement, filled with large boxes and tables covered with strange alchemical alembics and flasks.

They found the Marshal, Lizzie, Homer, and Madame Olonsky in the parlor. Also present was Doctor Bowen, who had arrived upon Lizzie's instructions, his eyes bleary from a full day's work and his shirt sleeves rolled up for business. The hostess was white as a sheet and trembling. She shuddered and groaned when she saw the state that Smedley was in. He collapsed onto the couch where Doctor Bowen ministered to him.

"I may have to give him an injection of bromo-caffeine," the doctor said. "He's suffering from a severe shock."

"Was he your devotee?" Lizzie asked Madame Olonsky bluntly.

The thin-faced woman glared at her with darkened eyes. "He was my mentor, my teacher, my prophet."

"Sounds like they were devotees to me," the Marshal chuckled.

"You are trifling with my faith," the woman snarled.

"And you two conspired to murder a man," Lizzie said hastily. "Even worse, you executed the deed, taking advantage of this poor man you called your husband."

"It was a legal ceremony!" Madame Olonsky boasted. "Performed by the Church of the Accelerating Veracity."

Homer slapped a palm to his forehead. "Ye Gods, how many secret societies are in this town?"

"As many as there are rays in a beam of sunlight," Madame Olonsky recited. "For the colors are many, but the light is one!"

"Speaking of light," Lizzie said, "why don't you illuminate us as to why Mr. Borden needed to be eliminated? And how did you trust this man to witness the event, far less record it with a Phemegraph."

"The Phemegraph was unexpected. Borden insisted upon it. He was fascinated by the technology and wanted Fenchurch to stick around and record them. The ritual was enacted in spite of his presence. We knew that his memory lapses were getting worse and that within moments he would have no record of the act in his head."

"But why?" the Marshal insisted. "Why did the man have to die?"

Smedley had lifted his head off his couch arm and grunted out an answer to the Marshal's question. "He violated his oaths!"

"And do the Ancient Order of Masonic Odd Men make a habit out of murdering those who break their oaths?"

"Ha!" Smedley roared. He lifted himself to a seating position. His face was crimson with rage. "The Odd Men are fools! Patsies! Simpletons who can only understand an emanation model of divine sustainment and can never penetrate into the multi-perspectival universe!"

"Hmm," Lizzie said. "That still leaves the motive very murky. Can you explain in plainer English?"

"He preached the Four and refuted the Three! One in Three! Three in One! There is no need for a Fourth! That is why the Southern Warden is missing. He was slain years ago when the first Grand Masters set the Minuscule Monad into Rotation around the Axis of Affirmation! Once every hundred years, the Fourth must be murdered to maintain the balance and to start a new cycle."

Madame Olonsky hissed and scowled. "Smedley! Your oaths! Are you mad?"

"The Odd Men are just a subterfuge, to throw them off the track!" Smedley raved on.

"What track?" the Marshal asked. "What in the name of Jupiter and Saturn are you babbling about?"

"The Arcady—" Smedley yelled, then fell back onto the couch, clutching his chest and breathing as if an elephant were stamping on his ribs.

"This man is having a heart attack!" Dr. Bowen said, ripping open his patient's vest. "Stand back! Give him space!"

Smedley jerked upon the cushions, grunting and snorting, spittle cascading down his chin. Then he settled into a strange somnambulant stillness, still breathing but with erratic rasps. Dr. Bowen checked his pulse and felt his forehead. "He's stabilized," he announced, "but he has suffered a severe shock."

Smedley opened his eyes and started to rattle off in a thin sing-song voice:

> *"Won't you come to my house?*
> *To my house! To my house!*
> *Won't you come to my house!*
> *There's lot of games to play!"*

His eyes fell on a particular automaton, a garish ape dressed as a French aristocrat, laced in silks and costly apparel, capped with a powdered wig. He rode a bicycle whose wheels remained eerily silent until Smedley darted forth and twisted the key at the base, setting it into grotesque motion.

"A mockery of the Enlightenment philosophy of the French Revolution," Madame Olonsky said. "Voltaire as Darwin's ape. Not the sort of thing Smedley would approve of in his ordinary state."

The Holy Hierophant of the Holy Order of Masonic Odd Men was now drooling with delight before the gyrating monkey-man.

"I fear also that his mind may be gone," the doctor announced sadly. "Whatever information he has about the murder may be lost forever."

"Not quite," Lizzie said. "Remember there were two more men present who still have their wits, presumably. I know them only as the Warden of the East and the Warden of the West. You will find them at the next meeting of the Ancient Order of the Masonic Odd Men, which I believe is tomorrow evening at eight on the clock at the Temple on Ferry Street, second floor. I will give you the proper steps and signs and secret passwords to obtain entry to the chamber. Either that or you can force your way in by lawful authority."

"A good old search warrant will do," the Marshal said. "Warden of the East and Warden of the West? Hmm. What kind of operation are they throwing there?" he asked.

"A most mysterious one," Lizzie replied. "Full of hokum and

wisdom twisted together into some strange set of unorthodox beliefs. I found much of what they said cogent and worthy of further meditation, but this twist in the affair, revealing the Holy Hierophant to have conspired to murder Samuel Borden and to have carried out the deed himself reveals that the Odd Men have been infiltrated by a much more secret group, one we know only as the Arcady Society. I have detected their presence before, and I suspect we will hear more about them in the future. The fact that they can resort to murder to protect their interests gives us pause to wonder if they are capable of far more ambitious crimes, such as vast conspiracies against our commonwealth."

"Well, for now," the Marshal said, pulling at Smedley's collar. "Let's get this idiot into custody."

"He needs medical attention," Dr. Bowen said. "I must attend."

"Fine," the Marshal agreed. "Lizzie, I'll return to break the news to Mrs. Fenchurch."

"No!" she said. "Leave Mrs. Fenchurch to rebuild her marriage. She must have no knowledge of this affair. Madame Olonsky will be charged with conspiracy to murder and there will be a public announcement that Smedley confessed to the murder of Samuel Borden. No mention should be made of the wax recording, the Phemegraph, or the man who operated it in the barber shop that Tuesday morning."

The Marshal hesitated, glared at Madame Olonsky who recoiled with a barely audible hiss, then motioned for the officers to grab her too.

"I'll return the poor Mr. Fenchurch to his wife," Lizzie said. "And within twenty-four hours, the city of Fall River will issue a warrant to enter the property line of the house on Franklin Street and destroy the backyard privy. It will be roundly condemned as a health hazard. Mrs. Fenchurch will not question the ordinance and Mr. Fenchurch will not even remember that the privy existed."

"Right," the Marshal said. "Is everyone in agreement? Can we get a consensus?"

There was a round of ayes about the room and the law officials began to handle their charges. Smedley resisted as the hand shackles were applied but he ultimately gave in, hardly sensible of what they were even for.

Before the house was vacated, Mr. Fenchurch slipped from the grasp of Officer Periwinkle and walked to where Smedley was sagging in the Marshal's grip. He inspected his face, touched his cheek, then turned and touched his own. Strange shadows passed over his countenance.

"Yes," he said. "Fenchurch. That's right. My name is Fenchurch. How extraordinary!"

"That's the first time he remembered on his own," Homer said. "Perhaps he'll remember the murders."

"Fenchurch," the amnesiac was muttering. "Arcady, was what he said. Yes, Arcady!" He snapped his fingers, "Arcady!"

Lizzie grabbed his forearm. "Mr. Fenchurch, what about Arcady? Do you know who they are? Where are they—"

Before she could finish, Fenchurch's face went through another transition and his cheery cheeks went limp. "Who?" he said. "Who are you? In fact, who am I?"

Lizzie sighed and pushed the man in the direction of the officer. "Return him to his wife. I'll instruct her in how to handle his peculiar condition. Perhaps one day we'll discover the bottom of this mystery. It is not the first time it has eluded me."

"For now, it is enough that we have the murderer of Samuel Borden," the Marshal said. "Huzzah for Lizzie! The constabulary of Fall River salutes you!"

"Fine," Lizzie said, distracted. "Just don't mention my name in any of the papers."

"As usual."

When all were vacated and Lizzie was left alone on the front porch of the Olonsky house with Homer, she pointed towards his kit bag. "Do you still have those cylinders we worked on yesterday?"

"Intact," Homer said, tapping the Phemegraph. "Sound vibrations from the past trapped forever in wax."

"Are you really going to patent that machine as your own? How much of it have you truly invented?"

"Lizzie Borden, how many times do I have to tell you? An inventor does not produce miracles out of thin air. He tinkers with the thousands of discoveries made before him, often by men more accomplished than himself. More than a fair share of this device is due to the work of Thomas Edison, the Wizard of Menlo Park, my hero, my mentor, my prophet..." His voice trailed off as he remembered the words of Madame Olonsky. "Perhaps I'd best leave it at that."

"That may be," Lizzie added. "But the Thesinger box is truly your own invention. It is simple and elegant, no moving parts, just two chambers, a presence and an absence. And a mirror between."

"Sounds like a parable of life. Or, at least, the life of Leonard Fenchurch."

They shared a good laugh and strolled together off the porch and into the darkening twilight of Fall River. The stars above were beginning their great curve towards midnight and the sun was sneaking into its night chamber to yield way to its most mystical twin.

A Final Visitation

In the wake of the Affair of the Audible Amnesiac, several critical details were withheld from the public. From the journalist perspective, Mr. Samuel Borden had been murdered in his shop by members of his own fraternal lodge, the Ancient Order of the Masonic Odd Men. The entire upper council of the Lodge was arrested and charged. The man known as the Holy Hierophant was deemed unfit to stand trial because of his mental instability and he was sent to Taunton Asylum for observation by the nervous doctors.

His real name was Arthur Jason Smedley and he was a cook at the Wilber Arms Hotel on North Main Street. He spent his subsequent days babbling incoherently and asking his warden if his padded cell was duly guarded. The warden invariably humored him by asserting that the padded cell was indeed duly guarded.

Mr. Leonard Fenchurch was returned to his wife and remained for the large part confined to his chambers, rarely leaving his bed far less his house for several years. His involvement with the affair at the barber shop was never publicly revealed, nor was the wax cylinder recording of the harmony quartet of the slaughtered man singing melodiously with his killers before he was catapulted into the infinite, never to return.

Another set of persons who were excised from the newspaper accounts were Lizzie Borden, the Girl Detective of Second Street, and Homer Thesinger the Electromachinician of Prospect Street. The two young investigators returned to their families with the profound renewal of faith in the marvelous inventions that men like Thomas Edison and Homer Thesinger were producing for the edification of mankind.

"It can double as a portable amanuensis," Homer explained one afternoon to Andrew Borden. They reclined on the mohair couch in the Borden sitting room, staring at the Phemegraph which rested on the table before them. Andrew was fiddling with the armature, testing its weight and range.

"You mean to tell me," Andrew marveled, "that I can record an entire correspondence on this contraption, and a secretary can write my words down for transcription? What other wonders can this perform?"

Homer flapped his hands excitedly. "You can send it to the opera for you, and it will return with the performance. Then you can hear the strains of divine arias in the privacy of your own home."

Andrew nodded in approval. "As long as it isn't Wagner."

"University lectures will be preserved, the speech of great men, Lyceum appearances. Immortal poems of antiquity will be yours for the playback, every play ever written. Shakespeare will come alive in the Borden parlor."

"And who will record all this literary bilge?"

"It's not bilge, Father!" Lizzie said, banging her knuckles against his shoulder. "And there will be no end of actors waiting to have their voices recorded for posterity."

A smile curled on Andrew's lips. "And with my capital behind the manufactory, we will all become wealthy beyond measure. Yes, the Borden Portable Amanuensis and Phemegraph. We must start producing models immediately."

"I'm afraid that's not possible Mr. Borden," Homer said, flicking at his pants leg. "I already have filed my patent caveat and sold it."

Andrew sank back into the couch as if air had just been released from his interior. "You sold it? We could have made thousands."

"I did make thousands. I sold the patent to the Wizard of Menlo Park."

"That goblin! He's the biggest fraud in the business! Homer, you have no business sense."

"But I am licensed to keep my prototype for amusement. We can record and play back our cylinders for eternity. Which reminds me Lizzie, isn't it time we resurrect the dead."

Lizzie glanced at the clock on the mantle. "If Mrs. Borden and Emma have finished with their shopping. I believe I hear them now."

The two women struggled in through the front door carrying packages of dry goods and dinner meats. Emma was indulging herself in laughing at some sort of humor that Mrs. Borden had expressed, but her face went stark still upon seeing Lizzie and Homer flanking her father. She rushed hurriedly through the sitting room into the kitchen as if being pursued by something dangerous.

As she did so, Homer slipped through the door into the parlor and closed it. Lizzie rose to greet her stepmother.

"Mrs. Borden," she announced, "you have spent several years mocking my detective agency."

"Not now, Lizzie," Abby said hastily, shifting her grocery bags to a more comfortable position. "There are chores to do. Dinner must be prepared and—"

"I would listen to your step-daughter," Andrew said, rising from the couch. "What she has to say is important. If it helps, I'll take that burden from you."

His hands went forward to carry the bags and Abby frowned at them. With confused silence, she handed them over and Andrew scuttled with a slight chuckle into the kitchen, closing the door behind him. Right before he did so, he gave Lizzie a puckish wink.

"What was that about," Abby puzzled. "Andrew carrying groceries?"

"As I was saying," Lizzie continued, pressing her hands together and rubbing them. "You have doubted whether my work with detection and Homer's backyard tinkering has been of any value to ourselves, to our community, or to humanity at large. Well, today I am proud to announce that we have perfected the ultimate device by which to bring our dearly departed back from the other world."

Abby gulped visibly. "My, Lizzie Andrew Borden. If I had any doubts about your sanity, now they are confirmed."

"On the contrary Mrs. Borden," Lizzie said, motioning to the dining room door. "Today we have a distinguished visitor. In fact, he is about to give a speech."

"A what?" Abby said, trembling.

Lizzie wrapped a knuckle on the door and shouted, "Mr. President!" after which the following voice came shrill and thin through the wood panels.

> Four score and seven years ago our fathers brought forth, on this continent, a new nation, conceived in Liberty, and dedicated to the proposition that all men are created equal.

A strange light flooded Abby's face. Her knees wobbled. Her eyebrows furled. With a shriek, she pushed open the dining room door, and desperation that had never before been exhibited by her in Lizzie's living memory erupted on the surface.

Once within the dining room, she ground to a sudden halt. Before her were Homer and her husband, Andrew, standing behind the dining room table. By their side was Emma, almost whimpering. They were the only inhabitants of the room.

Unless, of course, you counted the Phemegraph which played on the table before them. The voice continued, lingering in its phrasing, delighting in its own logic, till finally it came to a dramatic conclusion.

> *...that we here highly resolve that these dead shall not have died in vain – that this nation, under God, shall have a new birth of freedom, and that government of the people, by the people, for the people, shall not perish from the earth.*

Immediately following the recital, as the cylinder came to a dead halt, Abby's eyebrows steamed, her lips pursed, her hands curled into fists. Then, as she perused the jovial faces of Andrew and Homer, she softened, and then slackened.

"Was that you?" she asked. "Andrew?"

Andrew grinned and nodded. "Guilty as charged."

"Why," she said, pondering her dilemma. "That was quite charming."

"I recorded it for you, Abigail," Andrew said, stepping from behind the table, advancing toward her and caressing her cheek. "I meant every word of it."

"My," was all she could say. "My!"

Homer and Lizzie exchanged playful glances, then they motioned towards Emma.

"Don't be so shy," Homer said to his best friend's sister. "We can record our voices for amusement; keep a record of the family preserved in wax for posterity to hear. One day historians will be anxious to know more about us, and what thrill these cylinders shall give them!"

"I'm afraid of that thing," Emma replied. "It may eat me."

"Nonsense, Emma," Andrew said, not removing his eyes from his wife. "It's better than a photograph, and more ingenious."

Abby poked him on the shoulder with a stubby finger. "You mean more profitable, you old coot! You have your eye on Homer's next patent."

"Well," Andrew quipped. "I can't say I do and I can't say that I don't!"

"That's a logical contradiction," Lizzie said. "But one that shall speak volumes for the human condition. Regardless, let us all partake of that excellent dinner that Mrs. Borden and Emma have so graciously brought home for us! I will enjoy some light hearted banter and some good food with my beloved family!"

With hearty chuckles, they strolled from the room, the last one being Emma who took one last eyeball jab at the contraption that disturbed her so. She approached it almost as if trying to make peace with a hostile force. She prodded it and after ascertaining its safety, pulled the wax cylinder from the playback shaft. There were a few more cylinders on the table, and she lifted a random one to the machine, sliding it on as if it were most intuitive. After a tense pause, she pressed her finger to the switch that she had seen deployed too often, and set the cylinder in motion.

There were the familiar crackles of static and the rough surface of the wax dragging under the playback needle. At first she thought it as dead as Uncle Sam Borden, but then it spoke.

"Hello?" it said. "Are you there? Can anyone hear me?"

Emma yelped and ran halfway to the door. Its subsequent silence stopped her cold. She jerked her head between the exit and the machine. Then it spoke again:

"I pray, can you please tell me who I am? You see, I have forgotten! I'm afraid I need you to help! Who am I?"

Within seconds, Emma was gone from the room, the door having slammed forcefully shut. In the echoing silence, the room was void of all human inhabitants, resting in its own solemnity.

But then the voice came again:

"You must tell me! I am so lonely here with only the voices on this wax to keep me company! I need you to tell me who I am so I can keep myself company and no longer need anyone else! Please," it said. "Please, sir."

"Who am I? And failing that," it said. "Who are you?"

The nearby church tolled the hour and the cylinder came to a halt, leaving the dining room now void of presence. The machine itself was as still as death, now failing to even mimic the traces of sorrow.

Faintly in the distance, behind walls of wooden paneling, came the sounds of merriment, a human family enjoying its private abode.

THE END

THE MELANCHOLY SCION

MAY 1927. FRENCH STREET, THE HILL, FALL RIVER, MASSACHUSETTS.

PRESSED IN LAVENDER

For Lizzie Borden, Andre de Camp will always be the Poet.

In all her sixty-six years on earth, she had never been known to pay such reverence, silent or otherwise, to any member of the male sex, whether to applaud virtue or to praise physical elegance. But Andre de Camp, scion of a wealthy French family that had relocated to Fall River in the summer of 1877, a tall, brooding and decidedly handsome bachelor of nineteen years, the product of private advanced education, brilliant, fastidious in his manly dress and precise in his manners and ethics, held a special place in Lizzie's estimation of the masculine half of humanity.

She first glimpsed him at a mid-summer charity event in the church hall of the First Congregational. Standing with his illustrious family—the father wearing proudly a decorated uniform, the mother and sister standing upright with pious concentration—Andre bowed his head towards Lizzie, just once, as if in humble supplication before a higher power. The gesture sent a chill through Lizzie's being.

She quickly became impressed with how the de Camp men were so very different from the money-driven barons who banked her city, the uncultured factors and industrialists who would never design a cathedral or build an opera hall lest they consider it "a foolish dollar spent." Andre de Camp may have been spawned from that same class, yet he brought with him all the cultured elegance of Paris and the dark mysteries of the southern Languedoc, locales that Lizzie had admired from afar through sepia photographs of the mountainous region with its lush outcroppings and deep-veined soil, a land she thought only existed in her dreams.

Andre was a graceful, aristocratic youth who, like herself, was more comfortable with the personal passions and the aesthetics of everyday life than with the complexities of commerce. She saw in him not the proud Marshals and Presidents of France's dusty past, nor the great Sun King in his splendid palace, but the simple shepherds from the paintings of Poussin, the noble musketeers of Dumas, and the provincial people of the tales of Flaubert. He embodied in his presence all the excitement, adventure and beauty that she had admired in the great French paintings and novels that made their way to various Fall River parlors. In her opinion, he far outpaced in every manner the grown men of his generation.

But for the rest of her days she would never speak his name aloud. Even as an aging woman of the Hill, secluded in her summer bedroom in the rambling Maplecroft, her manse and hermitage, alone as she looked back upon a dark and hidden life, she would only speak of Andre as the Poet, and then briefly, and then only to a chauffeur or a domestic who was not of her generation, who would never have heard of the de Camp family, or would never repeat her words to anyone in town who may have known them, and then only when she was caught off guard with some seizure of nostalgia for a Fall River that had once been and now was no more.

But when the glimmer came in her aging eyes, and she spoke of the Poet, when she made oblique references to faces and places now lost to time and memory, when she hinted that once she had loved and felt within her breast a singular passion the likes of which had never been repeated, it was the summer of 1877 and the Case of the Melancholy Scion to which her thoughts took her. Back to a time before she was the secluded spinster on the Hill, before she sat alone in church because no fellow citizens would occupy the pews adjoining hers, before she was accused of that terrible crime whose shadow she would never escape, back when she was young and fresh and alive; to the time when she walked the streets of Fall River with Andre de Camp, who also was young and fresh and alive, and who, despite her unwillingness to let her heart be so directly touched, had truly loved her.

Back when she was Lizzie Borden, Girl Detective.

UNSETTLING REVELATIONS

1877. South Main Street, Fall River.

Andrew Jackson Borden took his pre-dinner constitutional from the front of his quaint little Greek revival house on Second Street towards the tonsorial parlor, the post office and the pharmacy to, respectively, get a shave, check for his mail and to inquire about the gastroesophe-geal disruption pills his wife Abby needed for her burning chest pains. Threading his way through the narrow streets, surrounded by the bustle of pedestrian traffic, the whinnying of nags, the clattering of buggies, and the hawking of the fish mongers, Borden turned to survey the town that had given him birth and had nurtured him through his rise to prosperity.

So many estate properties, he thought to himself. *So many empty lots. If only I could possess them all, to have that locus of power over the domestic and commercial fate of every individual in Fall River.* He allowed himself this one pure moment of magnitude, imagining an inflated likeness of himself that lay unrealized by his business colleagues, and then with a wistful grin that barely moved the edge of his mouth pushed on towards the barber for his weekly trimming.

At that very moment, a short squat man with a bulbous nose and bristling mustache stopped in front of Andrew, ungraciously blocking his path.

"You're A.J. Borden, I believe!"

Andrew lifted his chin proudly. "I do have that honor."

The man's mouth made a strange mumbling motion and then before Andrew could take refuge in flight, the man bellowed an almost incomprehensible "Feeeyaaaah!" and a large wad of saliva came flying across the distance between them, landing with a sickening thwack on Andrew's cheek.

"Here's for your thievery and your damned Ullsworth!" the attacker shouted. "Take a rest in one of your own flimsy coffins, why don't you? Hang ye be to Arcady!" And then the man was gone, leaving Andrew to wipe away his indignity with a hastily drawn handkerchief.

Ullsworth? Andrew pondered as a few passers-by giggled and pointed. Could that be the family he had driven from the Anawan Street property? Better for them, they couldn't afford the rent, not on the cloth doffing salary that Tobias Ullsworth had settled for after the end of his whaling career. The wife and seven children were much better off as wards of the city, where at least they could be assured that they would be fed every day. But who had been his attacker? And what connection could he have with this Ullsworth? Surely it took a dedicated passion to accost and insult a prominent citizen in broad daylight before gawking pedestrians.

Andrew turned to head home but was surprised to see his young daughter Lizzie standing on the street corner in a pretty pink and white striped fantail skirt and polonaise fresh from *La Mode Illustre*, topped off with a cunning chip hat laden with silk pansies perched high aloft her curly hair. She was positioned by a lamp post with a far twinkle in her wide blue-gray eyes.

"Daughter," Andrew said, pointing in the direction of the fleeing assailant. "I am afraid you had to witness my unexplained ignominy."

"Father," Lizzie said, her voice thinner than usual. "I did not see anything, for I am adrift in a waking reverie."

"You are indeed adrift. I don't think that I have ever seen you in such ponderous daydreaming. What distracts you from your daily duties?"

"I have been to the charity event this very hour on Saturday past."

"Yes, indeed. You accompanied myself and Mrs. Borden. Emma, I believe, was home with a complaint."

"And at the Church I had occasion to see the party of Frenchmen who have recently joined our community from abroad."

Borden nodded, his mouth clenched. Rubbing his unshaven cheek, he explained. "The de Camp clan…mighty proud people. They bought the Durfee Estate and are in the process of establishing an import-export concern. The Comte de Rennes, the father, is an enterprising gentleman, albeit a bit taken with lofty matters such as art and music, subjects not quite befitting a man of his industrious character."

"They are highly cultured then," Lizzie said, her eyes widening. "Oh Father, do tell me that they are versed in all matters of aesthetics. Poetries, romans-a-clef, sonnets and concertos, painting and architecture. Tell me that young Andre can dance to a rondo as easily as he can recite Shakespearian soliloquies, that as a family they have that spark of creativity within which transcends the ordinary particulars of our daily labors and occupations."

Andrew heaved an unpleasant grunt. "If you mean do they listen to operatic clap trap, or read the ramblings of word mongers, then yes, Daughter. They are aesthetes."

Lizzie smiled, her face reddening in the afternoon sunlight. "I am glad of it. Young Andre has caught my fancy, but I think you must tell not a soul about my feelings."

Andrew struggled to process this evidence of his daughter's awakening womanhood. He knew in the past that she had been distracted by boys, but she always maintained a short temper and a feigned indifference, perhaps to avoid complications. And she had socialized with strange, undeveloped male specimens like Homer Thesinger the Boy Inventor who presented himself more as a child despite his recent attainment of standing six feet tall. But Andre, the handsome youth who had been introduced as Jacques de Camp's scion, he was altogether different. He was stern and determined, calm and centered. He was also several years Lizzie's elder, and seemed strong enough to conquer her coquettish behavior if such was his will. No, this would not do. The de Camp boy must be denied access to Lizzie by any means necessary.

"Daughter," Andrew said, his mouth tightening against the emerging words. "Need I remind you that the Count is a Roman Catholic? They attend Mass at St. Anne's, don't you know?"

"Father," Lizzie smirked. "By now you should know that when it comes to spiritual matters, I ascribe the choice of worship to be up to each and every man's conscience. Besides, I am told that the Count has a Protestant mother."

"Yes," he grumbled. "Well, what, then, would you say if I told you that there is much scandal surrounding young Andre?"

"Scandal?" Her eyes peered purposefully, trying to discern his meaning. "What ever could you mean?"

"Much has been discovered about the family since their appearance in town. I have already heard word from my fellow stockholders at the Mill, who make it their business to investigate the background of newly arrived immigrants, that Jacques de Camp, the father of your beloved boy, has cleanly sailed through their careful scrutiny; but I fear to say that young Andre has not fared as well. The boy is known..." Andrew paused for dramatic effect "...he is known to frequent Houses of Assignation. He is a Sporting Boy."

Lizzie felt the fluttering in her head long before she could digest her father's statements. "Assig..." she muttered. "Sporting..." then she lifted a hand to her forehead and began her downward spiral towards the sidewalk. Andrew leapt forward and caught her in his arms. Her eyes were shifting violently back and forth under her lids.

A man in a bowler hat with trim mutton chops emerged from the moving traffic of pedestrians and offered his services. "Is this young lady aright?" he asked. "I am a doctor. Ah, Borden! I see Lizzie has taken ill."

Andrew recognized his Second Street neighbor, Dr. Seabury Bowen and watched breathlessly while the doctor brought a cracked tablet to her nostrils. She groaned, showing signs of life.

"Will she live?" asked Andrew grimly.

"Examine her pallor," said the doctor, pointing. "She has merely fainted. Nothing more."

Andrew scratched at his beard. "I suppose you want some brass for your services, Seabury."

"I am in your service," the doctor said, trying to haul Lizzie to her feet and tip his bowler simultaneously. "No coin required. Let us just get the poor girl home."

Andrew hesitated, assessing Dr. Bowen carefully. "You do not mean to clap me with a summation upon our arrival? I will not honor it!"

Dr. Bowen took a patient breath. "I have heard of you, Mister Borden. You need not fear any trickery from me. I am concerned only for the girl's health. Your daughter, I presume."

"Yes, it is Lizzie," Andrew huffed. "Be about your business, man. It is a harsh day when I confront an honest doctor. But I will tolerate your aid for my Lizzie's sake. Spring to it, man!"

As he helped Dr. Bowen carry Lizzie the two short streets to their home on Second Street, Andrew pondered Lizzie's reactions to the revelations about the de Camp boy. He felt a brief pang of guilt over distressing his daughter to the point of fainting.

"But my actions were all correct," he rationalized. "No good could come out of Andre de Camp. Not for my daughter!"

A DESPERATE VISITOR

Lizzie awoke in her cramped bedroom on the upper floor of the Borden's modest Second Street house. Fully clothed and reclined on her bed, her forehead beaded with sweat, she struggled to make sense of the tolling of the church bell. The small walls and their flowered paper caved in on her as she fought for her breath.

"Lizzie Andrew!" came a sharp cry.

Springing to her feet, she felt a disorienting rush of blood to her head as she nearly fell back onto the mattress. Her shoulders were caught fast by two hands that emerged from below a thin and chinless face that was now coming into focus. Lizzie's elder sibling, Emma, was standing before her, a frown upon her brow.

"My Sister," Emma sighed. "Sometimes I fear that you have the falling sickness."

"No, Sister," Lizzie said, bringing the back of her hand to her forehead. "It is Fall River that has the falling sickness!"

Emma waggled her head as if trying to dislodge a disturbed thought. "I have ceased to attempt understanding your inane ramblings. One would think that you had been secretly dropped on your head when you were a child."

"Would that the act was repeated to clear my mind of these worries."

A flash of recognition came across Emma's face. "You are pursuing your consulting services again. I swear by all the heavens, Lizzie, that is all nonsense. Pay more attention to your proper duties."

"Emma," Lizzie said earnestly, "I have heard this day that our town is host to Sporting Boys. And where there are Sporting Boys..." Her eyes took a quick dart about the room "...there are Fancy Girls."

Her sister flinched with great discomfort at the phrases that she was hearing. "If such matters go on in this town," Emma said with a shrug, "it is the province of the law to sort it out and the mandate of the Almighty above to judge their sins. For now, all we can do is suffer our mundane tasks upon the earth."

"Mundane tasks?" Lizzie suppressed a spontaneous chuckle.

"Yes, mundane. Mrs. Borden has some paper wrappers for us to address. And I believe there is a buggy to bring to Swansea Farm. Do you not remember that today is Wednesday? Now be downstairs in a few moments, composed and alert." And she darted from the room, more frustrated than concerned. Lizzie stood alone, staring into space, thinking.

After changing her downstreet ensemble for a cotton calico and stout tie oxfords, clothing more suitable for scrambling after eggs in a chicken coop, Lizzie came down the front stairs of the house to find her stepmother, Abby Borden, by the front door. Abby was a plump woman of fifty-two, with a dour and haggard face, as if she had spent the better part of a lifetime trying to feign cheerfulness with little reward.

"I am glad to see you well," Abby said cursorily, handing her a stack of paper wrappers. "Mr. Borden is hiding in his room fearing Dr.

Bowen's summation. One day that man shall be the death of us."

From the sitting room door emerged a smart and handsome man, his warm eyes twinkling above his mutton-chopped mustache. "Miss Lizzie," he said, nodding his chin respectfully. "Dr. Seabury Bowen. I trust you are feeling much better."

"Very fine, doctor. I have never felt better. Are you the man who aided me in my time of distress?"

"I have that honor. Even I, a poor medical man attempting to establish himself with such modest resources, has heard of the great Lizzie Borden, the Girl Detective of Fall River."

Abby groaned, her hands fleeing into her apron. "What nonsense! Girl Detective indeed!"

"Your daughter is quite an accomplished woman, Mrs. Borden. I am pleased to see her fine and healthy. Now it is for her father I fear. He seems to be in a state of apoplexy, as if something is weighing upon his mind. He muttered about a man who accosted him in the street."

"I believe Father said something about it," Lizzie said, "but I do not think that I remember."

Abby sighed. "Your father does indeed have many enemies since he has elevated his station in life. No doubt many of them wish him harm."

"I believe it was an English bard," Dr. Bowen added, "who described the King that must wear the crown as having an uneasy head. Sleep comes dear to such a man."

"Amen," Abby concluded. "Now, Lizzie you have chores to run. Emma's in the barn harnessing the rig. I suspect she'll call for you shortly."

Dr. Bowen removed his bowler from the standing rack, bid the ladies good afternoon and took his leave. Abby bolted the door after him.

"There are some doctors in this town who are decent at heart, Mrs. Borden," Lizzie said smugly. "Don't let Father begrudge such a man."

"To your chores!" Abby quipped. "Don't dally, there's much to be done. It is Wednesday you know!"

Lizzie took the wrappers and entered the kitchen where the stove was ablaze and some papers were already burning. Staring into the grate, Lizzie could see that they were legal documents touching upon property estates. For a brief moment, Lizzie thought she could discern the name Ullsworth on one of the papers. Something flickered in the back of her memory. Something she had heard while drinking her Ayres' sarsaparilla at the pharmacy with her friends, something about a whaling man who had vanished and his indigent wife and children. She was about to reach in and try to salvage the paper when she sensed a fluttering in the air behind her. Spinning about, Lizzie was facing her step-mother who stood with her hands thrust into her apron, a look of astonishment on her face.

"Lizzie Andrew," Abby said, her voice humbled. "There is a gentleman to see you. I do believe he is a gentleman despite his garish appearance. Although I doubt your father would ever allow such a person into his home."

"Garish? Is he fancied up like a saloon performer?"

"No, he is…well, perhaps you'd best see for yourself."

Lizzie came back to the parlor to find a very tall man standing by the piano. He was jowly and broad, covered in a red brocade of fine military threads, his feet planted firmly on the carpet, his strong arms bent behind his back. A domino mask obscured his eyes and nose, and a broad cape flowed like a theatrical curtain behind him. His mustaches extended below the mask and stood firm and proud like they were testifying a profound Yes to the vagaries of life. And while his mustaches were displaying defiance against darkness, his jutting chin was mastering the art of adjuration, a proud opulence that spoke of an abandoned country and a melancholy exile. Here was a man that radiated energy, masculine and forceful. Lizzie felt self-secure enough to stand firm before him, and to extend her hand without diverting her eyes from his piercing gaze.

He gave a brief smile. "Miss Lizzie Borden, the Girl Detective."

Lizzie held out her hand and he gently pressed his lips to it. "Forgive my forgery of identity," he continued, "for I have a high position in this town's industry and I must keep it secret, even from you, my potential consultant."

"I am intrigued." Lizzie waved towards the pillowed sofa. "Please have a seat and explain to me how I can be of service."

"I prefer to stand," the strange visitor exclaimed. "It provides extra labor for the legs, but my circumstance is such that at a moment's notice I must spring like a lion for shelter. I cannot be too safe."

"I see," said Lizzie, occupying the sofa with a coquettish descent. "Please explain to me how I can be of service to you."

He executed a hasty cough, his mustaches quivering, and then he began: "I represent a rather large number of Fall River businessmen, many of whom are aware of my identity but none of whom know that I am consulting with you. Besides yourself, your most polite mother, and the coach man who is in my private employ, no one knows of my visit here today."

"That is Mrs. Borden," Lizzie corrected him, nodding towards the door that Abby was, no doubt, pressing her ear against. "She is not my mother." Lizzie raised her voice to proclaim, "My mother is dead."

"Ah, I see. You must forgive my faux pas."

"No offense taken, Mr...uh..."

"You may call me Chace. Yes, that name would be suitable. But I may resume with the narrative of my situation. I am in communication with a large number of European concerns that are investigating the Fall River market, primarily interested in buying up stock in industry here. Some of those concerns have ties with the royal families of Eastern Europe. As you may know, there is quite a fuss going on abroad due to the conflicts with the Ottomans over the Slavic lands. England and France are quite busy with their espionage and intrigue, both of them taking sides one way or the other with the Russians over this terrible conflagration in Bulgaria. The Russian army has crossed the Danube and is laying siege as we speak to the city of Plevna. The death toll is mounting, and there are those who wish to see a hasty end to this campaign."

Lizzie nodded. "I read the Fall River Herald on a daily basis, Mr. Chace, while I heat my irons. I have perused some editorials about the affair with the Turks."

"Then you are aware that Europe is now a powder keg waiting for a match to fall upon it. And when that happens, there will be a conflict such as the world has never before seen."

Lizzie sighed, meditating upon the foolish games of powerful men and all their silly armies and conflicts. "There does seem to be quite a large amount of consternation. I can imagine the outcome of such an imbroglio. But what has this to do with anything concerning which I can help you?"

Chace rocked on his heels. "A Russian noble of some reputation has bought up large amounts of textile stock in order to raise funds for a private army to fight the Turks. I was to be the liaison between the Russian and a certain European government. He has sent an agent, an inventor, to speak on behalf of Russian industry."

"What could this Russian possibly have to offer the foreign government that could be so valuable?" asked Lizzie. "And why Fall River?"

The eyes under the domino mask darted from side to side as if scanning the room for spies. "The Russian inventor has laid out the plans for a new self-acting Mule which, when it was combined with the new Hayes and Drumpet Throstle Spinner and put into production at his test plant in Moscow, quadrupled his yarn output and tripled his pick per yard. We intend to sell this patent for the self-acting Mule to the highest bidder in Fall River while retaining a commission on each yard spun using the technology. This particular Mule technology will revolutionize the entire industry. The first manufacturer who adopts it will become wealthy beyond his imagination and the Russian shall have his privately funded army to fight the Turks and raise the siege of Plevna."

Lizzie shrugged. "Personally, I prefer the simple pleasure of a summer's afternoon eating pears in the yard, but I can see that when money and power are involved, men will do anything to exploit the common mill worker."

"Yes, it is very true. But if Herr Marx should have his way...well..." Mr. Chace raised a handkerchief to his sweating brow. "That is a story for another time." He stared in reverie at the far wall, his mind lost in some anguished internal debate.

"So you tell me that this Russian inventor is in Fall River with the plans for his invention?" Lizzie said, picking up the thread of conversation.

"Yes, but there is one particular that he did not count on. His plans have been stolen!"

Lizzie raised her hand to her mouth. "My Lord!"

"Yes. There has been perfidy of the most sinister kind. This Monday last at ten in the evening, while the Russian inventor was asleep in his hotel, a scoundrel entered the premises and stole the plans."

"Did he not have them locked up somewhere for safe-keeping?"

"Ah, that is the embarrassing part. He had ingeniously stowed the plans inside a medical...uh...how do you Americans say it? A pessary? Which he inserted into a chamber of his own anatomy. Modesty forbids me to locate the particular chamber in which the pessary was stowed."

"I see," said Lizzie, blushing slightly. "I believe it is a suppository you are referring to."

"*Mais oui!* Yes, indeed. A pessary! The fiend put him to sleep with liquid ether administered with a cloth over his nose, and then went to work extracting the container."

"Such a hiding place would not easily be accessed," Lizzie sighed.

"But when a man is unconscious, all sorts of violations are possible."

"Yes, that is exactly what I said to the foreign government. But they did not find such comments amusing. They told me I had twenty-four hours to find the plans, with or without the pessary; and that if I did not produce them before the arranged time for the meeting with the mill owners on Friday afternoon, I shall be removed immediately from my position as liaison. In such a case, I shall return home a ruined man, all my investments canceled, and my prospects in America reduced to nothing. Hence the desperation with which I approach you."

"Time must be of the essence," Lizzie suggested.

"More than you can imagine, Miss Borden," Chace confirmed. "Even more at stake than my own reputation is the fate of Europe. If the patent negotiations break down with the Russians, the balance of power will shift to those nations backing the Ottomans. All the stresses and tensions that are holding Europe in check will unravel and there will be a violent and bloody war amongst the nations. Shall I say, a world war, to coin a phrase."

The tall mysterious man paused for dramatic effect. Out in the street, a nearby church was tolling the hour. The clopping of horse hooves and the crying of the fishmongers lingered in the room. A darkness came over Mr. Chace's masked face as he waited for her to respond.

Lizzie took a deep breath. "But why come to me?" she asked. "I am merely the youngest daughter of a furniture salesman. I have no particular aptitude with which to deal with industrial politics, far less military wars abroad."

"But you are Lizzie Borden the Girl Detective! Amongst the board members of the leading mills you are notorious for bringing down Livermore, the mill owner who killed his own plant manager. You have shown fortitude, intellect and powers of detection that some consider uncanny. I come to you as my last hope to save not only my paltry self, but to help maintain the balance of power in Europe."

"Yes," Lizzie shrugged. "I did perform quite well during the Case of the Purloined Curio, and I was commended by no less than the Mayor himself for the Adventure of the Antiquated Blunderbuss, but I still don't agree that you have to hide from me, Monsieur Jacques de Camp, Comte de Rennes!"

"*Zut alors!*" came the bellowing reply from the sturdy giant. His cheeks went slack, and his hands fell to his sides. "I am undone! How did you know?"

"It is simplicity itself," Lizzie proclaimed. "You are doing an appreciable imitation of an American accent, but there are certain nuances in your nasality that bespeak a French origin. Further, your mustache is of a particular cut that I have seen only in Daguerreotypes of gentlemen from the hills around Carcassonne in the Languedoc. And I do believe I see embossed on your forefinger's ring the characteristic coat of arms for the Merovingian lineage, long since vanished from the Franco-Monarchial scene, but forever bound with honor and respect within the de Camp line, which I have studied at my local lending library, exhausting its modest resources on the topic.

"As for all your tales of Russian and Turkish conflicts, one need not go further than the few scraps of articles that can be read while heating flats for a grand session of handkerchief-ironing to know that England is attempting to stop the Russians from going to war against the Ottomans, while France is wholeheartedly backing the Russians' campaign. Further, the French government has recently investigated land grants in the Taunton River area for possible development of mills that would be run by France's own interests. One cannot put all these facts together without deducing that you are indeed a French investor recently imported into Fall River, and the only French investor I know of who fits that description is Jacques de Camp, whom I have scrutinized at a charity event this Saturday past; and who has the same hair styling as you, not to mention the same mustache, jowls and green-gray eyes. The domino mask and the perfected American accent did not fool me one jot, for I am a Girl Detective!"

De Camp was thunderstruck. His mustache puffed with his cheeks. "How extraordinary," he roared, his French accent becoming more apparent. "And in one so young! How can you doubt your abilities after such a display? The Russians are almost assured that their precious self-acting Mule plans will be retrieved. My commendations!"

He bowed low, almost to the ground.

Upon his upsweep, Lizzie said with a wry smile, "How delightful that a cultivated man of such stature should bow to me, a poor little girl in such a modest little house." She laughed and raised her hands to her mouth. "Oh dear, that is precious! Well, Monsieur le Comte, you may relax and remove your disguise. How may I be of assistance to you in this very strange affair?"

With all pretense tossed to the wings, the French aristocrat, with a sweeping gesture, removed the mask to reveal a handsome if not rugged face and deeply intelligent eyes. "I want you to find the Mule plans," he announced.

"But where do I begin? The thief must be miles from Fall River by now."

"No, I believe him still to be in this city. The only clue we have is this signet that was left behind at the scene of the theft, presumably by accident." De Camp lifted up a ring that glimmered in the sunlight shafting through the parlor window. Lizzie took it for inspection and saw a crimson letter A centered on the ring's face plate.

"I have not seen this before," Lizzie said, a shudder coming over her.

"I have. It is the sign of a secret society that operates right here in town. The Arcady Society. I'm not quite sure what their objectives are, but it seems likely that they are nihilists whose only goal is to topple the Czar from power and bring about a worker state in Russia. They have a vested interest in preventing the Russian expansion into the Crimea, and God alone knows what their plans are for Fall River."

"And this ring is a symbol of their Brotherhood?"

"Yes, the letter A is a symbol of the sudden violence that will erupt when the common man is ready to rise above his masters. They are no doubt influenced by Bakunin and his lot. I do believe elements of their society, inspired by the successful assassination of your President Lincoln in 1865, are planning the same fate for the Czar. They are aware that my mission in Fall River is an obscure but crucial step in the Czar's plan to reinforce his military victories."

Lizzie curled her fingers around the ring and sighed. "I find this all most fascinating," she said. "I would most heartily love to work on the case."

"I can reward you handsomely. Money is not an object. My purse is open for your use."

"No need. My consulting services are done purely for the good of all people everywhere. I have no material needs to compensate. I do, however, have a few questions regarding the robbery. How big is this container?"

"About the size of a peach pit. The plans, which have been printed on delicate tissue paper, are folded very tightly. But recall Miss Borden that the plans may no longer be in the pessary."

"I am aware of that. Of what material is it made?"

"Solid iron, embossed with the Romanov coat of arms and with a hinge that opens into its cavity."

"This Russian inventor, from where does he hail?"

"St. Petersburg. He has been sent straight by the Czar himself to secure the contracts with the Fall River businessmen."

"Where did the theft take place?"

"At the Hotel Wilbur, not more than ten minutes walk from this very house."

"Do the textile men know of the unfortunate robbery?"

"*Mon Dieu*, that would mean disaster. They are currently under the impression that we will be presenting the plans for the self-acting Mule by this time Friday morning."

"That is most unfortunate. This ring that you found in the hotel room of the Russian, was it simply lying on the floor? I find it unusual that a ring can so conveniently slip off an intruder's finger."

"Ah," de Camp said, screwing up his eyes as if trying to find the exact words. "The ring was not exactly lying on the floor. It had fallen off inside the Russian during the process of extracting the pessary."

"Oh," Lizzie said with a shudder.

"Yes," de Camp sighed. "Please do not ask for details on how we discovered it. I am not used to discussing such matters with a young lady. Needless to say, the Russian is mortified beyond words and for security purposes has been sequestered in a safe place far from this town."

"We shall save the details for another day," Lizzie agreed. "I would like to see the hotel room where the Russian was assailed."

"By all means. Be at the Hotel Wilbur this very afternoon. I must exercise discretion and disappear from the scene. So you shall rendezvous with my son, Andre, who will represent me in this matter. Report to the lobby of the Wilbur at three of the clock."

Lizzie's chest tightened. "I don't believe I have had the honor to meet your son before."

"Andre is a fine *garcon*, just turned nineteen. He has a bit of a fiery disposition and he is very strong in his opinion about foreign affairs. We often clash over such matters, but he is loyal to our *famille Languedoci-enne*. The bloodlines run very deep and he is a proud scion."

Lizzie rose to her feet. "I shall meet your son then at three at the Wilbur Hotel."

"Three o'clock!" The Comte de Rennes bowed once more, tucked on his domino mask, and ushered himself towards the front hallway. "*A bientot*," he said wistfully.

From up the hallway came Emma's thin voice. "Lizzie, I have rigged up the buggy, with no help from you, thank you!" Then she appeared in the parlor, dressed in a flowery hat, just as the Comte spun on his axis. Emma had barely caught a darting glimpse of the man in the cape and the mask, when she let out with a bellowing shriek. All the color drained from her face and her hands raced towards his face.

"Emma!" Lizzie said, just as startled. But it was too late. Lizzie's older sister had bolted for the front stairs and was stomping upwards towards the safety of her bedroom, making strange whimpering noises.

"I am profoundly apologetic," de Camp said, with a nod towards Lizzie. "If I had known…"

"It's all correct, Monsieur le Comte," Lizzie said. "Emma is used to far worse."

Lizzie stared at him through the window of the parlor as he descended to his waiting carriage in the street. She sighed, thinking of the boy she most dreaded, and most wanted to meet.

THE SPORTING BOYS

The Wilbur Hotel was up North Main at Granite Street. Lizzie managed to get there without a buggy and arrived just before three as a work team was unloading water barrels from a horse-drawn cart. A large banner straddling the main entrance boasted of the hotel's finer qualities:

FALL RIVER'S WILBUR HOTEL
An Ordinary of Most Excellent Attributes

Today: The Boston Barkeep Furniture Corporation Conclave
Displays of Stools and Mirrors by Master Craftsmen

Fine lodging for transients and permanents
Beer, oysters and horse-keeping
Elocution lessons by Professor Joseph Maple, Esq. of New Bedford

Rooms Available
Restaurant Attached – Victuals At Most Excellent Prices

King Darius Wilbur, Proprietor
Samuel Samways, Bar Keep

The lobby was bustling with an influx of folk from as far away as Providence, Boston, and even from the wilds of northern New Hampshire, for the Wilbur was playing host that weekend to a convention of saloon-furniture salesmen. They paraded around the lobby, these men of varnished wood and beveled mirrors, their top hats nestled in their forearms, their mustaches glistening with wax, their rattling wives beside them. In the center of the lobby was a large casket, presumably filled with beer, and a burly bartender in a bleached cloth smock was handing out samples in hardwood mugs.

Lizzie was surprised to see her father wandering the crowd, not particularly connected to anyone, but occasionally giving a grim nod to a passing gentleman. He twitched imperceptibly as his daughter appeared before him, planting her parasol firmly between her feet.

"Father, I did not think that you took an interest in the latest fashions in bar stools."

Andrew twisted up his brows. "I am merely memorizing the faces. They are competition, you know. But what brings you to the Wilbur, Daughter? Certainly you have not been seized with the desire to sample Master Samways' Home-made Hops?"

"No, Father. I am on a case."

"That nonsense business you started. I sincerely hope that you are being paid well for your troubles. A penny worked for is a penny in the pocket. I wouldn't have it any other way."

Lizzie smiled as the nearby town hall clock tolled three o'clock. A thin beardless bell boy in a small hotel jacket approached Lizzie.

"Miss Borden?" he asked in a voice crackling with adolescence as if he were growing upwards before her very eyes. He handed her a note which she unfolded. Noticing her father staring at her intently, she reached into her purse and pulled out a coin which she tossed to the grinning bellboy.

"Here you are, my hard working lad—a penny from my pocket." He hopped away merrily as Andrew scowled at her wasteful habit.

"Room 209," she read, and then bade her father adieu with a tilt of her head. She headed for the staircase, leaving Andrew Borden fish-mouthed.

"My own daughter, not yet eighteen," he stammered. "Unescorted to an upstairs room. What more horrors can this modern world bring?"

As Andrew turned to leave, he spied in the corner of the lobby three young boys dressed in lean long broad coats, watch chains and high boots, laughing and spitting their cigar smoke into the choked air. Two of them were fitted out in bowler hats and the tall, lanky leader in the middle was balanced under a tall opera hat that served to exaggerate his height. It was the Sporting Boys, the nattering nabobs of Fall River, grinning and roaring with chummy ostentation. Andrew noticed that as Lizzie ascended the staircase, the Sporting Boys were poking each other and pointing in her direction, their eyes filled with boyish leers. They were commenting upon Lizzie's elegantly draped posterior as it sashayed up the staircase, much to their amusement.

Their thin leader pumped his legs up and down as if he were a strutting rooster. "B'hoys!" he chortled. "Need we neglect Miss Lizzie Borden of Second Street and the fine young hams she's leaving behind for our viewing pleasure?"

The Boys roared. "Get out me tape measure, my skenchbacks!" one of them shouted. "My, what gazing stock!"

"She'd make a good Bowery G'al at dragging time! I mind you!" the leader shouted.

Andrew bit his lips and took a few awkward strides across the lobby to where the Sporting Boys were posturing, staring them down as their laughter subsided. The leader in the opera hat patted his chest.

"Andrew Borden I believe," he said proudly.

"Who may you be?" Andrew bellowed. "Your countenance is vaguely familiar."

The boy tipped his stove pipe and grinned. "Frank Rivers, how may I be of service?"

"I have heard of you, Rivers," Andrew growled. "You and your associates here are mere sensualists. But I'm not afraid of your secret language and your fancy airs, and I am appalled by your rendezvous with women of fallen characters. Your libertine antics may go over in fancy cities, but not in Fall River; this town is full of respectable folk! Be gone immediately and take your rabble with you!"

The smile on River's face was defiant. He tossed a side glance to his two companions who seemed to be hovering around his facial expressions looking for guidance, then he plastered down his soap locks, stepped forward and leaned in towards Andrew's sinking eyes. "No time for curtain lectures, I have a right to be in this public place," he said wickedly. "I paid my coins for a room, and so did my B'hoys here. And don't go apple bonking our fuzzle talk. We adopted it right from Paradise Square in Manhattan Island and it's proper for all my skenchbacks."

Andrew raised a straining fist. "No matter where you obtained your wicked speech, I cannot allow your vulgar remarks touching my daughter."

The thin wobbly-eyed boy next to Frank Rivers stepped forward. "Hi hi, cousin! 'Ol' Frank here won't be remarking anything touching your daughter before he can remark on anything worth touching."

Andrew's head went hot and he shook a curled fist. "Don't go near my Lizzie or…" His eyes turned red with anger as he bellowed, "Or I'll twist off your heads!"

And then, having expended his courage and energy, Andrew seemed to vanish into the air only to reform at the center of the lobby, heading towards the street. Frank Rivers turned to his chuckling companions and smirked. "Lam him, B'hoys!" he howled. "I am trembling in my boots!"

At his lead, they broke into laughter as Andrew disappeared between the endless displays of bar stools and spittoons.

Deductions and Romance

At the top of the staircase, Lizzie found herself looking down a long hallway that stretched southward between two parallel rows of doors. Halfway down, a man in a dark brown suit sat on a stool slanting backwards, humming wistfully to himself. As Lizzie alighted onto the landing, he straightened up, then scrambled to his feet and respectfully removed his hat. He was a large bear of a man, middle-aged and paunchy. His mouth was obscured by a dropping mustache. He wore a long dark-brown greatcoat that seemed unseasonal and was stained with the dust of the road.

"Miss," he said, blinking at her.

"Are you the detective from Pinkertons?" Lizzie asked.

"Pinkerton, Miss," he said proudly.

"I don't believe I catch your meaning."

"The name's Pinkerton, Miss. Fred Pinkerton of Pinkerton Brothers Private Security Firm."

"I see, your name does inspire confidence," Lizzie said, chuckling slightly into her gloved hand.

"The French boy is waiting," he announced.

On the door paneling behind him were the gilt numbers 209. With a soft touch, Lizzie pushed the door open and stepped inside.

The room was dark and stuffy. Only a few beams of sunlight slanting through the closed shutters enabled her to see a shadowy man standing in the corner. At first she considered her situation to be one of immediate danger, alone in a hotel room with a stranger who had not yet identified himself. After all, this was the room where the Russian inventor had been scandalized. But trusting in the delicacy of the moment, she swung the door shut behind her.

The shadow moved into a shaft of sunlight and Lizzie recognized immediately the bespoken Saville Row suit jacket, the youthful attempt at a military mustache, the twinkling eyes. Even the West Indies Bay Rhum that danced in the air between them whispered the name and title: Andre Louis Jacques de Camp, the Vicomte de Rennes.

"I know you," she said, remembering her father's ominous words about Andre's Sporting Boy life style. Why would the Comte send her into such a dangerous position?

"I know you too, Lizbeth Andrew Borden," Andre said with slight merriment. "I assure you that there is no danger here. Be at ease and join me in solving this wretchedly complicated and ever-deepening puzzle."

Lizzie's breathing came more easily. His voice was fine and equally well-mannered. This comforted her. "The name is Lizzie," she corrected him.

"Then Lizzie shall it be." He pointed towards the brass bed and the carpeted floor. "*Mais bien sur*, this is indeed a strange field upon which we are now treading. Here we have a room where a crime took place. A man was assaulted and something was stolen from him. What do you see in this room, Lizzie Borden? What scenarios can you deduce from the remains of Monsieur Tchakorov?"

With a daring flourish Andre drew back the shutters and let the bright sunlight flood the room. Lizzie was suddenly overwhelmed with an intense amount of detail. She paused, put fingers to her chin, and peered about. Then, while Andre stood at attention with a wry smile, she perambulated the length and breadth of it, peering into corners, examining surfaces, bending her knees to see beneath the furniture. She picked up nothing, but examined everything, maneuvering her body to change her line of sight before cuspidors, bed posts, cabinets, and the writing desk. She sat in a chair, smelled a bouquet of flowers in a vase on the dressing table, cast a winking eye at some framed pictures on the mantle, waved her fingers over a clump of charred wood in the fireplace, and pressed her shoes heavily against randomly selected floor boards. She nosed through the clothing lying on the rumpled bed sheets and the heaps of linen lying on the floor. A pile of papers in the waste basket occupied her attention for several moments. Lastly she inspected a painting that hung upon the southern wall, a copy of a rustic scene by Poussin of several shepherds gathered about a stone tomb. The painting stared back at her with an unsettling feeling of mutual fascination.

She came back to the center of the room and stood proudly before Andre. "I have comprised a scenario," she proclaimed. "For your amusement I shall state it."

Andre gave her a permissive wave of his hand.

"I did not know the name of the Russian until you just uttered it," she said. "But I can say with confidence that he is a proud man from a wealthy family that has recently come upon hard times. He was forced into the business of selling mill technology by the unfortunate death of his wife, which has left him with two small children to support."

Andre stared blankly at her. "Go on," he said.

"He was in this room for two days before his unfortunate assault. During that time he indulged in real estate speculation. No doubt he felt that migrating to America and bringing his children to Fall River would provide them with a future that cannot be realized in Czarist Russia. He also sees Fall River as an excellent town for his new bride-to-be since her career as an equestrian acrobat has come to a very tragic end."

"Excellent," Andre said with a reserved smile. "I can't imagine how you perceived many of the details in that portrait, but I did witness you examining the postcard upon the dressing table from the Louise Soullier Circus with the inscription from Marie confessing in French her deepest love and the prospects that await her in America."

Lizzie nodded towards the dresser. "Moreover, the clothing that you had laid upon the bed and the charming but sad bouquet of flowers on the writing desk have provided me the opportunity to reconstruct his recent past. As for the clothing, the fine quality of the suit shows a man of some means, but it has in the past year been washed so often its colors have faded, showing a recent downturning of his luck, no doubt happening simultaneously with the passing of his dear wife."

"What does the bouquet tell you?"

"Through a correspondence course with the Ophelia Society of Boston, I had the opportunity to study the fine art of florigraphy and floral management within parlors and sitting rooms. After completing the Home Guide To The Secret Language of Flowers, I had trained my eye to perceive the elegant messages that were being scripted within the combination of floral arrangements. Tchakorov, being from St. Petersburg, takes a very romantic European approach to this art. In this bouquet he has blended together crimson tea roses that show a melancholy loss, something that he has vowed never to forget. The presence of the scarlet nasturtiums led me to believe that there was a military death, perhaps a brother in the Bulgarian campaign, but the nasturtium also symbolizes patriotism, perhaps reflecting a period after the profound loss where he attempted to regain his emotional composure through world affairs. The pheasant eyes and blue periwinkles that are so mournfully laced at the corners show a sorrowful remembrance, that his feelings once so potent and devastating were mellowing into a sublime melancholy. The white Poppies whisper of a striving for forgetfulness, a moving on, so to speak."

"So far," Andre confirmed, "this is 'all correct' as you Americans are so fond of saying. What about the equestrian bride-to-be?"

"Ah, the full-blown red rose in the center that blooms above the rest speaks loudly of a return of hope and the dawning of a new happiness after a long sojourn in a wilderness, no doubt a wilderness of a mental nature. One can only guess that Tchakorov has felt a new love dawn. The enthusiastic postcard from the French horse woman that bespeaks a life together in America fulfills all my florigraphic interpretations."

"And the real estate speculation?" Andre asked.

"The caked mud on his boots is peculiar to a lot that is being developed just around the corner from Anawan Street, one that Mister Southard Miller has put up for sale. Near this lot is a tobacco shop that sells the Louisiana Perique that has a moist vinegary smell, the same smell that hangs so pungent in the air about us. No doubt the property came to his attention on one of his trips to obtain his treasured tobacco and he managed to get access to the property through the builder's agent."

"He may have been strolling for relaxation and entered the property out of mere curiosity."

"Ah, but his beloved Marie claims that she will be very happy in America. There are also the three books on the bureau, clearly obtained from the Stone Street lending library, one of them a French-English lexicon, another a picture book of famous horses of North America, and the last a treatise on the domestication of the recently married couple by

Professor Horatio Tiverton of Swansea. Finally his waste basket contains papers where he has been practicing his English letters, writing out phrases like, "My dear sir, which way are the horse stables" and "What are the most excellent children's schools in this neighborhood?" This shows me clearly that he was contemplating the rebuilding of his family with the French equestrian woman and his orphaned children right here in Fall River."

Andre clapped his hands in rhythm to a hearty laugh. "I can tell you with great confidence, Lizbeth—and may I be permitted to call you Lizbeth? It is far more suited to your dignity and grace—that your portrait of Monsieur the Russian is perfection itself, a small gem of analytical reasoning that does you very proud. But, alas, such details are useless when it comes to solving this riddle. For here we have a room where no intruder entered before the infamous deed, and no intruder exited. It is as if the Russian were attacked by *une fantome* of his own imagination."

"I don't understand," Lizzie frowned.

"Behold the testimony of the security agent." Andre went to the door and rapped three times in quick succession. A moment later, the large mustachioed man from the corridor entered awkwardly at a glacial pace, nodding respectfully at Andre and Lizzie in turn.

"Miss," he said.

"Mr. Pinkerton, I have a few questions about the evening before last," Lizzie stated. "I believe you were on duty when this deplorable theft occurred. Would you mind relating your version of the affair?"

He rubbed his chin as if trying to stir memory. "I'm not a man of very many words," he said, "but I can oblige if it will help bring about a conclusion."

"There will most certainly," Andre said defiantly, "be a conclusion, Monsieur Pinkerton. By your leave..."

"Well, it was before all this barstool nonsense. Hardly anyone was occupying this second floor but them Sporting Boys that make all the commotion a'nights with their Fancy Girls about. I was at my post at ten o'clock. I remember one of the girls yelling down the hall that her gentleman caller needed a bowl of hot water. Then all the doors were shut and everything was quiet. King Darius had turned down the lamps and you could hear all that slumbered snoring along the corridor."

"Fall River descending into twilight," Lizzie said softly.

"Yes, Miss. And that's when I do confess a profound lapse of character. I'm almost a'feared to lose my commission if I relate what I have to tell."

"You need not, I can guess. You were imbibing."

"At my post, it is true. The intent was to keep the fire going inside me, because the dark night in a hotel corridor can be mighty cold, despite the summer. I'm not a vain man, but this drinking is one act I do fear the judgment upon—especially considering its sequel."

Andre raised an assuring hand. "You need not fear prosecution since my father did determine that the whiskey was drugged."

"Drugged it was. After just a few sips, I felt myself slipping off. But I'm a stubborn man as well. I fought it all the way. On the exterior you might have just witnessed a big oaf of a man snoring in his boots. But from the interior angle I was wrestling with mighty demons. And I do declare, Miss, I won the battle. I forced myself awake."

"How long was your interval?"

"I can't rightly say, but it seemed enough for someone to have filched the key in my jacket pocket, and then slip by me into this here room to do his immoral deed. When I realized what had been done I got to my feet, roared almighty hellfire, and ripped this door nearly off its hinges, to find the Russian fellow lying on the floor with his southern exposure aiming out as bare as a babe's."

"Did you raise an alarm to the desk clerk?"

"Immediately, Miss! I figured the footpad was on his way out the front of the hotel so I bounded down the steps."

"Are there any other steps down to the lobby?"

"None, Miss. Those are the only ones from the second floor, and I blocked it with my girth the whole time. Then King Darius called the constabulary and I went upstairs to help preserve the Russian fellow's dignity."

"How long before the police came?"

"About three minutes by my reckoning. And they filled this room. They knew this was an international affair, although none of us, including myself, know the truth behind it. Something about foreign wars. I don't rightly care about those crazy tangles as long as my pay is regular, I keep my nose out of it. Leave it to the fancy politicos."

"How long were the police here?"

"About an hour, and then my brother Fred came to relieve me."

"Your brother's name is also Fred?"

"My daddy did have a hankering for that name. And when we came out twins, it seemed only right to consider us as one unit."

"I see. So Fred your brother took the second watch?"

"Right so, and we have alternated since at twelve-hour intervals. I told Fred to keep a right smart watch and to take no drink in fear it would mean the death of his ambitions."

"What about the Russian? Where was he taken?"

Andre answered, "Where no one can get at him. Needless to say he does not wish to be interrogated. You can learn nothing from him for he remembers nothing, but has a distinct soreness that may take some time to overcome."

Lizzie nodded. "I understand. Mr. Pinkerton, are you absolutely sure you saw no one leave this room?"

"None, Miss. Unless the fiend slipped out before I had awoken myself. But no one downstairs saw any man excepting myself come down those stairs. It's as if the assailant appeared from thin air and vanished into likewise."

"And the desk clerk, he saw no one go up shortly before the striking of ten?"

"No one," Andre added. "It seems as if the Russian's attacker was a passing shadow of no substance."

Pinkerton huffed. "No shadow could have taken the key from my pocket or pulled the Russian fellow off his bed to separate him from his night pants. There was flesh and blood involved, I assure you of that."

Lizzie put her two forefingers to her chin and drew in deep breath. She glanced about the room, carefully examining the walls, and then before her silent observers, walked up and down, counting her steps. After a few perambulations she turned to Pinkerton and said sternly, "I must ask you to stand guard over this room at all costs, to make sure that no one enters or leaves without your awareness."

His mustache dipped with his face in agreement. "I shall, Miss. Excepting at various times of the day or night I may be my own brother. We do take turns, and being that collectively we look like one person staring into a mirror, no one really cares if we swap out to give each other a chance to catch some snores, you understand."

"Understood," she concluded and then darted for the door, exiting into the hallway. Andre followed her out to find her walking a straight line along the corridor, pausing before each door. Then she turned about and came back, carefully putting one foot before the other.

"Curious," she said, leaning over to make sure the security guard had not followed them into the hallway. "Does he know about the pessary?"

"Not a bit."

"Does he know about the Arcady ring?"

"Even less."

"Good," Lizzie said with a nod. "Let's keep it that way. What do you know about this ring?"

"It is the signet of the Arcady Society. According to the locals that I have interrogated, it is the secret club of the Sporting Boys. Despite my father's fears that they are anarchists and assassins, I believe it merely to be a small group of rowdy youths who sample the opiates of the Orient and women of low character with equal impunity."

Lizzie furrowed her brow. "The same Sporting Boys who were present here at the time of the affair?"

"The same. Do you wish to talk to them yourself?"

"No, for now I'd like to see the desk clerk, this King Darius that everyone is talking about. He may hold an important key to this puzzle."

"I believe he is in the lobby tending to the Conclave." Andre pushed past her and led her down the steps towards the lobby.

KING DARIUS' SECRET CHAMBER

King Darius Wilbur was a man buried under burdensome mustaches that demanded far more energy and labor to keep in their pristine state than any one man could be expected to produce. Nonetheless, he wore his whiskers proudly and gave one the impression, as one talked to him, that his head was in the midst of being swallowed by them. Lizzie, facing him directly across the main desk of the Wilbur's lobby, experiencing the full impact of his face in the slanting sunlight, found herself visually lost in his whiskers' magnificence. It had been observed by many that the Wilbur hotel, a recently prospering concern, was growing in exponential proportion to King Darius' facial masterpiece and that local speculators feared that the further expansion of his business would result in the complete structural collapse of his head, which was itself already buried under the weight of his facial hair. Beyond this peculiar trait, he was jovial enough, and he seemed eager to provide Lizzie with information.

"I am quite alarmed," he confessed, "that such intrigue would go on under my roof. I did not think that the Russian would be at such risk in my own establishment, I dare say, I now do."

"And you saw no one go up those stairs at ten on the clock, or slightly before?"

His eyes hovered together near his nose. "No, Miss Borden. I was keeping watch, being mindful of that Rivers boy and his shameless carryings on with the harlot Miss Jewett. They've been keeping company here for quite some time, and always in the same room. God's teeth, but I dare say Rivers was enraged when the Russian fellow came to town."

"Rivers? Why would he be upset about the Russian?"

"Because he took his room, he did."

Lizzie leaned forward, quite drawn in by his statement. "You are telling me that Room 209 is usually occupied by Frank Rivers and his Fancy Girl?"

The mustaches bobbed with the face. "Dare say, I do! And it was a mighty strange manner in which it transpired. I had the Russian fellow booked by order of the French Count into a right proper room, one that hadn't been darkened in spirit by these nattering nabobs. I had him in the Commonwealth Suite and was prepared to dandy him up with all sorts of linens and soaps, but at the last minute a messenger boy comes from the Commons House. Seems like there was a mix-up, a right proper one, and personages unknown have insisted that the Russian be lodged in 209. Who was I to question it? I think to myself, I did. The letter came with all sorts of city seals. I don't know this fellow's business, but I know if a French Count is involved and orders come from the Commons House, then who am I, Darius Wilbur, who possesses nothing but an humble Ordinary of quality and stupefying face brushes, to question the properly embossed seals and signatures?"

"Do you have the letter?" Lizzie asked anxiously.

King Darius poked his face about under the desk, pulling up some boxes and peering into some sliding drawers. "God's wounds but I know it's here somewhere." His eyes brightened and he brought up a folded paper. After snapping it open he handed to Lizzie, who took one quick glance at it, then handed it back.

"It's a forgery," she observed. "It's not from the Commons House. Look at the paper: tan, mere butcher paper. And the signature says Larson E. Whipsnade. Who do you know in this city with the name Whipsnade?"

King Darius's mustaches were trembling as if they had their own nervous system. "I feel the fool, I do. Like if God has a fool all His own, it would be me."

Andre took the paper from Lizzie and let out with a small chuckle. "Tchakorov was being set up for thievery. They needed him in that room."

Lizzie peered up at the ceiling, measuring with her eyes. "Mr. Wilbur," she asked, stepping back to get a cleaner view of the expansive molding. "Would you say that Room 209 is just about....there? Right near that fancy plaster cornucopia coming forth from the ceiling above?"

"Sounds about right."

"And how many feet would you say between that cornucopia and the fancy swirls by the southern face?"

"Looks to be about two or three feet, no more or less. But I can't reckon without climbing up there with a mason's rule."

"Is there another room between 209 and the southern face?"

"Not that I know of, but I do believe there's crawl spaces all over the building. That's where the Weirds reside."

"The Weirds?" Andre asked puzzled.

"Ah, pay no attention to my fired imagination. It's a folly of my besotted brain. Too much mustache wax, I presume. But there are strange noises a'nights, especially since the Russian fellow's been pinched. From my post, I hear the thumping and the cursing."

"Cursing?"

"More like the wailing of a lost spirit. I can't bring myself to go searching the corridors. Perhaps the night watch Fred would be able to tell you. Perhaps it's some suicide from long ago who's up there wandering to find his closure."

"Not being a spiritualist," Lizzie announced, "I would sooner think it was just an intruder walking about."

"But the guests are all accounted for, they are!" Darius said. "Believe you me!"

Andre produced a small calling card that had a light trace of perfume. "King Darius, you have given us valuable information."

"Right so," the bewhiskered manager beamed. "When you decipher any of its meaning, let me know what it was that I did tell you, for I'll be danged if it makes sense to me right now."

"We will. And if anything of interest comes up, here is my card."

Darius took the card just as a horde of furniture men stormed the desk, all demanding their telegrams and directions to the nearest saloons. Lizzie and Andre stepped to the side, her eyes practically glued to the ceiling. Her lips were moving silently as if she were counting.

"You think there's an extra room?" Andre said. "But you can clearly see from the corridor that 209 is at the southern end of the building."

She took her gaze from the ceiling. "Oh Andre, this is foul play indeed. For now we have to prepare ourselves for a most unpleasant encounter. Bring me to the Sporting Boys."

Andre directed her towards the dining room from where bellowed forth a loud strain of youthful, impetuous voices.

LIZZIE GETS FUZZLED

Frank Rivers and his Sporting Boys were having their mid-afternoon cigars in the attached dining hall behind the Wilbur's lobby. They sat at their usual table along the western wall before large paneled windows, Frank with his tall opera hat flanked by two bowler-hatted youths, looking like a chimney rising above two slag heaps. A flustered waiter was racing back and forth bringing them victuals while they stamped their firemen boots and howled racy ballads.

A furniture salesman at a nearby table, distracted by the boys' obnoxious hoots, boldly shouted, "Please be quiet! Decent people are trying to digest!"

"Cheese them, B'hoys!" Frank said to his crew. "They're envious of us crapulous folk who live by our own tables of morality. But I say, stockjobbers be they!"

The salesman huffed and nervously went back to his coffee just as Lizzie Borden and Andre de Camp entered the hall. As if on cue, the Sporting Boys quieted down, stifling their laughs and straightening their legs under their table.

"Frank Rivers," Andre said with a bow. "Miss Borden and I require a few moments of your time, if you would allow."

"Hi, hi!" the Sporting Boy proclaimed. "It would be our honor to host such a fine lady and her dandified beau at our table. Chas and Buster here won't mind, will you my gutterbloods?"

"Nay," Buster explained. "Ladies of quality are always welcome to take maw-wallop with us."

Rivers raised his cane and waved it delicately towards the two chairs opposite him and his gang. As Lizzie and Andre took their seats, Rivers stuffed his cigar into his mouth, removing his stovepipe hat to reveal garishly plastered soap locks running down the sides of his scalp. He spat a wad of saliva into his hand and ran his palm along the glistening locks. As he replaced his hat, Lizzie felt a displeasing stirring in her stomach.

"Have a go at us, Lizzie Borden of Second Street," Frank said. "If we're colt's tooth enough for you."

"I could judge that a bit more for myself if I knew what 'colt's tooth' was," Lizzie said smiling. "But for the moment, I'd like to bring your attention to the evening before last."

Chas let out with a rude laugh. "That's the night the Ivan sizer got bully-whacked in the renterfuge."

Frank grimaced. "Now, now, my skenchback, don't go quanking out our guests with our fuzzle talk. For in her gumbling through, she may take beastly interpretations. Miss Lizzie, renterfuge is the room I keep with my prancing pony. I got tumbled by that mustached jarkman who runs this hovel. One day I'll divorce him from his facial for that bumwush."

"He gave the Russian your room," Lizzie said plainly. "The room you frequent with your whore Sarah Jewett."

Frank jumped in his seat and glanced about. "Don't go speaking it plain-like, there's bound to be a bit of scandal-brothing by local malifuffs."

Andre leaned in close to Lizzie. "From the German words mal meaning 'speech' and pfuffen meaning 'to blow.' Literally, someone who blows speech. I suspect he fears gossip."

"My," Frank chortled. "You are indeed bent upon deciphering us, ain't you?"

"Yes, Frank Rivers, we are," Lizzie said, her patience wearing thin. "You can hide behind all your fuzzle talk, but you can't get away from suspicion. And when a crime is committed within yards of your sleeping quarters, indeed within a room to which you have a key, your account of the affair is of great interest to those trying to find the conclusion of this affair."

A shadow fell across Frank's face as a cloud interrupted the sunlight. "You want to know the unfarded truth," he said calmly, "unmistified by false beauties. Well, I'll be the first to admit I'm a scoundrel of a carpet-knight. Many a fancy girl has fallen under my glamour. But that doesn't make me a thief. One may hazard from my fuzzle talk and sporting ways that I don't have a gall of bitterness within me, that I would just as soon steal the metal from my dying grandmother's teeth for a few tankards and a romp with a tweeny maid. Yes, I have my own morality tables that I draw upon, but I do have my limits. And I don't go bully-whacking gentlemen even if they are Ivan sizers. I don't go filching and I don't play hunt-the-whistle, and I don't send any old rake juggler off to Fiddler's Green for lampoons."

"What do you know about that night?" Lizzie said ignoring his obscurity. "What did you hear and see touching this affair?"

"That Pinkerton flonker," Frank spat. "He was guzzled and fell to sonorating. We heard his guzzle moans and then the next we heard he was all in a twee over it and went stomping to the jarkman. Next we know the badgers are all about and there's talk of this Ivan sizer being glorged."

"Yeah," said Chas. "Glorged by the insensible. You ever hear such gruff?"

"So who you got testifying? Drunkard pinks and bully-whacking ghosts?" Frank said with a gentle nod to his gutterbloods. "You ever hear such mulch before?"

"So what do you think occurred that night?" Lizzie asked.

"This is my reconstruction: the big office pinks had some malifuffs trinkling on the Ivan and knew his habits. So they waited till after dragging time and all the b'hoys and g'hals be in their stables for billy winks, then they pulled a filch party on the old pink and the sizer. They got more than one maw-hole to climb in since the b'hoys like to viz their sport." He held up his left hand, the thumb and forefinger tips pressed together, poked his eye through the ring and grinned. "Who doesn't like to viz a bit of the acrobatics."

Lizzie was taken aback by his garish gesture. "But you didn't answer my question," she added. "What did you hear and see?"

Frank leaned forward, his brows pressing together. "I was strumming a'loft at the time and wasn't quite paying apple bonkers to an Ivan and a pink who was sonorating a half hallway apart from my stable. Despite what you may hazard in your think hole, my ears ain't quite that big and my eye stalks ain't that protruded. So you got a bit of a problem distance-wise."

There was a long pause while Frank Rivers and Lizzie Borden sat locked in a frozen state, their eyes pressed together over the space between them. Then Lizzie broke the moment with a small crooked smile. "I think I've had enough information, Mr. Rivers. I take my leave knowing that the prostitute Sarah Jewett is safe in the custody of a boy who considers her a 'prancing pony' and names the hour she is taken to her 'stable' as 'dragging time' and that courtship and courtesy must take a holiday to 'billy winks.' I only hope that when I am of age to take a husband, he would use less flowery imagery to portray his affections for me."

Frank touched his cane handle to his forehead. "Pleased to have educated you, Miss Lizzie. Since we were educated at different high schools, I'm glad we can still understand each other."

Lizzie and Andre got to their feet. As they were leaving the dining hall, they could hear the snorts and sneers behind them. The flustered waiter was just entering with a full silver tray of maw-wallop.

"What did you divine from that parody of a conversation?" Andre asked Lizzie as they slowly strolled across the Wilbur's lobby.

Lizzie laughed nervously, "It is comforting to know that he draws the line at playing 'hunt-the-whistle.' I was beginning to fear for the female population of Bristol County."

Andre gave a dismissive wave. "They are mere pretenders. Just wealthy children who are too lazy to adopt their father's enterprises. They fashion their life styles after the New York City gangs who haunt Five Points and the Bowery. There is much suspicion here."

"Not necessarily," Lizzie added dramatically. "I don't suppose you noticed his left hand. When the sunlight hit at the right angle, I could clearly see the skin on his fingers."

Andre clicked his fingers. "The Arcady Ring. I did not even think to look."

Lizzie reached into her purse and brought forth the signet which she held up for Andre's perusal. "Your father let me have it. I was thinking of producing it for Mr. River's astonishment, but felt best to keep it discreet. Nonetheless there was no discoloration upon his fingers. I do not believe this to be his ring."

Andre stared at it, his jaw clenched.

"Does something strike you?" Lizzie asked.

"No," he said, rubbing his temple. "Only a headache. Shall we promenade down street? It is a striking August day, and I would very much like to know you better, Miss Lizbeth Borden."

LIZBETH OF LIGHT

As the sun sank behind the gently rolling contours of Swansea, beyond the river and the moving barges of bale, Lizzie and Andre walked along the dockside by the Troy Manufactory buildings. Already stars were beginning to appear in the firmament as the sun lowered beyond the horizon.

"I am sorry," Lizzie said humbly, "that I am so flustered. Whenever I see those youths, their futures filled with promise and possibility, their family offering them resources and capital, instead turning towards a wasteful life of mere libertinage and sensuality, I cannot feel but despair for the next generation."

"I believe," Andre said, "Frank Rivers is a nephew to Wellington Rivers, the paper mill tycoon. Needless to say, he has been disinherited. The boy is living upon the good graces of an aunt who is too old and senile to know what he is doing with her money. I still declare that he is our most likely suspect. It would explain why no one saw the thief come or go from the lobby. Rivers would have had to merely slip back into his room after the robbery, thus giving the impression that the thief had vanished into thin air."

"I cannot be fully sure, but the real thief took great care to put suspicion on Rivers and his boys. The ring was so placed to further that suspicion."

Andre shrugged indifferently. "What about the Pinkertons? Although my father puts enormous trust in them, there is no working man that cannot be bought if the price be high enough."

"No man is above perfidy," Lizzie agreed. "But my instincts tell me that the real culprit has yet to reveal his face to us. Such a pity, since your father needs a conclusion by the day after tomorrow."

Andre stopped and stared upwards into the darkening horizon. "My father," he sighed. "For him, it is all about money, I believe. Don't listen to his nonsense about the balance of power in Europe and anarchists lurking in the shadows. The man is merely concerned for his own stock portfolio."

"Is that such a crime?" Lizzie asked.

Andre was about to answer but then he pointed towards a twinkling star. "When I look upon that sky," he mused. "I realize we are but dust, mere motes of dust, compared to the vast wheels of creation. As a small boy, I would walk by twilight in the hills by Rennes-La-Chateau, past the old castles and the haunted graveyards, and watch the stars appear one by one, like celestials' candles on some vast birthday cake. Then I would lie on my back in the midst of the field and let the great spiral move about me. I would fix my gaze on one particular star and throughout the night notice how it would spin about as if on the rim of a perfect wheel. And I would feel as if I were pinned to the center, and that all of creation was whirling about me. At moments like those, my father and all his fortune would seem so inconsequential, like a forgotten dream that once had so much importance, but now was just a shard of memory."

Lizzie watched his face closely as he spoke. "You certainly have your thoughts lifted above the daily affairs," she answered. "I did not think a man of your means and title would think of anything but commerce and management of property."

"Perhaps it is the soil of my native land," he said. "There is mystery in its deep veins. It makes one yearn for something beyond the thin veil of daily sorrows. I am at heart a poet."

Lizzie sighed. "You are so very different from any man I have ever known. I have only known men like my father, and he is so very different from your own. My father never had a title, and his wealth is so small compared with your family's grand fortune. My father stands in relation to your father as we all do to the big wheel you point out in the sky. There is hierarchy indeed in this vast creation."

Andre's voice grew thin and modest. "But, Lizbeth, I see those stars reflected in your eyes. So by mirroring the light from above, you are becoming one with it. And then the modest Lizbeth who feels so unimportant is now the most exquisite being that exists."

Lizzie blushed. "I wouldn't go so far. I'm just a girl from a small family. There's nothing special about me."

"But we are all stars," Andre announced, lifting up a hand towards the heavens. "We twinkle on the great wheel of life, and we all move together in a perfect circle. I have written a poem to that effect. I call my composition, Lizbeth of Light."

A smile curled on her lips. "Why, that's my name."

He nodded in the affirmative and began his recital:

> *I call these bold words to draw your breath*
> *And to drum a beat on your warm heart*
> *I call upon life and its handmaiden death*
> *To give our child its earthborn start*

This child formed from the air betwixt us
That takes a first cry from the sorrows of life
From the darkness of spirit that surrounds us
But mews a bold Yes in the face of the strife

Against gray evening, the dawn weaves its charm
And something billows on the horizon's lip
'Tis the hope and the beauty and the inner calm
That we have won and must never let slip

So if verse be the beating pulse that fashions
A heart that shall sing strong and bright
Let me sing on through the daybreak that passes
Across my eternal Lizbeth of Light

A paralyzed silence fell between them. Andre stood by Lizzie's side, his shoulder barely touching her. She could feel the heat through the fabric and a chill transported along the length of her trembling body.

"When did you compose this poem?" Lizzie asked, her face turning red.

"After seeing you at your church this Saturday past."

"I did not think that you had noticed me."

"I asked my father who you may be and he answered, 'That is Andrew J. Borden's younger daughter. She is a clever, wise and commanding girl. She runs her own consulting business and has trapped several wrongdoers and corrected many harms to common people. She is indeed a flower of a girl in the midst of a rough crop.' And then I knew that I had found the one girl in Fall River in whom I could find a trustworthy soul."

"I am flattered indeed," Lizzie blushed. She was about to say more but could not find the words.

"Do you believe, Lizbeth Borden," Andre asked, "that perhaps our ancestors, on the lush fields of Carcassonne, enjoyed each other's company as we are enjoying ourselves on this most enchanted evening?"

She was stunned, standing frozen without speech, fearing to breathe.

"Perhaps they did," Andre continued. "And perhaps they partook of the dark blood of the soil, tasting together the richness of the earth into which they were born, and into which they shall pass. Perhaps a Bourdin and a Duchamps lay together under the mysterious stars and held hands as I hold yours."

And she felt a soft fluttering about her fingers, and then they were pressed together. Lizzie stiffened and found that she was no longer breathing, which embarrassed her and Andre smiled. "You have nothing to fear," he said peacefully. "I am a perfect *gentilhomme*." And he lifted her palm into the air and took a slight bow in her direction.

"There is beauty in you," she said in a bare whisper. Inwardly she blessed the darkness for hiding her blushes.

In the long distance the wail of a bale barge sang across the cloudy darkness like a leviathan of the deep calling for its home waters. Andre's face was only lightly illuminated by the hanging lamps but she could see his deep eyes sparkling with the waters below as the moonlight reflected upwards towards the pier.

There were never eyes more beautiful, she thought, nor a face so noble.

Lizzie pressed her free hand to her cheek to catch her tears.

"You are not a Sporting Boy at all, my dear Andre," she said. "You are a melancholy soul of light."

A Sudden Revelation

At breakfast the next morning, Andrew Jackson Borden sat with his family at his dining room table nibbling on some leftover codfish balls, his bead-like eyes staring distantly to the wallpaper as if he were contemplating the insensible. Abby Borden, seated near him, inhaling a cup of coffee and chewing gustily on a molasses cookie, seemed afraid to draw his attention towards the present moment; while Emma stirred restlessly upon some difficult secret that was bubbling inside her, causing her to shift her posture every few moments, a gesture accompanied by uncomfortable sighs. Lizzie, like her father, sat in a grim trance, her utensil barely grazing her dish. Only the Irish maid showed signs of animation, flittering in and out of the kitchen with the various courses of their breakfast.

"What is this gloom that descends on us today," said Abby finally. "It is like being seated at a funeral viewing. My dear Andrew, where is your mind wandering?"

"What?" he said, his eyes jerking back to the present. "My apologies, Mrs. Borden. I was trying to remember Tobias Ullsworth. I cannot imagine what ill tidings he harbors towards me."

"Ullsworth?" Abby frowned. "That's the cloth doffer that you evicted for non-payment of rent. I can't imagine what *glad* tidings he would harbor towards you. I told you that being so strict with him over one month's rent was not good for your reputation."

"I was merely protecting my property rights," Andrew said with a start. "That Ullsworth was particularly unsavory." He slurped at his stew, staining his beard. "I cannot abide slackards and layabouts."

"That slackard," shouted Emma, rising to her feet, "has disappeared from the face of the earth!"

There was a harsh moment of silence broken by Lizzie coughing delicately into her hand. "It's true, Father," Emma continued. "I have heard word from my contacts down street that Tobias Ullsworth has vanished. Last Monday morning he was seen wandering down by the Durfee Mill and at noon his boots were found by the side of the Quequechan. His wife and her seven children are living in a state of despondent impecuniousness."

"They should have considered themselves fortunate when they let the place!" Andrew sputtered. "It is not my concern."

"Heartless man," Emma muttered. "You don't know their fortunes, both before they let from you, and after their cruel eviction. You don't know the vagaries that have befallen them."

"I do know," Andrew said pointing a spoon towards his elder daughter, "that I have been fined by the bank for late payment of the mortgage. Ullsworth doesn't give a fig for that, nor should I care a fig for his dilemma."

"The man is dead!" Emma howled, and then fled towards the door, her hands moving towards her face. She collided with the maid who was entering with a tray of molasses cookies. "Out of my way, Maggie," she shouted, and a moment later her feet were heard clomping up the front stairs. Flustered, the maid ran back into the kitchen.

Abby patted the table with her palms. "Well, Andrew," she said solemnly, "you have certainly topped the program this time. I have never heard such disregard for another man's plight."

"Bah. I have my rights. Landlords have rights."

"But you have no poetry," Lizzie said suddenly.

"Eh? What?" Andrew spluttered. "What kind of nonsense do you speak?"

"You see no lights in my eyes," Lizzie announced. "You see no great wheel in the sky. There is only one letter separating your name from his, but the other differences are vast and deep. His blood runs with wine, yours with sawdust!"

Andrew looked towards Abby as if trying to find an anchor of sanity. "My daughter is speaking like the inmates at the Taunton Asylum."

Abby's face went slack. "I believe I know what Lizzie is saying," she said grimly.

"Ah, you are all insane," Andrew stammered. "No one knows the humiliation I felt! Spit at me in the street he did! In front of my own people! In front of my own daughter! Told me to go be hanged in Arcady, whatever the devil that means!"

Lizzie froze, her eyes widening. "What did you say?" said Lizzie.

"He told me be hanged in Arcady. I suppose he thinks I would travel all the way to Greece to dangle myself from some fruit tree."

Lizzie bolted to her feet, her arms shaking. "Who was this man? Do you not know? Oh, Father! I must know who he was."

"Tall, mustache and beard, spectacles. I don't care one jot who he is, as long as he keeps his spittle away from my brow!"

Lizzie ran from her table, leaving behind a full bowl of codfish stew. She pushed her way violently past the Maggie, who stood in the doorway staring at the remaining Bordens sitting silently at their table along the northern wall.

"For the love of Mike," she said merrily, "did your daughters not get seized by some turned milk? You're a right queer family, I declare!"

A Clue in the Midden Heap

The stable yard behind the Wilbur was filled with the whinnying and musty smells of the clientèle's beastly transports. The stable doors were wide open and the rank odors overwhelmed Andre, forcing him to hold a fine-clothed handkerchief to his nose. Lizzie's mysterious note had asked him to meet her back there at noon, and the eager anticipation that she had solved some part of the affair kept him at attention down wind of the stables' midden heap.

Lizzie appeared as if from the cabinet of a stage magician, her face bright and cheery, with a calm and ease that had not existed in her the day before. Andre greeted her with a slight kiss to the back of her hand.

"Lizbeth," he said, which made her smile.

"I have good news," she announced. "Another piece of this puzzle has fallen into place, and I am ready to test a hypothesis."

"I was hoping as much." Andre gestured towards the back door of the hotel. "Shall we?"

As they started towards the olfactory safety of the Wilbur's interior, Lizzie's eyes narrowed in on the large and distasteful midden heap upon which a dirty young girl in a patchwork dress clamored with an iron hook, digging into the tangled mass. The girl looked up with ferocity in her hungry face.

"Biddy Doren, if I am not mistaken," Lizzie exclaimed. "What are you doing far from Bishop Street? And digging in filth, no less."

The girl lowered her iron hook and stood erect. "The man said there's gold in here."

"The man? What man?"

"The man with the funny hat. He told me that I can stop my mommy being hungry if I can find her some gold." She held up an egg-shaped item that gleamed in the sunlight. "He found this and said 'Bah!' and threw it to me. He told me there's more in there if I were dog enough to scrounge for it!"

"*Bastarde*," Andre whispered. He reached forward and took the small ball that the girl was holding. It was the size of a walnut and looked like it had been forged roughly from tin. A small hinged top swung open to reveal a folded piece of paper inside. Lizzie reached in and grabbed it, eagerly unfolding the paper. In childish scrawl it read:

HANG BE YE TO ARCADY
ANDREW J. BORDEN

Without a moment's hesitation, she stepped back into the center of the horse yard and started scanning the tall back wall of the hotel, examining each and every window and small opening.

"You believe it was tossed from above?" Andre asked.

"I have been a fool! Of course! The pessary did not make it to the master criminal behind this. It is still in the hotel."

"But this is good news. That means there is a chance of finding it."

"I wonder," she said with a curious twinkle in her eye.

Lizzie unbuckled her purse and reached in, pulling out a large silver coin, and held it forth to the small girl. "Perhaps this can help with your mother's hunger." The girl stepped forward cautiously and snatched the coin, her fingers trembling as they wrapped around its circumference.

"Now run along and let your mother have the coin," Lizzie ordered. The girl sped from the courtyard, dust rising behind her.

Lizzie held the tin pessary in her hand and peered intently at the back wall of the hotel. "This is far more than I could have hoped for. Yes, I think I know what to do. Andre, I must ask you to tell your father that I have solved the case. But you must gather together the following people: the Comte de Rennes, Fred and Fred Pinkerton, King Darius Wilbur, Deputy Sheriff Wixon of the Bristol County police, and Dr. Seabury Bowen."

"A doctor?"

"Unless I am horribly mistaken, I believe we may have need of a medical man for a delicate procedure."

"I trust your instinct, Lizzie Borden, Girl Detective. Andre de Camp is at your service." And he gracefully withdrew from the courtyard, leaving Lizzie to ponder the odorous midden heap of Biddy Doren.

The Weird in the Wall

An hour later, a small coterie gathered in the lobby of the Wilbur, clustered about their host, King Darius Wilbur, who twirled his mustaches furiously. The Comte de Rennes, clearly uncomfortable with such a public appearance, glanced about with suspicion as if he expected a bomb-hurtling anarchist to be behind every pillar and post. One of the Fred Pinkertons stood like a stone sentinel with his hanging whiskers and dusty bowler. Deputy Sheriff Wixon of Bristol County, looking very mystified, tipped his cap to Lizzie Borden and asked politely, "I don't know what this is all about, but I bet it's a pretty how-dee-do."

Lizzie laughed. "It is very simple, Deputy. The Comte de Rennes has had something stolen from him, and now we going to retrieve it. I shall want you to arrest the culprit."

"Then you have found it!" the Comte said with bated breath. "*Mon Dieu*! You must tell me where it is without delay!"

"I am waiting for one more personage in our little drama, a man whose role may turn out to be of great importance. Ah, I see Andre, your *jeune fils*, has indeed located the good Doctor Seabury Bowen."

Andre and Dr. Bowen came in through the front door, the expression on the doctor's face betraying as much confusion as the deputy's.

"I have been informed you require my services," he said politely. "Is someone ill?"

"That is yet to be seen," Lizzie announced, then waved a gloved hand towards the stairway to the upper floor. "Gentlemen?"

A few moments later they had all regrouped outside of Room 209 where the other Fred Pinkerton, dressed in the same brown suit and bowler hat as his twin, stood by his wooden chair at attention. King Darius peered at him with puzzlement. "Are you you?" he asked, "Or are you your brother?"

"I'm the other one," he replied.

The entire crowd moved into the room, which was exactly as Lizzie had last seen it the previous afternoon, down to the flower bouquet on the writing desk and the French circus postcard on the dressing table.

"Gentlemen," she said, clapping her hands. "We are now in a room where four evenings ago, a robbery of great ignominy took place. A Russian inventor had a possession stolen from him as he lay unconscious, the victim of etherization. For the last twenty-four hours I have been greatly puzzled over this theft. For the thief did not seem to have entered or exited the room, or at least that was the impression of the good Fred Pinkertons and King Darius Wilbur, all three of whom I consider to be men of impeccable reputation and honesty. It vexed me greatly how the thief made his escape, and I have torturously pondered every possible solution. Then it occurred to me that perhaps the thief never made his escape at all. Perhaps—and I beg your indulgence for a moment—he is still here."

Everyone in the room shouted out with surprise, glancing suspiciously at their neighbor. Lizzie raised her hands to quiet them down. "And I am not suggesting that any one present in this room is the culprit."

"But it seems impossible," King Darius exclaimed. "Do you suspect supernatural agencies? I heard the weirds and their hideous calls in the night, I did."

"Nay, Mr. Wilbur, one need not resort to supernatural explanations. I will demonstrate the source of your nocturnal weirding calls." She reached into her purse and produced several slips of paper on which were handwritten phrases of varying lengths. She began to distribute them to her perplexed guests, keeping one for herself. Then she turned and faced the southern wall. The Poussin painting of the rustic shepherds about their tomb now seemed a bit crooked in the stark noon light. Everyone faced the wall with her.

"I may be wrong about this," she said. "But there is no other solution. Will everyone please be so kind as to read out the phrases on the paper I have given each of you? Read the phrase with a voice pursuing dramatic emotional ranges, like an actor upon a stage at a variety saloon."

The Comte de Rennes looked down at his assigned script. "But this is madness. What manner of words are these?"

"Trust me," Lizzie said.

Everyone stood staring at her, so she pumped her hand in the air and demonstrated in a loud and boisterous outburst. "It's a spouter boys! Off the bow sprits! Crank the boom lines!"

After an awkward pause, the rest of the men followed her example in loud theatrical voices as if they meant to be heard by a far-flung balcony of patrons.

"Abandon the house boys!"

"Come on, ye green-skulled dolts! Make fire-flies to the booms!"

"Ignite the blubber works! There's a goodly trough of oil to be had!"

"The winds are crossing swords, o me hearties!"

"Far to starboard the spermaceti awaits!"

"Harpooners to the boats! There she blows!"

For a few moments the men in the room raised this mighty cacophony, so much so that they began to hear feet stamping and the sound of alarm in the hallway outside. As their boisterous cries started to wind down, Lizzie egged them on. "Keep at it! Don't mind the innocents! We're almost there!"

Andre felt absurd and was the first one to stop. Just as he was about to protest and quiet the others, there was a horrific cracking noise and the entire wall before which they stood started to shake. The Poussin painting crashed to the floor, revealing more rose-flowered wallpaper, but dead in the center of the faint rectangle where the color had been faded by sunlight was a curious peephole, like a tiny eye in the middle of a rose petal. Then a thin crack appeared along the edges of a long, thin painted vine, and there was the creak of rusty hinges. Before everyone's startled eyes, a large section of the wall was pushing outwards. There was now a door where previously there had been no door, and it was swinging towards them to uncover a man-sized opening behind.

The figure that bounded from the newly exposed orifice was thin, grimy and dressed in filthy rags. His hair was wild, his eyes aglow with some feral madness. His whiskers flared out at insane angles and his cheeks puffed as he pumped against the wooden floorboards. He tried to race towards the door, but Deputy Wixon stepped forward and grabbed him.

"Lord salvage me!" the man was shouting in a creaky voice. "The spermaceti is spouting and I'm below decks! Where be my harpoon boys?! Spring, my lads! Spring!"

"How? What's this?" Wixon said incredulously, holding fast to the man's jacket tails. "Confound it, but it's our missing man!"

"May I introduce," Lizzie said, breaking out with a prideful laugh, "Mr. Tobias Ullsworth of Anawan Street. Deputy Wixon, I believe this is the man who has been missing for three days now?"

"*Mon Dieu, je ne comprend!*" The Comte de Rennes shouted, twirling his mustache. He stepped forward and peered into the wall cavity. The rest of the men stepped forward a pace to take a glance over his shoulder. Inside the wall was a tiny nest, about four feet by three feet, barely enough for a man to lie down in. Its back wall was exposed wood, through which could be heard the sounds of animals in the stable yard. On the floorboards lay a filthy pallet and a kerosene lamp, next to which rested a plate covered with insects, which had devoured what little morsels of potato and beans had been there to sustain the prisoner.

"You mean he's been in there?" Wixon said, staring at the filthy crazy man in his grasp.

King Darius let out with a howl that was both amused and offended. "Indeed he has! That's the Sporting Hole I heard slip from the skenchback Buster. Their way of spying on their Fancy Girls. I wouldn't have believed it, but there it is as evidence. And in my own ordinary, much to my chagrin."

"Frank Rivers," said Andre triumphantly. "This is proof conclusive. Shall we arrest that rogue?"

"No," Lizzie said. "We need to hear from the thief himself."

"Let go my arm so I can scratch my beard," Ullsworth shrieked. "I'm all a'crawling with critters!" Wixon released his grip, trusting that his charge wouldn't bolt for freedom, as the man savagely attacked his own facial hair like it was bursting into flames. "Oh, Flukes and Blubber! I ain't been so infested since I last went a'whaling! Damn that Rivers! Promised to send my children to school with their betters! Promised me that Tobias would never have to go to sea or work the cloth again! But he wanted me to swap the egg, he did. Give him a tin forgery, he said and let Borden take the blame! I say, let him rot in his own blubber works! Damn that Rivers!"

Lizzie nodded in silent agreement. "Wellington Rivers, the bank manager and paper merchant, is the mastermind behind this affair?" she asked directly to the hairy face before her.

Ullsworth snarled. "Aye, the ruffian! I'll savage his head, I will. He'll not suffer more in all his days!"

Andre raised an enlightened finger. "I suspected as much. Rivers must be in the employ of the British. They wish to prevent the Bulgarian expansion. Perhaps they hope to raise the siege of Plevna! Wellington Rivers is their puppet!"

King Darius snapped his fingers. "Aha!" he exclaimed. "And this Wellington Rivers was the investor behind this hotel. During the construction, he must have personally customized room 209 for his nephew Frank's lurid frolics. Dare say, that's it!"

Ullsworth focused his bloodshot eyes on the Pinkerton Brothers who stood glaring at him. "Galloping ghosts! Now he's split in two he is! I waited all these days for him to go away, now he's split in two!"

One of the Freds smirked, "That split happened a long time ago, my friend."

"But this is all getting us nowhere! Where is the pessary?" The Comte de Camp shouted. "Where are the plans for the self-acting Mule?"

Lizzie smiled and pointed a finger at Ullsworth whose face was now bloated with red swells. "Doctor Bowen," she said, "I believe if you examine Mr. Ullsworth, you will find what you are looking for." She leaned over and whispered a word into Bowen's ear, after which a strange gloom passed over the good doctor's face.

"I will do what I can do," he said resignedly, and then pulled Ullsworth across the floor and into the hole in the wall. The wallpapered doorway slammed shut and for a few uncomfortable moments the occupants of Room 209 were treated to a symphony of howls and curses, giant whoops and prayers to various North Atlantic whales and their Leviathan god. Then, after what seemed like an eternity, the doorway opened once more and Ullsworth appeared, more disheveled than before, holding up his belt-less pants so they wouldn't plummet to his heels. He stepped forward carefully with jackknifing legs giving the appearance that he was walking over gravel.

"Flukes and Blubber!" he bellowed, fleeing back to Deputy Wixon as if the policeman were some form of safe port in an otherwise hostile ocean. At that moment, the Deputy took out some metallic wristlets to bind the whale man's hands.

Dr. Bowen appeared back in the room with his jacket removed and one sleeve rolled up past the elbow. In his hand he held a shiny metallic egg about an inch in diameter. He held it aloft with delicacy.

"Careful," he said. "It must be washed."

"The pessary!" the Comte de Rennes roared and raced forward to toss both his arms about the befuddled doctor who collapsed like a boneless fish between the Frenchman's mighty timber-like arms.

Lizzie stepped before Ullsworth who quaked in his gumboots. "Aye lassie, you may think me a filthy and despicable codger," he groaned, "but I had my reasons."

"Your family is starving," she said in a whispery and sad voice. "After my father evicted you, you had no choice but to take up Rivers' offer. You have been twice betrayed."

A sparkle came into the man's desperate eyes. "Here's a girl who speaks righteous! You tell 'em!" He tugged at his shackles. "You describe how a man's beloved wife and children can be tossed into the street like so much offal! It's not a sane world, is it? Locked up in a disgusting hole for three days! I was told what would be done to my lads and lassies if I gave up the game, so I hid. For many days now, I hid and saw the sun go up and down through that accursed broken board. My life has been darkness and horse dung, I tell ye! And not even a place to empty my slops. You can imagine what I'm going to say to Rivers the next time I sees him! Yes, I'll walk right up to his fancy house and knock on the door, and when his high and mighty butler comes to toss me by the seat of his pants, I'll let loose my slops all over his European carpets! You'll see how he stands up to that! Yes, Mr. Rivers! Send me to do some bottom's up surgery on a poor defenseless Cossack! We'll see! Who'll now take care of ol' Tobias Ullsworth's poor starving lads and lassies?"

Lizzie gave a slight nod and the barest trace of a smile.

"Justice shall be done," she promised, and startled the old whaler by taking his hands in hers.

Everyone present stared in shocked silence.

A PLOT REVEALED

Lizzie Borden held court at the same table in the Wilbur's dining room as had been occupied the day before by Frank Rivers and his two skenchbacks. Bar keep Sam Samways, late of South Bethlehem, PA, provided some hops and spirits for the men while Lizzie drank a fresh cup of Orange Pekoe. The Comte and Vicomte de Rennes sat together, a large mountain and his smaller, thinner copy, flanked by the two Pinkerton Brothers, Fred and Fred, who resembled each other in both countenance and attire down to the last link on their watch fobs. Deputy Wixon was nursing a beer, having decided that being off duty was a much better position to be in than having to file all sorts of complicated reports, or explain to his superiors that he had solved a theft while making no arrests. Doctor Bowen was off tending to the physically ailing Ullsworth whom they promised to both morally reform and nurse back to prime health. For those present, the relief of recovering the plans for the self-acting Mule had unleashed a wave of merriment that manifested much laughter and friendly banter.

"Lizzie, you must tell us what led you to discover the whaleman Ullsworth in the wall" requested King Darius, his mustaches bristling.

"As soon as I saw the tin pessary in the midden heap," Lizzie proclaimed, "everything was absurdly simple. The message within the tin was an insult hurled at a man in the back alley from a broken plank in the outer wall of Ullsworth's hiding place. At that moment I knew that the plans had not only never left the hotel grounds, but no doubt were still in the room from whence they had been stolen. How that could be, when the entire room had been thoroughly searched, was still a mystery to me. But there was also this unnamed man, no doubt a stooge working for Wellington Rivers, who verbally and physically abused Andrew Jackson Borden on the street yesterday morning, believing my father to have been behind the betrayal. Yet his assault upon Mr. Borden provided the vital clue." Lizzie produced the folded paper from her purse and held it up for all to read. "Hang ye be to Arcady!"

"The whale ship Arcady!" Fred Pinkerton the Elder said with a start. "Sailed out of New Bedford in August of 1875, went down with all hands except for one whaler who returned in disgrace to Fall River to work as a cloth doffer to feed seven children."

"Tobias Ullsworth," Fred Pinkerton the Younger concluded. "Vanished this Monday last and not seen in physical form again until he emerged from a hotel wall this very afternoon turned into a gibbering lunatic by his long ordeal."

"The man who wailed in the night," King Darius said bemusedly. "The weird in the wall. Never again shall I ever suspect supernatural agencies when there is always a perfectly natural explanation. Indeed I won't!"

"It all does hang together," said Lizzie. "Wellington Rivers, President of the Tiverton-Rivers Paper Mill and co-chairman of the Fall River First National Bank, was suspected of sabotaging the whale ship Arcady to collect on insurance. It was his holding company that was found culpable in the sinking of the ship due to a faulty manufacturing of its hull planking, a finding that was buried under graft and corruption and never became public knowledge. The circumstances were known only to insiders like my Father who did not judge the man, and even admired him for his thrift. Tobias Ullsworth must have felt the need for vengeance against the man who destroyed his life."

"And Rivers," the Comte de Rennes said with a chuckle, "was unsuccessfully attempting to buy up stock in a certain unnamed textile mill that I was to negotiate a technological contract with, one that would seal the fate of the Crimea. Being a paper pulper, Rivers was looked down upon by those men of cloth who run the looms and spindles of Fall River. He would have the perfect motive to steal the plans. He would have been able to open his own textile mill and triple his wealth with his exclusive use of a revolutionary new type of Mule."

"Not to mention," Andre said triumphantly, "he wanted to cast the shadow of suspicion on his nephew Frank who had taken to the Sporting Boy life, and so disgraced the family name."

Deputy Wixon breathed a deep sigh. "I am hearing all that you folks are saying, but I have a pretty predicament here. I can't just march into Rivers' Paper Mill and arrest him, don't you know? What crime has the man committed that we can prove? Ullsworth can only be charged with breaking and entering and his ramblings about Rivers will be dismissed by folk who would sooner believe a man of wealth than a common cloth doffer."

"I'm afraid Wellington Rivers is untouchable," Lizzie mused. "His only punishment shall be his failure to procure the pessary."

"And what about Frank Rivers?" King Darius said with an evil twitch in his eye. "I can ban him and his likes and their libertine ways from under my roof, but they shall continue to roam the streets of Fall River, spreading their sensualist ways, and provoking our finest women into lives of wanton decline."

The Comte de Rennes stood to his feet. "The Rivers boy and his scurrilous gang shall be dealt with accordingly. Perhaps I can persuade some local men of substance to form a committee to abolish this social issue of Sporting Boys and their Fancy Girls once and for all. Why

Lizzie, I shall even recommend that your father be appointed as a committee member since he has confessed to me in confidence his outrage at these acts of youthful folly."

"I thank you on behalf of Mr. Borden," Lizzie said. "I'm sure he would be most eager to join your committee."

"More appropriately," the Comte said, getting to his feet and bowing politely in Lizzie's direction. "I must thank you, Lizzie Andrew Borden, on behalf of the French government, as well as the Royal Czar of Russia, for the recovery of our most valuable industrial asset. I will apply to my superiors for a special rate of compensation for you and your entire family, which will come from the sale of the self-acting Mule technology."

"*Merci*," Lizzie said, winking at Andre who smiled back at her.

Fred Pinkerton the Younger shrugged. "If you fancy folk would only have told us simple folk about all these Russian intrigues, foreign wars, and golden eggs from the very beginning, perhaps the Pinkerton Brothers would have been of more use. Perhaps we could have shared in the glorious wealth of this Mule, whatever the blazes it be!"

Lizzie laughed. "Have no fear, Fred and Fred. Payment for your services shall be paid liberally from my family's profits. And young Biddy Doren, the poor girl with the consumptive mother on Bishop Street, shall have a trust set up for her from the Lizzie Andrew Borden Fund for Destitute Children, as shall all seven sons and daughters of the lamentable Tobias Ullsworth. Nor shall I forget the orphaned children of Tchakorov, the poor Russian inventor, or his lovely new equestrian bride, who yet needs the funds to travel to America. I shall donate my entire share of the Mule plans to that effect."

"Hear, hear!" King Darius said, snapping his fingers in the direction of the corpulent Samways, motioning for a round of rice beer. "Let us all congratulate Fall River's most excellent Girl Detective!"

When the drinks had been brought, all cheered and raised their tankards to Lizzie Borden. "Hooray for Lizzie!" they shouted as one.

Lizzie sat smiling against the white wash of the tall dining hall windows, her hands cupped around her warm mug of coffee, since she was of the temperance and did not drink spirits.

The bellhop from the front desk appeared holding a letter stick which he extended across the table to Lizzie. She jumped in fright at its appearance before her nose, snatching the note while the bellhop receded into the lobby. She read the hastily written words and then turned to her assembled friends.

"You must forgive me, but a Mr. Butterworth of the Saloon Furnishing Corporation of Keene, New Hampshire is requiring my presence in the horse yard. I suspect he wants to engage me as a liaison between him and my father's business. Excuse me."

Everyone continued to banter and drink as Lizzie stepped from the room and disappeared into the lobby. Andre, his instincts inclined toward her protection, eyed her through the dining hall windows as she turned the corner of the building, her hat bobbing, and disappeared behind the building.

A moment later, King Darius twirled his mustaches, a sign that he was perplexed. "Strange," he muttered. "Mr. Butterworth was representing a furnishing concern in Boston. I think that he did leave early this morning."

"Butterworth?" Andre said, lifting himself from his seat.

"Exactly," Fred Pinkerton the Elder added. The man's face leapt into animated life. "By Jupiter, he did leave this morning! I carried his baggage to the waiting coach!"

"Zounds!" Andre howled, and reached behind his chair for his slender walking stick. Before anyone could comment, Andre had bounded away from the table and was sprinting towards the door of the dining hall, his cane swirling before him.

KIDNAPPED!

Upon entering the stable yard, Lizzie immediately sensed an unusual quiet; only the sounds of traffic and pedestrians from the other side of the tall hotel broke the stillness, but within the yard itself there was a strange vacancy of sound. Her instincts told her to run, that a horse yard was no place for a furniture salesman to meet with a lady of quality. She had encountered fake notes before. Why had her instincts failed her on this occasion?

"Butterworth!" she shouted, hoping that her voice would reach her friends through the dining hall window.

"I'll give you your worth of butter," came a familiar sneer. Out from behind a lumber shack came a swaggering figure balanced under a stovepipe hat, walking carefully in stocky fireman boots. "Don't be all in a twee, my dear. This ain't no dragging time; I have arranged for safe transport to a place where you can fuzzle with a man of great import."

Frank Rivers raised his arms above his stovepipe and upon this cue the yard's stillness was broken by the roar of a thumping horse. Before Lizzie could form any estimation of her predicament, a large barouche had entered the yard from the street, but unlike any barouche that she had seen before. It was an imposing four-wheeled high flyer pulled by a feverish white quarter horse, its nostrils blazing with wind. The bellowed hood formed a self-enclosed space over the carriage seats and draped black curtains hung down from exposed protruding dowels to conceal those who sat within. A pair of hands holding leather reins emerged from the curtain that draped over the outside box seat to drive the quarter horse that thundered before it. The barouche very quickly overtook Lizzie as she spun to make her escape. Frank Rivers had raced forward to grab her, and the flailing arms of Sporting Boys emerged from the hidden recesses of the concealed cabin to pull her up towards the gaping curtains.

"Mercy!" Lizzie cried, her body flush with panic. Before she knew it, she was inside the shaky cabin surrounded by Chas and Buster, their faces convulsed in vulgar leers. The barouche was bouncing up and down with ridiculous exaggeration as she struggled. Surely, she reasoned, anyone witnessing this from outside would think it peculiar and raise an alarm. All she had to do was to keep her limbs flailing.

Frank Rivers popped through the curtain like he had been swinging on a vine, his hat missing from his head and his soap lock grease dripping down his cheeks. "Quiet, my lamb," he said. "I am playing mere stumpet usher this afternoon. There's a man on the Hill. Yea, he's got reason to maw-wallop with you. Snaggle her to me, he said. And so we snaggle you."

"I'm going to scream," Lizzie said. She could feel the barouche starting to move into the traffic of North Main. Knowing that her chances to salvage her situation were rapidly diminishing, she broke one arm free from Buster's grip and lashed out at Frank Rivers, her finger nails which had been grown to a fashionable length, tore across his cheek, slipping off his sweat and soap lock. "Gaaaah!" he cried, raising a palm to his slashed flesh which had started to ooze blood. "You boggled dolly! You monster!"

"You're the monster," she said defiantly, and feeling the barouche gallop into full speed down North Main Street, she spat in his face.

"For that," he said, wiping at his nose, "you will know a grand rib roasting."

Lizzie closed her eyes, expecting the worst, but was immediately surprised to feel the entire balance of the carriage lean backwards, as if it were tumbling over. Sunlight splashed her face, and she opened her eyes to see the vast expanse of the afternoon sky flanked by the moving tops of buildings. Some one, or some thing, was pulling back the collapsible half-hood above her, ripping it aside as if it were made of tissue paper, and the draped curtains to her left and right were falling to the street. All the grips holding her were loosened. She fell back as the barouche tipped and for a brief moment, she saw Andre de Camp, stripped to his shirt sleeves, locked in a tangle with Frank Rivers against the clouds, then all was a spiral towards the ground and she felt the hard road beneath slamming her knees and elbows.

Rolling over to prevent her face from hitting the dirt, she saw the broken pieces of the barouche and a sad image of the collapsed quarter horse lifting its whinnying head upwards. It took but a moment for her to realize that Andre de Camp had chased the vehicle of her abduction and had overrun it on foot. Somehow he had managed to get on board and rip apart, seemingly with his bare hands, the collapsible hood, at the same time knocking the Sporting Boys off the vehicle. She caught a brief glimpse of Chas and Buster racing down the street, limping and screaming, until they crashed into a solid wall of Pinkerton Brothers.

"Apple bonkers!" Chas cried.

"Fancy some friendly fuzzle!" Buster said in a panic.

"Let bygones be made," Chas pleaded. "No rib roasting for us, my skenchbacks!"

Within second, the Freds had chosen their targets and the two Sporting Boys were air bound, hurled and twirled under. They fell like lifeless lumps to the ground, where they were assaulted by heavy workman boots. There was a gathering crowd on both sides of the street full of respectable men and women in their fine dresses and suits, all of whom were cheering on the melee.

Then Lizzie saw Andre and Frank Rivers standing arm's length apart from one another in front of the phaeton's shattered carriage, their feet in angry boxing stances, their hands up and curling into fists.

The startled crowd was now frozen in suspense as the two boys circled about an invisible center between them. A woman screamed, another fainted, dogs were barking, a gentleman cried out that someone should call the police. Far in the distance came the screeching of birds as they flew their indifferent path against the clouds. The entire scene was suspended in space as if it were part of some famous painting, as if

Andre and Frank were two titans wrestling in some mythical moment that existed outside of time.

"You think you know this stockjobber!" Frank Rivers snarled, and Lizzie realized to her horror that he was talking to her. "Not in a sloven's year! Let him tell you the truth! Hang ye be to Arcady!" Then he lashed forward violently, his arms swinging in graceful and powerful arcs.

Andre stepped into the punches and reached for Frank's soap locks. At first his grip slipped right off them, but in that instant he managed to disorient the Sporting Boy. Lashing out again, he seized the locks like they were horns on a rampaging bull and pulled with all the full force of his physical being.

"Yoiks!" Frank Rivers cried, then sped forward, pulled by his own hair. Andre brought a knee up into the boy's abdomen, which brought another exclamation, one that could not be represented by any word, and then Frank Rivers was limp and defenseless. Andre spun him about and kicked him full in the seat of his trousers, sending him in a comical arc over the stunned quarter horse. Frank Rivers hit the ground with a graceless thud, his face landing in some equine feces that his own animal had treasured the street with, and then lay disturbingly still, the only sounds being a very thin and listless muttering of some random fuzzle talk: "Glorged I be…gored to the bumwush…all in a twee, my skenchback…" And then he was silent.

Lizzie forced herself to her feet, which turned out to be the easy part. Staying upright was a task she started feeling was beyond her capacity. Her pulled muscles dragged her downward as a frightful state of shock began to pass over her startled body. Andre stood before her, his face covered in dirt, his shirt torn, his body still braced for action, not exhausted or weakened but strong and virile.

Warm waves spread downward from her head into her limbs, a delayed reaction to the fear, the anxiety, the deathly grip that had taken hold of her body ever since her ordeal had begun. But she was held together by the sight of her brave soldier, her beautiful Vicomte, drenched in sweat, heaving with fear for her safety. Her feelings were very shameful, but in Andre's presence she couldn't but surrender to them.

She ran forward and into his arms, her face trembling, her tears staining her cheeks, her arms grabbing desperately at him, begging to be embraced.

For a moment there was warm comfort, like she was falling through soft down in a summer's breeze with no physical pain, no fear, no danger.

Her reverie was broken only by a startled yelp that dispelled the waking dream. "Lizzie Andrew!" She lifted her eyes from Andre's shoulder to see her sister Emma in an afternoon dress at the periphery of the startled crowd, her face aghast, her hands raised to her ovaled mouth.

"It is all correct, Emma," Lizzie said, not even loud enough for her sister to hear, "Andre is my skenchback."

Then she fell into blackness, her last impression being Andre's arms catching her as she plummeted.

JUSTICE AND LOST LOVE

The conclusion to the affair held little comfort for Lizzie's shattered heart. Despite the justice that had been executed and the financial reward reaped by the suffering innocents who had been involved directly and indirectly in the affair, there was still the small matter of the signet ring with the scarlet A embossed upon it.

All else was neatly concluded. The pessary with its enclosed textile technology was returned to the Comte de Rennes. A few months later, a new textile mill owned and operated by a Russian industrialist became operational along the banks of the Quequechan, to much ballyhoo and a titanic flood of profits due to the introduction of a new self-acting Mule that increased production and the pick of the yarn. All who held stock in the venture, including Lizzie Andrew Borden and her father Andrew Jackson Borden, had more money flow into their accounts than they previously could have dreamed. Lizzie, in turn, donated all her proceeds to a charitable fund for destitute children. The Doren woman in Bishop Street was able to find a proper home for her small child Biddy, who Lizzie saw every Saturday afternoon thereafter for ice cream down street, and who eventually matured into a fine young woman, the first in her family to study at a university. In later years, Lizzie heard that Biddy Doren wrote serialized novels about social issues that gave Upton Sinclair a run for his money in the literary market place.

Tobias Ullsworth was set up in a proper apartment and, much to her father's disconcerted grumbles, given a job as a clerk at Borden and Almy's furniture concern, where he had responsibilities ranging from taking warehouse inventory to swaying customers' buying instincts towards certain preferred items. The more difficult concession that Andrew had to make was to allow Ullsworth to hang the copy of Poussin's

The Shepherds of Arcady that had been salvaged from room 209, the most enduring symbol of his long ordeal, on the store's back wall over a field of rose-colored wallpaper.

Frank Rivers and the Sporting Boys were arrested and brought up on charges of kidnapping and assault, plus the theft of a barouche from a carriage yard in Tiverton. Wellington Rivers attempted to persuade anyone who would listen that his nephew Frank had been under the spell of a charlatan mesmerist named MacAlister Mundi, and so, Rivers contended, could not be held accountable for his deeds. However, Lizzie came round to Rivers office one afternoon, spending no more than one half-hour sequestered privately with the paper tycoon, after which all claims of his nephew's innocence were inexplicably dropped. Rivers produced one statement to the local newspaper in which he said, "Frank is indeed of bastard stock from a degraded branch of the family. My sister found him on the steps of a local saloon wrapped in fish paper. I cannot with clear conscience defend his kind."

After serving a spell in prison, Frank Rivers, along with his Bedford Street B'hoys, effectively disappeared from New England altogether. It was rumored that years later Chas and Buster were hanged at the Tombs, the large police dungeon in New York near Paradise Square, where they had been charged with "crimes of innumerable unpalatabilities." It was believed that Frank Rivers became the notorious Bowery Boy Strangler who terrorized Mulberry Street in the late 1880s, writing taunting letters to the police with phrases like, "I am only at my lick-for-leather for the last was for colt's tooth. The next one shall be a grand rib roasting!" But that could have been mere coincidence. The Strangler was ultimately caught and strangled to death by a vigilante mob, but the photographs then taken by the New York Herald of his corpse in an upright coffin are no longer extant.

As for Andre de Camp, Lizzie saw him on a Tuesday afternoon one week after the affair at the Wilbur. For several days, her father had prevented the two from meeting, for he was seized with a sudden suspicion of the boy's intentions towards his daughter, and also embarrassed by the publicity that the public beatings had drawn to the Bordens and the de Camps. Disregarding the fact that Andre had quite possibly saved his daughter's life, Andrew bolted shut his home and stayed indoors during his normal business hours, just to make sure that Lizzie sat in her room all day, alone and despondent. He was hoping that some sense could be driven into the French boy who still, despite the father's precautions, insisted on calling at the Borden home every day at noon.

By the seventh day, Lizzie had howled at her father to let him in, and Andrew reluctantly consented. "Ten minutes," he said. "I give you ten minutes with the boy and then you are to forget you ever knew him."

She found Andre in the sitting room, standing near the piano. He looked as dashing and well-kept as always, his facial scuffs a mere phantom of the past. His eyes brightened when he saw Lizzie cross the floor. He moved forward to embrace her but she held her body back. She was giving the impression that there was an invisible line on the floor between them beyond which he was not allowed to cross.

"It is madness that we are kept apart so," he said, tears forming in his eyes.

"No," she said, her face cold and blank. "It is best."

"*Mais mon Dieu*, what can you mean."

"I know you have the best of intentions, and I do believe, Andre de Camp, that you love me. I have never doubted it. And I have committed your poem Lizbeth of Light to precious memory. But I can never let you any closer than you are now. Perhaps not even this. We shall see each other in church, we shall see each other at the board meetings for the textile concern, but outside of indifferent and necessary encounters, we shall never talk again. Never, do you understand?"

A dark shadow passed over his face. "*Pourquoi?*" he asked.

"Because you lied to me. You deceived me. In your attempt to save your father's reputation, you tampered with the truth. That was your ring that was found in the poor whaleman. The A on the signet stood for Andre, not Arcady. It was you upon which Wellington Rivers was attempting to cast suspicion. In your clever machinations, you conceived of this Arcady society, an anarchist cabal targeting Fall River, to divert suspicion from your own guilt in the affair."

He was horrified. His mouth trembled as he struggled to find the words. "I was only trying to retrieve the pessary. I didn't think that my father's obsession with this Arcady Society was of any consequence. In France he saw them lurking everywhere, and here in the wild land of America he is even more fearful."

"I do not believe that this society even exists." Lizzie's face went dark as she contemplated something even more unthinkable. "Or perhaps you are the Arcady Society. Perhaps you have attempted to bring this French breed of political unrest to our ordered community. Perhaps Rivers was trying to wipe out this pestilent breed of revolutionary activity before it could get a foothold in our town." She paused, trying to read the shifting shadows on his face. "Or perhaps I shall never know the truth. Andre de Camp holds many secrets, and this secret society that bears his initial is his best kept."

"I wish I could tell you the truth," he said, puffing up his chest. "But I am bound by oaths. If you only knew, Lizzie Borden. If you only knew."

"It is best," she replied, "that I never know. For the past seven days I have tormented myself over this decision, and I must now reveal that I choose not to have anything to do with you. I care not if the Arcady Society is a mere figment of everyone's suspicions and you are blameless. But after your painful lie, I can never trust you again."

He lowered his eyes towards his feet. Somewhere in the distance a fruit peddler was hawking his wares, and a bale barge blew its horn across the deep waters of the Taunton.

"I am sorry," he said solemnly, "that you feel that way."

"But I shall never forget your kindness," she said assuredly. "And I shall never forget your poem. And I shall never forget the melancholy boy who once upon a time did indeed have love for me."

Andre nodded, forcing back his anguish. He stared at her for a moment and then spoke very lyrically: "'Tis the hope and the beauty and the inner calm/That we have won and must never let slip.'"

She moved slightly towards him, as if she were ready to embrace, but then stopped. "Yes," she said. " 'Never let slip.' And I never shall."

"I cannot live without you," he said languidly.

Her eyes widened as red came across her face.

"Oh, yes you can!" she replied angrily, and left the room as quick as a whirling tornado.

On her way to the staircase she met with her father who stood broad-shouldered, his chin jutting forward, a look of triumph on his countenance. "What did I tell you," he said smugly. "The boy is obviously a liar and a..."

"Say nothing more Father," she cautioned him. "Do not talk to me for three weeks or I shall twist off your head!"

Andre-Lude

It was not the last time that she would meet with Andre de Camp, le Victome de Rennes. Their paths were to cross again in several more of her cases, most notably the Adventure of the Phantom Thespian and the Strange Affair of the Hottentot Venus. And it was only a matter of time before she had cracked the code of the dreaded Arcady Society and discovered Andre's true role. In a strange tender way he was eventually redeemed, but she would never again open up her heart to him as she had done the night that she first heard the words to Lizbeth of Light.

Indeed, for all these long and sad years, Lizbeth Andrew Borden kept the words to the poem in a locket about her neck. It stayed with her throughout many an adventure, kept her company at night in the cruel days of her incarceration, provided inner strength when all around was darkness. And occasionally, when pressed by the rare Fall River resident who was old enough to remember the Comte de Rennes and his daring son and the summer of 1877, she found herself transported back again to that time indelibly marked upon her inner soul by Andre's lyricism. As the sun descended over French Street and the sloping shadows amidst the elms reminded her of the faded evenings of yesterday, all she could do was to sigh and stare into empty space, perhaps inwardly numbering the years to see if it were even indeed possible that he could still be alive and upon the earth, and remark with confident melancholy:

"This coming summer I shall be sixty-seven, which means I do have a chance of perhaps talking to him again, of walking by the river and remembering. To see that Great Wheel in the sky and wonder...and wonder...for we are but passing shadows and shall soon be gone. To see him once more, before no more. Yes.

"The Poet really did find a hope and beauty that he wanted to share with me. I turned my back upon it, and perhaps that was the gravest mistake of my life. But I have never let it slip. I have held it right here, in this locket, for all these lonely years.

"Perhaps it would be nice to see him again. Very nice indeed. Yes.

"For I was very fond of him when I was a Girl Detective."

THE END

THE TRAUMATIZED
METALLURGIST

1876. FALL RIVER, MASSACHUSETTS.

VANTAGE POINT

The Wampanoag Iron Works consist of a series of granite buildings grouped in a majestic compound along the curve of the Taunton River at Mount Hope Bay. The walls, which had originally been hewn from the quarry beds of a nearby cascading stream, define with precision the Iron Works' machine shops, engine rooms, furnaces, forges, and administrative building. The collective whole of these purposeful spaces breathes in the rich ore of the Earth, and from thence exhales the artillery cannons, barrel hoops and nails, iron castings, and ammunition which are destined to be consumed by other industries for other human activities. Like the textile and cloth manufactories that cluster against the river shoreline and back along the stream, the Iron Works bear witness to the indomitable will of their human creators and their unquiet domination of the once-primitive land.

Now consider this industrial enterprise from the perspective of the spiraling goshawk, who, breaking from the New England wilderness in search of the perfect crag on which to perch and survey its dominion, thus comes across this tangled plain of brick, wood, stone, and metal. What can be happening here? In times past, this landscape was a furry carpet of wood, a sprawling forest of cedar and oak, cut through by a falling stream, all bearing little evidence of the strange animal called man. Now the trees have been beaten back; instead, the great granite edifices that belch the hot breath of smelting iron arise in the clearing, themselves surrounded by a dense and filthy hive of ground dwellings. From such structures an army of servile men, women, and even children, emerge each dawn, their faces bent towards the dusty ground, joylessly marching through the gateway of the compound and not reappearing until the sun has set beyond the western horizon. To our long-tailed hawk, this entire cycle of human labor must be baffling indeed, being so against his free nature and unbounded spirit.

By coincidence, the sentiments of our airborne observer are being shared by a man who stands in the upper-floor window of the administration building, his attention fixated upon the rail yard and the small trains that puff and clatter, bringing their heavy loads of iron product to the shoreline and the cargo steamers that await their burden. The man in the window stares at the yard stacked with pig metal and coal bins, his eyes widening as if he were seeing for the first time a world he previously would not have thought possible. Perhaps he, like the hawk above, had also gazed into the wide plain off Mount Hope Bay, expecting to find familiar fertile earth, fresh water, lush trees, deep green, and blue skies, a bountiful land that would feed the needs of his species; but he has instead discovered the crowded dwellings and the polluted refuse of human life. The biblical Adam has not left the garden, but the garden has been transformed about him into one of blasted earth and painful labor.

Let us examine this human observer for a pace, pondering his immaculate cotton suit, his fine threaded pants and shiny leather shoes. Let us take note of the gold ring on his left hand, and the resemblance he bears to the suited figure in the mighty oil painting that dominates the eastern wall of his office. We quickly recognize that here stands the owner, president and chief agent of the Wampanoag Iron Works, Colonel Richard Ulysses Anthony: grandson of a legendary founder of Fall River's industry, and one of the wealthiest men in Bristol County.

Now that we have identified him, let us wonder why his face has turned sullen and distraught; and why he suddenly turns like a startled child, racing from the window, his legs folding beneath him as he curls on the floor beneath his desk, his knees to his chest and his eyes filled with anxious tears.

What can be the matter with this man that he should tremble so? With all his power and wealth, should he not be content and joyful in his existence? As he sobs, he reaches out with one hand towards the window, as if yearning for something forever beyond his reach.

This is a mystery that we must ponder.

THE PHYSICIAN'S ADVICE

June, 1876.

The Colonel had not been seen all morning, but it was known to his administrative staff in the outer offices that he was hidden behind his bolted door. He had arrived at nine on the clock, his furrowed brows, framing very odd facial twitches. He withdrew into his office, saying nothing, but having established a gloomy unrest amongst his clerks and accountants as they continued with their labor, all the while gossiping in hushed voices. "What can be wrong with the Colonel?"

After a time, they knocked politely, hoping to hear his familiar voice, but receiving only silence. So they pounded harder, barking petitions for him to come forth and demonstrate that he had not been hurt in any way. Sensing possible danger, his executive secretary had finally called for Doctor Ames, the only man who was allowed to discuss delicate matters of health with the Colonel.

The doctor alighted from his horse-drawn buggy before the red-bricked administration building and walked stolidly through the arched entrance, his black satchel by his side, a pince-nez straightened across the bridge of his steep and narrow nose. A rigid beard jutted outwards, itself a hairy extension of an enormous chin, and preceded him as he walked forward. A group of nervous factors followed him up the main stairs and through the outer rooms. "He has not been himself," they told him hurriedly. "Such moods he has shown." "His demeanor has been sullied!" "You must help him, Doctor Ames!" And so on, straight to Colonel Anthony's door. "He won't open up," confirmed the chief day clerk. "We've tried everything short of battering it down."

The doctor grasped his leather satchel with both hands for assurance, and then let forth a battery of knuckle raps upon the wooden panels, shouting at the margin of his lungs, "Richard, you'd best open up or I shall treat you quite indelicately at your next physical."

Within a moment, the bolt unlatched and the door was quite easily opened. The doctor raised a hushed finger of silence to the gathering crowd of workers before slipping into the office, swinging the door shut behind him. Once inside, his eyes began to adjust to the harsh contrast between the dark mahogany of the furniture and the sunlight streaming from the tall bay windows. The room was replete with wooden cabinets stuffed with ledger books, with endless bundles of accounting reports, and with large leather-bound volumes whose slightly unpleasant smell testified to how many years they had been sitting unopened on their shelves.

The Colonel was standing like a wounded child in the center of the room, his back slumped, his knees weakened. "Help me," he said plainly.

"My dear Colonel," the doctor said, appearing calm. "Whatever could be the matter?"

"I only wish I knew," the man lamented, staggering for a chair that rested against the side wall. The doctor helped him into its seat and then touched his anxious patient's forehead.

"You are cold as ice. I surely hope this is a purely emotional affair. Your health has been impeccable and I intend to keep it that way."

The Colonel pushed back his forelocks. "Ames, you and I have known each other for many a year."

The doctor's smile was small and slanted. "Your entire life, in fact. I caught you with both hands when you leapt into the world." He lifted a tight fist. "Why man, where has fled the zeal and optimism of that primal moment? You stand before me like a ghost."

The Colonel turned his face towards the sunlight, revealing watery eyes. "It happened suddenly, at midnight. All these years, all the bone-crushing work, the endless hours laboring to build this enterprise, to please the stockholders, to balance my interests against the operatives and the labor agitators. It all came crashing down. I can no longer think of it. No, my mind cannot go there!"

"Go where?" Dr. Ames asked, solemnly. "No one is asking you to go anywhere."

"Not a place, but a word. I cannot utter the word any more, nor look upon the hoops and nails and cannon into which we have cast it."

A beam of understanding came over the doctor's mind. "You mean the metal upon which this factory has been built?" The Colonel nodded, his face trembling. "Don't worry, Richard, I won't utter the word. But you must explain: it truly terrifies you? Surely this is the result of a prolonged and painful stress. Your job has driven you to the ground. I suggest you get away from it all. When did you last spend a day with your family? Or at a watering hole doing some swimming? Since when have you spent an afternoon on the shore of Gardner's Neck practicing your artistic skills with the paint brush?"

"Such pleasures are beyond my reach," the Colonel admitted.

"How long have you felt this?" asked the doctor, sternly. "You have been hiding it from me?"

The Colonel lowered his eyes ashamedly. "Do you recall when the operatives took to strike, and filled the courtyard waving their hammers and I hid myself in an abandoned reverberatory furnace? At the time, I explained my behavior by claiming I had been struck on the head with a ball-peen and had become senseless. However, it was far more than that. I was in my rational mind, of sorts."

"Do the workers frighten you so?" the doctor asked, his voice softening.

"No, it is not the workers I now fear; it is not they whom I am unable to look upon without being consumed by horror. It is the metal, the product." He turned his face and raised a forearm over his eyes. "Do not make me speak of it, if you treasure my humanity!"

Doctor Ames let out with a hearty chuckle. "Richard, you are showing your humanity at last. There is nothing inherent in the substance in question nor any product of your factory that will harm you. Your mind is producing danger where no danger exists."

"But it is all around me," the Colonel shivered, drawing in his knees. "I dare not leave this office for fear of confronting it everywhere. In the wrought fencing through which I must pass to get to the street; in the frame of the buggy I must ride to reach my home; in the railing that leads to my upstairs bedroom; in the nails that hold my family portraits upon the wall! Indeed, that substance is one of the most common elements upon the earth, and the molten core of this planet is said to be swimming in it. Alas, the meteorites from the furthest stars show that the Heavens are composed of it, and perhaps God himself is cast in moulds beyond our imaginings. No, Doctor Ames, there is no place on Heaven or Earth where I am safe!"

The doctor's mustache twittered as he removed his glasses, fogging the lenses with his open mouth and then wiping them with a noserag. "Richard, I understand such anxiety, but I can assure you that you are in no such danger, these being merely irrational emotions. The cure is not to retreat into a rarified world where the substance does not exist. You merely have to take a vacation to calm your nerves."

The Colonel ran his fingers over his flaccid face. "Eh, what?"

"Two months in Europe shall do you well. Yes, that would be my perfect prescription. When you return, you'll see that your tolerance for the substance shall be restored to normalcy, and you can once more drive your buggy, ascend your staircase, and hang your family portraits with joy in your heart. And upon your death you may enter the Kingdom of

Heaven fearing nothing from the metal framing the pearly gates."

"But I can't abandon my business," the Colonel said, desperation seizing his voice.

"Nonsense, there is no time like the present to just abandon it all. Everything will be here when you return. There is no matter of business that is so important that you should risk your sanity over it."

"Yes, yes, you are wise, Ames, I see that now. Oh, what a fool I have been! How ingenious the under-pinnings of the human mind are, that it would make something so repellent to us we would flee from it, even if there is no danger. Ames, I feel the courage now to test this theory. Say the word, freely and unhindered as if you have never played witness to my anxiety."

"Iron," said the doctor plainly.

For a moment, the Colonel held his stoic ground, his face frozen in the aspect in which it had hung before the syllable had been uttered. Then, with little transition, a broad panic erupted on his brows, and he let loose with a harsh yelp. Before the doctor could stop him, the Colonel had dashed across the room, his long legs flapping about him, as he scurried for the velvet window drape, far to one side of the expansive bay window, behind which he sequestered his body.

"It is no use," he wept, "I cannot abide to hear it. To Europe I shall go, and pray that my ship shall not have any railings or wrought fences upon its decks! Oh, Ames, I am lost without you."

"I concern myself solely with your well-being," the doctor announced, lifting his pince-nez. "Is there anything else I can do for you?"

The thin voice came from behind the curtains. "Yes, send in Rogers. I'll need him to take my place and organize my affairs in my absence. And find Latham the Furnace Foreman."

"Latham," the doctor said ominously. "Isn't he the agitator who led the strike?"

"Yes, yes, but you see the extent of my mania, that I would rather face the strike leader than even catch a glimpse of...I cannot even say the word. Bring them now, man!"

Doctor Ames cleared his throat and quietly opened the door to the office. Standing before him, staring at him madly with various degrees of concern, were the assembled staff crowding the outer office. With a few hasty words, a boy was dispatched to the factory floor. After several nervous moments filled with ambient mutterings and stifled questions, two men appeared and approached the doorway. They were of very different demeanor, one being a stormy-browed, well-suited man with oiled hair and a wide tie. The other man was short, stout, and calloused, his rough face showing the harsh years, the cloth cap and baggy trousers revealing his relative rank in the hierarchy of the mill. Just outside the door to the Colonel's office, they halted and peered uncomprehendingly at each other.

"What's he doing here?" shouted Latham in a muffled Yorkshire accent.

"Is this a strike?" asked Rogers the sub-agent, rigidly. "I'll be damned if this is a strike!"

"The Colonel wishes to see you," Doctor Ames said, lifting his palm towards the open office door. Once they were inside, they stood confused at the empty space behind the desk.

"Where is the Colonel?" Rogers asked the doctor, as if talking directly to Latham was a forlorn option.

"I am here," came the voice from behind the drapes, now gaining in confidence.

"Is this a joke?" Latham asked, as Doctor Ames closed the door, cutting off the curious eyes and ears of the office crowd.

"I admit this is an awkward situation," the doctor consented. "It is too complicated to explain at the moment, so I would suggest you just listen to the voice of your employer."

"Thank you, doctor," the Colonel said again from his hidden nest. "The short of it is that I will be going away, far away, for quite some time, perhaps a couple of months, perhaps half a year. Rogers, you are now charged with complete and absolute power over the workers and staff of this mill. You are to act with decisiveness and unity of will."

The sub-agent blinked, as if facial movement was a prerequisite to mental understanding. "As you wish," he began to say. "But…"

"There is no but, you have to perform exactly as I described. Latham, you are to receive a doubling of your current salary if you promise not to cause any more labor unrest. Double, man!"

Latham stared blankly into the red texture of the drapes, raised a finger and opened his mouth, but then remained silent, his finger trailing downward as if it were representing the thought that had just dissipated in his head.

Rogers scratched his chin. "I don't suppose I can get double my salary as well?" he asked.

"Absolutely not, you are not indispensable to me, nor do you threaten

my business on a daily basis. Latham here is intelligent, infinitely patient, and cruel in his long-term plans. Like a glacier during the age of
ice, he moves slower than the human eye can detect, but in the end, he
destroys landscapes. You, Rogers, are weak and derive all your virtues
by imitating my gestures. In that respect you are like a monkey to my
organ-grinder. No, you are to remain at your current salary and your
only directive is to keep the profits flowing and the workers happy. Do
you hear me?"

"Yes, I hear you," Rogers replied. "But I still don't understand why
you're hiding."

"That's my business!" came a cruel howl. "Now get back to work you
two and I'll see you in the winter when I return. Begone!"

Confused, the two men stumbled to the door and the doctor dispatched them back into the outer office. Once the door was bolted again,
the Colonel walked shakily from his perch and gained the relative safety
of his desk chair. "Do you really think Europe will do me good, Ames?"
he asked.

"Splendidly," the doctor replied. "Go to Italy and take in the ruins
of Pompeii. And perhaps the island of Elba, where a man who once
conquered the world became a powerless prisoner. Ponder the transient
nature of all human vanity. Visit many ancient tombs and destroyed cities, and view the broken pottery of history's most glorious empires, now
gone in the dust of time. Yes, make it a tour of power's consequence.
Soak in the lessons that the vanished empires have to teach us. Then
you shall see that all this..." and the doctor waved a hand towards the
window, his fingers extending towards the granite buildings beyond,
"...is but wind...yes, but wind."

"Perhaps," the Colonel said, wiping the sweat from his brow with
his cotton sleeve. "But keep an eye on Rogers and Latham for me. They
don't take such a lofty philosophical view of things. Make sure they
don't kill each other."

"I shall," Ames said, peering at the door, and imagining the scene
that must be playing its course in the outer office. Then the two men
fell into silence, interrupted only by the beating pulse of the metal works
that vibrated in the floor beneath their feet, the walls about them, and
the entire building, a surging and repetitive roar of a beast wallowing
in liquid fire.

THE WIZARD OF PROSPECT STREET

September, 1876.

"They call me a boy inventor," boasted the petulant young man, seated with a comforting mug of medicinal sarsaparilla at the front table of the apothecary shop. A bowler hat bestrode his forelocked head as his almond eyes danced merrily over his inner thoughts, more so than upon the pretty girl before him. "But," he explained, "much of my work is the invention of small improvements to existing technology, such as an optimized relay in a telegraph machine. It's more accurate to call me a scientist, as my father does, and true, I use the scientific method, rigorously and with tremendous results. But I aspire to more than just being another inventor or scientist. I want to be a Wizard!"

"That's precisely the type of arrogant nonsense I'd expect from you, Homer," Lizzie Andrew Borden, the Girl Detective of Fall River, snorted, with a spoon balanced in one hand and a lump of ice cream melting in a glass before her. She had never heard Homer wax so pontifically, nor with such self-assertive luster in his voice. "I don't suspect you could even define the word 'wizard'," she challenged. "To me, it evokes a picture of a tall bearded man, his cap and robe decorated with astrological symbols, holding an ancient manuscript that describes methods to turn metals into gold."

"No," answered Homer Thesinger, excitedly. "That's some farcical court magician. My Wizard is a man who can control the elements, harness the powers of the water, divine the secrets of electricity, and provide insight into the nature of light itself! I'm talking of men who are shaping the new world that we live in, men like Thomas Edison, the great electromechanician, who is performing great miracles in New Jersey."

"Never heard of him," Lizzie sighed. "I swear, Homer, you produce the most unusual and obscure people."

"Edison is far from obscure. He's experimenting with electricity to provide an alternative to the oil lamp, one that will run automatically on a current of energy. No more shall we butcher the whales of the world's oceans to illuminate our nights. Soon, we'll merely toss a switch, and the light will flow from hot wires; you shall read your book upon a midnight without any oil at all, and no fear that the wind will blow the fire upon your sheets."

"Perhaps," she said between licks of her spoon. "I'd rather take my chance with an oil lamp than have a hot wire dancing about my head.

And besides, how does making a wire hot make you a wizard?"

Homer held up his hands to the air before him and grasped the emptiness. "Can you touch the light? Can you move it around and make it do your will? Try that, and then tell me that a man who can conduct the course of light rays is not a true wizard."

"But he hasn't done it yet," she was quick to exclaim. "By your own admission."

"Well, he already invented the Quadruplex telegraph. From your puzzled frown, I conclude that you have never heard of a Quadruplex."

Lizzie forced her puzzled frown to dissipate. "I know what a telegraph is," she announced. "True, it is a remarkable device to carry words across vast distances. But there is nothing remarkable about this, certainly not anything to cause this man in New Jersey to be so adulated."

"Mr. Edison's Quadruplex," Homer said, breathlessly, "can carry four telegraph messages across one wire. Can you imagine this?"

"But I'd only want to send one at a time," Lizzie shrugged. "Where is the advantage?"

"Think of a world network of wires," he mused, "bringing the human word across vast distances, across oceans!"

"This is what you want to do with your life?" she asked. "It sounds rather lofty for a boy from Fall River."

"And Edison was just a boy from Milan, Ohio," Homer smirked. "Now he has a big contract with Western Union and a marvelous laboratory in New Jersey. Where would any of us be without ambition? The acorn would never become the tree. Lizzie, think of what you can do with a Quadruplex? What if you are in a situation where you must send a message to four people at the same time?"

"I shall send them all telegrams," Lizzie huffed.

"No, four telegrams would need to be drafted; that would be laborious. Imagine that you could enter some words into this machine, and then with one press of a button, you would send those words to four separate people."

Lizzie peered downwards, dropped her spoon into its glass, and drummed her fingers on the tabletop as if she were composing type. "So let us say that I must tell my sister back on Second Street what meat to buy for supper. I should merely compose the words as if I were setting the type, and then..." She reached over beyond her lunch and stabbed the table cloth with a forceful fingertip. "I shall send the message along its path, on the wire, and my sister and others shall receive it if I will it?"

"Yes," Homer nodded, enthusiastically. "It becomes more marvelous than that. One day we will even abandon the typed words and shall harness sound the same way that we will harness light. The human voice, political speeches, entire pieces of music, will be carried over networks of wires moving into all the towns across America. We shall even send the signals across the trans-Atlantic cable. One orchestra playing Beethoven's Fifth in the Academy Building will be heard by the entire world!"

"Who will be conducting?" Lizzie pondered. "That matters, don't you think?"

"For artistic purposes, yes. But Mr. Edison will create machines that will capture the music, encode it onto sheets of metal, and then be capable of playing it back, long after its recording, long after the orchestral players are lying in their Oak Grove tombs. The ordinary man shall carry this music around in his vest pocket, and bring it out and listen to it when he chooses."

Lizzie sat back against her chair. "Well, Homer, while all you wizards go off on your great visions of scientific conquest and playing Beethoven over the Atlantic ocean, I'll still be carrying in the milk, ironing the laundry with my flats, and complaining to the Maggie that the morning muffins are burnt. Perhaps I'll be amazed when it happens, but until then…"

"We will all benefit from the coming revolution," Homer concluded. "And I'm not talking about socialism! Excuse me; I'll get us more sarsaparilla."

He marched from the table to the front counter where A.E. Dobbs, the proprietor and inventor of Dobbs' Medicinal Syrup Water and Sarsaparilla Health Notion, stood in subdued conversation with two bowler-hatted gentlemen. Lizzie watched Homer cautiously, subtly agitated by his arrogantly optimistic philosophies, by his masculine pomposities that were straining through the undergrown limbs of a mere boy. From the growing industrial culture about him in Fall River, Homer was learning how to desire power on a vast scale, to think in a large way that tried to encompass the world and all its powerful forces. It seemed only yesterday that Homer was merely tinkering with some rubber tubing and Bunsen burners in his father's barn on Prospect Street; now he was shouting about sending the human voice around the world over electrified wires. It had not been enough to fashion himself an electromechanician, toying with electricity and machinery. Now he was a wizard transmuting metals in his alchemical alembics.

It all comes down to metal and power, he concluded wistfully. *They want the metal in their money, in their telegraphs, in their mighty ships on the river and in their cannons for war. The world of men is the world of metal. I'm glad that women have cloth and linen and silks to balance them out!*

Homer returned from the counter, visibly distracted, his hands empty and tense by his side. He pointed towards the front counter, where Dobbs was putting down his wipe rag and joining his two new customers before the counter. Several more persons came in from the street, accompanied by a babbling buzz of voices. Through the dusty window, Lizzie could see that many men and women had gathered, and seemed to be staring down street, all talking, some pointing with puzzled looks as if they had not a clue as to what was happening.

"What's this?" Lizzie asked.

"Trouble at the Wampanoag," Homer said. "A.E. heard that someone was murdered."

Lizzie stared before her, seemingly focused on nothing, then started to pull on her cotton gloves. "Yes," she said. "I suppose my planned afternoon of dress shopping must give pause, for I believe I shall be of service to Fall River once again as a Girl Detective. Homer, I beg your leave: I'll see you again on Thursday, for more banter about the marvelous machineries of the future."

"You're going to the mill?" he asked, incredulously. "The police will take care of this. No need to put yourself into danger."

"Your sense of wonderment comes from the sciences," she explained. "Mine comes from the unsolved mystery. This murder at a mill may yet prove to be unsolved."

"It sounds very serious," Homer said, fidgeting with his hat and peering about at the gathering crowd. "I'd best accompany you."

"If you wish, but I doubt that the man was strangled with a Quadruplex wire. More likely it was something more mundane, a stabbing or a bludgeoning with a monkey wrench. It all seems so beneath your marvelous wizardry."

They joined the growing stream of people heading off down South Main. There were pedestrians of leisure, servants with armfuls of groceries, peddlers pushing their carts off their beaten paths, and business owners leaving their establishments puzzled over why so many people were abandoning their shopping and heading towards the river. They filed past several granite mills, where the thundering noise of the looms shook the earth under their feet, and where sad-eyed girls and blank-faced older women stared plaintively out the tall windows on each floor, unable to either enjoy or afford the commerce of Main Street, or take part in the curious march towards the Iron Works. A calm afternoon enjoying sarsaparilla was not their luxury. These mill women, enslaved by the machines of their masters, could not find the time to gossip about marvelous inventions in fantastical futures. They could only spare a fleeting moment to watch the migration of people westward, all that would be allowed by their foremen, and then turn back to their ever-demanding looms, the silhouettes vanishing from the windows as the thunder of industry continued unabated.

The sidewalk before the mill was obscured by the crowds that had gathered, and Lizzie and Homer had to elbow their way through to the main entrance. What magnetic energy has drawn them all here? The very talk of a murder was but a visceral pull that drew them into a wide-eyed tangle, buzzing like a hive before the gates. With reluctance, Lizzie tried to imagine what it would be like at her father's small house on Second Street, so quaint and unassuming, if the Borden home were ever the scene of a dramatic killing. So many neighbors clambering to get a view of the body, so many policemen crawling like insects about the rooms, entering her closet, disturbing her dresses. In less than a second, she had wiped the unsettling image from her mind, focusing on the situation before her.

Several policemen were holding back the crowd at the gate, the officers growing impatient and braced for action. Lizzie recognized Officer Beck, the bushy-faced man who had so generously helped her during the case of the Portuguese Reprobate. She caught his attention with a wave of her hand, then pulled Homer forward by the flap of his jacket.

"Miss Lizzie," Officer Beck said gravely. "This is not a place for you; go on home where it's safe." He tipped his hat at Homer, flashing little recognition.

"Most of Fall River is here," said Lizzie, pointing a gloved finger at the crowd. "Why should I be the exclusion, particularly since I have experience with crime detection?"

"There's no business here for a detective," Beck said, biting his lip. "Chester Rogers, the acting agent, took a gun and shot John Latham, the furnace chief, dead in the skull. Happened in front of everybody, so there's no doubt as to the course of events."

"I'm sorry to hear it was so simple," Lizzie commented, noticing that Homer's face had gone pale upon mention of the shooting. "Do you know the motive for this murder?"

"Well, that's a bit of a puzzle at the moment," Beck confessed. "But I don't think we have to stretch our imaginations too far. Latham was one of those English agitators, always stirring up trouble with the operatives. Straight Yorkshire tradition, and as socialist as you can paint him. I suppose poor Rogers just reacted to his politics in too expressive a manner."

"So this Rogers hasn't made a statement?" Lizzie asked impatiently.

"No, he's as quiet as a rock, I expect stunned to silence. The only thing he's agreed to is to identify the dead man and admit that he was holding the gun when they caught him."

Lizzie frowned. "You said a moment ago that he was seen by everyone. Now you are saying that he was caught with a gun. Did anyone witness the murder or not?"

"Oh, Miss Lizzie this is not one for your casebook, believe me. It's a simple act of murder." His cheeks twitched and his eyes softened. "Or so they say."

"Officer Beck," Lizzie said, a pert little smile dancing across her lips. "you are holding something back from me."

"Well," he confessed, "there's some poppycock I've heard that doesn't make any sense. They say that Rogers pulled the trigger and shot the man dead, but they also say he wasn't the one holding the gun. None of this adds up, believe me. But there were witnesses; and good ones too."

A solid bewhiskered man in a broad officer's tunic came forward, his shiny boots stirring beneath him. Officer Beck shrank back, visibly outranked. "Marshal," he said, tipping his hand. "I was just talking to Miss Lizzie Borden here…"

"Yes," said the City Marshal in a deep-toned voice. "I'm familiar with the Borden girl and her peculiar occupation."

"I was telling her that her services may not be needed," Beck said, nervously. "We got a real cut and dried one here, don't you think, Marshal?"

"Perhaps," he said, wistfully. "Or perhaps we can use an extra set of eyes and ears. Miss Borden, do you have a few moments to talk to a very apprehensive mill agent?"

"I don't have any other pressing engagements," she said. He motioned for her to follow him into the building and she moved forward, pulling Homer, whose face was still deathly white, behind her. The

Marshal paused and cast a crinkled brow at the young boy. "This is my assistant," Lizzie explained, chuckling. "He's writing my adventures up into short fiction for a very prominent women's magazine."

"Perhaps," the Marshal said, stepping down to Homer, who seemed to grow shorter in height as the officer approached. "You're the Thesinger boy, aren't you? You distilled guncotton in your backyard."

Homer nodded and said with a whiff of pride, "Nitroglycerine, to be truthful."

"Either way you phrase it," the Marshal said, "you were in violation of city ordinance. And I turned a blind eye because you claimed you were...uh...making a 'valuable contribution to science that the brutish behavior of policemen should not corrupt.' I believe those were your exact words."

"So they were," Homer laughed nervously. "But it was a most valuable contribution."

"One that ended with a thunderous explosion which propelled an oak tree ten feet into the air, a tree which came crashing down on your neighbor's backyard privy, smashing it to bits."

"Yes, well, that was a mistake," Homer blubbered. "I'll be more careful next time."

The Marshal nodded to Lizzie then turned darkly to Homer, holding out a finger towards the boy's trembling face. "I'll let you in this mill, even into the crime scene, but you keep in mind I'm watching you with every eye in my head."

"Yes, sir," Homer said, then sank forward, his knees weakened, and trailed Lizzie and the Marshal in through the front gates of the Iron Works, away from the increasingly agitated crowd.

THE SINGLE BULLET

The administration offices of the Wampanoag Iron Works were elegantly designed and tastefully decorated. Lizzie, who had visited the board rooms of banks, was impressed with the beautiful interior, the burnished oak and maple furniture, the paneled walls boasting a few framed art prints depicting Biblical scenes in an Italianate style, desks and swivel chairs, and filing cabinets and potted palms all competing with one another for wall space. The clerks, accountants, and secretaries had a calm, studious environment in which to work, quite in contrast to what Lizzie had always imagined inside an iron mill. There were no odorous heaps of slag, or half-naked, sweating workers scorching their forge clamps and pounding their hammers upon tremendous anvils. Instead, Lizzie witnessed the white-shirted day workers who moved paper and totaled numbers, who labored with their brains, not their brawn, who came from good stock and wealthy families. These were academy graduates and university scholars, who, despite their academic calling or degree in life, were still sacrificing their daylight hours in service to the manufacture of metal.

The staff was standing at attention behind their desks as the City Marshal paraded across the expanse of the outer office, leading a smirking young girl and a frazzled school boy. His mature gait resembled a morning drill, giving the day workers another dramatic moment in a work day that had started so uneventfully, but which had since been transformed into a mystery play, with a plot that unfolded with each passing moment, complete with a gruesome murder and an endless roster of colorful characters.

The Marshal approached the open door to Colonel Anthony's office and motioned for Lizzie, Homer, and Beck to follow. Two men were standing inside, silhouetted against the sunlight of the bay window. As Lizzie's eyes adjusted to the contrasts in light, the two silhouettes gradually crystallized into two men, dressed in gray and brown worsted suits with high collars and string ties.

The broader of the two, sporting mutton chops which were slapped onto the sides of his face like metal plating on a gunboat, erupted with a furious bellow whose energy seemed to slam shut the office door behind them. "You have brought in children! Mere children! Mr. Marshal, are you mocking us?"

"Mr. Brayton," the Marshal addressed him, "I introduce you to Lizzie Andrew Borden, the Girl Detective. With the understanding in mind that you expected a mature investigator of the male gender, I ask you to consider that this is a girl who lays claim to great reasoning ability, and a sharp mind that may well penetrate the mystery that confronts us."

"Who's the other one," asked the shorter man in a nasal tone that bespoke a lingering head cold. His pin-pointed eyes were huddled together, both ever so slightly out of balance.

"Homer Thesinger," answered the boy, stepping forward and extending his soft hand. The two men stared at it with cold detachment until he withdrew it. "I am Miss Borden's biographer," he added.

"What do we need a biographer for?" Mr. Brayton said, raising his palms to his lapels. "This is not child's play, this is..."

"Mr. Brayton," the Marshal interrupted. "I understand your trepidation in this delicate matter, but I do assure you that I have brought a most excellent detective, and she shall hear testimony in a manner she sees fit. Lizzie, I introduce you to Mr. Thaddeus Brayton, chairman of the Wampanoag Board of Directors, and the mill's legal attorney, Mr. Conrad Twillie."

"I am most honored," Lizzie said, bending her head. "I assure you both that I will take this matter with the utmost seriousness. I have done great service to private industry, the people of Fall River and our duly appointed law enforcement officials. One must only be reminded of the Case of the Portuguese Reprobate or the Affair of the Unexpected Exhibitionist to register confidence in my abilities."

"You brought down Livermore," Mr. Brayton said, peering forward, his brow tightening. "I confess that the man's actions were reprehensible and un-Christian and I do give you credit for exposing his darker deeds. But I hold great suspicion against you. I don't know your loyalties."

"My loyalties are to justice," Lizzie said proudly. "I abhor all crime."

"I'm not talking about crime," Mr. Brayton said, impatiently. "I see you as a woman who hasn't worked a day in your life. Neither has your pale companion here. This case involves a subtle knowledge of the cunning philosophies adopted by labor and the moral complexities confronting management. There is a war of constant turmoil below the surface of our enterprise, Miss Borden. Many powerful men who bear your name in this city struggle with it every day. We must keep constant vigil, or else the forces of anarchy will overwhelm and strip us of the wealth and property that we have forged over these past seven decades. That danger is at the heart of this murder."

"You are saying," Lizzie said in a measured tone, "that I am not qualified to understand the political dynamic between the killer and the murdered man? In that case, how would a detective who is on the city payroll understand any of it better than I? He, too, would be neither labor nor management."

Mr. Twillie's eyes floated closer together. "A decidedly clever girl with quite a belligerent arrogance. Perhaps she is a useful resource, Thaddeus, what say you?"

"I say throw it all before her!" Mr. Brayton hoisted his arms upwards.

"What can come of it? Either she solves the murder or she doesn't, and those are odds that would apply if Marshal had brought in the entire police force. Forge and foundries! Throw it all to her!" He turned his back and walked to the window, locking his fingers behind him.

Mr. Twillie coughed into a fist and with the other hand brought forth a silk handkerchief to wipe his palm. "Miss Borden, I ask only that you refrain from disclosing anything you learn about the internal workings of the mill or the unfortunate murder that has occurred here today. This is to be undertaken with strictest confidence. The same applies to your biographer. This is one chapter he shall not be allowed to write. Such restrictions will be lifted should there be a determination of guilt and a public trial. But until this becomes a public affair, you have no freedom of press."

"That is not an issue," Lizzie said, nodding towards Homer. "Should I fail to solve the case, I shall not be interested in publicizing its details."

"Granted," Mr. Twillie said, his face lengthening into a bold, stark statement of indifference. "I shall monitor all and provide legal punctuation as I deem fit. Mr. Brayton shall also bear witness to the investigation."

"Agreed," Lizzie said. "Having said all this, I wish to start with the murdered man and the weapon that killed him."

"Yes," the Marshal said, gesturing towards a door against a far wall. "Both are within, but I must warn you that Mr. Latham's visage is quite disturbing."

"I have seen many a cadaver in my day," Lizzie said, waving for Homer to follow her. They all filed into the smaller chamber, which seemed to be a private meeting room dominated by a long polished wood table fringed with high backed chairs. No doubt in this space, without windows and having only one communicating door between itself and Colonel Anthony's office, high level meetings of great sensitivity were conducted that decided the fates of hundreds of employees and shareholders. Now, upon the table, where many a secret financial report and profit statement must have been displayed, was a long white sheet stained with much blood in the area that gracefully curved over what seemed to be a man's chin, nose, and forehead. They nestled about the table, squeezing themselves into the space for a closer examination.

"The man was shot in the outer office," the Marshal said grimly. "He was brought in here to prevent ghoulish onlookers from watching the attempts that were made to save his life. Unfortunately, there is much emission from the wound."

The Marshal pulled down the sheet to reveal a face locked into a contorted state of horror, the eyes closed, the mouth distended, the tongue slightly protruded, and the cheeks twisted. A bullet wound punctuated the right temple, a clean opening that showed all signs of being a point of entry. It was the damage to the head down below, just behind the left ear, that told the gruesome tale. Small, sharp fragments of skull had fallen like cracked eggshell to the table, along with some brain matter and coagulated blood which had seeped down from this larger wound. Lizzie bent to look at it, but Homer kept his distance, his face whitened and non-expressive. She examined the man's head quite closely. "Clean face, other than the blood." She pressed a fingertip to the skin just above the wound on his temple, distending it from its natural shape. "In through the front, and out through the back," Lizzie noted.

"And there is the weapon that Rogers was holding over the body," the Marshal said, pointing towards a wooden tray that had been laid out at the foot of the table. Upon it was exhibited a shiny hand-firearm, an inert piece of metal that radiated its own haunting messages of turmoil. "You may examine it," the Marshal added. "The bullets have been removed, but take note that there were five left in the barrel. Only one had been fired."

Homer broke his trance and stepped forward to place his hand upon the gun. "Colt .45," he said, lifting it by its dark wood handle, the muzzle pointed towards the ceiling. "Single-action revolver, beautifully manufactured. Army issue," he proclaimed as he pointed it upwards, peering up the barrel and cocking the hammer. Lizzie lurched upwards on her toes for a brief second as he fired the trigger and a sharp metallic burst clanked in their ears. "They call it the Peacemaker," Homer said, snapping open the loading gate and examining the barrel. "I would not want to be staring into its orifice," he concluded, and placed the weapon back on its tray.

"There is no other entrance to this room?" Lizzie asked, gazing around at the three walls that were quite occupied with everything other than doorways. "Then at least we know the killer could not have possibly escaped through here."

"The killer escape?" Mr. Brayton glanced angrily at the Marshal. "What have you told this girl?"

"Not much," the Marshal replied. "Perhaps we'd best retire back to the crime scene, and there we can brief Miss Borden upon the perplexities that confront us."

THE STONE BRIDGE

The east wall of the main office was dominated by the large bay window overlooking the central complex of the Iron Works. Here Lizzie stood, staring through the glass begrimed on the outside by the vaporous pollution of the furnaces. Below, the various buildings, workshops, and furnaces glowed like a cluster of firebugs within a jar. The sounds of vast enginery, metal upon metal, echoed from the machine shops, and teams of men moved about on the pathways, some pushing carts of pig iron, others pausing in their tracks and looking blankly up at the window where Lizzie stood. She marveled at the many laborers, men who were engaged in such arduous toil that her daily tasks seemed petty by comparison. How readily would they trade their livelihoods for her comfortable world of domestic trivialities, to instead have a roof over their heads without having to count the pennies for their rent and to obtain a salary from how many metal casts they can perform in an hour. The value of their lives was measured by the tons of steel placed into the shipping yards of the Anthony family, a brutal equation from which there was no escape. She withdrew from the window, troubled by such thoughts and feeling reluctant to be observed by any of the workers below.

"To begin," Lizzie said, seating herself in the polished swivel chair behind Colonel Anthony's desk, "I need to know the facts, as they stand."

From across the room, Mr. Brayton and Mr. Twillie examined the young girl with frowns, offering more puzzled silences than answers.

The Marshal sensed the stressful pause. "Facts," he began. "One would hope that facts are solid things, like rocks or doorknobs, presenting a surface to the world that is hard and impermeable, and not subject to refutation. But here we have something troubling that causes us to question the nature of facts. There are indeed facts in this case: Mr. Rogers and Mr. Latham were seen through this very door quarreling. There are ten witnesses alone who saw Latham pull a revolver from his pocket and swear that he would do the deed. Six witnesses saw Latham point the gun straight at Rogers' head. And one witness saw the gun explode."

"So *Latham* pointed the gun at *Rogers?*" Lizzie asked.

"Correct, according to six witnesses."

"And Latham pulled the trigger."

"Equally correct, according to one witness."

"But it was *Latham* who was found with a bullet in his head."

"Yes," the Marshal affirmed. "And Rogers standing over him, holding the gun."

Lizzie drummed her fingertips on the desktop. "Could Latham have misfired, and Rogers grabbed the gun from him?" she asked.

"That was our first impression," the Marshal confirmed. "But according to the witnesses, only one shot was heard, and our analysis of the murder weapon shows only one bullet was discharged from the barrel."

"Is it possible that the Colt was not the weapon that was fired?"

"It was still smoking when Rogers was caught holding it aloft over Latham's corpse."

Lizzie pondered this for a moment, her eyes resting squarely in front of her as if she were trying to recreate the scene with her imagination. "So Latham fires a bullet in the direction of Rogers, but somewhere in the course of the bullet's travel to Rogers' forehead, it reverses direction and kills the man who fired it."

"The six witnesses," Mr. Twillie suddenly announced, "swear that Latham was holding the gun point blank at Rogers."

"Did anyone see Latham fall?"

The Marshal shrugged. "As soon as they saw Latham aim the gun and heard a cry of 'No!' from Rogers, they fled for their lives, thinking that the gun would be turned on them next. And yet, one minute later, when the security guard on duty entered the room, Rogers was standing over Latham's body holding the gun, with one bullet discharged. Latham was lying on the ground, his skull shattered and his life removed from his mortal remains."

"So one discharge, one bullet, one dead body." Mr. Brayton emphasized. "Nothing can be clearer."

"There is a definite narrative here and gaps to fill in," Lizzie stated. "We need to know how Latham arrived at the office, how he got into the room, and what was his business with Rogers. Perhaps we should begin with the executive secretary."

"That would be Miss Borden," said the Marshal. "We have her waiting downstairs." He snapped his fingers at Beck, who stood in some vaporous cloud of thought. Then the officer jumped to the occasion and fled out the door.

"What were the two men quarreling about?" Lizzie asked.

"It is undetermined," Mr. Brayton said. "But there is no doubt that labor agitation is behind this all. Latham was an old-time 'ten-hour' man, a supporter of universal suffrage. Back when he was a young mill worker in Pawtucket, he was a prominent member of the Dorr Rebellion. And he wrote anti-capitalist tracts for *The Monitor* all throughout the troubles. There was no rougher beast than Latham when it came to speaking up for the rights of operatives. Print cloth or iron, no matter the industry, he claimed to be the spokesperson of all the oppressed."

The Marshal scratched his beard. "Personally, I would not know whether to vote the man to be President of the United States or to have shot him myself."

"What is that supposed to mean?" Mr. Brayton said, his eyebrows flaring.

Lizzie ignored the chairman's comment, and asked the Marshal, "We believe that Rogers was arguing with him over some principle of workers' rights?"

"Hard to imagine, but the passions were undeniably strong," the Marshal said, staring down at the blood stains on the carpet.

Officer Beck reappeared with a small, peevish woman, bespectacled and awkward. She wore leg-o-mutton sleeves, tapered waist, and modest bustle. Her eyes widened when she laid them upon Mr. Brayton, and her body shrank back towards the door.

"It's alright, my child," Mr. Brayton said, paternally. "You may speak your mind and tell the truth."

"I shall do that and more," she said, her voice expressing a hesitant confidence.

"Miss Elizabeth Borden," Beck announced, "Miss Lizzie Borden."

"My," Lizzie said, holding two finger-tips to her smiling mouth. "It seems we are close in name as well as blood. Are you from the Richard Borden branch?"

"No," Miss Borden said. "That's a different Borden."

"And you are executive secretary to Mr. Chester Rogers?"

"Yes, or at least I am now, since the troubles with Colonel Anthony."

"Troubles?"

"Yes, Colonel Anthony has been working day and night on this mill since he inherited the ownership from his father five years ago, and I fear that he underestimated his own capacity for endurance. Three months ago, he suffered a nervous breakdown, right here in this office. He became morbidly afraid of iron, couldn't even say the word. He had to be whisked away to an Italian retreat to recover his senses."

Lizzie took a sideways glance at the Marshal. "Were you aware of this?"

The Marshal nodded. "I had some understanding that the Colonel was not well. We were told to keep an eye on his house for an indefinite period."

"Morbidly afraid of iron?" Lizzie said, suppressing a giggle. "How does this happen?"

"The demands of his job created tremendous stress in his mind," Miss Borden said, her face as blank as a fresh sheet of paper. "There is nothing more horrible than to feel your humanity sinking under the weight of industrial responsibility."

"Why?" Lizzie added, "Did the Colonel actually mine the ore? Did he work the furnaces? Did he pour the casts? Did he engineer the trains to their shipping destinations?"

"No," Miss Borden sighed. "But I'm afraid that there are other ways of feeling the weight of the business. His entire family fortune was resting upon his success, and the pressures on him were enormous. Not to mention he took a highly personal role in the labor disputes. Confronting the very people who toiled for his wealth, whose physical stamina determined the success or failure of his investments, was quite taxing on him."

"Any man in his position would feel a weight of responsibility," Mr. Brayton added. "There are many concerns suffered by management that are simply swept up in the undertow of labor agitation."

"Mr. Brayton," Lizzie said, holding up a palm. "I am asking questions and expect the answers to come from Miss Borden. Please curtail your commentary." She nodded to the secretary. "You may proceed."

"His nature was truly sensitive," Miss Borden continued. "He never meant to be elevated to such a position, and to be in a field where the laborers worked half-naked over burning furnaces, pouring hot liquid metal, toiling in the fields with their dynamite and drilling tools … well, I should add that the irony of it all did not escape him. He was looking for redemption, for a way out of his predicament."

"But he did not wish to lose the money of his investors?"

"I don't believe that was a consideration for him in the end. He was haunted by what had once been his dream, which was to be a romantic poet."

"A poet?"

"Yes, he was a big admirer of Wordsworth, Shelley, and Keats. He even admired William Blake, despite the man's revolutionary beliefs. Yes, Colonel Anthony was a true poetic soul, and would much rather have been far from these Satanic mills, instead enjoying the bounty of nature and dancing with the wood nymphs rather than cracking a bull-whip on the backs of men who were his social inferiors. He had also meditated deep and hard on the moral implications of the cannons, am-munition, and armaments supplied by this company to the war effort, and the amount of human blood shed by our product. Despite what many may think, Colonel Anthony's true nature was closer to an angel's than to a murderer or a man capable of enslaving others."

"That's quite a claim," Lizzie said, "considering that the Wampa-noag Iron Works has tripled its output and profit shares in the last year alone, due to a decrease in wages and the additional unpaid hours forced on the workers. Can a poet at heart be so calculating and profit-driven?"

"That was a decision by the Board of Directors," Miss Borden ad-mitted. "And not one that the Colonel took to heart. In fact, it was that very directive that led to his breakdown."

"So he had a soft spot for the operatives," the Marshal said be-musedly. "You would never know it from his behavior."

"Not quite," Miss Borden said, staring blankly. "The Colonel kept his feelings to himself. Perhaps that was his undoing, and a circum-stance leading to his gravest crisis. The day that he had his collapse, he was curled in a ball like a child, under his desk, refusing to talk to anyone except his physician, Doctor Ames."

"Was he examined by this Doctor?" Lizzie asked.

"In this very office, and immediately the Doctor prescribed the trip to Italy. As far away from the production of iron as the Colonel could possibly go. He suggested the Colonel visit ancient ruins so he could ponder the vanity of man's existence. The Colonel knew the poet's words quite well. 'Look on my works, ye Mighty, and despair!' Shelley."

"I always wanted to see the shores of Calabria," the Marshal mused, tugging at his mustache. "It would beat the hell out of Rocky Point."

"What is your recollection of the actual shooting?" Lizzie asked Miss Borden.

"Alas, many of the pertinent details I did not hear or see; however, I feel my narrative could prove valuable. It was early this morning, just as the ten o'clock whistle blew, and Mr. Rogers came into the office late. Then he quickly gave me orders to leave him alone until further notice. He closed the door, and was silent for a time."

"For how long?"

"I would say half an hour by the clock. Then Mr. Rogers suddenly flung open his door, looking all angry and fierce, waving his arms and calling out for me to get Mr. Latham immediately. Then he said something unusual that I have not forgotten. He said, 'Tell Latham to make haste to the Stone Bridge! No dilly-dallying!'"

"Dilly-dallying?" Lizzie repeated. "A curious phrase. What do you think he meant by the Stone Bridge?"

"I am not sure of the exact allusion, although I took it all to mean that Mr. Latham should expedite his arrival. *Tout de suit*, as the French would say. So I dispatched a boy to find Latham down in the machine shop, since he was on shift."

"Did you tell the boy to repeat the phrase, word for word? Including the Stone Bridge part?"

"I did everything that Mr. Rogers ordered me to, word for word, most assuredly."

"How long did it take Mr. Latham to arrive?"

"About five minutes, I would say. I have no understanding if five minutes constitutes 'making haste to the Stone Bridge.' but Latham seemed to rush into the office, paying no attention to myself or any of the other assistants, and walked quite confidently up to the door. Without hesitation, he opened it and stepped inside, leaving it just barely ajar behind him."

"The door was not wide open?"

"Not at that point. But we did start to hear the shouting, muffled shouts with both men talking over each other in a heated way. We all became concerned and it was myself who swung his office door open. My concern was entirely with Mr. Rogers' safety. I did not care what Mr. Latham thought or felt of my actions."

"How far open did you swing the door?"

"Almost completely, as far as it would go. Far enough for me to see Mr. Rogers by the desk and Mr. Latham standing before him holding the gun."

"How was he holding the weapon?"

"Outward, like this. Almost point blank. Several of us screamed at that point, I must confess. It was truly a gruesome sight. I never hope to see such another."

"So at that point, you ran?"

"Yes, I did run for the door to the outer office. I did not care to be in the general area when the firearm was discharged."

"Did all the people witnessing this with you run at that same time?"

"I believe we ran in stages: some of us at first, the rest upon the following moments. But I did not make it out the door to the hallway before I heard the shot."

"So the interval of time between your witnessing Mr. Latham holding the revolver towards Mr. Rogers, and your hearing the gunshot, was a mere matter of minutes?"

"Not even a minute. I would say as long as the time it would take for me to run halfway to the hallway."

"What happened then?"

"There was a frightful silence, like all time had come to a halt. Then we looked back, frightened, at the office. The door was open, and Mr. Rogers was nowhere to be seen. But neither was Mr. Latham."

"Both were gone from sight?"

"Yes, at first I took that to mean that Mr. Rogers had fallen to the floor, possibly mortally wounded, and that Mr. Latham had somehow fled deeper into the room. But then we saw the poor man's feet on the floor. And then Mr. Rogers appeared back where he had been, holding the gun, looking startled. He glanced down at the body, then at the weapon in his own hand, and then at us. He spoke to us: 'Have no fear,' he said. 'He is no longer a threat to us.' This filled us with a tremendous sense of relief, and we all felt safe enough to enter the room."

"Everyone entered into the office at this time?"

"Yes, about ten of us. We all wanted to know if Mr. Rogers was unharmed. His body was certainly in prime condition, but his mind seemed a bit frayed, as if he had just been through a terrible ordeal and his nerves were sundered."

"And that is when the police were called?"

"We didn't see any resistance to the idea from Mr. Rogers. In fact, we all thought it to be a clear case of self-defense." Her eyes darted swiftly towards the Marshal. "Apparently, our opinion was not shared by those who had the authority to declare it so."

Lizzie quickly asked, "Who was the last person to actually see the two of them before the gun was fired?"

"That would be Mr. Howard," the Marshal jumped in. "The Pig-Iron Puddler."

"A Puddler?" Lizzie asked, curiously. "He was standing in this office?"

"I had first noticed Mr. Howard just before the explosion," Miss Borden continued. "He ran back into the office with us and stood over Mr. Latham's body, staring down at it like it was some curious artifact he had found during a naturalist hike. He did give me a nervous shudder."

"Did he speak at the time?"

"No, he remained silent. And yet..." Miss Borden paused, her voice wavering as she raised a finger towards her cheek. "There was something peculiar going on. Mr. Howard was standing over Mr. Latham, and yet when I turned away, feeling greatly disturbed over what I had witnessed, I happened to peer into that mirror—"she gestured towards a slanting oval mirror that stood sentinel next to the office coat rack, "—and I saw Mr. Howard over by the door, standing behind the crowd, moving backwards as if he were inching his way across the floor."

"Was it at that point that he left the room?"

"I suppose so," answered Miss Borden. "I'm not quite sure why it struck me as odd. Perhaps he had gotten to the door a bit too fast, like he had run from the body. But a moment later I turned around and he was still standing in the room, talking to one of the office staff and pointing back towards the body. It was as if he couldn't decide if he wanted to flee the scene or not, which made me suspicious of him. Very odd behavior."

"Why would he want to flee?"

"I have not a notion on that. However, I am positive he was in the outer office when the shot rang out. He is not the killer, I am certain of it. I just remember how strange it felt when I saw him in that mirror..."

"I have one last question for Miss Borden," Lizzie announced. "Do you believe that Mr. Rogers had any true motivation to murder Mr. Latham?"

"I know they were not on the best of terms because of Mr. Latham's agitation, and how he wrote vitriolic diatribes against mill management in the columns of *The Monitor*. And he sent angry letters to *Iron News*, which has the audacity to publish them. I can think of many men of Mr. Rogers' social standing who would like to have seen Latham rotting in a jail cell or dangling at the end of a rope."

Lizzie put her fingers together below her chin. "But even if we take that as motivation for a murder, why would Mr. Rogers do this in broad daylight, in front of so many witnesses?"

"It was not characteristic of Mr. Rogers," Miss Borden observed, "to have put himself at such risk, or to have murdered anyone for that matter. However, even if he were to contemplate such a heinous act, I do not believe he would have done so with his own hands, even if those hands belonged to the man he murdered."

A muffled cough was heard and Mr. Twillie spoke: "Pardon me, Miss Borden, Mr. Brayton and I have taken note of some of the dubious allegations in your account, yet we are willing to overlook these due to the tragic nature of the events. However, we have a question of our own, one that Miss Borden here, no doubt, cannot ask because she does not even know that the question exists."

Lizzie raised an eyebrow, trying to comprehend Mr. Twillie's statement. "A question that I do not know exists?" she asked. "That is very odd."

"Most definitely," Mr. Twillie continued. "But now I must pose it to Miss Borden: are you aware that Mr. Latham was said to have been a member of a strange society, one that would stop at nothing to overthrow the owners of this mill, and to surrender the very means of production to the hands of those who would destroy it?"

Miss Borden's face went slightly pale, her cheeks thinning. "I know nothing about such a society," she said, "except strange rumors, and I certainly do not know if Mr. Latham had any involvement. But when I did witness Mr. Rogers and Mr. Latham poised to combat each other, I thought immediately that something unspoken had been brought to a boil, that the conflict between them was symptomatic of that deeper conflict."

"This is most interesting," Lizzie said, stroking her chin. "A secret society within the mill?"

"One dares not speculate," Miss Borden said plainly. "As I have already told you, there are only whispers."

A long pause followed her statement, while all the inhabitants of the room eyed each other with the strange anxiety that overcomes a group of intimates who suddenly feel that everyone else has become incomprehensible strangers. Lizzie swatted some dust from the desktop. "I will follow up on your suspicions."

"That is entirely your affair," Mr. Twillie cautioned.

Miss Borden nodded with a faint trace of respect, and then jerked a thumb back towards the outer room. "I must return to my desk," she muttered, glancing furtively at Mr. Brayton. "I fully expect to be relieved of my employment and sent home without a job within the hour. Truthfully, that shall be a relief, if you must know." And then she vacated the room, leaving behind a shadow as if she were still standing in the path of the slanting sunlight.

"A secret society," the Marshal said, breathlessly. "Of all the confabulations…"

"What do you know of this?" Lizzie asked the stoic lawyer. "If such an organization is behind this murder, you must tell me immediately."

"We were not suggesting we knew anything about a secret society," said Mr. Twillie, hastily. "We were merely asking if she had any such knowledge."

"Even so," Lizzie said firmly, "you have taken a perfectly coordinated and balanced interrogation and derailed it with your political paranoia. I must ask the two of you to remain silent from here on in."

"I have even a better idea," the Marshal said. "Hide inside the meeting room."

"What?" Mr. Brayton said, tugging at his mutton chops. "I have to remind you that I represent the presiding board of this mill and I will not tolerate your impudence."

"Regardless," the Marshal said. "Behind the door, both of you. And speak not a word. Be grateful that I am allowing you to hear anything." The two men looked at each other with skittish alarm, and then tromped to the meeting room, Mr. Brayton muttering a few syllables while Mr. Twillie gave the Marshal and Lizzie purposeful stares. As soon as they were secure inside the room, the Marshal pulled the door to within an inch of being closed.

"What do you make of that?" he asked Lizzie.

"I'm not sure," she mused. "When we embark on the murky sea of secret societies, simple facts take on even more insubstantiality than that which we have previously suspected. Indeed, each fact does turn into its opposite, and all hope at recovering a solid truth can be lost."

"But we are not talking about the supernatural here," Homer said, sliding from his chair and advancing to the center of the room. "Even in science, forces that appear to be ghostly and beyond our physical senses do, upon closer examination, begin to follow rigid laws that enable us to make predictions. Although we cannot see a secret society, we can yet detect its presence and trace its behavior."

"In my mind," the Marshal added, "the society does not even have to exist to exert a force. The mere rumor of its existence causes people to behave oddly. It is an angry ghost haunting the mills, turning brother against brother, manager against operative."

"Careful," Lizzie said, jerking her head towards the meeting room door. "As we proceed, we must determine for ourselves if this is a deception, or whether Mr. Twillie actually does have cause to be paranoid."

"One cannot blame him," the Marshal sighed. "If iron mongers can become morbidly afraid of their own metal and discharged bullets can turn about in mid-flight, anything can happen. Where do we go from here?"

"It is time to visit the exact moment of the crime," Lizzie asserted, "or as close as we can to it. I believe we must now speak with Mr. Howard, the Pig Iron Puddler, he who is described as being the last witness. In his words may lie the answer to an unfathomable mystery."

THE BATSTO GHOST

The man who entered the room accompanied by Officer Beck was medium in height, unassuming, swathed in overalls, clutching a cloth hat between his hands. His mustache drooped down towards rough stubble on his wide chin. "Thomas Howard," Officer Beck announced, and the man dipped his head in deference towards the Marshal and the girl behind the desk.

"By your leave," he said with a lumpy voice. "Mr. Marshal, you do me proud. Interrogated twice in one day, what an honor!"

"Mr. Howard, at this hour I am a mere spectator," the Marshal announced, thrusting out a gloved hand towards Lizzie. "Here is your inquisitor."

The man's eyes sparked and he raised them towards Lizzie directly. "I'm sorry if I seem a bit twitchy, but you caught me at a delicate moment. Seeing what I have seen isn't a common occurrence. And now to have to take off my hat to a young girl who has more authority than the City Marshal, that's quite hard to fathom."

"You show respect to Miss Borden, Howard," the Marshal cautioned.

"Yes, I shall." The man rotated his hat between his dirty fingers. "I didn't mean to imply I won't take part in this interrogation. I suspect she'll review the same points of order that I've been revisiting over and over with various policemen and investigators down below. Unless, of course, she's creative and has some new angle to pursue."

Lizzie suppressed a smile and folded her hands on the table. "I admire your pluck," she said. "I'm not sure if my questions will compete in originality with the other investigators, but they are my questions, not theirs. To start, from where do you hail? You don't have a local accent."

His lips pulled back into a slanted smile, his teeth obscured by his mustache. "Yes, that is indeed a different sort of question. No, Miss, I'm not from around here. Rather I hail from the bog-lands of New Jersey. I'm an old Batsto man working the furnace in the Pines, you better believe it. I spent twenty years hauling the bog iron out of Batsto. I bet you never had to spend two decades of your life lifting rocks, did you Miss Borden?"

"I have not been alive for two decades," Lizzie said with a giggle. "But I assure you, I have nothing but the utmost respect for your labor. The fantastic marvels of today's modern age would not be possible without the selfless work that you performed in the bogs of New Jersey."

Howard rubbed his chin and said blankly, "Perhaps I did contribute to fantastic marvels. Perhaps some houses up on the Hill have some banisters cast from my bog-iron, or some cannonball I gave birth to in the furnace actually won a battle for General Grant. But in actuality, the only fantastic marvel I experienced in my day was to get a dollar into my pocket at the end of the week, so I could buy food for my family. And even that didn't last long. Pennsylvania came around with its fancy furnaces, and we were out of business. We left the Lake, and even now the bog-iron's growing back, but no one wants it. They just want the Lake water for drink in Philadelphia. And suddenly there's no more Lake, no more Pines, no more village. So me and my wife and my poor son had to come here, to work for the Colonel. We live in two rooms and the landlord takes everything we got. But I keep pouring the casts, and tending the puddling furnace. Is that fantastic enough for you, Miss Borden?" He grinned widely, crinkling his cheeks.

After a nervous silence, Homer Thesinger, seated in a guest chair against the far wall, cleared his throat. "Mr. Howard, that furnace at Batsto that you so diligently kept burning for two decades. Did you run this by a water wheel?"

"Why yes, we had our dam, and the spillway turned the wheel."

"And you fed the charcoal and the ore through the top?"

"Yes, layered with shell flux, and it would melt down to the crucible. We'd grab the run-off from the bottom, and paddle it into the casting shed."

"I saw a picture of this in a trade journal, and I believe it was the Batsto Furnace."

Howard's face soured. "What do you care about these furnaces? You're but a boy, never saw one in your life."

"But I examined the output of your fine castings," Homer said, gleefully. "My family has a whole collection of kettles and skillets from Batsto and I so admired the craftsmanship I did some research into the manufacturing process. In the library stalls I discovered a monograph on the Old Jersey Furnace that explained the entire process to my great satisfaction. Indeed, I have enjoyed many a meal made in your hallow-ware."

The man's eyes moved closer together. "How do I know you're not fabricating this story? My kettles couldn't have been distributed this far north!"

"Indeed they have, and I invite you and your wife and your son over to my father's home this very evening to enjoy a fine meal and an elegantly brewed pot of tea from the implements we are discussing. The meal will be delightful and the tea will reach a fine degree of subtlety, all enriched by the iron products in which they are to be cooked. And that, Mr. Howard, is a fantastic marvel, more lasting and more valuable than any fancy beds or staircase railing up on the Hill."

The old bog-iron man looked at the boy with a twinkle in his eye, parted his lips as if he meant to reply, then turned sharply towards Lizzie. "I have my own supper plans, thank you kindly, so I'll have to turn down that offer. In the immediate, I'd like to answer this young lady's questions, if you please."

Lizzie nodded towards Homer. "Mr. Howard, I would like to return to the moment in question, when Mr. Latham is quarreling with Mr. Rogers and he pulls forth a revolver with the intention of murdering him. You witnessed the actual shooting?"

"As sure as daylight streams through that window, I can see that gun pointed straight into the face of Mr. Rogers."

"But you did not see the actual moment of contact?"

"No, I can't say I did. I was too busy running for my life. I didn't have enough passionate curiosity to watch a man die."

"But you heard the report of the gun?"

"Surely, I did. We all heard it, but no one was clear whether it had gone astray or not, and we all kept racing towards the door."

"You heard the explosion while you were running for the door?"

"Most definitely. I would not be standing there like a slack-jawed fool, knowing that the bullet would fire at any second."

"Mr. Howard, I ask you one more time, did you actually see the bullet leave the gun?"

His mouth twisted under his mustache and he blinked cryptically. "Well, how can someone see a bullet leave a gun at all? It travels so fast, you wouldn't see it even if you stared at it. When I said I saw the gun fire, I suppose I was condensing a bit."

"So your answer is no, you did not see the gun fire."

"I heard it sharp and clear, Miss Borden. As for seeing the bullet suspended in space long enough for me to identify it as a bullet, I can't vouch as clearly. But you can believe me when I say that barrel was taking a long hard look at Mr. Rogers' face, and within a second or two of me turning to run for the door, there was an explosion, only one. Only one gun was fired and I know who was holding it and to which point of the compass its barrel was pointed."

"After you heard the report, you came back. You even entered this office and examined the body?"

"Why, yes, I was following the crowd. Mr. Rogers was holding the gun, and we weren't afraid of him, so I examined the scene."

"Did it strike you as odd, after what you had witnessed, that it was Mr. Latham with the bullet in his head and not Mr. Rogers?"

"It's not my business to puzzle that one out," Howard said, "being that I'm just reporting what I witnessed."

"Mr. Howard, why were you here in the first place?"

"To feed my family of course. A man must work."

"No, I mean why were you up in the offices of Colonel Anthony? You work on the casting floor, your crew make nails and hoops and kitchen ware from the iron that flows from the furnaces. What were you doing on the third floor of Colonel Anthony's administration building?"

He stared grimly at her. "Why do you ask?"

"It's an innocent question, I believe, and quite fair in my estimation. You merely have to state your business with Rogers, or anyone else in the office."

"If you must know, I was determined to ask for a pay raise."

"Was it typical protocol to leave your furnace down below and to walk up to the private offices of the executive Agent of the mill at midday to ask for a pay raise?"

Howard's face tightened. "My father brought me up to be direct and to raise my eyes to the man in the big house. When we were unhappy at the Lake, we would march right up the road to the owner's front porch and confront him as he sipped ice tea with his daughters. Put the man on the spot! Demand your due! I may be in a New England mill now where a man's labor isn't worth the metal that our pay is stamped upon, but old habits die hard."

"Yes," Lizzie said. "Quite so. I do admire your gumption."

"May I go now, Miss Borden?" Howard asked, scratching behind his ear, and nodding towards Officer Beck. "If my interrogations are over, I'm planning on taking the afternoon off, being that my foreman is dead and my boss is under arrest for murder. I don't suppose casting some barrel hoops would be profitable under these circumstances."

"Good idea," the Marshal said, his smile broadening. "Enjoy the afternoon sunlight."

"Can't say I'll see much sunlight," he said. "I have some business to discuss with the wife, in light of all this. Not often that we're both at home at the same time, it may be an enjoyable experience." And with a wink of his eyes and a flurry of his cap, he paraded out the door, pushing his fists into his pockets and whistling a casual tune.

"There's something about that man that's not quite correct," the Marshal said, peering at the empty space where the Puddler had stood.

"How so?" Lizzie asked. "Was his story consistent with his earliest interrogation?"

"Decidedly so. Except for the part about asking for a pay raise. Earlier today he told us that he came up here to resign his position, that he wanted to 'spit in the face of the man who drove him like a slave.' Yes, those were his exact words, weren't they, Beck?"

The officer who stood like a sentinel near the door, stirred into motion. "Yes, sir. When we first nabbed him down on the floor, he made it sound as if he were ready to kill the man himself."

Lizzie's eyebrows lifted. "You nabbed him on the floor? You mean, he went back to his station?"

"He was the only witness who didn't wait around for the police," the Marshal explained. "Beck had to go fetch him."

"Why did he leave the scene of the crime?" Lizzie said, puzzled. "And why did he change his story?"

The Marshal shrugged. "Prestige, perhaps. His one moment to shine in the light instead of hovering in the shadows of the machine shop."

Lizzie glanced over at Homer. "Would you really have had the Howards over for their supper?" Lizzie asked. "Without consulting your parents, you would invite over a complete stranger?"

"Without a doubt," Homer beamed. "He would have made a great smash with my mother. She always boasted about how she had the sturdiest and most excellently crafted iron skillets in all of Bristol County. Indeed, the entire Commonwealth. Meeting the man behind such a beloved work of art would have been her greatest pleasure."

AN AGENT'S SECRET

Chester Rogers was slight and nondescript, his thin face revealing little of the turbulence that must have been crackling like fire within him. The two policemen who flanked him, the Marshal who stood behind him and Officer Beck who guarded the office door, both seemed fidgety, as if at any moment they expected an outburst or a threatening move. They could hardly be blamed for their vigilance: before them sat a man who only an hour earlier had fired a bullet into another man's brain. His calmness, under such troubling circumstances, was what was most disturbing about him.

The irony that his interrogator, a young girl of no seeming consequence, had the outrageous audacity to sit behind his own desk as she questioned him, did not escape Lizzie. She began carefully, "I have been informed that you were engaged in an argument with Mr. Latham, and, in the resulting confusion, the poor man has been shot in the head. Can you deny this?"

Rogers eyed the Marshal. "Where is Mr. Brayton? Who is this girl? I don't know her, why should I speak to her?"

"You'll answer her questions," the Marshal said with measured tenseness, "as if I were asking, do you hear me, Rogers?"

"At least tell me her name."

"I am Lizzie Andrew Borden," she said proudly. "And I suspect you would have heard that I fared very well in the past investigating crimes both high and pedestrian. In the Case of the Purloined Curio, I brought about the downfall of Livermore, the mill agent."

A strange light appeared in Rogers' eye, and he looked at her intently. "Livermore," he said. "Even more of a reason why I should not discuss anything with you."

"Why would you be so critical of my actions in that case?" she asked. "Do you condone murderers and would prefer to see them go unpunished?"

"Many crimes have gone unpunished," Rogers said with a sneer. "Why should that one have been different?"

"Because the man who Livermore murdered was a good man, while Livermore was vile and uncivilized. Just because he was a mill agent doesn't mean..."

"I don't care if he was a Methodist minister," Rogers snapped. Then he paused as if asking her to contemplate his words carefully. "I have nothing further to say about that," he added.

"What do you mean?" the Marshal asked, his brow furrowed. "What do Methodist ministers have to do with..."

"I think this can all be reduced to a simple question," Lizzie said, shelving the snippet of conversation in her mind for future examination. "Did you or did you not shoot Mr. Latham in the head with a Colt .45?"

"You mean the Single Army?" Rogers said, disdainfully. "Latham brought it into my office and made all sorts of threats."

"What kind of threats exactly?"

"I have nothing to say about that, or the whole incident, except that the gun went off during a struggle."

"Who fired it?"

"I have nothing to say."

Lizzie hesitated, waiting for any further comment, but the man had closed his mouth and turned his face to the door. "There is a witness who saw Mr. Latham pointing the revolver in your direction," she explained, "almost at point blank range. Then a second later there was a loud report from the discharging of the gun. So how did the bullet not reach you? What magic did you perform that would have reversed its course and sent it spiraling into Mr. Latham's head? Are you a magician, Mr. Rogers, who can bend the course of a piece of metal hurtling at close to one thousand feet per second?"

"No," he said. "I'm not."

"Then what happened? Can you put our minds at rest and show us what transpired in that brief second after the revolver was fired?"

"No," he repeated.

"Can you at least tell us the reason for your quarrel?"

He breathed deep, considering some inner thought, then proceeded. "We received a rather large order from New York, of such a magnitude that to fulfill it would tax our resources. To meet the order, I directed that the teams were to work overtime, one extra hour a day, with no increase in pay."

"And Latham, as fiery as his agitation was, opposed this directive?"

"He loathed it, said that I was a harsh monster who should be destroyed."

"Would you disagree with that assessment?"

"I was put into this position suddenly, without warning, forced into a system of responsibility for which I cannot take blame. It is my duty to keep these mills running, and to turn a profit for our stockholders. I recognize the humanity of the men and women who labor in my name, but I cannot simply let empathy for their plight ruin the production of the iron."

"But the men and women who produce that iron for you are human beings, and they have families to feed."

"They are free to come as they please, and to go as they please. They are not slaves."

"No," Lizzie said, pondering. "I would not think they were slaves. But how can they go as they please when they have no other place to go? That's like telling a man who is deposited without a boat in the middle of the Atlantic Ocean that he is free to swim to shore if he chooses."

"I am not here to argue politics," Rogers said. "I have had enough of it listening to men like Latham."

"So, are you pleased to see him go?" Lizzie asked.

"I was staring down the barrel of a gun," Rogers said. "The weapon was aimed to kill me and I had to act fast."

"No man can act as fast as you claim to act," the Marshal shouted. "It's physically impossible."

"How do you know how much time had expired?" Rogers answered. "Because of a few secretaries and clerks who barely understood what was happening? Why do you favor their memories over mine? Latham pulled the gun on me, and I had no choice but to turn it back upon him."

"Through the power of your mind alone?" Lizzie asked. "Somehow, you reversed the direction of the bullet?"

"I will answer no more questions," Rogers said. "If you wish to arrest me for murder, that is your prerogative. However, if you cannot prove that I pulled the trigger, if you have no witnesses, and by your own admission, I cannot possibly have fired the gun, then you'd best let me go this instant and judge Latham's death a suicide." He closed his eyes with a brief flutter. "I shall say no more until you make your own decision."

"Make our decision?" the Marshal cried, his voice thundering. "Why, of all the impudent..."

Lizzie took a breath and rose to her feet. "Mr. Rogers, what is the significance of the Stone Bridge?"

Rogers gave no answer, but his brow furrowed. Lizzie walked to the front of the desk, her dress trailing about her, and leaned in close to Rogers' left ear. "The Stone Bridge," she repeated. "Was this some kind of code? Did he bring a gun with him because you had somehow instructed him to bring the gun?"

"Why would I tell him to bring a gun?" Rogers said, keeping his eyes shut. "That would be suicide."

"Suicide for you?" Lizzie asked. "Or for him?"

"It was merely an expression," Rogers said between tight lips.

"There is a stone bridge that connects Fall River to Aquidneck Island, is there not? Can that be the bridge in question?"

"I have no idea of the origin of the expression, I just find it useful when asking a man to double his pace and make haste. I leave the history lessons to others more versed in the events surrounding that bridge."

"Mr. Rogers, I have an important question for you, and I am most eager that you will supply your very first answer, since you have effectively avoided giving any up till this point. I have heard rumors about a secret society in this mill, perhaps a workers' conspiracy, one designed to seize the means of production from the owners and to give it to those who toil to create the wealth. Do you have any knowledge of such a cabal?"

"It sounds like rank socialism to me. I pay no attention to those European political fads, although I suspect Latham, being from England, had some knowledge of it."

"Was that the subject of your quarrel? Did such talk provoke him to pull a revolver upon you?"

"Discussing politics with Latham was an ineffectual experience. When I attempted to reason with him, explained to him my position, defended the economic system that drives society, I might as well have been talking to a brick wall. He was unwavering in his beliefs to the point of losing touch with the blunt realities of life."

"You didn't answer my question."

"I suspect I have," Rogers said, his mouth slightly twisted. "I have answered every one of your questions, perhaps too much so. May I go now? Or shall I be put into shackles and dragged to the police station to sit behind bars and shout my innocence to the mob below my solitary window."

"Mr. Rogers, what do you know about Thomas Howard the Puddler?"

His eyes darted away. "He is of no consequence to me."

"What was he doing in your office at the time of Mr. Latham's death?"

"Perhaps you'd be best off asking him. I know nothing of his business."

"Did you see him in your office after the shooting?"

"Yes, I did, in fact. He came in with the rest of them, ghoulishly observing the scene."

"Did you not think it unusual that he was there?"

"I paid it no mind. My attention at that time was occupied with more important matters. I had no truck with a puddler. But wait, yes, I did have a thought in my head regarding him. And it was this: Why is he here in my office, and not at his furnace station increasing my wealth? Yes, that was my very thought, but it was as brief as a single moment, a fleeting thought."

Lizzie turned to the Marshal and waved a diffident hand. "He is entirely at your command."

"Damnation," the Marshal said, pulling forth a pocket watch and noting the time. "Mr. Rogers, I cannot find any means by which I can link you to the crime. There is no material evidence, outside of the fact that you were holding a smoking gun over a dead man's body after it fired a bullet into his brain. You are free to go, for now. But don't leave town. We may require you for further questioning."

Rogers smiled and got to his feet, his cheeks blushing. "I'm happy to have helped in any way to illuminate this affair. Now that you have given me the pleasure of my freedom, I do have a statement of fact to make, one that I was unwilling to make when I assumed that my fate lay behind bars."

"And what may that be, Mr. Rogers?"

"One bullet cannot come from two different directions; it is a sheer impossibility. A gun can only be aimed in one direction. If the bullet came from a direction that was contrary to the direction in which the bullet was fired, then either the gun was not in the position where it is believed to have been, or the bullet itself was not as it seems. Both gun and bullet came from a furnace of fire, and back to the furnace they shall go. And there may be a puddler at both ends of the affair."

Lizzie, Homer, and the Marshal simultaneously blinked and pondered his words, attempting to straighten them out in their heads. "That's what you call a 'statement of fact'?" the Marshal asked. "I have half a mind to beat the truth out of you, Rogers!"

The sub-agent sauntered to the door. "I have no more to say except that upon my arrival at home, I shall consult with a lawyer, and next time you shall find me better prepared to not answer any more of your useless questions." He took one last glance about his office as if to soak up a scene that was not confined to memory, and then disappeared from view.

"What do we make from that?" the Marshal huffed. "Not exactly a signed and sealed confession, is it?"

"On the contrary," Lizzie said excitedly. "I believe we did hear something akin to a confession."

"What, you think he pulled the trigger?"

"I am not inclined to reveal my theory as of yet. There is another person I will need to interrogate."

Her thoughts were interrupted by the sight of Brayton and Twillie standing in the meeting room doorway, their proud faces stoic and silent. They advanced into the room like synchronized dancers, or perhaps bonded Siamese twins, afraid of stepping apart lest their connection to each other be compromised.

"We have listened and observed," Mr. Brayton boasted. "And we must restate our suspicion that dangerous and secret forces are at work within the mill. Perhaps this man Howard knows more than he is saying, or Miss Borden is in collusion with the conspirators. Whatever transpired in the small amount of time between Mr. Latham's firing of the gun, and the arrival of the bullet at his forehead, is not of any consequence. Our only concern is that Mr. Rogers defended the mill, its principles and well-being, against dark and savage conspiracies."

"Perhaps," Lizzie said. "Or perhaps your theory about the secret society is mere paranoia."

"There is no proof to confirm that," Mr. Brayton said, clanking his cane against the ground. "Your science and deductive reasoning are of no use here. We highly recommend abandoning the case, and simply letting the lack of evidence decide the outcome. Let it be determined in a court of law. A guilty man is dead, an innocent man and defender of the faith is walking in his liberty. Is that not enough to redress the balance and put all this to rest?"

Lizzie rubbed her forehead as if to stimulate further thought, turned to the Marshal and Homer for some modicum of personal support, then leveled her gaze at the two well-suited men and answered with a plain and unassuming voice, "No, not really."

"Eh, what?" Mr. Brayton huffed.

"A man lies dead," Lizzie said, pointing to the room behind their backs. "His life stolen from him. For all your pretended proclamations of justice and the role of your business in the larger affairs of mankind, I fear that the integrity of your iron mill and the safety of your investments is not a consideration here."

"Such talk is not trivial," Mr. Twillie said. "We can order you off the premises as a suspected member of the secret society. You will never be able to disprove us."

"Nor can you prove such an allegation," said Homer, unexpectedly. "Sir, I am but a young boy, steeped in science and not quite as well-versed as you may be in the practical affairs of industry, although I do follow the technology in various trade magazines. So my opinions may fall short of intellectual profundity, but it does seem to me that regardless of whether this secret society exists, and regardless of whether it played a role in the killing, you have hosted in your factory today a highly publicized murder. The entire city is witnessing these events unfold, and all revelations will be subject to public scrutiny. If you fail to present to them a solution to this mystery, word about ill-doings in the mill will spread about the city, perhaps the entire commonwealth. Agitation will increase, for Mr. Latham will have become a martyr, a common working man murdered by management, and management will doubtless be perceived as having heartlessly allowed his murderer to go free. So, I think you should permit Miss Lizzie to pursue this investigation to its proper conclusion, lest you turn your factory into the spark that would light the fires of revolution, perhaps even on a global scale. Do you want to be known as the industrialist who initiated the downfall of industry?"

Mr. Brayton's eyebrows had somehow joined above his nose. "Not particularly," he answered. "No."

"Then perhaps," Homer concluded, "Miss Lizzie should be allowed the run of the mill. Let her work her magic."

THE CRUCIBLE

The thundering of the steam hammers and the relentless roar of the furnaces, beasts of burden groaning under a yoke of unimaginable heat, filled the hallows of the factory floor, drowning under its tidal wash of energy the singular voices of the men who labored at the machines. As

Lizzie walked with her company across the wide open floor, crowded to the walls with piled machinery, immense castings and moulds, and jagged mounds of slag, she raised her hands to her ears, attempting to quash the pressure that was building inside her head. Both the Marshal and Homer made some gestures to her, perhaps to redirect her course, or to convey some information, but their words were lost in the deafening din.

A row of workstations against the northern wall was manned by workers who stood holding long strips of metal that they were awkwardly feeding into hungry machines. The men were constantly making adjustments to the angle of the strips as the metal teeth ate at them, thereby spitting them into a hopper below. What emerged were metallic spikes that Lizzie took to be nails. Often she had seen her father procuring these nails for his furniture business, but now she marveled at their birth, seeing how they were cut from whole metal by the machines, and so quickly, to produce hundreds of them within minutes, ready for use. She ran to one of the hoppers, to the surprise of the worker who manned the operation, and drew forth one of the spikes, holding it before her in the light, and smiling. The worker gestured for her to get out of the way, tilting his head towards the machine as if warning her about a dangerous creature.

The next stage of the factory floor was populated with a variety of unfamiliar machines that were all stamping and shearing, cutting and stripping. The cacophony of noises rose like the ear-bleeding murmur of several off-key choirs, dancing in rhythm but continually slipping about each other's measures. It was more bearable, more fluid, than the nail factory, but nonetheless taxing upon the ears.

A worker maneuvering a wheelbarrow of machine parts appeared before Lizzie, blocking her path. He stumbled for a moment, angling to get around her, then stood firm and straightened his back. For a moment, their eyes met, and Lizzie felt a strange wash of feelings. Acknowledging the presence of this man felt wrong, as if she were establishing the grounds for a confrontation. He clearly wanted nothing more than for her to get out of his way to give him easy passage to a particular area of the shop, but Lizzie somehow felt as if he were angry, thrown into ill humor by her dress, her frilled hat, her gloved hands and rustling skirt. She was as out of place on the factory floor as a sunflower would be growing from the middle of a board room desk. With her will paralyzed and her body frozen into place, it was left to the Marshal to step forward and gently guide her onward by pushing her shoulders.

As they approached the furnaces, the air grew hotter, smokier, and more rank with the vapors of metal. Blasts of heat made their breath more labored, pressured the surface of their faces, reddening their cheeks, warming the floor, indeed the entire earth, beneath their feet. Liquid metal, spitting off embers in sprayed arcs, poured down chutes, directly towards large moulds, there to be cast into various shapes. Men stripped to their waists, dirt-crusted and dripping streams of perspiration, channeled the metal with long poles that they deftly stroked with all the vigor of a gondolier moving his precious cargo through a canal.

Other men raced to and from the large banks of fiery machines, pushing before them their barrows that glowed with the white-hot metal, itself comprised of ill-formed bricks and logs with crude edges, of unpounded spongy fire masses that belched embers as they sped. One wheelbarrow full of coal, navigated by a scurrying worker, nearly ploughed into Lizzie; she just managed to step aside, her hand flying to her open mouth, her shoes tripping on her long skirts.

"The Devil!" the man cried out. Was his frantic gaze, his rapid pace, merely to work the iron, to get it from the furnace while it was still burning hell-fire and malleable enough for hammering? Or was his sense of panic more acute because his foreman had been murdered and he was not allowed to stop production? These men, who had labored under the supervision of Latham, knew he was dead, and that his body was lying mutilated by an iron bullet, perhaps of their own manufacture, in a meeting room above. Yet, here they were, still working, still driving the wheels of industry. What manner of place would not even allow one of them an afternoon of contemplation, or even of grief for the tragic loss of one of their fallen men? What irony would put them right back into the rolling wheels of producing wealth for the very man who may have murdered their boss, their fellow worker, their friend?

She turned to the Marshal and gestured that she needed to talk to him, but he insistently pointed onwards, driving her towards an area past the furnaces. Beyond the full blast of heat was an array of workers settled at their anvils, lifting their proud hammers aloft and driving them down heavily upon the burning products of the casting floor. Some had helmets and goggles, some braved it alone with bare sunburnt faces. Their random clanks and hammer strokes all played against each other in a symphony of metal clashing against metal.

Lizzie absorbed all the sights and sounds about her with a wide-eyed naiveté, as if she were experiencing the birth of her own awareness of the world. Here was the origin of so many of the things she took for granted. The anvils, kettles, skillets, and nails were being born in a painful agony of cutting, shearing and pounding. Bins of pig iron lay inert, waiting to be re-melted and transformed into casket hoops and fencing. Common sense had always told her that the manufactured items about her, whether they were at home in her kitchen on Second Street, or in some public place like Dobbs' Apothecary, were made in some factory—she was always mindful of this; however, the industrious labor before her was also colorful and adventurous. The flowing metal; the searing heat; the seemingly random, but highly organized flow of men and workers and machines; the ingenuity that was deeply invested in every moving part; the centuries of labor and skill and accumulated knowledge on how to work the metal, on how to transform its state to liquid, on using heat to change its nature and qualities, working its shape and stamping upon it the forms of the things we need in the world, all this activity and knowledge and hard physical labor, all whirled in a vortex of mind-numbing, tremendous energy about her.

Homer, too, gazed about him like a child in a confectionery shop, his mind awash in lightning-quick observations of the gear cranks, the fly-wheels, the steam hammer fittings, the flying belts, catwalks, ladders, and furnace designs. He had never seen such an industry of labor and technology working together on such large a scale, and was embarrassed to admit that he had lived in relative ease in the same city where such labor was being driven, yet had never even glimpsed any of these scenes before. These men were not a group of comfortable middle-class dabblers in scientific observations and experimentation, nor were they students trying to impress young women with Bunsen burners and chemical reactions inside test tubes; they were brawny and lusty men who savagely swung the hammers, pumped the bellows and paddled the burning metal with precision and skill honed to the level of art. Here was the end path of science, the practical application of its principles, the user of its chemistries and physical laws of nature to effect the production of goods. In his library books, in the privacy of his own studies, he had known such worlds existed, but to stand in the midst of it while it danced about him, his mind and imagination turning with the fly-wheels, was a most extraordinary experience. For a moment, in the center of the blasting room floor, he was spell-bound. He gently extended his arms and closed his eyes, feeling the vast power and industrious magic happen about him.

"Move on," the Marshal shouted over the din. To the policeman, the scene about him was about as aggravating as one could experience during the course of a working day. And yet there was a sense of comfort in witnessing the precise regularity with which the workers turned the wheels and kept the mills rolling. If only the men who drilled under his command would be so machine-like, what benefit they could be to the city. It was very well to patrol the streets for lawbreakers, investigate murders, track down criminals, and hobnob with politicians; but, in essence, the ultimate mission of the Fall River police was to maintain a lawful balance, to ensure that the wheels turned, the mills rolled, the assembly lines produced, and that the daily labor did not stumble. The Marshal glanced at Brayton and Twillie, who walked across this floor as if it were a front lawn and they were about to chastise the gardener for not trimming the hedges properly. Their only concerns seemed to be whether these half-clothed Vulcanists about them were focused enough on their work. Did they even consider what equilibrium was being held in check, what forces of anarchy were being contained in their Pandora's Box, and how petty their profit margins seemed in the face of such chaos? All life, mused the Marshal, was a constant tight rope walk between the towers of Order and Disorder, and money had as much to do with it as a carrot dangling before the mule had to do with the purpose of the cart ride.

They passed down a long corridor, echoing with the steam hammers and anvil strikes, then came to a larger cavernous area. There hordes of finished product, small parts and larger complete machines, lay about in rows and columns. To Lizzie's untrained eye, these were packed shipments, ready to be rolled off to train cars that were visible through a tremendous opening in the wall. Beyond the freights, she could see the tracks that curved in towards the glistening water of the Taunton River. The schooners were at dock, the water was glistening, and the vast assemblage of iron product, now having reached the end of the production line, huddled like uncertain immigrants about to embark on a perilous journey to some unnamed continent.

"Where's the Howards?" Mr. Brayton snapped at a thin dock foreman who stood with an inventory book. The foreman waved towards a far wall where a small glowing furnace flared and fizzled, angrily eating the coke and ore within. Before it sat a small child, barely six years old, on an upturned barrel, his body clad in overalls, a cloth cap atop his begrimed face, and his coal-stained hands holding a shaft of iron which he turned about, examining it like it were a creature of strange fascination. He lifted his face warily towards the odd assembly of policemen, mill management, and youths who approached him, expressing no small agitation of mind.

"Erasmus," said Mr. Brayton abruptly. The boy snapped to his feet, tossing aside the iron shaft which clanked against the ground, sending an uneven echo through the cavern of the room. "Where is your father?"

The boy's eyes darted to and fro, as if trying to calculate the dangers inherent in his potential answers. The Board Chairman asked his question again with a harsher bite, bringing the boy, it seemed, almost to the verge of tears.

"Erasmus?" Lizzie asked, glancing at Mr. Brayton, who nodded. "Erasmus," she repeated, kneeling down so her face came level with the boy. "You work this furnace? What do you do here?"

His lower lip trembled, then withdrew, as if he were attempting to stifle his own words. Then he muttered, so faint that Lizzie had to tilt her ear inwards to hear, "We get rid of the slag." Then after a pause, he added, "And the broken bits."

"You melt the slag?" Lizzie asked, and he nodded his trembling head. "Where is your father now? Did he go home? Why didn't you go with him?"

"Not allowed," he said, darting his eyes frantically at Mr. Brayton. "I'm a bad boy if I go."

Lizzie walked closer to the furnace and peered into the fire tongues that danced in the heat blasts. Picking up an iron stoke, she shifted it around inside the belly of the machine, turning about chunks of coal and ore, causing a run-off down into a crucible where the molten metal bubbled and burned. Evidently, quite a bit of slag had been melted down in the past few hours. She tossed the stoker aside, and backed off, brushing down her skirts, assuring herself that no fiery ember had nested inside her clothing.

"This child is in much danger," she said directly to Mr. Brayton. "He should not be manning this station, or at least he should be clothed for protective measures."

"It is very safe," said Mr. Twillie mechanically, as if repeating a speech that he had made on several occasions. "Do not fear that he will burn or be injured by the furnace. If it happens, it is because of his own negligence."

Lizzie felt her own breath cease, and she looked immediately towards the City Marshal. His eyes were dimmed, his lids pressed half-closed, his stern face telling her that her argument was best left for another time, another forum. She slapped her hands together and said loudly over the grinding roar of the factory: "I believe I have solved the murder!"

Her audience all stirred, glancing at each other, their faces flushing with expectation. "At least the mechanics of it," she added. "But now I have one last detail to fill in, which, with a little bit of luck, will tell me the identity of the individuals involved."

"Involved?" the Marshal asked, surprised. "Mr. Latham and Mr. Rogers were the individuals involved."

"Not quite," Lizzie said. She lowered a hand towards the mouth of the furnace. "I need to see the Howard boy's mother. She is the key to this entire mystery."

"Mrs. Howard?" Brayton bellowed. "Are you serious? What has she..."

"Yes," Lizzie said, proudly. "I am quite serious. I believe a few questions posed and a careful consideration of the answers will reveal to us the length and breadth of it all, including who pulled the trigger that launched the bullet that ended Mr. Latham's life."

"How would she know that?" the Marshal asked. "It was her husband who was present at the scene of the crime. Do you suspect that he confessed the truth to his wife?"

"I believe," Lizzie replied, "that Mrs. Howard knows more than we think, but understands little. Now, Officer Beck, if you would please take charge of this young boy and entertain him for an afternoon. Buy him some ice cream at Dobbs' Apothecary, get him a proper outfit of clothing, a scrub bath at the police station, and then return him to his home. Charge all expenses to my father at Borden and Almy's on South Main. After his proper grooming, I shall induct him into the Lizzie Andrew Borden Trust Fund for Destitute Children. My charity shall provide what his parents have withheld."

The young boy looked up at her, his eyes widening, his cheeks trembling. Then he lifted a blackened hand and poked out an index finger, his other fingers curling against his palm. With his mouth he made the sound of a small explosion.

"Pop," he said.

"We shall see," Lizzie said, her smile vanishing.

THE MOUSETRAP

Two separate buggies transported the company up the steep slope away from the mill, turning onto Columbia Street to where homes grew more clustered, huddled together as tents would be placed in a strike camp, fraternizing against the oncoming winter cold. The buildings rose upwards, some floors seemingly accessible only by way of unsteady wooden stairs that snaked up against the windows. The streets were eerily empty, in sharp contrast to the crowded Second Street where Lizzie lived with her family. The men of this neighborhood were all absent, away at their machines in the various mills, as were perhaps the women and children, too. Whoever remained here enjoying the privacy of their homes between the factory bells was no doubt busy with washing, ironing, cooking food, dusting, scouring, chopping wood, chipping ice, tending to small children (only the tiniest were exempt from the mill work), and otherwise engaged in activities that their spouses could not perform when they returned from the prolonged work day, exhausted and half-dead.

They alighted on the street before a house that rose upwards several stories. The wail of a mourning dove cooed over the backyard fence; Lizzie caught a glimpse of the wings as the creature ascended beyond the neighbor's yard. It was as if some part of her own spirit had flapped outwards and away, the unbounded part of her beating heart that dreaded witnessing under what conditions the Howards actually lived.

As they ascended the front porch towards the main door, a haggard face appeared in the second-story window, a round but fleshy and begrimed face. A bolt of recognition crossed Lizzie's mind: "Mr. Howard!" The face twisted into a state of panic, the eyes bulging and the mouth widening into a silent scream, and then withdrew so quickly that they all blinked as if doubting what they had seen. "That was Mr. Howard," Lizzie repeated. "But..." she said, closing her eyes and attempting to see in her mind's eye what had been wrong with the face. Perhaps it was that he had been wearing spectacles? Or that he had shaved his beard stubble?

"He didn't have his mustache," the Marshal said. "By Jupiter's Scepter, he went right home and shaved off his mustache. Now, does that strike you as a perfectly innocent thing to do after being the main witness at a murder?"

The Marshal banged upon the front door. After a brief but hushed argument from within the building, one that was barely loud enough to distinguish any words, or to determine even how many people were disputing, a thin and humorless woman opened both the door and the screen. She had on a plain gingham dress with a dirty apron, upon which she wrung her hands; and her eyes were reddened with distraught tears. "You are here to arrest my husband?" she asked, immediately spying the Marshal's brass buttons and authoritarian mustache. "He will cooperate, I dare say he will."

"We interrogated him at the mill," Lizzie said. "Has he explained to you the situation that we face?"

"He is not a murderer," she said, her voice disintegrating, her fingers rushing to her cheeks. Upon the buckling of her knees and the start of her downward spiral, the Marshal stepped forward, cradling her as her posture disintegrated.

"We shall be destitute," she was muttering. "All is lost!"

"Get her off the street," the Marshal said, and the officers, with the help of Homer, carried her into the front hallway and up the staircase to the dank kitchen on the second floor.

"The bed," Lizzie commanded, and they followed the rapid movement of her eyes towards a door that led deeper into the apartment. Lizzie noted, with dark forebodings, the faded rose wallpaper, the splintered furniture, the coarse and matted rugs, and the variety of insects that raced down the hallway on scuttling legs. Here, in these impoverished and destitute quarters, lived the Puddler and his family. This was the abode of a man who scooped the slag and poured the molds needed to create the cheap trinkets destined to decorate the homes on the Hill; a man whose credibility and veracity she was threatening to destroy; a man who had never done her any wrong, and, indeed, seemed to be engaged in only one activity: the provision of security for his family through the hard work that a pampered middle-class girl like Lizzie could never comprehend, far less execute on her own. The reaction of Mrs. Howard to their arrival bespoke a misplaced guilt, of a good man trapped in untenable circumstances.

By the time they had laid Mrs. Howard out on the lumpy mattress in the bedroom, under a painting that appeared to be the single attempt at decoration—a lighthouse astride a seashore hill at twilight—Lizzie had regretted her approach. What comfort could she afford this innocent woman now that she was here to implicate her husband in a savage murder?

"Mrs. Howard," Lizzie said, tapping the back of the woman's hand. Her eyelids fluttered and opened, focusing on Lizzie's slight smile and large soft eyes. "We do not wish your family any ill will, but we need to discover the truth about the affair at the mill."

"He is not my husband," the woman said, and Lizzie noticed that Mrs. Howard's eyes were not resting on her, but on something over her shoulder.

"What?" the Marshal shouted, and the two police officers joined in his outburst. All was fury and flailing arms, while the assembled lawmen scrambled for the dusty shadow that had unexpectedly darted across the room towards the kitchen door. The Marshal's arm hooked around the runner's neck, while Homer, darting downwards, grabbed his knees, forcing him to buckle and collapse. There was a brutal mêlée of men, of uniforms and hats, all clattering apart and together, and next an outcry from an unexpected and unfamiliar voice, then a groan and a gradual settling. All of the men present were splayed on the floor, breathing heavily, seemingly secure in their capture of the now-suc-cumbed individual. Lizzie was puzzled to see that the subject of attack was Mr. Howard, the Pig Puddler; only at this moment, he was snorting hotly over a bushy mustache that somehow had managed to adhere itself back to his bristly face.

"Can't a man leave his own home!" he was barking. "I won't stand still for another interrogation; you have all you need to know!"

"Except for who you really are," Lizzie said. Noting that the man was pinioned by the assembled lawmen, including Homer, who was still clasping him tightly by the shins, she knelt down, rustling her skirts, and picked with nervous fingers at the man's facial hair. For a fleeting moment, the man struggled with his nose, twisting it sideways as if attempting to prevent Lizzie's actions; then, realizing that he had no physical way to halt her, he sighed deeply, his two eyes coming together in the center of his face as Lizzie peeled away the mustache, revealing a rudely shaven upper lip.

"God's wounds!" the Marshal cried. "What is the meaning of this?"

"I can tell you the meaning," Lizzie said, holding up the strip of hair as if it were a trophy. "But I think we should allow him to speak, should we not? You will not be of any more trouble to us?" she asked politely.

"No," the man said, his limbs deflating, his rigidity vanishing. "I will not struggle, let me go."

With some reluctance, the men released their prisoner. Realizing that he was being afforded his freedom, the man shook his limbs to test their agility, and then, along with several lawmen, scrambled to his feet. He stood before them, wiping the dirt from his vest, smoothing over the creases in his pants. "I will no longer resist in any sense of the word."

The Marshal looked at the man and froze, his body stiffened into an awkward pose of disbelief. "Begging your pardon, Colonel Anthony," he said, his voice crackling with uncertainty. "I may need to arrest you in a moment, but feel free to provide an explanation for this behavior."

"Thank you, Mr. Marshal," spoke Colonel Richard Ulysses Anthony, thrusting his chest forward in its denim worker's shirt, his hands outward in a gesture of good faith and show of non-violence, and his eyes perched stonily upon Lizzie. "I require an equally compelling explanation from Miss Borden."

Lizzie was about to respond when a rustling at the kitchen door turned all heads towards another man, previously unseen, walking slowly across the creaking planks.

At first, the figure seemed a replica of the Colonel, dressed in his worker's threads but sporting the bushy mustache. A closer look at the pock-marked face, the crinkles around the eyelids, and the grizzled chin, collectively confessed the identity of Thomas Howard, Pig-Iron Puddler. He stood stock still and apart, blinking at the tableaux before him. "So," he said in a whisper, "is it over?"

"Evidently," the Colonel responded, his hands patting his sides. "And I don't see any need to put your good wife through any more of this torment."

Howard nodded, took a glance at his trembling wife, whose face was already radiating a profound sense of despair, and then, with grappling fingers, reached up to his bushy facial hair. With a deft twist of both his hands, Howard pulled the mustache from his lip. Without the hair, he looked no closer to the Colonel in aspect or general flesh tone, but Lizzie could now see how the addition of the mustache on both men could deceive the executive secretary or a startled accountant whose awareness of a passing stranger's facial hair would be secondary to the event of Mr. Latham's murder.

Mrs. Howard, stirring from her troubled swoon, gazed at her husband's bare lip, her mouth shutting tight, her eyes widening. "Thomas," she said, in a voice surprisingly calm. "You look ten years younger, I dare say."

MELTING POINT

The two men, the Mill Agent and the Pig Puddler, sat behind the kitchen table facing the company, their faces as contrasted as night and day. Mr. Howard's cheeks were drawn with sorrow and long labor, while Colonel Anthony's smile was crookedly smug and confident. Before them lay the two bushy mustaches they had pulled from their lips, displayed as if they constituted evidence being offered in a courtroom trial.

"I find it amusing," Lizzie chuckled, absorbing the scene, "that they can only resemble each other with the fake whiskers. It shows how the human mind does filter out what it chooses not to see."

"It was damned hot during the castings," Mr. Howard complained. "I'm glad to be done with it."

"You did the correct thing," she replied. "How you must have suffered these past three months, knowing that your life has been compromised for the benefit of this murderer."

"Murderer?" said the startled Marshal, his hands grabbing at his belt. "Do you mean to suggest the Colonel?"

"There is no need for me to be evasive," the Colonel said. If he were haunted by any guilt, his countenance and tone of voice did not betray it. "I did kill Latham with my own hands, and I shall sign a confession to that effect. I only ask that you send for Doctor Ames immediately, for he is the only person who can guide my tortured mind back to a position of equilibrium. Until then, anything I pronounce is under the provenance of a deranged manner of thinking. Isn't that right, Mr. Brayton?"

The Chairman, slumped in a corner upon a three-legged stool, held his face in his hands, making slight billowing noises. His lawyer, Twillie, standing by his side, his face thin and expressionless, with one hand upon his employer's shoulder, appeared to be jolted by the Colonel's inquiry. "There is little I can offer you, Colonel," the lawyer said, "except to advise that you have already stepped beyond the boundaries of my purview. I can offer no more than minimal advice on how to proceed from here."

"The Iron Works shall be dust," Mr. Brayton whispered through his fingers. "Dust in the vapor of time."

"More of that anon," Lizzie announced. "What we need to do now is untangle the knotted evidence and reveal this plot for what it is. For, although I am confident of the mechanics of the crime, it is only the Colonel who can explain to us the motivations that drove the affair. And

I suspect that it will be harder to extract that confession of motive than it was to obtain the confession of having committed the deed itself."

"Hang it all, you think I care a fig for why?" the Marshal said. "If he will sign a statement to the effect that the gun smoked in his hand, I'll stop asking for the why."

"Yes," Lizzie consented. "That would be sufficient, but we can at least piece together a rather simple explanation from a complicated set of evidence. For future plots and murders may depend upon our work here today. If Mr. Brayton is correct about the conspiracy within the mill, then this murder may be symptomatic of a wave of violence that may engulf the industry. And in that context, the motivation behind this is of great interest to us."

"Granted," the Marshal added, humbled. "Far be it from me to discourage the uncovering of a criminal society. Proceed."

Lizzie glanced at Homer, as if trying to draw inspiration from her silent friend. He stood under his bowler by the bedroom door, one elbow drawn up to the wall, one leg casually crossed over the other. However, when Homer saw Lizzie's face with its so-familiar expression of a dam about to burst and thereby reveal the secrets of its contained water, he stood to attention, adjusted his hat and placed his hands at his sides. "Edison," he repeated. "It started with Mr. Edison."

"Yes," Lizzie said. "And the idea that a signal can flow in multiple directions at once. Pure information, unencumbered by what that signal actually means. A telegrapher sends off the message, 'Come quick, I need you!' in a series of electrical dots and dashes. To the metal wire on which the signal moves, that message is merely a change in current, meaningless to the untrained machinist. What is needed at the other side is a human mind to place those dots and dashes back into a set of symbols that have actual meaning—such being the nature of words."

"You are a born Electromechanician," Homer complimented her. "Edison could not have explained it better."

"And for every transmitter," Lizzie said proudly, "there must be a receiver. Observe Mr. Howard and Colonel Anthony who we see before us. Both were Pig Puddlers, one in the management office, the other in the furnace room melting and casting the pig iron. The highest office and the lowest dungeon. And a flow of information between them. 'Tell Latham to make haste to the Stone Bridge! No dilly-dallying!' Why was this message sent? And what exactly is the Stone Bridge? These questions I asked myself.

"I do not think it wrong to assume that Mr. Latham never pulled that trigger. But a bullet was fired! Was it Rogers himself? How did he get the gun? It is very simple: the gun seen in Mr. Latham's hand was not the gun that had been fired at all. And the gun found smoking in Mr. Rogers' hand is not the same gun that was in Mr. Latham's hand. There were two guns in that room, and the one that fired into Mr. Latham's forehead was in the hands of Colonel Anthony."

"I confessed," the Colonel said hotly. "Is that not enough?"

"No," Lizzie said. "I want to demonstrate how you did it, to dispel any notion that it was a miraculous piece of magic. There was nothing magical about it, it was mere mundane luck, dreamed up in the flash of a moment, executed with little thought, and then covered up with some simple deception. Once I explain the mechanics of it, you will seem more of a lackluster mind, than appear a criminal genius."

"I did not aspire to criminal genius," the Colonel said. "I simply acted, and then I ran. Yes, like a rank coward. But now, I wish to face my fears, look Madness and Death in the eye, and so laugh at their dark mysteries."

"Your fears," Lizzie echoed. "Like the fear of metal, the irrational terror brought about by the very substance that creates your wealth? Perhaps the metal is just a substitute for a deeper fear, that of the workers themselves who fire and cast the metal for you into products that you can sell. The metal represents, at least in your mind, the accumulated hatred and violence building in their hearts as they labor day and night to grow your fortune. You are more afraid of them than Death itself, and all that fear was poured into the casting mold of your imagination. So you decided to conquer your fears by taking on the guise of a puddler and working the metal yourself. I have seen this before, men hurtling themselves directly at the very situation or person who troubles them most."

"I thought you were in Pompeii," said Mr. Brayton to the Colonel, his eyes darkening, "looking at dead people to remind yourself of the ephemeral nature of life. That is what you said."

"That is what my doctor suggested," the Colonel said defensively. "But do not fault Ames; he is innocent in this affair. He counseled me, and I saw a way of tending to two problems at once, my own mental breakdown, and the rumors of a secret society of syndicalism within the mill. I have previously built up a rapport with Mr. Howard, being that I studied well in the history of the bog iron industry, and Mr. Howard had much to contribute to the subject. I met with him secretly, and conversed often about the furnaces of New Jersey, from the days before the anthracite flowed out of Pennsylvania and the face of modern iron production changed forever. Remember, Thomas, the many hours we sat with our corn cobs before the fire and wove endless tales of pulling the iron from the bogs, of pouring the shell flux, or of crucibles and boshes, of charging the furnace, of rolling and slitting the sheets? How we envied our ancestors who pounded the hammers on the anvils to produce the perfect nails for wardrobes and cabinets and chairs. How free they were, producing with their own hands, callusing their palms and fingers to produce the goods that they would then sell directly to the customer in his humble home. Those early men of metal forged a revolution, Thomas, building an iron industry to flout the British with all their manufacturing. We were no longer a nation of cash crops, tobacco and cotton; we were now makers of iron! And steel! Yes, Thomas, we talked of steel, and the new processes and blends that would help this nation grow to gigantic proportions. How we dreamed of our metal plated against the hulls of giant ships crossing the Atlantic, of metal capable of defying the icebergs of the frozen north, of buildings in the midst of our cities rising to fifty stories tall, of hardened war machines that would fright the souls of fearful adversaries and drive our conquests home! Do you remember, Thomas? Say you do, and I shall be vindicated."

The other man at the table eyed him furtively, his lips tightening, then said, "If I had known what you are capable of, I would have found a place to stuff that corn cob pipe."

"Now, Thomas," the Colonel said meekly. "That is unkind."

"Nonetheless," Lizzie continued, "a devil's pact was made between the two, and instead of fleeing to the Mediterranean, the Colonel went straight to this home. Here, he confided in Thomas his plans to work the metal. Tell me, Mrs. Howard, was this the time, three months ago, when your husband decided to grow his mustache?"

The woman stirred, at first hardly aware she was being addressed, then flashing recognition of Lizzie's question. "It came suddenly, almost overnight. I did not question, for I am a simple woman, and know little about men's ways."

"It did not strike you odd that such a bushy mustache can grow overnight?"

"He gave a muddled explanation at the time," the wife observed. "With hindsight, it does not make much sense. Oh, what a fool I have been!" She lowered her face into her weakened hands.

"Do not draw out her humiliation," Mr. Howard implored. "I did explain to her, later in the month, that to carry out this deception with exactitude, the Colonel would need to take more liberties in my own home, eating dinner in my place, tutoring my young son his letters, even..." He paused for a moment, forcing his eyes upwards to daringly fall on his wife's crumpled posture. "...sleeping in our bed."

"My God," the Marshal whispered. "What perfidy is this man not capable of?"

"Do not judge me!" Colonel Richard Anthony shouted. "For I had a higher purpose in mind."

"Higher?" Mrs. Howard said, raising her face with a renewed sense of dignity born from outrage. "You call that a higher purpose?"

"Exactly," said the Colonel. "Once I was within the mill, laboring at the furnace with the pig iron, I began to gain more information about the society of which we have talked about only in whispers. It may have been a stray voice from the casting floor, or a rumor carried by train rail into the charcoal house, or a fragment of truth brought to me by a child stoker. But I incrementally came to gather my evidence against Latham and the evil forces that pulled his puppet strings. After a time, I knew the extent of his plans, the scope of the conspiracy, and I knew I had to act."

"And you forged a deal with Rogers," Lizzie said hastily, "for him to take the blame for the murder, did you not?"

"As I have already said," the Colonel bemoaned, "it was not well thought out. It happened all in a matter of moments. I brought the Colt to the office the night before, smuggling it past the guards, explaining it as some iron to be melted in the blast. I then brought it to the office, where I spent a sleepless night huddled behind my own curtains, strangely believing that the events of the past several months had been nothing but a dark dream. I wanted to rest in the halls of Morpheus, only to awaken upon the dawn seeing my tweed suit upon me, and my morning reports on my desk; it seemed as though it was June, and none of this nightmare had even occurred.

"Yet, I was awakened by Rogers entering the office. It was a strange moment, for I assumed he thought me to be Howard the Puddler, come with a gun to assassinate him in the name of the society. He would have raised the alarm from the start and forced me to abandon my plans, but I ripped off the mustache. By so doing, I assured him that all was correct with the world, and that he was in no danger of falling prey to any assassin's plot. It took a long time, but I slowly convinced him that the death of Latham was necessary, that it would send a message to all anarchist assassins everywhere their syndicalism would not be tolerated in our society. I described a plot in which Latham would be shot in this office and it would be believed that Rogers was the culprit, but that he acted in self-defense. To alleviate his fear of being imprisoned for the rest of his life, I cited several popular cases of the past where a man accused of murder would be set free after a dramatic and very public trial, found not guilty of all charges although common sense and even some hard evidence spoke otherwise."

"Nonsense," Lizzie snorted. "I know of no such cases. You are talking fantasy."

"You have not heard of the Reverend Avery," the Colonel said hotly. "Look into your own backyard history, Miss Borden. In 1832, a Methodist minister of Bristol strangled a poor mill girl in Tiverton. He had secretly made her pregnant, and she was in turn blackmailing him. One night he met her under a hay pole at a Durfee farm and tied a rope around her neck, killed her in cold blood. He was subjected to three trials, Miss Borden. Not one, but three, in Bristol, Tiverton, and by the elders of his own church. And in all three cases, despite the majority of evidence against him, he was set free."

"The Methodist minister," the Marshal echoed. "Rogers told us that to our face. He was reaching out with the answer and we were too blind to see it!"

"I have heard of the Reverend Avery," Lizzie said. "But he spent the rest of his life in shameful ignominy, living under assumed names and witnessing his own effigy burned in the streets. Why would Rogers agree to such a future?"

"We were in the midst of discussing that possibility, how we could effect the crime in such a manner as to instead establish him as a virtuous hero in the eyes of management. He would be the man who stood up to the society and cut it down at its root."

"You mean," the Marshal said bitterly, "you aimed to kill a man in cold blood and then let one of your inferiors take the blame."

"Latham would be a sacrifice," the Colonel said breathlessly. "One death would put an end to the society and avoid decades of warfare between labor and management. I asked Rogers to call Latham to the office, where we could shoot him at point blank range within the hearing of a dozen office workers. There would be no doubt that Rogers shot Latham in self-defense."

"But you did not expect," Lizzie said solemnly, "the Stone Bridge."

"Yes, the Stone Bridge. There was the crack in the scheme, the thought that Rogers was a member of the society himself. How agitated he must have been in that office, talking to a crazy man with a gun, knowing the plan was that he was to be arrested for murder on the flimsy promise that I would find lawyers to free him from prison." He cast an unctuous glance at Mr. Twillie, who was still nursing his pale employer.

"Let it be read into the record," Mr. Twillie insisted, "that I knew none of this. I honestly thought the Colonel to be staring into some dead volcano somewhere."

"But what is the Stone Bridge?" the Marshal said, pulling at his cheeks. "What message did that convey to the furnace room?"

"We may never know the meaning of the Stone Bridge," Lizzie offered. "Rogers will never tell, and Latham is dead. And the others that are part of this conspiracy will never cough up their knowledge, even under pain of torture."

"Rogers part of the conspiracy?" Mr. Brayton said, his face rising into sudden renewed interest in the proceedings. "Why, all the confidences I have made in that man! All the business secrets and development plans! They were being fed directly to the secret society?" He went deathly silent, and began to tremble as if an eruption of his intestines was imminent.

"No doubt," Lizzie speculated. "We evidently have here a group of scoundrels of no moral suasion. Confidences are betrayed as easily as children play games in the gutter. Such is the flow of intelligence through a network of spies and assassins. There is no honor amongst thieves."

"Rogers was part of the conspiracy," the Colonel conceded. "But I did not know it at the time; how foolish I had been! I had not heard of the Stone Bridge, nor the secret message within the expression 'dilly-dally.' Latham came armed, and the real Thomas Howard came with him, but stayed outside. I was sequestered behind my curtains, and watching this ugly scene unfold before me. Rogers engaged Latham in some sort of debate, shouting about production and lengthened hours; and Latham, knowing this all to be some sort of ruse, replied in kind and shouted about workers' rights and increased wages. In the midst of this charade, Rogers must have made some sort of gesture to indicate to Latham that the danger implicit in his Stone Bridge message was behind the curtains, at which point Latham pulled forth his gun and pointed it in my direction. To the witnesses looking through the door, they must have believed the gun to be pointed at Rogers, due to the angle at which they were watching. At this point, I had no choice but to fire. It was an act of self-defense, one can argue. If I had not fired, it would be me lying dead in the mortuary, not Latham."

"You fired at a very lucky moment," Lizzie explained. "When Latham pulled his pistol, the eyewitnesses peering in from the front office had started to run, fearful that they would be caught in a spray of bullets. With those witnesses, no one would guess that it was not Latham's gun that had fired."

"Excepting myself," Mr. Howard lamented. "I did not even believe that the Colonel could be in that room. I truly believed that it was Latham who fired. My hatred for Rogers was such that I held contempt for those investigating, attempting to prove otherwise, or so it seemed from my vantage. Now that I see the Colonel's plot so clearly, and my role in the matter, I humbly beg your pardon and throw myself at your mercy."

"No grudges there," the Marshal nodded. "But how do we know this to be true? We still have no witnesses but Rogers and the Colonel, and their words are suspect."

"Without a doubt, a forensics report from the coroner," Lizzie offered, "will reveal that there was no gunpowder burns or powder upon the victim, something that would have been quite evident if he had been shot at such close quarters. Add to this that the angle of the bullet from the bridge of the nose to an area right behind the left ear showed that it had not been fired at him from directly in front. Evidently, Latham was shot from the area by the bay window."

The Marshal huffed and paced about, grabbing at his mustache and muttering. Then he raised a gloved finger as if to make a point, but sighed and said, "So how did the Colonel, disguised as the Pig Puddler, get out of the room after firing the gun? And how did the gun get into Rogers' hand? And by Saturn's rings, what happened to the gun that Latham was about to fire?"

Lizzie cast a glance at the Colonel whose strange smirk had returned. "Here he was clever," she said, "but still very simple. Taking advantage of the confused circumstances, and noting that there was not a soul in the outer office standing by the door, the Colonel came out from his gunman's perch, and slipped the smoking Colt into Rogers' hand, all according to plan, although I doubt that Rogers had much time to consider his alternatives. Then he reached down to Latham's body and snatched up the gun – whether it was a Colt or not is something that seems to be lost to posterity. It seemed fitting to the Colonel to leave only one gun at the scene, and that it'd best be one that had been discharged. Then he just stepped back behind the open door, hiding his presence, as the returning workers, including Thomas Howard, entered the room. At this point, there were two Pig Puddlers present, and in the confusion, no one really noticed. Except for Miss Borden. I recall her one bit of testimony that Mr. Howard seemed to flip from one side of the room to the other. She noted this phenomenon in the full-length mirror by the coat rack but dismissed it as an optical confusion. Yet she actually did see two Pig Puddlers, and remains the only witness who did so."

"So there were two gunmen," the Marshal said, "but only one bullet fired, and it was not from the gun in Latham's hand. So, what happened to Latham's gun after it was snatched by the Colonel?"

"I can guess that it happened as follows," Lizzie said proudly. "The Colonel slips from the room, bringing Latham's gun with him, proceeds down the administration steps, into the hallway and up towards the furnace room. There he tosses the weapon into the fiery chamber tended by Mr. Howard's young son, Erasmus, who by now must be quite confused over the true appearance of his own father, having spent several months being tossed back and forth between the real person and the subterfuge. By the time we have examined the furnace, all traces of the gun have been removed, the fire reducing its form to liquid, to be scooped from slag and drained into new moulds to provide domestic trinkets for Fall River households."

"You are all correct," the Colonel said. "That is exactly how it happened."

"Perhaps," Mr. Twillie said, raising a palm towards the Colonel, "we'd best keep our mouths shut from this moment on."

"The man who should be doing all the talking," the Marshal observed, "is Rogers. He can verify this story one way or another, if he tells the truth."

"I don't suspect he will be talking much," Lizzie observed, "for if he is truly a member of this anarchist society, then he will continue to protect its secrets. For example, you will be hard pressed to discover the true meaning of the Stone Bridge, or the hidden message inside the phrase 'dilly-dally.' Latham took that to his grave, and so shall Rogers or any other member of the society."

"Isn't it best," inquired the Marshal, "to take this man into custody on the strength of his confession, and to lock him away for his crime? Why should we chase after motive if the proof of his guilt is enough?"

"No doubt it is best," Lizzie answered. "Secret societies are difficult to detect, even more so to expose. And they will counteract our investigations with more violence. Yes, we shall heed the Marshal's advice; we must allow justice to balance what she can, and leave those political battles for another time."

As Lizzie finished with a flourish of her hands, there was a clattering on the stairs, and then the sound of heavy boots ascending. All eyes turned towards the kitchen doorway, where Officer Beck, his beard flecked with the white smear of vanilla, appeared. He was holding the hand of a small boy by his side whose entire mouth and nose were buried in a generous glob of ice cream on the top of a hearty sugar cone. Erasmus Howard had been transformed from the filthy waif of the furnace room into a bright, cheery, and well-groomed young lad, clad in checkered knickers, a clean pressed shirt on his torso hugged by suspenders, and his head bearing a flattened cloth cap. His skin was cleared, his hands a healthy flesh tone, but the biggest alteration to his previous incarnation was the broad smile that shined across his face on both sides of the ice cream cone.

"Pop!" he said, pointing towards the pocked-marked Pig Puddler at the table. The man, who since the arrest, had not smiled or cast any gentle eye upon any man, now gave forth a comfortable chuckle. He crossed the room, kneeling down to greet his son with a warm and intimate embrace.

"He has been cleaned and fed," Officer Beck stated, then glanced back upon the stair behind him, twisting his hands. "Yes, and there is one other matter. As I was procuring this iced delicacy for young Master Erasmus, a gentleman approached me and demanded audience with the Marshall immediately."

"What kind of man?" the Marshal asked. "What business does he have with me?"

"Not any particular kind of man," Officer Beck answered, staring with blinking eyes at the Colonel. "Sir, is that who I..."

"Don't be so agog, Officer," the Marshall said. "I'll explain later. Summon the man you speak of."

The Officer motioned down the stairs and a soft ascent was heard. The sound culminated in a lanky figure appearing at the doorway, his bushy beard thrust forward, his pince-nez balanced on his cautious nose, and a leather satchel clutched in his bony hands. "Doctor Ames," the Colonel whispered. "Dear Lord, you are my salvation."

"Not quite," the doctor beamed, making an odd hand gesture with two fingers before his chest. "Marshal, I would like to have ten seconds of privacy with the Colonel, if it pleases all and one."

"Ten seconds," the Marshal said. "You have petitioned your own time limit, proceed."

The Doctor crossed the room and stood beside the Colonel who stared at him with awkwardness. The physician then knelt down, and placed a cupped hand over the Colonel's ear. All the company could see his cheeks bellow with his lips and then he was silent, his hand removed, his form moving away from the Colonel towards the door. "Thank you, gentlemen," he said, then made a slight waggle of his fingers at Lizzie, who stood defiantly behind the seated Mrs. Howard. "And ladies, adieu!" And he was gone, departing with just a clattering down the stairs and a rusty creak of the front door of the house.

"What do you suppose that was about?" Lizzie asked, disquieted, then turned towards the Colonel. "Can you explain? What did he tell you?"

"Professional confidentiality," the Colonel retorted, gazing towards the begrimed window, pretending a profound disinterest. Somewhere in the far distance, a mill tower was tolling the hour, and Fall River was beginning to fall under a veil of dark northbound clouds.

The Last Cast

The young pair rode their buggy back to the apothecary on South Main Street, their intellects contented, a sense of justice having been served permeating their peaceful afternoon. The Girl Detective and the Boy Inventor strode into the nearly empty store, caught the eye of A.E. Dobbs, Proprietor, and demanded two more sarsaparillas to quench their late afternoon thirst.

"What did you hear about that trouble at the iron mill?" Dobbs asked, his hands behind the spigots. "Was it indeed a murder?"

"Truly," said Lizzie, proudly. "And I solved it."

The proprietor twisted his cheek and shook his head playfully. "I suppose I'll read about it in the papers, or get some stray gossip from customers, but I don't think I'll ever know the truth behind it all until I hear it directly from you, Lizzie Borden."

"*Il n'y a pas de quoi*," Lizzie said, taking her mug and turning towards their street-view table. When she blinked at Homer's startled expression, she explained, "I'm studying French privately, to prepare for my trip to the continent. Father keeps suggesting the Grand Tour." They sat together with their drinks.

"Europe would be quite illuminating," said Homer excitedly. "You can stop in at the Royal Academy in London. I hear that they are attempting to complete Babbage's designs for a computing machine that would carry out the processes of the human brain through electrical relays."

Lizzie looked distraught at his pronouncement. "Really, Homer, first the light of the human eye is captured by a machine, then the human voice is captured, now the human brain is being reduced to…a machine! Did not your trip to the Iron Works teach you anything about how technology dehumanizes people? If I go to London, I shall visit the National Gallery, and take a tour of nearby Windsor Castle. I shall witness art and architecture that is immortal."

Homer sipped at his drink, visibly dismayed by her comment. "I did notice the demands placed on the workers, as well as the unfair conditions and the political complexities that arise from such inequality of wealth and labor, but I also saw men who were putting their hearts into the work; I could see it."

"Perhaps," Lizzie conceded, "the truth is somewhere in between. We shall meditate upon this."

"In the meantime," Homer said, "I have a new chapter of your biography to compose. Yes, I shall record this case for posterity," he laughed heartily. "The Adventure of the Doubled Pig Puddler."

"One can think of a more sensible name than that," Lizzie suggested. "I'm afraid the affair didn't have the same sense of completion as my other cases, largely because we never discovered the true nature of what we may confidently call The Stone Bridge Society. It would have been a sweet moment indeed for me to have done at least that. For now, I feel as if I have solved the mechanics of the crime, not the motivation."

"What makes you so sure you solved even the mechanics?" said Homer, surprised. "You only think that the Colonel was the man who pulled the trigger."

"Why would you make such a statement? It's readily evident.

Besides, the man confessed, you were there, you had ears in your head at the time."

"True, but anyone could have said anything. No one knows for a fact that the Colonel was walking around with a Pig Puddler mustache in that office room. What do you base that on? That Elizabeth Borden saw a reflection in a mirror? And even if we do put a puddler in the room during the shooting, how do you know that it wasn't Mr. Howard behind the curtains, and Colonel Anthony in the outer office?"

Lizzie felt a wave of tension along her spine, reaching her neck and tightening her face. "Homer, you are beginning to frighten me. Don't you think that the Colonel's confession is authoritative enough?"

"Well, let's examine for a moment what he said. According to him, he was in the office explaining to Rogers that they have to kill Latham, not realizing that Rogers was really part of the conspiracy. So Rogers gave some sort of signal telling Latham to come with Mr. Howard and to bring along a handgun for self-defense."

"And where is the fault in that scenario?"

"Who was sitting next to the Colonel when he confessed?"

"Mr. Howard, the real Mr. Howard."

"Right, and what if it was Mr. Howard and the Colonel who were plotting to kill Latham, not the Colonel and Rogers? Or what if Latham himself was plotting with Rogers to kill the Colonel but they didn't expect the Colonel to have a gun as well. What if, Lizzie Andrew Borden?"

Lizzie took a deep sip of her sarsaparilla, swallowed, and closed her eyes to accompany a long sigh. "I am going to totally ignore," she confessed, "everything you just suggested. I consider it all to be irrelevant to the case and more typical of your skeptical approach to life."

"Fine," Homer said, and crossed his arms. "Have it your way. The Colonel killed Latham after being betrayed by Rogers. It's a good scenario, and one that suitably accounts for all the facts."

"Yes," Lizzie said.

"And besides, the Colonel confessed, and will go to jail of his own free will."

"Correct," Lizzie said.

"Then why," Homer quipped, "did Doctor Ames have on a false beard?"

Lizzie lowered her mug and stared hard at Homer. "A false beard? How do you know this?"

"Because the real Ames is a friend of my father's and comes quite often to the house. I've had the pleasure of witnessing the man up close dozens of times. And I can assure you that the man who came to the Howard house this afternoon was NOT Dr. Ames."

Lizzie blinked and then followed the curved path of a fly over her head. Turning towards Homer, she shut her lids, then fluttered them open as she responded, "I see little reason for you to lie to me, but given the fact that someone unnamed, no doubt a member of the Stone Bridge Society, has staged a hoax right under the very nose of the City Marshal as well as the Most Excellent Girl Detective of Fall River, would it behoove us to make light of this? Should we tell the Marshal? Would it make a difference even if the Colonel is acquitted on the grounds of self-defense? In sum, Homer Thesinger, does it matter a fig?"

Homer nodded briskly. "I don't suppose, but I did want to give you that observation."

"Yes, well, we can keep that observation under our hats for now. Besides, there's very little we can do about it." She drummed her fingertips nervously on the tablecloth. "Imagine, Homer. The case is still not solved. We don't know any more about what happened in that office during those few seconds than we did before the investigation. Should I be concerned about this? Will my reputation be tarnished? I had a perfect record of solving the crimes I've investigated, now I must live in shame that I am not perfect."

"Lizzie," Homer said. "In this particular case, we should just leave it well alone. There's politics and interactions here we can't possibly comprehend, and with which we should not be getting involved. There is a time and place for everything, and if this Stone Bridge Society does in fact exist, and if it is growing in strength and gaining a foothold in the mills, we shall hear about it again. And perhaps then we shall confront our Doctor Ames impersonator and rip his fictional beard from his face, exposing the conspiracy and bringing them all to justice. But now is not the time, I agree. We shall remain quiet and humble, in the light, but watching the shadows."

The bell atop the front door tinkled and a thin man in a gentlemen's coat entered, his eyes staring widely about as if he were attempting to test out his vision for the first time after a long blindness. A.E. Dobbs jumped to the service counter to see to the newcomer's needs, but the man held up a hand, forcefully, and sat down.

"I saw a terrible thing today," he said hauntingly, "and had a horrific vision."

"Would you like some sarsaparilla?" Dobbs enquired. When the man didn't respond, the proprietor shrank back to his seat. Lizzie called out across the table. "What was the terrible thing?"

"A man was killed today," the man said, his bearded face turning towards her. "In the mill. The Iron Works. "

"We have heard news to that effect," said Lizzie, solemnly. "What did you see?"

"I saw the body being removed," he continued. "The sight pierced me, and propelled me into a deep trance. I was spiraling over the city like a great hawk, and the human world was below me, in those dark mills along the river and the stream. I flew unencumbered by any ordinary restrictions, soaring over the heights, looking for a crag on which to perch. Yet I could not find anything but stacks and steam and brick and metal. There was no natural cliff, nor gorge, nor ravine, nor even a towering tree on which to perch. I circled and circled, longing to land, desperate to find in that valley of industry, some resting place that I could temporarily call my home before I migrated once again to the feeding grounds of the far north.

"Then, as I was bemoaning my plight, there was a mighty rush of wind, and a fire storm, and a great conflagration assaulted the city. The citizens ran to the streets, hoping to escape the inferno of their homes and places of business as they exploded in the hellish flames. But there was no escape. As they huddled against the river, attempting to save themselves from being burned alive, a terrible wind came in from the north and hurled the flames to the very lip of the river. Women died with their sons still clutched in their swaddling clothes; men of great wealth were consumed; children even, and animals also were all eaten up by the ravenous hunger displayed by the great storm.

"Then all was smoke and ruin, and not a living thing stirred. I alighted upon a singular stack still rising from the burnt rubble and rested my weary wings. There was calm once more, with all that belonged to man in ruins. All the human presence had been erased as if the entire race, with all its atrocities, its wars, and its art and science and culture had never even existed upon the planet. The forest was growing back; the mighty mills were sinking into the dust, ready to be cast forever into the timeless abyss of eternity.

"I could do nothing but weep, as only a hawk would weep when it sees no place called Home, but longs to be at rest. Yes, I will never again be the same."

The man's head sank to his breast and he heaved a tremendous sigh. Lizzie carefully stepped across the floorboards and touched a fingertip to his shoulder, causing him to shudder. "Forgive me, my young lady," he said, his eyes rising with an unexpected twinkle shrouded by watery tears. "I shall arrive on the other side of my melancholy, and anon be myself once more. Good day to you, gentle people. Good day." And he replaced his hat, adjusted his watch fob, and ironed out with flat fingers the creases in his jacket. After a final nod of his head that bespoke a reluctance to surrender to despair, he stepped out onto the street to the delicate tinkle of the apothecary bell.

"Don't tell me," Lizzie said, refusing to turn her countenance towards Homer.

"But I must," Homer said, no trace of pride or satisfaction in his voice. "Now you have met Doctor Ames."

"I gathered as much," she said, bemusedly. "I have solved the case, but I have not fathomed the mystery."

Then she turned, clapping her two gloved hands together. "Homer, I believe we must meet again next Tuesday morn for some more sarsaparilla and some most excellent banter about science and technology. Yes, I believe I would enjoy such a discourse. And I am most curious about the discoveries of Mr. Edison in New Jersey."

"I shall be delighted," Homer said, bowing slightly and replacing his bowler. The two paid their bill to the proprietor, and stepped out into the busy foot traffic of South Main Street. They then disappeared into the busy stream of traffic that flowed, as a river would into an ocean, into the endless parade of human life.

THE END

THE AGITATED ELOCUTIONIST

AUTUMN, 1875. FALL RIVER, MASSACHUSETTS.

THE MANTELETS

Throughout most of the summer of 1876, I had seen precious little of my favorite cousin, Miss Lizzie Borden of Second Street. My family held her in great esteem for her triumphant handling the previous summer of the Case of the Purloined Curio. That regrettable incident had involved the murder of my father by a charlatan spiritualist and a deranged mill owner. Lizzie, acting as a sleuth in our employ, had brought the murderers to justice, restoring not only my family's honor and inheritance, but creating her reputation as New England's most excellent consulting detective. Thereafter, we treated her like one of our own, despite how remote she was on the family tree.

In late September, while shopping down street, I had a chance meeting with her that not only reconnected us socially, but also served as prelude to a whole season of involvement in her most singular cases. While attending a slaughter sale at Hodges & Son's Ladies Apparel, I found Lizzie in the midst of choosing between a cotton fur-trimmed cape and a silk mantelet. She was overjoyed to see me and gave me a warm and welcoming embrace that was quite the remedy for my forlorn mood.

"Come, Cousin," she said happily, "Let's each buy the cotton one, both you and I together, and we shall resemble twins upon the street."

We had just purchased our capes and wrapped them about us to wear out of the shop, when I asked the proprietor for a neck clasp. As he displayed several varieties of the requested item, Lizzie coughed into her fist and hurried me out of the store and into the busy street. "Don't bother," she said, and reached into her cape pocket, withdrawing two silver collar clasps with embossed lilies.

"Lizzie," I said. "Have you been taking your Fancy again?"

She dismissed my chastisement and helped me fasten a clasp to my collar. "No need for alarm," she assured me. "My father pays a great deal of money on my accounts. It shall all even out in the end."

I was rather taken aback by her behavior. This was a quirk of hers that was well known by most merchants in Fall River, and about which there was an eerie conspiratorial silence. Lizzie Borden took her Fancy when she was in a particular mood, and her father made the appropriate adjustments with the tradesmen who had fallen victim. That much was recognized, but as long as the bills were paid in the end, there was a willingness to look the other way.

Despite this distressing incident of shoplifting, I enjoyed being once more in the company of my cousin. I do confess we made a picturesque pair, strolling along in brand new identical capes, clutching at each other like silly schoolgirls. I had never seen her so happy and talkative, boasting of her many accomplishments, and bragging incessantly about her successful cases. She claimed that her detective skills had evolved, now that she was systematically studying the criminal mind and its methods. She was even working toward a certification of some sort, sponsored by her contacts within the police department.

"Oh, Lizzie," I cautioned. "Don't let your face be printed all over the newspapers. Otherwise, how can you work undercover when you are so well known to the criminal world?"

"I have already taken that precaution," she assured me. "I work in secret, contacted only by referral. I requested that the City Marshal keep my involvement off the public record. I do not fight crime out of pride or for any worldly vanity such as fame; I do it to help my fellow man, to bring bad people to justice, and to give comfort and hope to those who have been wronged."

"Your life is an exciting one," I told her. "I spend my days making sure the twins don't soil themselves. And occasionally, I take Mother to Father's grave and watch her weep. Such a dreary life."

"That can be remedied," Lizzie said excitedly. "Join me on my new mystery. I was offered one this very morning."

"Your cases sound dangerous," I protested. "All this talk about a professor who tried to murder you with a bow and arrow, and a secret society of anarchists who shot a mill foreman. I can't be brought near to anything of that kind! I'm delicate and easily disturbed."

"Nonsense," she replied. "I can assure you that this case is fit for a novice. You can come along as my biographer, my Boswell so to speak. When I wish to pen the casebook of my career, I will need such a one as Sarah Borden, whose meticulous notes and sharp recollection will provide volumes of dramatic memories."

"I'll try my best," I told her honestly. "But I don't want to encounter any midget gunslingers. That affair sounded most unpleasant."

She gave a titter of a laugh. "That was the Adventure of the Minuscule Monk, and the gunslinger was mummified, most harmless. This new case involves a petty act of burglary, a mere trifle of an incident but not lacking, I trust, in a few thrills."

MRS. ARBUTHNOT'S PROBLEM

So it happened that I was invited back to 92 Second Street, that small, charming residence down under the Hill where Andrew Jackson Borden, the furniture merchant, maintained his household. Here Lizzie lived with her father and her older sister Emma, a dour woman who didn't take to my charms very well; and Abby, the stepmother, a pleasant enough soul who seemed to always be on her feet doing housework, from sun up till down, an accomplishment that Lizzie did not emulate. While Abby was taking our capes in the front hallway, she spoke to her step-daughter in a tired voice: "You can have the parlor if you insist on doing that detective nonsense again."

"Yes, Mrs. Borden," replied Lizzie, coldly. She handed over her cape without even looking at her.

By ten o'clock we were seated in the parlor, ready to receive the client, when Lizzie made a most surprising statement: "The woman you are about to meet is worth about half-a-million dollars. She is the owner of the Star of Swansea, that glorious sapphire whose presence in this city has been publicized by the newspapers, a horrible mistake if you ask me. There is no better way to magnify its vulnerability to the criminal element. They might as well have printed the combination to her safe, as far as I am concerned."

"Is she hiring you to protect the gem?" I asked breathlessly.

"Quite the contrary. She is hiring me to find it. The Star was stolen from her house yesterday evening."

"Good Heavens!" I exclaimed. A knocking came at the front door, disrupting our chat. Then Mrs. Borden, wiping her hands on an apron, ushered into the room a proud, opulently dressed woman. "That one is Lizzie," she said before withdrawing. "You are now on your own."

We rose to greet the newcomer who was tall and distinguished, swathed in a magnificent daytime walking suit of dark umber-striped serge and a close-fitting brimless hat, decorated with a jet-black raven's wing rising as a cockade behind her. Her presence was strong and dominating, punctuated by a stern face that spoke of a hard life and accumulated wisdom.

"Mrs. Arbuthnot," Lizzie said, giving a slight bow and encouraging her guest to sit in the room's finest chair. The woman gazed at us with pinched eyes over a drooped nose, and then took her seat, almost reluctantly. As she adjusted her pince-nez, she digested the quality of the furniture and the wall decorations.

"This is the residence of Borden," the woman finally said in a husky voice. "I may have a settee that was manufactured by the man. Yes, I believe it is the one in my guest bedroom."

"I'm Andrew Borden's daughter," Lizzie said, without breaking her smile. "I must thank you for coming to me in your time of need."

"They told me you were good," said the woman. "Otherwise, I would not have ventured south of Bedford Street."

"I am honored by your confidence in me. I conversed with Officer Beck just two hours ago and I believe I already have the particulars in this case." Lizzie paused momentarily, but the woman did not so much as flutter an eyelash. "Nonetheless, I wish you would present the facts to me as if I were a blank slate."

"Who is this other one?" Mrs. Arbuthnot asked, nodding towards me.

"This is my cousin, Sarah Borden. You may speak freely to her as you would to me; you can trust her implicitly."

"Yes, well, that remains to be seen. Miss Borden, I am not a woman who cares for silly particulars, but here is my story. I am an elocutionist, perhaps one of the best in the country. I can restore any man's lost voice, correct an accent, prepare one for public speaking or performance, and train vocal cords for operas, lectures, sporting announcements, auctioneering, even Swiss mountain yodeling. I have certifications from top schools in Europe, having studied with some of the most recognizable names in the field of phonetics and vocal anatomy. Clients come from all over New England, entering through my front door as stuttering idiots, and emerging several weeks later capable of reciting any Shake-spearean soliloquy. I am so well talented in this field that my clientele has included a politician of such world-renown that I have been sworn to secrecy, otherwise I would parade his name before you. He was inca-pable of pronouncing the sound of the letter M when in the company of women. He is now cured and converses quite fluently with any existing phoneme no matter what the gender of his audience."

"I am convinced that you have considerable skill in your field," Lizzie said, waving a diffident hand. "I can tell by the quality of your clothing that your income must be considerable."

"Yes, I am a rich woman. I spend my money liberally—quite liberal-ly—going so far as to have procured the Star of Swansea, a magnificent sapphire, one of the most perfect of its kind in the known world. There-fore, it was with great horror that I woke up this morning to discover that it had been stolen!"

"Officer Beck tells me," inquired Lizzie, "that you know the iden-tity of the thief?"

"Yes, he is Arthur Tinge of Bedford Street, an unremarkable philol-ogist with an undistinguished degree from some shabby Rhode Island college. I had an un-spirited elocution lesson with him yesterday eve-ning, working on his stuttering. At one critical point of the evening, I needed to excuse myself from his presence; I regret to say this left him alone with access to my entire first floor, including the kitchen where my evening toddy awaited. This drink is prepared each evening by Banters, my valet. I now know that Tinge had once apprenticed as an apothecary and had the requisite knowledge to administer a potent sedative. A police chemist has already examined the half-finished toddy by my bedside and verified the perfidy.

"Tinge left at the end of our session, but after giving enough time for Banters to retire to his attic room, and for my drugged toddy to plunge me into unconsciousness, he broke into my house, discovered the secret hiding place of the Star, and disappeared into the night. Upon awakening at dawn, and noting the absence of the gemstone, I called for the police and told them all about Tinge. Subsequently, he was routed from his bed and questioned. The gem could not be found in his posses-sion, he denies having it, and I fear that he will be presumed innocent."

"How do you know that Banters was not the culprit?" Lizzie asked. A stunned moment of silence announced outrage that such a question could even be asked. "He is a man," Lizzie continued, "who is already in the household, knows your nightly routine and, I suppose, the hiding place of the gem. Wouldn't he be...?"

"Preposterous!" came the inevitable cry of protest. "There has been a Banters with an Arbuthnot for generations, going back to the War of Independence. This particular Banters has traveled extensively with me throughout Europe and the Middle East. One time in Cairo, he took a bullet from a Persian bandit that was meant for me. No, if he were destined to betray me, he would have done so years ago. Besides, despite your assumption, I did not share with him the location of my Star."

"Then how could Tinge know it?"

"Because I told him!" Mrs. Arbuthnot said alarmingly. "It hurts my very pride to think it, but during my lesson, a clue to the hiding place just happened to make a rather difficult tongue challenge for his stuttering. I handed him the information without a thought. I now suspect his entire set of lessons was a ruse to enable him to get inside my house and to steal the gemstone. No doubt he had read that wretched article in the *Herald* announcing my possession of it. His request for an elocution lesson followed hard upon that column's publication."

"It would help me immeasurably if you would tell me the tongue challenge," Lizzie explained. "I need to know all pertinent data, if I am to be of any help."

Mrs. Arbuthnot thought for a suspended moment, twisting up her lip and fluttering her eyes. Finally, she said, "How many stars shall a swan see stark when the sea swan sees stark stars?"

"And that provides enough information to reveal the hiding place of the jewel?"

Her words emerged from a rigid, impassive face. "In retrospect, yes."

"Mrs. Arbuthnot, I would have presumed that you had invested in a security safe or a bank vault rather than leave the jewel in such an obvious location as behind a painting. I am more than familiar with the 'Stark Swansea Swans' by New England's most excellent master, Henry Lloyd Dunstan, having seen the original of that work in the very studio where it had been painted during the Case of the Draconian Antiquarian. Due to its subtle beauty and evocation of local flavor, many an affluent lady of this city has a print of it hanging in her parlor. I would have one myself if my father did not find it a vanity to admire art. But surely, you must have realized how vulnerable your Star would be in a niche behind a painting?"

"Refrain from your chastisement, my dear girl, the jewel was not hidden behind the painting. On the back of the canvas is a hasty pencil scribble referencing a passage from Scripture that, when properly deciphered, leads one to a shelf in a certain cabinet in a specific room where a musical box, that I had obtained in Jerusalem during my linguistic travels in the Holy Land, contains a key that can be used on a sliding panel in a place revealed by calculating the numerical beats of the box's music. That panel concealed the secret hiding place of my Star."

"Then why did you give Mr. Tinge this particular tongue twister? There were many others that may have sufficed for his particular impediment. 'She sells sea shells...' for example."

"Despite my excellent judgment of character that has hitherto protected me from swindlers and confidence tricksters, I still would not have believed Mr. Tinge to be such a rascal."

"But where is your proof other than you gave him the tongue challenge?"

"Alas, I have none. The police found evidence of forced entry, but not a footprint or anything physically denoting that Mr. Tinge had been on my property after I went to sleep. They consider my claim to be mere guesswork, and Mr. Tinge is looked upon as the innocent victim of my miscalculation. This is why I sit here in your small house, awaiting your offer to help me bring Mr. Tinge to justice."

"How may I do that? If there is no physical evidence..."

"Just apply that brilliance that has gained you such a reputation," the woman barked. "I cannot spend more time talking! I must go and restore my residence to normalcy before I receive any more clients. Banters is very disturbed and is now imagining a jewel thief behind every doorway. I turn this matter over to your more than capable hands. Go see Mr. Tinge," she commanded, extending a calling card. "Bring this deplorable business to its conclusion. I expect the Star of Swansea to be returned to me before the end of this week, or I shall tell the world that Lizzie Borden, Girl Detective, is a weak-willed fraud."

"Are you blackmailing me, Mrs. Arbuthnot?"

"I do not blackmail. I either speak truth or I do not, that is all."

"May I inquire how you heard about my services? I operate only through referrals."

The woman blinked and gave a small wry smile. "Word travels fast in Fall River. You may not be as secretive as you may believe, Miss Borden."

Lizzie closed her eyes for a brief moment, and I momentarily feared that she would lose her temper and say something to the woman that we would regret when we read it verbatim in the next day's newspapers. However, she looked up boldly and stated, "I will find the Star of Swansea for you, and I will bring this to a conclusion."

"Most delightful!" our guest proclaimed, her face shifting to a bright and almost cheerful disposition. She started for the door. "Now if you will excuse me, at three o'clock this afternoon, I have an appointment with a man who cannot speak without stamping his feet. He plans to ask a woman's hand in marriage, and would like to do so without endangering her toes."

"Mrs. Arbuthnot," Lizzie said, raising a finger. "Beyond staining my reputation, what would you do if the stone cannot be found?"

The woman closed her eyes momentarily. "It would have been a pleasure to raid the treasure house of the insurance company. First Mutual of Massachusetts has fed upon the fat of the wealthy for a good many years. But you'd sooner be able to squeeze blood from the Star of Swansea than an insurance pay-out. Only one hour ago, they sent over a thin, weedy man who barely showed any trace of being human. I believed him to have been born to a calculating machine. He told me, in my own living room before the assembled police officers, that I could not collect on the policy because I had willingly let the thief into my home. I tried to explain that I had sent Tinge home and that he came back later for the burglary, but he would not listen. This is why retrieval is of the utmost importance: if I cannot have the insurance money, I must have the Star back or there shall be no consolation. If you need me, I will be at home."

She left swiftly with a dramatic flurry, not even bothering to shake our hands or to thank us for our time. When our visitor was properly back in her stanhope, and several dozen yards down the street, Lizzie turned to me and said directly, "What did you observe about her?"

"Obviously, not a happy woman," I suggested. "Proud, to the point of mania, stubborn, and vain. She makes too much of her profession, no doubt an inflated impression provoked by an excess of money and no family on which to squander it. Obsessed with material objects, lacking in any heart-felt insight into her fellow man, and possessed by the singular compulsion to always be right in any matter, even when she is clearly wrong."

"Yes," Lizzie said hastily. "You do pick up the essentials of her personality; but I fear, Cousin Sarah, that you have missed all the important details."

"What?" I gestured. "How can I have been more...?"

"Did you not notice her excessive anger at First Mutual?"

"Anyone in her position would be outraged. Imagine if you..."

"Or her insistence on my involvement in the affair."

"Perhaps your reputation has grown by word of mouth, as she has said."

"Nonetheless," Lizzie said, clapping her hands and smiling broadly, "we need to hit the streets. Yes, this will be grand, Sarah. We shall follow this trail to its conclusion, no matter how unpleasant."

"Do you really think you can find the Star?" I asked.

"That is entirely dependent upon what the Swan sees on a starry night," she answered cryptically, but before I could question her further, she had headed for the front hallway to fetch her cape and hat.

THE SPEECH CLIENT

Out on the streets of Fall River, our matching capes kept us warm from the encroaching chill, and two pairs of three-buttoned kidskin gloves kept our fingers quite toasty as well. As we passed the shop windows on South Main, I saw Lizzie glancing at the brooches, parlor fans, and winter sundries that were displayed behind the glass. I felt a twinge of nervousness that her mind, no matter how focused it may be on the present case, was drifting towards her Fancy again. It was an unpleasant feeling to have to fret over such things, much as it is when a loved one takes to drink and performs irresponsible acts without any regard to consequences. I tried engaging her in light conversation to take her attention away from the window displays, but she remained forever peering with one eye at the knick-knacks and trifles that were ever so tempting to her weakness.

We arrived at the address on Bedford Street given to us on Tinge's card, a modest half-house that clung to its neighbor with an air of insecurity. In answer to our bell, the resident appeared in the doorway, a small, thin man who seemed to be cowering as much as his house. "I suppose," Arthur Tinge said, after we had introduced ourselves, "that you are working for the police."

"I am an independent consultant," Lizzie clarified. "The police do not yet know I am here." We removed our capes and handed them to our host who hung them on pegs in the front hallway. Shortly thereafter, we were roasting before a warm fire in the sitting room.

"I must confess that I am here at the request of Mrs. Arbuthnot," Lizzie explained.

"Ah, that harpy!" he said, not too surprised. "I rue the day that I ever met her; she has been a canker sore on my existence."

"I detect something bitter between you?" Lizzie said, tapping a finger to her lower lip. "Perhaps you can illuminate your relationship with her."

"There is not much to tell, other than I have been a stuttering idiot since the day I met her. I merely wanted to get some elocution lessons so I could address the local chapter of my philology club. We are a small group, only ten of us, and we have failed for several years to draw in one new member. I don't suppose philology can be very popular around here, being that you have to master at least two dead languages and three of Indo-European descent before your application is even seriously considered. In a mill town such as Fall River, that is asking a bit too much."

"So you went to Mrs. Arbuthnot in preparation for a public speech?"

"Yes. The opportunity to give such a recruitment speech at the Anawan Mills came up and I was terrified."

"At the Anawan Mills? Such an odd venue for a philology club."

"Their chief Agent was obsessed with bringing culture to the workers. In fact, it was he who recommended Mrs. Arbuthnot. He told me that she had helped his son overcome a complete inability to recite poetry in the presence of a dog."

"Peculiar. That must have been an accomplishment."

"She came so highly recommended, I expected not only that I would overcome my fear of public speaking, but that I would gain the power to shatter wine glasses with my new-found vocal bombast. In fact, within one lesson, she had me orating like Cicero, and feeling mighty empowered about it. It was only natural, at the end of the lesson, that I offered to pay her handsomely and promised to recommend her if ever a friend of mine had a speech problem. But it was then that she destroyed my life."

"At the end of the first lesson?"

"Yes. She began to order me about, telling me how slovenly I was, how my posture was abominable, and that all the progress in elocution couldn't live up to the fact that my voice sounded like a rodent being strangled. As a consequence of her chastisement, I became a stuttering idiot. I could barely get out a sentence, I was so tongue-tied. I tried to tell her it was mere intimidation, being that I was shamed by her observations, and too aware of my imperfections. I simply wasn't comfortable enough with myself to speak confidently anymore."

"But you went back for more lessons?"

"I had paid for six lessons in advance, two a week for three weeks. She not only drained my financial resources by raising her rate on the second lesson, but my stuttering got worse, and, before long, I was almost incapable of saying anything. That was when she began to rebuild me, from the ground up, as she phrased it. She gave me some wicked tongue challenges, and before long I could only speak the tongue challenges. Ordinary speech like 'How are you?' and 'What a fine day' was completely beyond my ability to utter, but I had no problems with such useless phrases as 'Bilberton Babbles Bubbles Blitheringly Between Bouts of Bilious Blathering.' In short, I was not fit to talk to anyone without some sort of radical verbal surgery."

"That is all very interesting, Mr. Tinge, but your speech now is fine, extremely eloquent. I have had no problem understanding anything you have uttered since we entered this room."

"That is because last night I finally put my foot down with Mrs. Arbuthnot and regained some of my confidence. I have an ancestor who fought with George Washington, you know: Thomas Tinge, the Plymouth glove-maker, who had literally put down his foot on a Hessian general at the Battle of Assunpink Creek and won the day for the Continentals. I have always wanted to perform an equivalent act of courage. This Circe had whisked me off to her prison island for the last time. I told her that I was done with her, that my speech would mend itself of its own accord, and that I didn't need her to see me as a bottomless money pot. It may have taken me almost ten full minutes to say all of that, and I'm sure I sounded like a lunatic, but I said it. Mrs. Arbuthnot took it very badly, told me that I was a silly man, far from perfect, and that my proposed lecture on 'The Philological Life As A Valid Venture In Less Than Three Dead Languages' would be a disaster. She openly put a curse on me, predicting that five words into the speech I would lose complete control of my voice, and all the audience would hear would be rasps and groans and futile attempts to form words. I told her to go to blazes. She stood and looked at me for a very long time, her eyes clicking back and forth as if she were not seeing me at all. Then she asked me to stay where I was and she promptly disappeared from the room for ten minutes. I had no clue where she went."

"Perhaps she went to freshen her toilet," I suggested.

"No doubt, but I'm not sure which end of herself she used to do so. She came out after ten minutes bellowing loudly and telling me that I would never see the swans on the Swansea, or some such nonsense. She kept jabbering and pointing at that damn painting of hers, for no apparent reason. I gathered up my courage and fled the scene, racing through the streets, hoping to get home before whatever vulture she had conjured over my head started to peck at my skull. I was in bed by ten o'clock and slept through the night, comforted by the fact that I was safe at home where no Medusa could turn me to stone."

"Then it was in the morning that you first heard of the robbery?"

"Of course; the police woke me up by nearly battering down my door. They asked me an uncivilized number of questions, then searched the place thoroughly, and found nothing. It was to my credit that my landlady saw me come in last night before the robbery, and that my next-door neighbor had been kept up by my snoring. If I had performed the robbery, there simply wouldn't have been any time for me to take the Star of Swansea anywhere else, unless, perhaps, I had swallowed the damned thing. I suppose the police want to follow me into the privy the next time I feel like discharging my dinner."

"Yes," Lizzie said, suppressing a giggle with her gloved hand. "I assure you that I am convinced that the Star of Swansea is nowhere on the premises."

"Thank you. You are my first convert. The City Marshal threatened to come back in an hour to tear up my floorboards."

"I am deeply pained to hear that such a tragedy has descended on you, Mr. Tinge. Would it bother you if Sarah and I were to be present at this second search?"

"Not at all. You two ladies have been most kind, and perhaps the only persons that I have met since sunrise who believe in my innocence. Come back at noon, and you shall witness the exoneration of my good name."

We rose to leave but Lizzie had one more question: "Was last night your customary time to see Mrs. Arbuthnot?"

"Yes, in fact. But there was a small irregularity. I tried to cancel due to a minor personal matter, nothing of great importance but one that was hardly less preferable to being humiliated all evening by a bullish woman."

"But you did not cancel?"

"No, she calmly explained to me that I would pay for my lesson whether I attended or not. The policy seemed fair, but I had never encountered it before. Perhaps it was nothing but a teacher's hostility towards a non-cooperative student."

We thanked our rattled host and went to get our capes. To our surprise, we found a man standing in the hallway. He was quite elegant in his dress, from his bowler hat to his leather shoes. When Mr. Tinge laid eyes upon him, he yelped and stuck his hands deep into his pockets. "W—w-w-what are you d—d-doing here?" he stammered. His eyes went into an uncontrollable fit of blinking, the worst I have ever witnessed, his face contorting and collapsing as if the stuttering were just an extension of some seismic facial earthquake.

"Lizzie Borden," the newcomer said, quite flatly. "I have been sent by my Lady to ensure your protection in the streets. Rogues and ruffians abound."

"Banters?" Lizzie asked, peering at his stony face. "There is no need for protection. We are in no danger."

"G-g-get that m-man from me," Mr. Tinge said, racing back to his sitting room where he collapsed into a chair, his entire body curling up like a ball. A series of immodest whines came from deep within him, filling the room with a pathetic dreariness.

"Very well," Lizzie sighed. "Shall we?"

SOLVED!

We took the streets, Lizzie and I walking before the tall tower of a man who drew stares on every block, until we reached Rogers, a small pleasant restaurant on South Main Street where we withdrew for private discussion. We required two tables since the manservant acknowledged our need for privacy. He subsequently ordered no food and spent all his time staring at us from a distance. The seating arrangement was quite awkward and drew more incredulous stares from the other patrons.

"Banters' protection is quite unnecessary," I noted. "Do you suppose Arbuthnot is up to something?"

"Protection is just a pretense," Lizzie agreed. "Perhaps he doesn't want us to be talking to the wrong people."

I felt an anger rise within me. "Arbuthnot is not telling us the truth!"

I proclaimed. "She humiliated that poor feckless man into submission and now she is trying to frame the theft of the jewel on him! And why else would she do that unless she stole her own gemstone?"

Lizzie produced a small, comforting smile. "You are reaching for wild conclusions. It could be that Tinge, being in reduced circumstances, made a play for the Star of Swansea, and now fears that the police will find it in their second search."

"But it would make no sense for him to keep it in the house," I implored her. "And he seems to be content to stay there until the police arrive."

"You don't know that," Lizzie countered. "He could be disposing himself of it right now. We would have done better to have watched the house rather than indulge in sarsaparilla and quahog sandwiches."

"That would make a fine picture," I mused. "Us spying on Tinge while Banters spies on us. Perhaps Arbuthnot will be spying on Banters and the police spying on her. Oh Lizzie, this is like a nonsensical merry-go-round!"

"It's about money, no matter who the thief," Lizzie said, resignedly. She looked down at her meal. "It's always about money."

After our dinner, we took back to the streets, Banters trailing behind us. When we stopped to look at a shop window, he stopped, and when we re-directed our steps to take an alternative route, he followed in due course. There was something decidedly sinister about him, as if he were an espionage agent working for some secret society. What I had feared had indeed come true: being in Lizzie Borden's presence had not failed to produce the potential for danger and adventure. Was Banters our ally or our most fiendish foe? To what lengths would the jewel thief go to avoid detection? Would some desperate criminal await us with mask and pistol around the next corner of shops?

I noticed that our walking path had taken us a bit far from the Tinge house, and I mentioned this to Lizzie. "I want to see how our traveling companion reacts to a small detour," she explained.

Down Columbia Street, a long string of shops in a row all displayed garish signs from which hung larger-than-life plaster gemstones, endless arrangements of cheap stones crowded behind the glass windows. Lizzie stopped at each one, glancing back without fail at Banters who seemed to be interested in what shops drew our attention, but it was hard to evaluate at the distance that he kept.

We had stopped before one nondescript shop when we happened to witness a most remarkable sight. One of the jewelers who stood alone in the middle of his display room seemed to be going through a violent spastic fit of some kind. His entire body was spiraling about, his arms flapping up and down, and his face was in a violent state of convulsion. His mouth was emitting some of the most hideous squawks and bellows that I had ever heard coming from a human throat. After several spirals, he stopped and clucked, forcing his tongue into all manner of contortions. Soon enough, he caught a glimpse of us looking at him through the window and it was then that his manner eased, his body straightened up, and his face remolded itself into a cheery and friendly shape, as he opened the door for us.

"What can I do for you young ladies?" he asked in a perfectly ordinary voice. Such contrast between his current demeanor and his previous inexplicable behavior had shocked us into silence.

Lizzie gestured that we were only browsing through the merchandise in the window. He went back to his counter and began to fiddle with his till. After a moment, he glanced up at us with a slight trace of suspicion and then began to move a large steamer trunk from the aisle of the shop to behind the front counter.

"It seems as if he is preparing to vacate," I suggested to my companion. "Do you notice, Lizzie, that there is a 'closed for business' sign on the window, and yet the shop is open. That trunk looks big enough to suggest he is going away for a long time."

"I have so observed," she replied, with a crooked smirk on her face. "But I do not believe he is getting ready to leave. On the contrary, it looks as if he is returning. Note how he moves the trunk towards the rear staircase; I believe his apartment to be above those stairs. And yet..." She glanced furtively about and then asked me, almost in a whisper, "Can you please glance back at our spy and see what he is doing? Be very precise in your description."

"He's walking about," I told her, "a bit flustered. He has lost his composure. Now he is calming down. I suspect that, if we move on, he will follow placidly."

She looked at me with a bright and relaxed smile. "Then, I do believe, dear Sarah, that I have solved the case."

"What? Based on what? The chicken clucks made by the jeweler?"

"It is all so clear to me now," she said, clapping her hands. "You must understand, I had my doubts, but I needed more data. Our time would now be best spent reporting what we know to the police."

"What we know? I know nothing."

"Ah, but you shall. Let's hurry to Mr. Tinge's fearful little abode to rendezvous with the City Marshal and set him on the appropriate course of action."

A Police Raid

We arrived back at the Tinge house to find the City Marshal and a trio of policemen before the front gate, clustered around the quivering frame of Mr. Tinge as he shook and stammered in the shadow of Fall River's most powerful public official. I had seen this tall, barrel-chested and heavily mustached man before, but never when he was standing with such authority, a full foot above the heads of other men, his baton slicing the air, his orders clear and precise with a voice that equaled his girth. When he caught sight of Lizzie he froze, a strange expression of uncertainty enveloping his face.

"What is this?" he said, lowering his baton.

Lizzie approached him, nodding, and gestured for him to follow her to the side path. He followed, waving with his gloved hand for his men to hold ranks and to wait for him. The two of them conversed quietly for a moment, the Marshal looking rather annoyed and then confused. Lizzie poked her fingertip several times into her other palm and talked excessively while the Marshal stood in rapt contemplation, his fingers stroking his chin. He then asked something that sounded like, "You are absolutely sure?" to which Lizzie nodded and added some more words. She pointed down the street where Banters waited, a grim pillar of dark clothing, motionless and silent.

The Marshal returned to the front of the house and mustered his men. "This may come as a surprise to you," he said, keeping an eye rigidly on Lizzie, "but we are not going to search this house. Instead we are going to pay a visit to Mrs. Ellen Arbuthnot."

The trio of officers muttered in confusion, responding with a flurry of desperate questions, but the Marshal was on the move, pointing his baton westward along Bedford Street, and leading his men like a roaring Light Brigade down a Crimean battle ridge. Mr. Tinge struggled to keep step with them, his face flushed with embarrassment and speckled with tears.

Lizzie and I fell in behind them and followed. A quick glance over my shoulder revealed Banters moving with us, not missing a single beat. The entire five block interval between one house and the other was occupied with my protestations that Lizzie tell me immediately what was going on, and why, after watching a Columbia Street jeweler prance about his store like a deranged barnyard animal, did she finally think that Mrs. Arbuthnot had been lying.

"All shall be revealed," she promised. "Trust in my methods."

At the home of Mrs. Arbuthnot, the police knocked upon the door. The famed elocutionist came outside, her words bellowing to the skies above, echoing over the yards of her neighborhood. "This is an outrage! What authority do you have? Do you have any idea who I am? You, Officer Beck, have you not forgotten that I have taken your useless son and cured him of his irrational phobia of multi-syllabic words? Have you no gratitude?"

"He may talk more," Officer Beck shouted back, "but I'll be hanged if I can understand anything he says!"

The Marshal stood before the woman, his thumbs hooked in his belt. "Mrs. Arbuthnot, I have given orders to search your house."

"And what do you propose to find there?"

"Some clue as to the identity of your thief."

"You have your thief!" she shrieked, pointing at Tinge who had appeared behind the officers. With her accusation, the man whimpered and darted about, looking for something to hide behind. "That sniveling nothing of a man," she protested, "has stolen the Star of Swansea! Did you search his house before you initiated this farrago of nonsense?"

"That is none of your business," the Marshal told her. "Now call over your valet. He needs to be searched as well."

After a suspicious pause, the woman nodded in the direction of her manservant and he stalked forward. Halfway to the front door, with a twisted face and an uncharacteristic howl, he hurled himself upon Lizzie, grabbing her with his large hands that pulled violently at her cape. She attempted to block her face with her forearms, but he snapped with his teeth, seemingly trying to bite her. Both man and girl collapsed in a tumble to the ground, while the Marshal yelled at his men to separate them. It required all three officers to pull the animated valet from Lizzie, while the Marshal personally helped her to her feet and dusted off her cape. Once subdued, Banters fell silent and gave no resistance to the men who escorted him into the house.

"Great Battering Rams!" the Marshal shouted, as perplexed as anyone else. "What could have gotten into him? It was as if he were trying to kill you."

"A terrifying testament to his loyalty toward his lady," Lizzie said, composing herself, and followed the rest of the men inside.

The attack upon Lizzie had put a good deal of incentive into the policemen, who now besieged Mrs. Arbuthnot's parlor room as if it were also a prisoner that needed restraint. They rifled through papers that had been neatly stacked on a writing desk, pulled up the rug, knocked over the center table, capsized the couch and chairs, forced books off their shelves and scattered them without any concern for the damage they suffered; they even flung about the framed photographs that lined the fireplace mantle. Then they headed upstairs. The damage could be heard through the ceiling: loud thuds and the scraping of beds and chests across the floors, the turning of tallboys, and the violent rifling of cabinets. Bed sheets were tossed down the hallway stairs and even a chamber pot was overturned and discarded on the landing.

The police officers came down empty-handed and renewed their savage assault in the sitting room, the kitchen, and the closet under the front stairs. Within ten short minutes, the inside of Mrs. Arbuthnot's dwelling looked as if it had suffered terribly during a hurricane. The Marshal stood in the middle, conducting the melee with his baton, while Lizzie stared with rapt attention, like a child let loose in a candy store, as if some profound meaning would be revealed with each violation of the elocutionist's personal possessions.

"I shall be financially recompensed for this," said Mrs. Arbuthnot, watching with elegant agony at the damage being done. The Marshal gave her a sideways glance and then dismissed her comment with great indifference.

The fury continued as hatchets were produced and floorboards were ripped up, wall panels were removed, paintings were taken from their mountings, including the Dunstan canvas of the stark swans, which had nothing written on its back. With each disappointment, a renewed energy invigorated the savagery of the search, and the police continued damaging everything they possibly could, overturning vases, tossing about valuable china, opening even a music box and cigar humidor. Albums of photographs were ransacked and tossed carelessly about. Even a pair of pince-nez lay shattered on the ground, trampled by a careless boot.

After forty minutes, the destruction seemed to be complete and the

Marshal reconvened his men in the parlor, their hands empty. Mrs. Arbuthnot and Banters stood with tense outrage convulsing their faces. Finally, the elocutionist asked tersely, "Are you satisfied?"

"No," the Marshall said, "I'm not."

He raised a finger toward Officer Beck who, in turn, nodded to the two men by his side. The three officers now grabbed the elocutionist and her servant forcefully by the arms, dragging them, despite their angered protests, into the kitchen. For several minutes, there came from the other room the most horrific shrieks, howls of protest, and what sounded like failed attempts at escape. When they all came back into the parlor, Mrs. Arbuthnot and Banters were disheveled, their clothing rather disturbed, and walking dizzily. The elocutionist's hair fell about her in disturbed strands, as if she had been the victim of an experiment in electricity gone horribly wrong. Banter's tie was missing and his collar extended as if he had been the recipient of a bomb blast. They resumed their standing position in the ravished parlor, now both quite subdued and impassive.

"Nothing," a policeman told the Marshal, who turned a face of frustration straight at Lizzie.

"It is here," she said nervously. "I know it. It must be."

"You have put my reputation on the line," the Marshal said. "Bring in Tinge."

Two policemen went to the front hallway and came back with the rather nervous and twitching philologist. He raised his arms as if to protect himself from expected blows of the Marshal's baton. "Don't h-h-hit me!" he implored.

"What have you done to this man?" the Marshal asked the woman, his stick wavering.

"Nothing that he hasn't done to himself," Mrs. Arbuthnot announced. "And I must protest the violation of my physical being while this sniveling worm is allowed to go without so much as a slap on the wrist. I insist that you search him the same way that you searched me, that you attack his house with the same violence that you have mine. I insist upon it! And while you are at it, search this impetuous and prideful girl here who calls herself a detective! Search her! In fact, search her even before you search Tinge! I think you may be surprised!"

"Why not search the Marshal?" Lizzie shouted, losing her patience. "Or innocent Sarah here or..."

She stopped cold, her face collapsing into a solitary scowl. Her eyes grew closer together, her brow tightened, and then she pouted. She was in the midst of some realization that had previously eluded her. All in the room became quite still, reluctant to even breathe, as the Girl Detective peered about, soaking in as much as she could, as if she were memorizing the position and attitude of everyone in case she had need of that information in the moments to come. With a silent solemnity, I watched as she lifted up one hand, then slipped it into the pocket of her cape, the fingers grasping about as if trying to clutch something that didn't have any realistic dimensions. Her hand came forth, empty, and she thrust her other hand into the other pocket of the cape, repeating the operation. With each clutch of her fingers, her face grew more perplexed. She then looked Mrs. Arbuthnot dead in the face and said with a defiance that startled even the Marshal, "I suppose they can search me now, for they will find nothing."

"Nothing?" Mrs. Arbuthnot said, startled. "Nonsense, look again, it must be there!"

"Why must it be?" Lizzie asked. "You are trying to get the police of Fall River to believe that I would steal the Star of Swansea?"

"You were in Mr. Tinge's house for quite some time," the woman said with a snarl. "My man Banters here will testify to that. Why shouldn't you be tempted to…eh…take your Fancy, as you so eloquently phrase it?" She gave a conspiratorial wink at the Marshal.

"But I don't have it!" Lizzie shouted, patting the empty pockets of her cape.

"You are lying!" the elocutionist replied, vibrating the room. "Marshal, search her immediately! Why do you stand there doing nothing? I shall do it myself!" She leapt forward and struggled with Lizzie, pulling at her cape in the same manner that Banters had done on the street, but with an extra dose of viciousness and desperation. Several policemen came forward, grabbing the woman and pulling her off Lizzie. "You must have it!" she was shouting. "If you don't have it, all is lost! Oh, all is lost!" Then she collapsed onto the rattled remains of her settee, heaving with tears.

Mr. Tinge, who seemed to have become more relaxed as Mrs. Arbuthnot collapsed into hysteria, said confidently to the Marshal, "This woman tried to make everyone believe that I stole the Star of Swansea, which is total nonsense. Now she accuses this innocent girl as well. But if I did steal the gem, then it must still be in my house. You may go with your men and see for yourself."

"Not so fast," the Marshal said, raising a gloved hand. "I need to hear from Lizzie what just happened, because I'm not so sure about it myself."

"I can easily explain," the Girl Detective said resignedly. "I suspected from the start that Mr. Tinge was wholly innocent, that his elocution teacher had, for reasons of her own, needed to steal her own gemstone and declare it lost so she could collect the insurance money. Perhaps her finances had gotten out of control, or she was too deeply in debt, or she was living too well for her own convenience. This was confirmed when your officers searched this room. Letters from creditors were found in great plenitude upon her desk, but since none of you understood their importance, they were summarily scattered on the floor. This was a woman who needed money, a lot of it, very fast. And her most valuable asset, the Star of Swansea, was her surest bet.

"I can imagine she was tempted to sell it legally, and get the market value for it, an amount which must be quite considerable. But she subsequently devised a more sinister plan, to pull a confidence trick on the insurance company, and to have it fenced in the underworld at the same time, thereby doubling its value and, from her perspective, harming no one but an insurance company that was, in its own right, greedy and criminal. The sincerity in her voice when she confided in me of her cynicism was so believable that I knew she had the ability to defraud First Mutual of Massachusetts without any guilty conscience.

"And so a plan hatched in her mind. She spent months turning Arthur Tinge into a sniveling worm, someone scared even of his own voice. The cruel manner in which she systematically destroyed his confidence can only mean she had targeted him from the very beginning to be her prime suspect. Last night, she reaped the harvest of her labor: when Tinge tried to cancel his lesson, she threatened to have him pay for her time which encouraged him to attend; once he was in her parlor, she awkwardly drew his attention to non-existent clues that supposedly revealed the location of the Star; then she deliberately left him alone for an inappropriate amount of time so she could claim that he had examined those clues. After his departure, the valet arranged the home to look as if a burglary had taken place, such as breaking the door latch and upsetting some of the furniture. He even drugged the night toddy to show that Mrs. Arbuthnot had been unconscious when the stone was allegedly taken from the house. In the morning, it was a simple matter of calling the police and informing them that Mr. Tinge had done the deed. The stone would never be found and suspicion would fall on Tinge forever more.

"I suspected almost immediately that Mrs. Arbuthnot had stolen the gem herself. What bothered me, which is why I dismissed my good friend Sarah here when she proposed such a solution, was why she would hire me as a consulting detective knowing that I would have the power to discover the conspiracy? Just now, when both Mrs. Arbuthnot and Banters attacked me, I finally saw her plan very clearly.

"Mrs. Arbuthnot knew that I have a reputation in this town for taking my Fancy. It is not something I am proud of admitting in front of the City Marshal, but they say confession is good for the soul, and I now am trusting in the truth of that proverb. I have given in many times to an urge to filch small things from their rightful owners. Nothing as serious as a gemstone, mere trifles, and the Marshal is no doubt familiar with some examples of my weakness. I believe this to be the reputation considered by Mrs. Arbuthnot as she struggled to extract herself from an impossible turn of events that had developed over the course of the morning. She had Banters follow me to Mr. Tinge's residence. Why did she do this? Something had changed this very morning; the plan had gone awry. But what could have happened? And what was Banters' mission? Only Banters can tell."

All eyes turned to the butler. There was a mere flicker of one eyebrow and a small twitch at the corner of his drooping mouth, but otherwise he remained silent.

Lizzie continued, "Mrs. Arbuthnot confessed to me that she had been humiliated by First Mutual of Massachusetts, that they had used a loophole to prevent her from ever collecting on the theft insurance: she had revealed to the thief the hiding place of the property and on that basis her claim was rejected. As for selling the stone to the underworld, the money involved was insufficient without the additional insurance money. Her only option now was to restore the Star to her possession so she can sell it openly. This would be most difficult: she could not suddenly claim that the gem had slipped behind some pillow shams. That would lead to gossip, rumors. Who would believe her? No, she needed to retain the illusion of robbery but have the Star make a dramatic re-appearance.

"After the police and the insurance agent left her home, Mrs. Arbuthnot and her valet must have conspired very quickly on a second, more improvised plan, and I believe, for reasons I shall reveal presently, it was Banters who suggested that I, Lizzie Borden, be targeted as an additional suspect, a suggestion that Mrs. Arbuthnot appreciated. Immediately, a note was sent to my house requesting a meeting later in the morning. As I was conducting my interview with her on Second Street, Banters was down on Columbia Street telling the jeweler who was going to fence the gem that his services were no longer required. After he finished there, Banters had a second destination.

"Mrs. Arbuthnot had made it very clear to me that I should be present at Mr. Tinge's home later that morning and was very precise about the time. This was because Banters' mission was to make sure that I would be found with the stone in my possession. I knew there had to be a reason for him to enter Mr. Tinge's house without knocking, something that made no sense in any other context. That had been his moment: he was temporarily alone in the hallway with my cape; he could not have devised a more perfect opportunity. Then he followed us, making sure that I remained in ignorance of my possession until he could arrange for me to be incriminated before the police. If you gentlemen had seen it emerge from my cape, you would have been convinced that I had stolen it from Mr. Tinge and you would have arrested me as a co-conspirator in the theft.

"But imagine Banters' confusion when I had the police search diverted to his own lady's house, presenting him with quite a dilemma. Attacking me in the street, even before an assembled police force, would provide him with the opportunity to extract the stone from my pocket, thereby preparing me for the singular moment of humiliation that Mrs. Arbuthnot so desired. Likewise, Mrs. Arbuthnot was attempting to retrieve the stone when she attacked me herself."

"Remarkable!" the Marshal applauded.

"Balderdash!" cried Mrs. Arbuthnot, thrusting up her chin. "The poor girl is seized by the fever of her imagination!"

"You!" Officer Beck cried out, raising his stick. "Shut your gob." The woman turned fish-mouthed and frozen, glancing painfully at Banters as if he would extract her from her humiliation, but the valet remained taciturn.

The Marshal scratched his chin thoughtfully. "But where is the stone if not in your pocket? If Banters put it into your cape at Tinge's house, and your pockets are now empty, where is the Star of Swansea?"

"That is something that no one could have predicted," Lizzie replied, her mouth curling into a smile. "Sarah, would you be so kind as to check your pockets?"

I placed both hands into my cape and immediately felt the gemstone, warmed against my body, hard to the touch, its presence simultaneously gentle and cruel. I withdrew it with my trembling hand and held it up against the light, shocking all assembled with its radiant beauty and perfect form. For a single moment, it shone like a blue star against the existing light.

"How?" was all I could articulate.

"Did you not fail to notice," Lizzie said, pointing with a finger, "that when we left Mr. Tinge's house, you took my cape quite by accident? Note the blue trim on the sleeves, how it is a different shade than mine? I did not even notice until just now, an oversight for which I will never forgive myself." Lizzie stepped closer to Banters, who stared back at her with a gruesome shade of rage on his otherwise impassive face. "Isn't this all true?" she asked quietly.

"I would have seen you hanged," the man said gruffly.

"I'm sure you would have," Lizzie replied. "There has been a Banter's in the Arbuthnot family for many generations; but I suspect that other families have had their Banters, and perhaps one of them has appropriate reason to seek revenge on the Girl Detective who exposed his perfidies. Who was it, Banters? A brother? A close associate? Is his employer now languishing in a prison unbefitting a man of his quality?"

Banters' cheeks twitched; then his eyes widened; then he retreated back into his silent world.

Lizzie nodded knowingly and turned back to the crowd. "As for Mrs. Arbuthnot," she stated, "let her be advised—the next time you communicate with a Fall River jeweler who is well-known for trading stolen gems to the criminal underworld, be so kind as to keep him out of your personal affairs. Mr. Gerard Gumley of Columbia Street, a man who is as well known to the police for his various speech impediments and vocal oddities as he is for his illegal fencing of stolen goods, was a little too ambitious with his elocution assignments. I saw him practicing his vocal exercises in his shop this morning, a clear sign that he had taken lessons. It had also been clear that up until this very morning, he had been planning to abandon his shop and to go to some remote country where the law could not reach him. I wonder how much money he would have gotten for cutting the Star of Swansea. Enough to buy a tropical island and never see Fall River again? Anyway, he is still in Columbia Street, perhaps a bit rattled from his disappointment. I am sure it would take little pressure from the police to secure his testimony that he had conspired in the theft of the Star of Swansea. Isn't that right, Mrs. Arbuthnot?"

"May your words choke in your throat," was the elocutionist's only reply. Then she turned to her stoic man-servant and breathed one short statement: "I would have taken a bullet for you too, you know."

One eyebrow lifted upwards, temporarily giving the impression Banters was experiencing an emotion. "I don't give a dash," he announced, and then his eyebrow descended, casting his face back into stoic placidness.

The Marshal cleared his throat and with a sweeping gesture of his hand to his assembled men, restored his authority to the scene. "Let's get these ruffians down to the station. I can't promise Banters that he won't have some discomfort, but I'll put it into the record that he was only following orders from his lady. I guess that will amount to something. As for Mrs. Arbuthnot, my only advice at this point would be to speak as little as possible, something I'm sure she will find difficult to enforce. Lizzie, I must commend you and add this case to your wall of accomplishments."

While replying to the Marshal, she gave me a heart-warming glance. "No need to give my name to the reporters," she said cautiously. "My services require no thanks."

The Marshal gave a polite bow before turning about to command his men. And so, once again, I had witnessed my good friend, Lizzie Andrew Borden, the Girl Detective, reduce hardened law officers to stunned silence. Whatever she had learned through her perilous work this past year had matured her into a seasoned sleuth with a relationship with the police that was more complex than I would have guessed. Perhaps an adventure with a mummified gunslinger wasn't such a preposterous notion after all.

I escorted Lizzie back towards Second Street so she could return to her mundane world of household chores and trivial conversation with her family. Admittedly, I was very nervous, almost frightened of her. Just three short hours ago we were best friends, romping down street and buying new clothing to protect against the winter chill. In those few hours, she took me on an adventure, one that involved intrigue, police maneuvers, various physical assaults, and a jewel theft. I could not believe that so much could be compressed into so short a morning, and it was not even time for dinner.

"How do you do it?" I inquired, as we turned onto South Main. "I mean, honestly, how do you do it?"

"Me?" she said, her eyes fluttering. "I told you many times, Sarah dear. I am the most excellent Girl Detective. Did you expect me to do otherwise? Come, perhaps when we get home I shall find a new client and we shall have a new adventure. The day is still young."

The End

THE PURLOINED CURIO

1875. FRENCH STREET, FALL RIVER, MASSACHUSETTS.

VOICES FROM THE SUMMERLANDS

Sarah Durfee Borden was growing weary of the pretense of mystery, of her mother's face glowing in the kerosene light, of the twins' cries of astonishment as each new trumpet blast sounded beyond the shadows in the far corner of the parlor. But what she was tired of the most was Elizabeth Wingate's flabby jowls nodding and chortling in some pathetic act of spirit possession. All in all, Sarah was sick of the endless séances and dancing flames, of loud snapping table raps and candle light, of cold wisps blasted from over her shoulder to make her believe that her dead father was somehow in the room.

Young Sarah, not quite fifteen years of age, born and bred in the Fall River parlors that were more suited for salons than spirit rooms, knew a charlatan when she saw one, and Elizabeth Wingate, despite her aristocratic airs and altruistic demeanor, was a fraud of the first order, a hoax mistress, a traveling snake oil peddler. How much money had the Widow Borden, her mother, spent on these endless rituals of hocus-pocus and supposed spirit visitations? How many textile dividends had been liquidated in sacrifice to Wingate's bank account? How many superstitions and weaknesses in her mother's character had been exploited by this fraud—this silly woman who had claimed that by using spirit visitation not only would she reunite Mrs. Borden with her dear departed husband, but would also locate his missing will?

"Jonathan Borden is but a mere whisper, a glimmering cloud passing through the Summerlands," the corpulent Englishwoman said in a low rumbling voice. "Mrs. Borden, you are the flame that is attracting him to our sphere of matter. He yearns only to be close again to your material manifestation."

"Where is my Jon?" Mrs. Borden cried, her face wet with her own burning sadness. "I want to hear his voice once more!"

The young twins cowered in their high chairs, small beings terrified by flickering lights and dark shadows that they could not understand. "Papa!" said the one on the left. They still could not comprehend his absence, and this farcical charade was only confusing them.

Sarah rolled her eyes and pressed her hands against the gilt table-cloth. "Don't forget to ask him to empty his slops. There's an awful smell."

The mother slapped an open hand down hard. "Sarah! Be still!"

Another trumpet blast came through the brocaded wall. The Widow Borden jumped at its sudden eruption. "What's the point, Mother?" asked Sarah impatiently. "This is all theater! There are no trumpets of the dead! I bet if you search the backyard you'll find an associate of this faker hunched behind your crunch berry bush with a small horn to deliver his blasts on cue." She poked an evil eye at Wingate who flustered in her seat, attempting to preserve an aura of solemn trance. "I would prefer you to attach your leech-like tentacles to some other poor widow and not my mother."

Wingate opened one eye and let it periscope towards Sarah. "Hush!" the Englishwoman said, raising a chubby finger to her lips. "Your father is just passing through the veil."

The Widow Borden said exhaustedly, "Stop insulting our guest, Sarah. She is not a fake. She studied with the Fox Sisters."

Sarah yelled out, "Fiddlesticks!" and fled from the table, pulling at the drapery and upsetting the candle that fell to the side and sputtered out. Within moments, she was in her bedroom, reclined on her lounge and sobbing liberally.

Now she was in a fine imbroglio. She had wanted to give Elizabeth Wingate a piece of her mind for several months now but remained silent while her mother's dwindling wealth had financed these greedy charades. If only her father had properly filed his will with the probate office. Surely he had anticipated his death by creating the document, so why had he hid it in a place where no could find it? Why did he take that secret with him to his grave?

Sarah knew that for her to expose this spiritual fraud, she would need help from an expert. But who could prove Wingate's deceptions? Or find her father's will?

As Sarah pondered these questions, she happened to glance at her writing table, and saw a framed photograph of her associates at the

Women's Temperance Society. In the center, beaming with pride and decked in her Sunday tulle finest, was Sarah Borden, her eyes glowing with the optimism of youth. She remembered the day of the photograph with fondness and nostalgia, for, at that time, her father had been alive to witness his daughter's accomplishments.

Right next to her in the picture was a plump distant cousin of hers, one of the less prosperous Bordens, with her smooth round cheeks and protruding blue-gray eyes. Here was a girl whom Sarah had shared a high school classroom with, had sat next to at temperance lectures, and to whom she had confided some secrets that only girls could share.

Yes, thought Sarah. How absurd. I should have thought of it from the beginning.

I shall consult with Lizzie Andrew Borden, the Girl Detective.

A Private Consultation

The Borden house on Second Street was a quaint example of the Greek revival architecture that populated the downstreet area. Each time Sarah came down from the hill, engaged on business, a social visit, or to help with her mother's banking errands, she was struck by how crowded and small everything seemed, and the Borden house was no exception. It was pressed against the bustling sidewalk where peddlers and pedestrians challenged each other for space.

Sometimes, in the downstreet area, Sarah would catch a glimpse of Andrew Borden, Lizzie's father, who was tall, thin and a bit spectral with his unkempt locks and grim straight-lined mouth that always seemed clenched. He radiated some intense and unsympathetic aloofness. It was known that this self-made man had sold coffins, and it was rumored that he was a penny pincher, that he kept his wife and two daughters on a tight leash, that he negotiated each and every coin in any business transaction and prided himself on never having spent a foolish dollar. Outside his house on Second Street, about to knock and call upon his daughter, Lizzie Borden, the Girl Detective, Sarah had to muster all her courage.

Fortunately, it was the mother, Abby, who opened the door. She seemed humorless, but pleasant enough. "Are you here to see Lizzie?" she inquired and Sarah nodded slightly. "She's upstairs reading her Plutarch, but I'm sure she is receiving."

Sarah was ushered up a high narrow and bending staircase to a second floor landing. Abby Borden, who was physically drained from the demanding climb up the stairs, pointed to what was presumably Lizzie's bedroom door. "Just knock and she'll answer. Now if you'll forgive me, I must lie down. I've been dusting all morning and I'm fairly exhausted." And then she disappeared into the guest room, a feather duster flicking about her like a tiny bird.

After knocking on Lizzie's door, it was opened a crack and Sarah saw those wonderful eyes peering outwards. "My word," came an exclamation from within. "Sarah Durfee Borden! My favorite cousin!" The door flew open and Sarah was confronted by a cheerful Lizzie. "What brings you here to brighten my day that is otherwise occupied with dreary Roman classics? Come on in, please, and sit with me."

The door widened and Sarah was ushered into the bedroom. A single bed was angled in the corner, covered with a blue embroidered bedspread. Behind it was what seemed to be a communicating door to another part of the house. To Sarah's right was a fainting couch in front of the right-hand window and a chest of drawers. To the left was a desk and chair with bookcase above. Another bookcase was against the far wall, liberally sprinkled with book spines, and draped over with a velvet portière. There were elegant prints of cathedrals and European edifices hanging from the walls. It was the bedroom of a cultured, intelligent but cloistered young woman.

"What a lovely room you have here," Sarah said pleasingly. "What wonderful southern exposure."

"Actually," Lizzie said with a sly smile, "this room belongs to Emma. The poor girl is visiting in Newport and I've temporarily taken over. If she ever suspects I'm using it as an office for my consulting agency she'll have a fit, she will!" Lizzie pointed to a room off to the side that looked small enough to comfortably stable a horse. "That's my room over there. But this is just our secret, now, isn't it?"

Lizzie motioned Sarah to the fainting couch. "Please," she said, and gracefully sank with her into the cushioned seat. "What can I do for you today?"

"Lizzie Borden," Sarah said, leaping forward with her clenched hands, "I am told you are a solver of mysteries."

"Why yes," Lizzie said with a wry smile. "I have been quite successful at solving some other puzzles that local consulting detectives have been baffled by. I helped the constabulary solve the case of the

Portuguese Reprobate, and I was quite useful during the Affair of Mrs. Wilmarth's Immovables."

"And," Sarah interjected, "I did hear gossip about your role in the Riddle of the Forlorn Maggie."

Lizzie chuckled as if she were recalling an amusing anecdote. "I did not even think that one made it into the record. Well, all of these affairs earned me commendations directly from the town judiciary." She pointed to a framed certificate hanging above her writing table. "I am considering a full blown career in criminal detection if my father will provide capital for my tuition."

"Your credentials are indeed impeccable, and that is why I am coming to you today. For you see, I have a mystery unfolding within my very house. As you may know, my mother, Victoria Borden of the Anawan Street Bordens is the poor widow of Jonathan Borden, of the French Street Bordens. Six months ago, almost to this very day, my father died under mysterious circumstances while managing one of the Livermore mills. We do believe it to be foul play. He was found in an apoplectic state and quite dead. The cause of the death was never confirmed."

"My word," Lizzie said, holding two fingertips to her ovaled mouth. "That would be foul play indeed. Is there anyone that you think would harbor such hateful feelings towards your father?"

"Yes. He is Thisbalt Livermore, of the Taunton Livermores, the owner of the mill my father died in. A fouler man I cannot suspect, with his odious cigars and his corpulent belly. As a little girl I felt my skin crawl when he entered the room. For years I endured his sly flirtations, and now we suspect that he hired the agent who terminated my father's life. To make matters worse, we cannot find my father's will. That document would have provided for my surviving family, but alas we are left with a legal morass that threatens to have all my father's property turned over to Livermore. Unfortunately, my mother seeks to solve this problem through supernatural agencies."

"Supernatural?" Lizzie said. "Give me more details."

"A British spiritualist, Elizabeth Wingate. Perhaps you have seen her lecture in town about the seven-fold rays of man's spiritual origins. She is a fraud, I believe, and possibly an agent of Livermore, attempting to infiltrate my intimate family circle and obtain information about the hiding place of my father's will. I cannot prove that Livermore is behind Wingate's fraud, but if I could, it would go a long way to proving that Livermore was behind my father's demise."

"This Elizabeth Wingate, has she come recommended?"

"No, she approached us after hearing of our plight. We inquired about town and found out that she has worked with the Fox Sisters in upstate New York, but it is doubtful that anything said about her has veracity."

"Has your mother shown any previous interest in the spiritual arts to warrant such gullibility?"

"Not quite," Sarah said, and then paused, pressing her lips together.

"Well," said Lizzie. "It seems you are remembering something of importance."

"Quite right, Lizzie. You see my mother has a Spirit Box."

Lizzie's eyes widened. "A Spirit Box?"

"Yes, a small curiosity Father picked up in a dusty antique store downstreet. Father was particularly afraid of it after he brought it home and was loath to touch it."

"Afraid?"

"Yes, it was said that it was haunted by evil spirits. Particularly an angry ghost of a savage Indian who wants revenge for the atrocities committed by the white colonists some 100 years ago when Fall River was not yet even a town. Some say the ghost is that of Awashuncks, Squaw Sachem of the Sakonnet. They say she was condemned to dwell within the box by King Philip himself!"

Lizzie shuddered. King Philip, a Wampanoag Sachem, had been killed almost two hundred years before during a very bloody war with the English. Many a time in her childhood, her father had told her, "Be a good little girl or King Philip will be waiting for you in your bedroom." The thought had always haunted her deepest dreams.

Drawing herself together, Lizzie uttered, "But one cannot truly believe the box to be haunted?"

"My father did, and he went to great lengths to train us from an early age not to touch it. It sits there, alas, in Mother's Cabinet of Curiosities in the parlor, collecting dust. No one, especially Mother, dares to touch it."

Lizzie's eyebrows furrowed. "Does this Elizabeth Wingate know about this Spirit Box?"

"Well, yes, Mother was particularly interested in getting Wingate's opinion as to its supposed possession. Wingate wanted to take it with her to examine it, perhaps to perform a spiritual rite that would clear it of any possession, but Mother became hysterical and told her that no human on earth should touch it or else it would unleash King Philip himself and we shall all be brought to woe. Wingate told her to leave it be for now and when they have contacted my dear father's spirit in the Beyond, they will ask his counsel on the nature of the Spirit Box's inhabitant."

"So Wingate is interested in this curio?"

"Very much so. We certainly hope the old woman has some truth in her claims for supernatural powers. We would certainly love to have that old Spirit Box cleared of spirits. I have had many nightmares about that damned box."

Lizzie Borden, the Girl Detective, glowered in the dusty afternoon light. She scratched her chin and then pressed her hands against her bengaline dress. "Sarah, in a few scant moments you have provided me with a complex mystery that will indeed be a challenge. I shall take this case, and I ask for nothing more in return than a most excellent and hearty meal and an evening's delightful banter with your wonderful family when the affair is finished."

"Why certainly, Lizzie Borden," Sarah said happily. "You are indeed a gem of a girl. When do we begin?"

"Right this very moment! I shall inform my father's wife that I am going downstreet. I believe he can help gain information about this Livermore character. I wish to assess him myself."

The two girls left the room and entered the guest bedroom which they were surprised to find empty. "Mrs. Borden must have finished her chores," Lizzie announced.

They were startled to hear Abby's dour voice come from behind the bed where she lay on the bare floor, invisible to their eyes. "Over here Lizzie! I seem to have fallen off the bed while napping. Can you take a moment to help me to my feet?"

"Lizzie," Sarah said with alarm. "Your mother is in peril!"

Lizzie took a deep breath, her eyes twisting upwards with a forceful annoyance, and muttered, "She is not my mother! She is my stepmother!"

AN INVESTMENT PITCH

Andrew Borden, a tall dark figure, grim like a provincial undertaker who had just come into some inheritance, ambled down the street on his way home for dinner. His thin emotionless mouth and cold marble eyes greeted his fellow citizens who bothered to tip their hats and say a kind word of greeting.

"Good day, Mr. Borden," said one corpulent gentleman.

"Good day, Borden," Andrew muttered back, nodding his head. He vaguely remembered the man: J.F. Borden. Or was it T.E. Borden? Or perhaps that was another Borden. He couldn't keep them all calculated in his head and it sufficed to just call them Borden. No one would question him since he was a man of means and could walk downstreet with dignity and respect.

He reached his home and climbed the steps, retrieving his key from his pocket. In the front hallway, he was met by his youngest daughter, who came up on him from behind and tapped his shoulder. He seemed more than a little perturbed as he placed his hat on a standing rack.

"Nay, daughter," the poker-faced patriarch muttered. "Coming at me in such a manner is not fitting. What is your business?" He stepped into the sitting room to get his newspapers and Lizzie followed.

She smiled devilishly and slid onto the low sofa against the far wall. "Nothing, Father. I am merely curious how your day went."

"Twenty seven dollars in revenue for the Maple Street property," he bemoaned, as he flipped through the papers. "Plus a plundering of my daily tills from Mr. Carpentiere who seems to have forgotten that his talents lay more in the peddling of feather beds than in the creative fiddling of my audits."

"I'm sorry to hear that Father. But I'm wondering if you are better off putting your energies towards the associations within the textile community, than building furniture that you sell at most excellent prices befitting our Commonwealth."

Andrew peered up from his news stories, his eyes twitching. "What the devil do you mean, daughter? Borden and Almy is doing well by me."

"Yes, but there is great money in banking and textiles. I hear that Mr. Livermore is without a partner these days. His former co-president is simply late of this world, having died at the mill a few months back."

"I have heard of such things. J.A. Borden was a far cousin of mine, and I believe he left his widow with sufficient funds. Livermore is not someone I ever had a fondness for. His reputation recently has been a bit scandalous."

"How so?" Lizzie asked.

"Many say it is a mistress. His poor wife does suffer. I say that these times are not befitting for a man of industry."

"I suppose there is no harm in offering him your financial services, Father. I'm sure he could be quite reasonable when presented with a flow of money. After all, he is one of the most important textile merchants in town."

Borden brooded by the fireplace, his fingers tapping on his watch fob. "I suppose you are correct. I shall pay him a visit anon."

"What better time than the present," Lizzie said. "I hear he takes his dinner in his mansion between eleven and noon. And it is within a short walk from here."

"Up the damned hill!" Andrew scowled. "I swear an oath, daughter, you are going to be the death of me!"

Lizzie smiled and patted the horsehair sofa that was so comfortable beneath her on this quaint summer afternoon. "Why Father, such a horrible thing to say," she coyly whispered.

THE DRAGON'S DEN

On the street, a bowler-hatted gentleman lifted his palm to his brim. "Good day, Borden."

"Good day, Borden," Lizzie's father replied, and then gave a polite nod to a passing woman. "Good day, Mrs. Borden."

"God's graces on you, Mr. Borden," she said with a solemn nod of her own.

"And how is Mr. Borden this fine forenoon?" asked Andrew.

"None too well. He is currently consulting for his health with Dr. Borden."

"Would that be the Dr. Borden of Borden Street?"

"No," said Mrs. Borden. "That would be the other Dr. Borden."

"My word, you are correct. Forgive me, Mrs. Borden."

"Think not upon it, Mr. Borden." And they were past.

"How many Bordens are there in Fall River, Father?" Lizzie asked, clutching his big knuckled hand.

"Not enough for confusion," Andrew said loftily, then tipped his hat to another passing gentleman. "Good day, Borden," he announced.

Eventually, Lizzie and her father stood before the stately Livermore mansion. Overhead clouds passed behind its gables with gaseous indifference. "If only," Lizzie mused, "you had bought us such a fine dwelling on this hill instead of that midget cheese box on Second Street."

"Hush," her father said, raising a single finger to his thin lips. "Be quiet daughter, do not stress my patience."

A harried butler answered the door and took Andrew's card, peering up at him as if he were his better. Andrew huffed his way into the house and Lizzie followed. After a time sequestered in a drawing room, father and daughter staring at a billiard table that was so large it wouldn't even fit into their parlor, the teakwood doors flew open and in strolled Thisbalt Ajax Livermore, holding a wide beer flagon, his mouth stuffed with a generously rolled cigar.

The textile tycoon was more corpulent than Lizzie had imagined. His face was a fiery splotching of skin disorders as if some fierce mold had hatched on his lower chin and spread across his muttonchops, ear and forehead. There was also the glistening of medicinal gel that gave his head the appearance of wet rotting fruit. Lizzie fought back the urge to turn away her disgusted eyes.

"Borden," he said, dipping his chin in Andrew's direction.

"Mr. Livermore," Andrew said with reverence and a bit of awe. Lizzie had never seen her Father humbled so. "How are you doing on this fair day?"

Livermore puckered his lips. "Pash and twaddle! Have you not heard of the unfortunate Mr. Tweed of New York? He has been apprehended and is now wallowing in a common prison cell." Livermore puffed on his cigar like it was an extension of his face. An inky cloud wafted about his speckled head. "Borden, that is alarming news. I do not believe men of industry are respected in this day and age. No good can come of that."

Lizzie took a breath and interjected. "I do believe Mr. Tweed to be of a criminal disposition unbefitting an elected political official. I do not think a cell can be low or dank enough for his kind."

Pin-pointed eyes emerged from the darkening smoke. "Borden, you must have a sit-down with this young lady and correct her misdirected thinking."

"I endeavor to acculturate," Andrew sighed. "Lizzie, however, directs her thoughts elsewhere."

"There is nothing misdirected about my thought," Lizzie said, pulling at her ruffles. "I merely suggest that no man, no matter how wealthy or industrious, should be above the law. If Mr. Tweed has robbed New York City of millions, he must be called to justice."

"The courts shall decide," Livermore said, choking on the dusty air. "Meanwhile, Tweed is indisposed to a chamber not befitting a man of his industrious character." He paused to sip from his flagon. After lifting his dripping face from the brew, he sputtered, "But such talk merely takes us from our purpose. What can I do for you today, Mr. Borden?"

"Lizzie here has advised me to hitch my wagon to your train, so to speak. She suggests that I invest my money in your textile interests."

Livermore took two puffs of his cigar and said with a grunt, "How much and how soon?"

Andrew fell back on his heels. "Well, I suppose we can set up a meeting at the Bank to discuss the particulars."

There was silence in the room for a space.

"No particulars," Livermore shrugged. "Just sign a check at the front office."

"For what amount?" her father stuttered. His legs were visibly trembling.

Livermore's eyebrows extended to the top of his pasty scalp. "How the blazes should I know; you're the one who made the offer. What's your game? I've seen you, Borden. You make feather beds and coffins don't you? You grew up on Ferry Street. You raised yourself from the shame of nothing to where you are today, just like myself! Give me all you can spare, and in return I'll give you a cut of the great expansion that is about to occur. Are you not a man of vision? Do you not have financial instincts?" He paused and savored his tobacco, then stared back at Andrew. "Is that all? What are you gawking at?"

Andrew's fingers clutched at his side. He seemed to be trembling from the top of his pate to the bottom of his congress boots. "Uh...yes, I suppose that is all."

"Hmmm...yes. Well, I do believe you have turned out to be a fine ally, Borden. I look forward to seeing your money."

"I suppose that would be advantageous to both of us. Good day, Mr. Livermore, and I thank you for your time."

"Yes, my time." Livermore turned towards the massive fireplace that dominated one wall of the room and stared up at the array of framed Daguerreotypes that fringed the mantle. "I have nothing but time, Mr. Borden."

Lizzie and her father interpreted the sight of his back and the smoke curling from his head that it was time to leave.

Back on the front porch, Andrew stared down at his daughter and pressed his lips together. "My fortune at a clap," he groaned.

"Nonsense, Father. Livermore will take good care of you. He'll treasure your contribution."

"What is this really about, Lizzie? My word, girl, you are never what you seem."

"Not what I seem, Father," Lizzie said, beaming. "But what I have seen."

The framed Daguerreotype of Elizabeth Wingate, nestled on Livermore's mantelpiece, sitting in the prized position dead center between images of illustrious colleagues and family members, had told her all she needed to know about the connection between the fake spiritualist and the textile tycoon.

A Widow's Predicament

Sarah Borden met Lizzie Borden downstreet at the apothecary as she was leaving with a string-tied bag of rat poison. Her most excellent cousin was beaming with rosy cheeks. "Did you discover something, Miss Lizzie?"

"I prefer to remain reserved on the subject, Sarah. For now, I wish to accompany you on a social visit to your mother. I have much to discuss with her."

An hour later, they were seated in the very parlor room where Wingate's ceremonies were enacted. Lizzie sat with the Borden family, the twins bouncing around the room with urgent energy, and the Widow Borden, grim and sallow looking, seated in her chair of mourning, her eyes begging for respite.

"It has been a trying ordeal," the Widow Borden was saying. "Elizabeth is doing the best that she can but these things take time. Once you have become a shade in the Summerlands, it is very difficult to maintain contact with the material world. But I'm hoping that Jonathan's resolve to fulfill his love for me is stronger than those incorporeal bonds that are tying him to the afterlife."

"Or perhaps," Sarah quipped, "we aren't paying Wingate enough money! I'm sure if we doubled her salary, suddenly Father would start yapping."

"Sarah!" came the maternal rebuttal. "Please be reverent towards Mrs. Wingate, especially in the presence of our guest!"

"You must consider, Mrs. Borden," Lizzie said boldly, "the possibility that the spiritualist is not quite as effective in her conjurations as she may have advertised."

"Nonsense, she comes with the highest recommendations. She..."

And Sarah joined her mother in unison, "...studied with the Fox Sisters!" and then added "What a load of horse droppings."

The Widow Borden's eyes went milky as she thought back into the past. "I went to a performance of the Fox Sisters in New York a few years back. They were performing at the Academy of Music and drew quite a large crowd. They brought back a young boy who had been crushed under a mule at a Nyack farm. He wandered across the stage with these large accusing eyes. It was the most frightful thing I had ever seen. But it filled me with the strength I needed to endure Jonathan's death. I felt for the first time that there is hope, that he is not forever lost."

Sarah said grimly, "Mother, this has gone too far. Lizzie Borden is here to help you find the will, not to contact the dead."

Lizzie's eyes strayed towards the Cabinet of Curiosities that flanked the far wall. It was large and heavy with bronze claw feet and decorative flanged framings. Inside lay various items, many of them primitive artifacts that the Bordens had picked up from Jonathan Borden's sea voyages when he was a textile merchant abroad: African idol heads, JuJu sticks, and other implements of superstitious value.

"Perhaps the will is hidden somewhere on the premises...perhaps in one of the curiosities in your cabinet. Stuffed perhaps into a voodoo doll?"

"Alas," the Widow Borden said, resignedly. "I have examined all those items."

"All of them?"

"With the exception of that..." she pointed with a trembling finger.

Prominently, in the center cube of the cabinet, sitting alone with plenty of breathing space on both sides, was a large rectangular box, noticeably Western in style, with shellacked sea shells delicately placed in a rim along the joint lines.

"The Spirit Box," Sarah said. She got to her feet and started towards the cabinet, but halted, her feet glued into place. "For someone so unbelieving," she confessed, "I am afraid of that thing. Father himself told me of the evil that dwells within."

"We must leave it for now," the Widow Borden said solemnly. "It is cursed and cannot be touched or moved. When we ever depart this house, for whatever reason, we must leave it behind. Let the next resident of 9 French Street inherit our heavy burden."

"How did the Spirit Box get in the house in the first place?" Lizzie asked. "Surely it didn't just appear one night."

"No, that it didn't. It was my beloved Jonathan who brought it home from work one day. He said that it must never be opened, ever. Except on one occasion."

"And what occasion would that be?" asked Lizzie.

"In case of his death. He said it must be turned over to his lawyer at once. That only Joseph Coffin of New Bedford, his life-long solicitor, knew how to undo the curse of King Philip."

"Odd, I never heard of a lawyer practicing the spiritual arts."

"It struck me as odd indeed. But Jonathan himself filled us with such fear that we cannot even touch it to give it to Coffin. We figured we'd rather let it sit there and contain its evil rather than take the risk of Coffin exposing us all to woe."

Sarah said quietly, "There may be a connection with Thisbalt Livermore and that box."

"Hush!" said her mother.

"There's no point in withholding information from the only person who can help us, Mother." She turned to Lizzie. "Livermore was over for dinner with his dreary wife, this raggedy thing he drags behind him whenever he wants to make a splash on the social register. And in the middle of cigars and brandy in the billiards room, Livermore excused himself and went to find the water closet. When he didn't return, Father set out to fetch him and discovered him in the parlor trying to break into the Cabinet of Curiosities with a hatchet. He was snarling like a dog, in fact. Father said it was the most frightful thing. A week later...he..." Sarah fell forward with a sudden sob.

Lizzie put her hand gently on her cousin's shoulder while she regained her composure. "Why would Livermore be interested in the cabinet?" she asked.

"He may have been after the box," the Widow Borden said. "I do believe he is drawn towards evil, and wants to corrupt us all by discovering the secret of the box." Then her face became more drawn than ever and she moaned, "A week later my poor Jonathan was found dead in his office. He was slumped back in his chair with the most hideous look of horror on his face. His hand was outstretched on the table pointing towards the far bookcase. We never knew the significance of the gesture. But I believe that he may have been visited by the shade of Awashuncks, Squaw Sachem of Sakonnet."

Her hands flew to her face and tears fell copiously from her red eyes. "Oh, I am the most wretched woman who ever lived! I yearn for peace! And for Jonathan!"

"Mrs. Borden," Lizzie asked. "Is there any reason to believe that Elizabeth Wingate is also interested in the Spirit Box?"

"Nay, in fact she seems to dismiss my fear of it as trivial. She claims that when we settle the affair of my poor husband, she will address the box."

"Address it?"

"Perhaps I shall let her remove it from the premises. She knows how to handle it, more so than Solicitor Coffin would. Yes, I'm sure Mrs. Wingate will know how to contain the evil of the box and then it will no longer be in our house."

"Yes," Sarah interjected. "Let her have it. Let the curse be on her head, the old fake!"

Lizzie Borden nodded thoughtfully. "Mrs. Borden there may be more to this than meets the eye. I do believe I can help you, but I need your cooperation."

"And what would that be? Anything to remove this curse from my life!"

"I need you to schedule a séance with Elizabeth Wingate, here tonight, and invite me along. I need to be present at the conjuration of your husband."

The Widow Borden composed herself by dabbing a handkerchief to her red cheeks. "Why yes, that can be arranged. Mrs. Wingate is always pressing me to make another attempt each and every night."

Lizzie pressed her hands happily down onto her knees. "Fine then, tonight it is. And with your leave, invite along into our company any members of the legal profession you happen to know, anyone with an open mind for such supernatural matters. Just send a note round my home with the exact time of our congregation and I shall be here a half hour before to set up."

"Set up? Whatever can you mean?"

Lizzie rolled her eyes to the ceiling. "Oh, I merely meant that I will prepare myself for the proper mood. You never know what will happen. It is not every day that I get to meet shades of dead Indians!"

THE ELECTROMECHANICIAN

Homer Thesinger was called by many in Fall River the "Boy Inventor," but his preferred term for his chosen profession was

Electromechanician, a word he had first seen used in *Telegrapher* magazine to describe Mr. Thomas Edison, Homer's most valued role model. He spent his days in his father's basement on Prospect Street tirelessly tinkering with his electrical and telegraphic apparatus, his endless flywheels, batteries, electromagnets, relays and receivers, determined to be one of the first to make marked improvements in multiplexed signaling. He was regarded by most as intellectually promising but lacking serious prospects when it came to a career.

In the midst of his stubborn and time-consuming work, he often joined Miss Lizzie Borden for some refreshments at the South Main Street Apothecary where he would boast about his own inventions and visions for machines not yet invented. He held a bit of a torch for Lizzie. He admired the way her mind sorted out a considerable amount of factual data, always managing to piece together a larger picture that was absurdly obvious once you divined the solution, but which had been doggedly evasive during the crime solving. He felt she accomplished, with the puzzling mysteries brought to her by her clients, what he was attempting to do when he engineered some electromagnetic device: to fit it all together into an elegant and obvious solution. For this reason, his inventive mind and mechanical competence had served her well in more than a few of her detective cases.

So it came as a pleasant surprise one afternoon when Homer received a note by messenger to meet Lizzie at the Apothecary on South Main Street and that he should bring his Sazaphone, a complicated contraption of rubber tubing and ear-shaped lozenges that were designed to project voices from one part of a room to another. Homer had invented the device for a school performance of *A Midsummer Night's Dream*, but it had never been used because it had been so effective that members of the rehearsal audience had trembled in fear of the spectral voices that emerged from its cups. The presiding theatrical director finally deemed the device infernal and had banned it from the school grounds.

Homer appeared in the Apothecary with his inventor bag slung over his shoulder, the Sazaphone protruding through the burlap like a bunched serpent coiled inside. Lizzie was up on a stool sipping her syrup water and tapping her toes on the cross bar. "Homer," she said with a sigh. "You have acted promptly. Once again I need you to aid me in my exploits."

"And what, pray tell, are those?" Homer asked. He was used to Lizzie allowing him only enough information about her proceedings that he needed to know, no more, no less. "I have a meeting of my Fluted Shaft Society at eight tonight," he explained. "We're designing a cylinder that will capture the human voice in coded format so it can later be reproduced mechanically. We're hoping to obtain a patent and make money selling it to industry. We believe it will replace the stenographer. We're calling it the VocoPhonometer."

"A machine replacing a human voice," Lizzie mused. "This century has brought nothing but technical marvels into our everyday life. But anyway, Homer, I believe I can have you at your Fluted Shaft meeting by its pre-ordained hour. Here's what I want you to do for me. How well can you climb through shrubbery?"

"I don't believe I have any practice in that area."

"No matter. The trick is to avoid getting the seat of your pants stuck on thorns. I have faith that you can accomplish that."

Homer rubbed his pants legs with a trembling hand.

"And," Lizzie continued. "I need you to rig up some sort of harmless explosion. Something with a snap and a bang to it!"

"What exactly are you proposing, Miss Lizzie Borden, Girl Detective?"

She smiled. "Well, I'll tell you. But you must follow my instructions precisely!"

After sundown, Homer Thesinger, hauling his burlap sack over his shoulder, entered the Widow Borden's French Street garden by the side path of the house and immediately encountered the crunch berry bushes that whispered in the wind below the brightly lit parlor window. Through the glass, he could see a gathering of people, including the Widow Borden and her children, and Judge Mason and his tiny wife. They were standing around the parlor table just as Lizzie had described, and within a moment or two, a rotund woman, dolled up in a head scarf entered the room fluttering her fake eyelashes. This, no doubt, was the phony spiritualist, Wingate. Homer didn't like her one bit. Imagine taking advantage of poor widow Borden's grief, and in plain view of the young twins.

His eyes lit up a bit as Lizzie Borden and Sarah Borden entered the room, nodding their heads in quaint curtsies and allowing Judge Mason to press his walrus mustache against the backs of their hands. After a few polite pleasantries, they all settled down around the table and the kerosene lamps were lowered as Wingate sat like an erect Buddha in

front of the massive Cabinet of Curiosities. Her candle flickered upwards, giving her face a ghastly glow as she threw back her head, her
eyes going pearly white.

Lizzie sat to the side, peering intently, her eyes darting over every minute detail of the scene. Judge Mason and his wife held their
silence, clasping each other's trembling hands. The twins hid behind
their mother's chair as the Widow Borden pressed a handkerchief to her
prematurely tearing eyes. Sarah looked as diffident as ever, just like she
did in Latin class whenever Miss Handy gave a particularly dull lesson.

With a scowl and a silent curse, Homer stepped awkwardly across
the dank undergrowth as his ankle caught on some root that arched
upwards from the soil. He noticed it was a lead pipe. There was a muffled gasp in the foliage and Homer froze in his tracks. Fearing it to
be a trapped animal of some sort, he trailed his fingers along it, and
began patting a rounded surface that crinkled like felt. He lifted it and
immediately saw he was removing a bowler hat from a figure that was
hunched in the bush. With a slight yelp, the person released his breath
and threw up his hands.

"By Jove!" Homer cried out. "Who the devil can you be?!"

The hunched figure trembled. "It's only I, poor Tom Crank! Don't
be stern with me, Master Thesinger. I'm only doing my contracted duty!"

Tom Crank was one of the more feeble-minded students at Fall
River High School. He had shared many a lunch hour with Homer
Thesinger where he had proved continually how slow-witted his mind
could be. Homer shook his head with disbelief and pointed at the pipe.
"What's this blasted thing for?"

Tom reached up, his hands grasping a tarnished tin trumpet. "It's
mere fascination, sir!" he said with alarm. "I've been paid my wages!
Wingate's got her subterfuge and I'm a cursed man!"

Homer grabbed the boy by his lapels and shook him until his
eyes went crossed. "You mean you're the one whose been blowing
these trumpets?"

"Aye, sir. I don't mean to be insensitive to the Widow, but I've been
paid a most excellent wage. And I always did want to be a musician."

Homer released the lapels and stepped back a pace. "You are nothing but a mercenary."

"Aye, that I am. And there's no shame in it when you're trying to
turn a penny for your hungry family."

"Whatever Wingate is paying you, it's tainted money. If you want some redemption for your part in this subterfuge, I recommend you do exactly what I tell you to do!"

Tom's face contorted, and then his eyes sparkled with some hope. "Oh to be sure, there's nothing more sublime than to correct crooked ways. Just show me what to do and I'll do't."

Homer reached behind him for his rucksack. With a cherry glow in his eyes, he dipped his hand inside and pulled forth his Sazaphone, now a tangled mass of rubber tubing.

"What in the name of the Twelve Tribes be that?" the trumpet hustler cried in astonishment.

Homer Thesinger, the Boy Inventor, just grinned.

A Spirit Box Opened, A Demon Set Free

Lizzie had noticed from the very first that Elizabeth Wingate was keeping her back to the Cabinet of Curiosities. It seemed to be a deliberate avoiding, rather than a casual ignoring. Up close, the spiritualist's face was flabby and pasty, and her eyelashes were obvious fakes. As soon as the lights were dimmed and the candlelight filled the room, the rappings began. They seemed to be coming from the table, but it could very well have been underneath the table. Those attending seemed too terrified of them to pay much notice to particulars.

"We are gathered here tonight," Wingate said suddenly, "to draw forth the specter of Jonathan Aloysius Borden from the beyond, from the Summerlands. May his presence here be potent and puissant."

"And don't forget to bring his checkbook," Sarah whispered into Lizzie's ear, provoking a sharp giggle. Wingate's eye flashed to the side, demanding silence.

Mrs. Judge Mason twitched in her seat. "I hope he comes soon. It's awfully cold in here."

Lizzie noticed the draft as well. No doubt the window just beyond the parlor door was kept wide open. If all had gone well with Homer in the garden, there should be a lozenge shaped cup snaking along the floor at this very moment.

"Jonathan!" Wingate cried out. "Come forth from the realms beyond!"

Suddenly, without warning, there was a haunting groan. The two small twins began to cry and Mrs. Judge Mason let out with a shriek.

"Victoria!" came a spectral voice. "Victoria! I have come back to you!"

The Widow Borden leapt to her feet and held out her arms, tears pouring freely down her face. She was too choked up for words.

Wingate stared, puzzled, at the parlor door. Lizzie suspected that she was baffled as to the nature of the voice. It certainly was different from the utterances made by her accomplice in the garden. Homer was being extremely clever.

"Victoria!" it continued. "This woman, Wingate! She is not a friend!"

Wingate snuffled. "Why, Jonathan," she said purposefully. "You must be confused. I am your familiar, your material basis in the waking world."

"You are nothing but a desperate fake!" the voice shouted.

There were muffled gasps, as Wingate sat poker-faced.

Lizzie pulled out a handkerchief from her dress pocket and pushed her nose into it, letting out with a sharp sneeze. Then, just on cue, as her hands came down from her face, a terrific noise filled the room. A new voice, warbling, deep and loud careened off the walls and echoed between the doorways. Lizzie smiled subtly. Homer's Sazaphone was working its magic.

"This is Awashuncks, Squaw Sachem of the Sakonnet!" it screamed. "The fires of tribulation are coming down upon French Street ready to consume utterly the misbelieving! Oh fly! Fly while you can! King Phillip shall have his revenge!"

The assembled guests stared at each other with alarm, then turned to Wingate who was sitting with a perplexed frown that outdid their own. "Wingate!" cried Sarah. "If ever there be a time that you confessed to fraud it must be now! You have either gone too far, or we are about to be consumed by the Tribulation!"

Wingate spoke with a choked throat. "Alas, I cannot say this is subterfuge."

The voice spoke again. "Let my words be a warning to your eternal souls!"

Mrs. Judge Mason gathered her composure enough to speak a single sentence. "Perhaps dear," she said hoarsely, her face getting paler with suppressed fear, "we'd best listen to her advice." Then she swooned into the arms of her husband whose walrus mustache bristled with rage and fury. "Wingate!" he puffed. "Stop this farrago immediately! We've tolerated your frauds because they amused us, but this..."

Wingate lifted her empty palms into the air. "I only wish I could."

The voice shouted over the din, "If you do not flee, the house will be set aflame and all within it shall satisfy the swollen appetite of fire." Then there was a small explosion that illuminated the room, followed by a smell of sulfur and charcoal. With this sudden assault on their senses, many of those present gasped and started violently for the exits. The Widow Borden gathered the twins, who were paralyzed with fear. Lizzie rose from her seat, fearing nothing of course, but curious to see what Wingate would do next.

As Mrs. Judge Mason was revived by the pudgy hands of Judge Mason, Sarah, right on cue and with a wink to Lizzie, motioned for everyone to head for the French doors leading to the main hallway. "Fly to safety!" she commanded, and everyone listened to her directive. All but one, of course.

Elizabeth Wingate ran straight for the Cabinet of Curiosities. From the folds of her blouse she produced a small claw headed hatchet which she raised with terrific violence against the Cabinet's glass front.

"Got you," Lizzie smirked.

The spiritualist deftly smashed the hatchet into the pane of glass that separated her from the prized Spirit Box. For a brief moment, the flabby woman stared through the shattered glass, then dropped the hatchet to the ground with a dull thud and with trembling fingers lifted up the shell-rimmed box in the air, muttering under her breath, "I have seized the prize!" She swooped it down to be buried within the folds of her blouse, then bolted for the door.

"The purloinment of the Spirit Box," Lizzie thought, "proves everything. This case is as good as solved."

Following Wingate out of the house, she came upon an odd scene on the front lawn. Deputy Sheriff Wixon, a tall handsome man with a generous mustache, was holding Homer Thesinger and Tom Crank by their collars with two respectful hands.

"Here's a pretty how-dee-doo!" Wixon was shouting. "What is this nonsense? Ghosts and trumpets!"

"Let my man go," Lizzie and Wingate said in perfect-pitched unison, then stared at each other as if they had both shown up at a ball dressed in the same gown.

"Deputy," Judge Mason said, holding up his wife who swooned with a near-fainting dizziness. "They are innocent. I think I know what has transpired here tonight." He pointed downward to the streamers of rubber tubing that were hanging from beneath Homer's jacket, and the bent tin trumpet that was dangling from Tom Crank's belt. "I believe the poor Widow Borden has been the victim of an elaborate fraud to obtain her money and to steal her husband's will."

"What?" Wingate sputtered. "My intentions towards the Bordens have been nothing but honorable." She lifted her hands up in the air as if to demonstrate the straightforward fact that she had nothing up her sleeve. Unfortunately, at that very moment, the Spirit Box emerged from its hiding space within her blouse and slid down her hooped skirt to the ground, hitting the lawn with an audible thwack and turning on its end twice before coming to a dust-stirring rest.

"That," Wingate said glumly, "was not quite to my advantage, now, was it?"

Mrs. Borden stared in horror at the Box, then glanced up at Wingate who was edging her way towards the garden path.

Lizzie stepped forward and pointed a stern finger at the spiritualist. "Mrs. Wingate, I'm afraid I must ask you to remove the slipper on your left foot and snap your toes."

The woman's cheeks went slack. "What a preposterous proposal," she blurted.

"No, I'm afraid that I have to ask you to do this toe-snapping right away."

Wingate peered about as if trying to discover some escape route from the garden. With a sudden grunt and a lurch she bolted from the crowd and headed straight for the path off the property. At first Deputy Wixon made some attempt to follow, but Lizzie lifted a single finger encouraging him to stay his hand.

Before Wingate could reach the safety of the street, there was a quivering sound as if a large strip of metal was being twanged, and her agitated body seemed to lift completely from the ground. For a second she hovered in space as if suspended by invisible entities, and then came crashing with a sickening crunch to the earth. She flopped for a moment and made a crude noise as air escaped from her orifices, and then lay very still and silent.

Wixon's eyes were wide with astonishment. "I don't suppose you can explain that," he said to Lizzie.

"I can," Homer Thesinger said, beating his chest with pride. "I have laced the path to the street with my Super Durable Elasto String. The sound you heard was its marvelous flexing ability, like a piano wire being plucked. I have merely set a very primitive trap to catch a sophisticated bird."

"Well done, Homer!" Lizzie clapped, while Deputy Wixon raced forward to manacle the stunned spiritualist.

"And now for the Spirit Box," Lizzie said, holding up the shell-encrusted container. The Widow Borden shrank back with an awful creep. "No, Lizzie! King Philip! Awashuncks, Squaw Sachem of the Sakonnet! We shall all be brought to woe!"

"Nonsense. This is nothing but a curio that Mr. Borden proposed to be haunted to protect its contents. I'll show you."

Lizzie lifted the lid as several present put up their arms to shield their eyes from any supernatural events. As soon as they could see that there was no spirit, no blast of light, no demonic clouds or shrieks of the damned, they lowered their arms and peered into the interior of the quite ordinary box.

Inside was a rolled piece of paper tied with a red bow tie.

"The will!" Sarah said.

The two little twins started bouncing up and down like one of Homer Thesinger's Vertical Amusement Shafts. "The will! The will!" they were shouting.

Mrs. Borden was reduced to tears seeing her little precious girls so happy. She knew that they understood little, but they knew enough to know that their mother would be made immeasurably happy by the appearance of what they knew as "the will." And here it was: the ultimate secret of the dreaded Spirit Box of the Curiosity Cabinet.

Wixon, who had been poking around the clothing on the inert Elizabeth Wingate, came back to the crowd with a wrinkled piece of paper. "Here's a nice how-dee-do," he chuckled, glancing at its contents.

The Widow Borden took the paper in hand and arched it towards the kerosene lamp that dangled from the back porch. After a moment, her eyes flickered and she looked as if she would faint. Judge Mason came forward to support her and Lizzie and Sarah hunched over the paper. It read:

Dearest Winnie,

The Borden family is in our proverbial grasp. As long as no one peers into the Spirit Box, we are safe. Snatch it while you can and we shall be done with this dreadful business!

I deeply regret having to procure the African potion to settle the Borden Affair, but the medical investigators were too dull-witted to see past the frightened look on Jonathan Borden's face. It was, indeed, the perfect crime!

Let Livermore be your paramour forevermore. My duckling!
My fine apparel of warm enswathed womanhood! I shall be
yours until the last trumpet sounds.

Doodles

Underneath was a crude line drawing of a man in a top hat and monocle with exaggerated lips puckered up for amorous activity. Three X's captioned the drawing. Sarah felt a shudder go through her skeleton thinking of Livermore being capable of such feelings. And worse, being the recipient of them.

Lizzie rubbed her chin. "Doodles? I never would have guessed. Not a logical extraction from either of his names."

Sarah nodded, tears forming in her eyes. "The man killed my father."

"Yes," Lizzie said, staring at her compassionately. "I can only imagine that feeling."

The Widow Borden snatched the Spirit Box from Lizzie's hands and held it aloft as if it were some accursed thing. "You have plagued my life lo these last few years, haunting my nights and making my own parlor a place of fear! Be done with you!" And she smashed it upon the ground under her foot. It splintered into shards and the sea shells rattled off into the grass. "Contact Joseph Coffin immediately!" she announced. "There is a will to process!"

"Lizzie Borden," Sarah said, placing a congratulatory hand on her cousin's back. "You have done fine work here tonight. Mother, we must reward our girl detective with a most excellent and hearty meal and an evening's delightful banter with our wonderful family. Even Tom Crank can join us if he chooses, despite his culpability in this affair!"

Tom snuffled nervously. "I'd be most obliged. Poor Tom's a-cold!" And he pulled his threadbare jacket tighter around his frame.

"Consider it done," Mrs. Borden said, holding up the will in a loose fist. The entire family, Lizzie, Homer, the Judge and Mrs. Mason and Deputy Wixon—all except for the inert Elizabeth Wingate and poor shivering Tom—joined in with a healthy burst of laughter and applause.

An Evening's Recap

The scene at the factory office had been chaotic. The Fall River police had approached Livermore directly, despite their fear of his stature and influence. When the coterie of officers and the arresting lieutenant entered his office and announced their charge, Livermore had cried out, "God's wounds!" and tried to spear one officer with a large fountain pen from his desk. As a result, he had to be tumbled to the ground and his hands tied behind his back with a shackle. As they dragged him through the lobby of the textile administration building, employees who were so used to seeing him cross the marble floors in an ermine coat and stately top hat, now saw him frog-marched like a snarling beast, his obscene curses echoing off the ornate marble ceilings.

Lizzie and Sarah went once to the county prison to see Livermore in his cell. He sat in the furthest corner, swathed in shadow. His eyes pierced the darkness to hit them directly with a cold shudder.

"The hag and the harlot!" was his only exclamation.

Lizzie shot back with, "Perhaps, Doodles, you will be joining Mr. Tweed in chambers more suited to men of your industrious disposition." From the shadows, they could hear Livermore choking with rage and vengeance.

Then Lizzie and Sarah retreated and went to the local apothecary to relax over a few mugs of medicinal syrup water, Mr. A.E. Dobbs attending.

"How did you know that the will was in the Curio?" Sarah asked excitedly.

"It was very simple," Lizzie Borden replied. "I knew from the start that Wingate was a fraud. The rapping on the table top can be achieved quite effectively by snapping one's toes, and I did notice that Mrs. Wingate had on padded foot slippers, the type you can cast off quite easily just by lifting your foot. She also walked with a pronounced slant towards the left, showing that it was her left foot that was employed in the toe snapping."

"Marvelously perceptive," said Sarah, enthralled.

Lizzie laughed. "The credit for the discovery of the source of the trumpet blasts I give to Homer Ulysses Thesinger, Boy Inventor. I was not surprised to see Thomas Crank of Rodman Street involved. That poor boy can be easily led by wolves into walking off a cliff. Fortunately, the law has overlooked his breach of conduct and he is now at home nursing his wounds. For his role in the affair, I shall honor him with a stipend that will offset his college education, advancing his status in life far beyond what a bobbin boy in a textile mill would accomplish."

"That is very generous of you," said Sarah with a broad smile. "Poor

Tom is merely a follower and was exploited by Wingate as much as my mother. We bear him no ill will."

Mr. Dobbs, polishing his glasses behind the counter, joined in with fascination. "But Lizzie, you still didn't tell us how you knew about the Curio?"

Lizzie smirked knowingly. "When Homer announced that King Philip was coming to enact his revenge, Wingate ran for Widow Borden's Cabinet of Curiosities. I found it quite significant that she grabbed the Spirit Box. I couldn't see how the Box would have been of any interest to Wingate. She no doubt wanted to keep whatever was in the box from being destroyed."

"Brilliant. So at that point you knew that Wingate was only after the contents of the box, and that she had no other interest in my mother or my family's affairs."

"Yes, and that she was in the employ of Thisbalt Ajax Livermore was obvious from the picture of her that was in his drawing room, proudly displayed on his mantelpiece. I knew there was a connection between the two."

A dark look came across Sarah's face. "But my word, Lizzie. Didn't your father hand over all his money to Livermore?"

"That is the beauty of the machinery I had set into motion," Lizzie smiled. "My father invested everything he had, so much so that when Livermore was exposed as a murderer, the Livermore Mill went into the hands of the investors. My father is now the de facto owner of the Mill! His fortune has quadrupled with one investment."

Sarah lifted her mug of syrup water and saluted her newly found friend. "Lizzie Borden, you are truly a girl detective of the first order!" Sarah exclaimed.

Lizzie nodded. "Yes," she said. "And a girl detective is what this world needs most at such challenging times as these."

The two Borden girls, joined by A.E. Dobbs, Pharmacist, engaged in hearty laughter and good company, sipped their syrup water and through the smoky glass of the apothecary front, watched the sun settle down on the quiet twilight of Fall River.

THE END

The Exhausted
Amanuensis

October, 1877. Fall River, Massachusetts.

A Competitive Nature

On the very morning that Lizzie Borden of Fall River first heard of the puzzling Professor Welles and embarked on one of her most baffling adventures as a Girl Detective, she was lounging about in her sister Emma's airy and sunlit bedroom. Reclining on the fainting sofa, she basked in the heat and light of the southern exposure despite the late autumn season. Holding a pearl handled mirror up to her face, she solemnly examined her pouty cheeks, her wide eyes, and short eyebrows, feeling with her fingertips the youthful texture of her skin.

"One day, Lizzie Andrew Borden," she spoke softly to her own image, "you shall be known all throughout this Commonwealth. Children shall be singing your praises in rhyme."

The bedroom door disrupted her reverie as it rattled hard against the chair that Lizzie had propped underneath the doorknob. This was followed by a low grumbling, and the sound of footsteps drifting away in the direction of the adjoining guest room. Lizzie put down the mirror and braced herself, knowing that the second door into the room, the one from the guest chamber, would soon open. When it did, it pushed aside a small dresser that groaned forward into the room, in its turn disheveling the carpet. In the dresser's wake stood Emma Borden, her older sister, who, as was apparent from the street dust in her dress hem dragging behind her, had been running errands. Emma stood fish-mouthed, her eyes lighting up as she soaked in the invasion of her private bedchamber.

"I suppose you are wondering," Lizzie said, getting to her feet and hand-ironing her skirt, "why I am not locked up in my own room." Her eyes darted towards the small closet-like space that sat just off Emma's bedroom, in which a large bed dominated the area below a dim window. "Perhaps your seminary education did not include the art of measuring walls," Lizzie scoffed, folding her hands before her. "But if you examined that little crawl space that has been designated as my own, you will find that its dimensions fall quite short of those of your own spacious quarters."

Emma's eyes ran rampant over her sister's face, as if she were looking desperately for some hint that sanity dwelt within. She then pointed a finger towards Lizzie's bedroom. The finger stood in the air like a flagpole, quite firm in its meaning.

Wisely choosing to remain silent, Lizzie nodded, lifted her skirt, and moved towards the room. She then slammed the door behind her. Just as she had seated herself on the bed, wondering how long her punishment of solitude would last, the door banged open and Emma appeared, her words flowing just as freely as they had previously been frozen.

"You pretend that you have the disadvantage!" Emma shouted, her voice passionately reaching an upper register. "You think it's easy for me, to know that at any time you feel like it, you can come charging across my room, disrupting my peace? There is no privacy in this house! I can't sit still for a moment, not a moment. And for what? So you can shirk all your errands and run around this city playing like you are some sort of crime detective? I can't even imagine why you would do anything of the sort!"

"Perhaps it's because I'm clever," Lizzie said. "I may have the tiniest room in the house, but I certainly have the largest mind."

"And what is that supposed to mean? I want to remind you that I am thoroughly educated, and I have intellectual talents of my own. Did it ever occur to you that I might be offended by your posturing and all the attention that your superior intellect has won you? I can do your job just as well."

A broad smile graced Lizzie's face. "Why Emma, that would be delightful. Fall River will be all the richer for that. There are, sadly, plenty of unsolved crimes to go around."

Emma thrust out her chin. "I have no doubt in my mind that I can do what you can do. There is no trick to it. It's all common sense."

"Common sense? Well, then let me demonstrate, dear Emma, why I am a Girl Detective and you have been making runs to the family farm to gather the eggs for Father. I have a puzzle for you, and I want you to solve it. It is a simple one, but very revealing."

Emma's eyes turned upwards as they narrowed. "Proceed," she challenged.

Lizzie cleared her throat. "I begin. You enter into a cabin in the woods that is dark except for the moonlight coming through the single window. You find on a table a single match, a candle, a kerosene lamp, and a log of wood for the fire. Now keep in mind there is only one of each item, including only one match. Which would you light first?"

Emma closed her eyes as if trying to crank the gear shafts of her mind. "That is obvious," she finally announced, staring proudly at her sister. "I suppose I should hang out my shingle as Emma Borden, Girl Detective, for I have solved your little mystery using simple reasoning. The candle will be the one to light first."

"Why so?" asked Lizzie.

"It is simplicity itself. The candle is the easiest to ignite, it takes but an instant. And besides: you never said the kerosene lamp has any oil, and the log of wood would need a fireplace, which you have not described. Thereby, confronted by a single match, a candle, a lamp, and a log of wood, I would first light the candle. Then if the lamp has any oil, I can transfer the flame to it from the candle, and if the cabin does indeed have a fireplace, I can set ablaze the log with the generous fire from the lamp. That, dear Lizzie, is how a seminary girl thinks!"

Lizzie smiled and began walking past Emma on her way to the hallway. "You would have to light the match first," she said as she rustled across the floor. "And that is how a Girl Detective thinks."

Emma stopped breathing as her hands curled into fists and Lizzie descended the steps, softly humming to herself. Somewhere in the distance, the town hall bell was tolling the noon hour.

THE PUZZLED PROFESSOR

Later that afternoon, a small nervous woman in a blue bengaline dress paced back and forth outside the Borden residence. As her wrung her hands together, the woman's anxious eyes were glued to the sidewalk as if she were about to make a monumental decision. As the horse traffic, street vendors, and pedestrians flowed around her, she gathered up her nerve as well as her skirts and ascended the steps to the Bordens' door. With newly found determination, she knocked.

"I must speak to the Girl Detective," she announced when a middle-aged woman, wiping her hands on an apron, answered the door. "Please announce me to Elizabeth, the clever one," the visitor said boisterously, as if she had rehearsed the line.

"Lizzie is her name," Abby Borden, Lizzie's stepmother, corrected her. "And if you must insist on indulging her in her sad fantasy, then so shall it be. Come in, please."

The woman, upon being ushered into the parlor, took a sweeping look at the small modest furniture and marveled. "I like your wallpaper," she said, pointing at the violet curls of flowers that snaked along the walls. "You have developed a tasteful interior."

"Thank you," Abby said. "I'm glad someone appreciates it. I'll go fetch the...uh... clever one."

A few moments later, Lizzie Borden entered the room, standing tall and stiff, a group of books in the crook of one arm. "I beg your gracious pardon," she said, smiling. "I didn't mean to keep you waiting, but I was in the middle of my mid-afternoon tour through these fascinating books on the medical sciences. I am taking a particular interest in the life story of Dr. Benjamin Rush, a man who, despite his erudition, experience, and wisdom, was a passionate advocate of bloodletting. It is a barbaric element of our medical climate, thankfully one that is in the process of disappearing. Why only the other day our family doctor told me..."

"Dear girl!" the woman said, stepping forward, encouraging Lizzie to move back towards the piano. "I come to you on most serious business; this is not about bloodletting, but my poor, insane husband."

Lizzie set the books down on the piano top and motioned the woman to join her on the lounge. "I apologize; it often takes moments to return from my studious trances. Please be seated, and I am all yours."

The woman nodded and began in a careful voice: "I am Julia Welles, the long-suffering wife of the great Professor John Wellington Welles, late of Brown University, now living in semi-retirement on Rock Street. We have been in Fall River for a full year now, and my serious wishes were for my husband to let his brilliant career fade behind him, and for him to enjoy his twilight years in domestic simplicity. For so long now has he been immersed in the study of mathematics. He has an almost unnatural obsession with the theories of infinity, although I fall short of understanding exactly what they are. All these years, I have taken pride in his excellence, his authority, and his natural ability to discipline his mind to solve any number of complex equations. In his prime years, he was a foremost expert on the paradoxes associated with these sciences, and learned men from all over the world would seek out his judgment and advice."

"Happily, I have heard of Professor Welles since he has moved to town," Lizzie confessed. "But my path has never crossed his, except for a paper he wrote on the speed of light through the ether that I may have read at the library. I am afraid that my knowledge of mathematics is not as strong as I would wish. However, I hold Dr. Welles in very high esteem. I am a little confused, however; do you come here with a problem relating to the Professor? I sincerely hope nothing is wrong."

"Nothing is wrong," Mrs. Welles announced. "But I am afraid that something may be wrong in the future. "

"I don't follow."

"I can barely follow myself. My husband has put too much of himself into his work, laboring long and hard. In his solitude, he has long occupied his mind with mathematical paradoxes. One time he attempted to explain the theory of accelerating infinities. I followed him at first, but soon got lost in the logic, or lack of logic, and I pitied him that he often has to spend long periods inside his own mind with such thought-twisting equations. Always I feared that he would lose himself and become severely muddled. Indeed, I'm afraid that time has come."

Lizzie rocked in her seat. "What has happened?"

"Recently, he has come to the conclusion that…" She glanced about, making sure that Lizzie would be the only person to hear her. "I know this sounds crazy, but you must understand that my husband has been under enormous strain. He is of the opinion, based on his own research, that time as we know it—the time that we follow like a straight arrow throughout the day, from the moment we sit up in bed to the late hour upon which we fall back asleep—is not as straight as one would think. He actually believes that time is moving in both directions, that some of us are moving in one direction in time, and that others, like himself, are moving in another direction."

"What exactly do you mean?"

"He explains it thus: what is tomorrow for me is yesterday for him, and what is yesterday for myself is tomorrow for him. He claims that he is moving in epicycles, as he calls them; and states that although he experiences each individual day in the same time flow that the rest of us are moving in, the progression of days for him is backwards. He also claims that in this manner, he can predict my future, because to him, it is his past."

Lizzie felt a surge of disappointment. Instead of a mystery, she was hearing a simple case of an overworked mathematician who needed a vacation. "He is obviously too strained from his work," Lizzie announced. "I believe this is beyond my talents. Perhaps he should see a doctor about his nerves."

"Well, it is not his mania about the flow of time that I have come to see you about, nor is it the mystery that I expect you to solve. You see, tangential to this theory about time is his insistence that he has committed a horrible crime. And to make things worse, my husband contends that crime is still in our future, although for him, he remembers it as if it were yesterday. Indeed, it may very well have been yesterday for him."

"A crime? Has he indicated the nature of this crime?"

"I know this sounds incredible, but he claims that there will be a day and an hour in which he will cross from one time flow to another, and on that particular day, he will actually meet with himself. He claims that in a fit of hysteria, he will kill himself, or has killed himself."

Lizzie nodded and flattened out her skirts. "Yes, I see. Well, Mrs. Welles, I don't know how I can help you. I have heard of lunatics in our Taunton Asylum who have received some very excellent treatment at the hands of trained professionals. But I am not of that profession."

"I know, dear girl. I am sorry to bother you with such a strange tale this early in the day, and I know it must be severely confusing. But I do believe that my poor husband is suffering such delusional mania that he actually believes that he will be killed by himself. I know that this sounds fantastical, but I would like to hire your services to solve a crime that has not yet been committed."

"How can I do that?" Lizzie sighed. "Clues usually appear after a crime, and not before. Further, when the culprit of the crime has already confessed that it will actually happen in the future, and that he himself will be both the victim and the murderer, where do I even begin? The identity of the murderer is already solved, and the victim will only be dead for a single moment since the murder will happen backwards, hence there will be no more victim after it is committed. And the only victim before it is committed is the murderer. So where is the need for a detective?"

"Nonetheless, I implore you to take the case. I want you to spy on my husband and piece together the twisted labyrinth of his failing mind."

"How can I spy on him? From what you tell me he is a recluse on Rock Street, and I cannot be occupied by creeping around the windows and peering in. I'll be picked up by the police."

"I can arrange to have you brought in as his personal amanuensis. He has already expressed the need to finish his current thesis called "Zeno's Paradox and the Arrival at the Zero Point Through Eudoxus' Method of Exhaustion" for the *Providence Journal of Mathematical Studies*. He is desperate to finish the paper and have it published before he corrects his direction in time and survives his own murder of himself."

"Am I qualified for being an amanuensis for a celebrated professor? I clearly do not know the math."

"All will be taken care of. Previous assistants hardly did any work at all. He merely wants someone to follow him around and jot down notes that he spouts at random intervals. Oh, Miss Lizzie Borden, Girl Detective, will you help me in this matter? From the stress of it all, I am going mad myself."

Lizzie stared into space, trying to imagine herself taking notes for a Brown University Professor. There was an attractive allure to it, a quality of accomplishment. Since she had never attended a university, this would be such a great opportunity for her to experience the mind of a brilliant, if not slightly insane, man.

"I do suppose I can spare the time," she said quietly.

Mrs. Welles beamed with hope, her eyes widening, and her hands reaching out for Lizzie's shoulders. "Oh dear, I know there may be not much more to this than my husband's drift into madness, which, in and of itself, is a tragic thing, but to think that I may be able to prevent, with your help, his own murder of his future self, that gives me great comfort."

Lizzie rubbed her chin. "If this will accomplish nothing more than to give you a slightly more balanced peace of mind about your husband's condition then I shall be glad to oblige," she said. "As you may have discovered from various sources, I do not charge any fee for my services, except the satisfaction that I am providing good deeds for my own community, by helping those who truly need help. That has been my reward."

"Yes, I have heard of your generosity. But I do insist on paying you a wage for your pretended work as amanuensis. It is only fair, since you will actually be providing my husband with the assistance that he needs. At least accept that small pittance, one dollar a day. Starting tomorrow morning at nine o'clock."

"Agreed." Lizzie was about to stand and walk Mrs. Welles to the door when she froze in place, a strange smile on her lips. "I do have one request," she said.

"Anything you wish, dear girl."

"I have an assistant of my own. Like me, she has a strong mind and is currently an apprentice to my detecting profession. I wish to bring her along, perhaps disguised as a cook or a maid. Do you have a position on your domestic staff that would suit a woman of about twenty-six?"

"Why, yes; indeed I do. The maid-of-all-work has recently fled the premises, disturbed over my husband's condition. We have put a notice in the afternoon paper, but have not yet received any responses. Do you think your assistant can handle a domestic job?"

"Without question. You have my word that she will provide impeccable service, both as the new maid and as a complement to my own investigation."

"It sounds splendid. What is her name?"

Lizzie closed her eyes, feeling for the answer with her mind rather than thinking it out. "Maggie," she finally announced.

"It is done," Mrs. Welles said happily, rising to her feet. "I shall see both of you tomorrow morning at nine. I will tell my husband that you shall be arriving in the morning."

Once Mrs. Welles was safely out of the house, Lizzie turned to ascend the staircase towards her bedroom, and spied Emma standing like a sentinel at the top of the steps.

"Maggie?!" Emma asked, her eyes rolling.

Lizzie lifted up her hands. "Now, Emma! I only had your edification in mind. I assumed you would want to take part in an investigation to improve your detective abilities."

"Maggie!" Emma repeated, her voice ascending.

THE IMAGINARY MAN

Early the next morning, Lizzie and Emma walked up Rock Street, their hands on their hats to counter the high winds that stirred about all the elegant homes of the more affluent families of Fall River. Lizzie was dressed in a tightly fitting dark blue Basque with a handsome row of buttons running down from a bow brooch under her chin. She was fretting over a pocket watch, which was nestled in her left hand, minding the time, pacing herself so they would arrive at their destination punctually on the hour. She seemed ever the intellectual young lady, straight out of school.

By contrast, Emma trailed her sister in a shapeless gingham dress with a stained apron that she had fetched from the cellar dustbin. A white cap bridled her head and a set of pockets flapped about her side flanks.

"I feel as if the entire city is laughing at me," she whispered to Lizzie.

"Nonsense," Lizzie said, not looking at her sister. "We are just a secretarial assistant and a Maggie out for a stroll."

They passed the elegant homes along Rock Street, distinctive dwellings with their gilded capitals and elegant balustrades, their Mansard roofs, and their sandstone walls and granite pillars. These magnificent homes, in which dwelt the mighty owners of the mills and the influential bankers of Fall River, were quite a contrast to the relatively shabby Greek Revivals to which Lizzie and Emma were accustomed, and seemed like Temples of Apollo by comparison. The two sisters paused before an imposing home that was graced with what seemed to be a mill tower proudly erect off the center.

"Here lives Jefferson Borden," Lizzie sighed. "Now, there is a Borden indeed."

"Did you not ever feel, Lizzie," Emma asked solemnly, "that Father could have secured us our place up here on the Hill? Perhaps if he had been far more ambitious, he, too, would have prospered as regally as Mr. Jefferson, and we would then be enjoying such a castle for our own."

"Father has done very well for himself," Lizzie said, pulling at her arm. "We cannot fault him if he has not risen as high as Mr. Jefferson, so there is no need to mourn our possible futures now."

They finally arrived at the residence of Dr. John Wellington Welles, an elegant and feminine pink house rising from the street. A narrow set of stairs led up to a small porch. They rang the bell and the lady of the house arrived, looking at Lizzie with a strange dislocation. "Ah, the new amanuensis. Professor Welles is quite anxious to get started."

"The pleasure is all mine," Lizzie said with a tiny curtsy, then ascended into the house. Emma, after a slight pause in which she detected she may be left behind on the porch, followed quickly before the door shut. Mrs. Welles looked at her with a discerning eye.

"And this must be Maggie."

"Yes," Emma said, pausing awkwardly then dipping her knees faintly. "I am...uh...Maggie."

"Fine," Mrs. Welles said coldly. "Before you do one moment of work, let it be understood that you are in service to our needs. There is one hard and fast rule here at the Professor's house, and that is the servants need to be ready at all times of the day and night to perform their duties. There is no such thing as having idle moments on your hands here. Having said that, you will now follow in the direction in which I am pointing. The kitchen is that way. Mr. Humphrey is waiting. He'll explain your duties."

Emma swallowed hard, took a desperate look at Lizzie (who seemed to be ignoring her), and started toward the kitchen with an awkward gait. When she was gone, Mrs. Welles broke out into a huge smile and poked Lizzie in the arm. "If that is truly not a maid, then she must surely be applauded for her theatrical skills!" she exclaimed. "I could not tell the difference. Come, Lizzie, I'll introduce you to the Professor."

They walked down the corridor by the side of the main staircase and came to a dark oak door that opened into a musty study with northern exposure, dominated by many bookcases. The volumes were laid out in long rows, so numerous that they obscured most of the walls, darkening the room. Centered upon the wide fireplace mantel was a marble clock, flanked by two golden lions. The clock's pendulum swung back and forth to an audible, persistent metronomic pulse.

Before the windows facing the street, stood a dark mahogany desk upon which lay mountains of paper, behind which rested a small man with an egg-shaped head bearing a fringe of white hair around the side. His face was obscured by an enormous shock-white mustache growing over his lips like a strange mammal that had deposited itself on his mouth for hibernation. The man's face turned upwards. Only the uplifting of the mustache gave Lizzie the suggestion that the man had smiled.

"This must be my new assistant!" he shouted in a thin and shrill voice, quite in character with his stature. To Lizzie's surprise, the man glided out from behind his desk without gaining any height. Apparently, he had been standing; his legs were comically short.

"Come, my child!" he said, a few stout fingers motioning her across the room. He stood in a frayed dressing gown with a tasseled cord, as if he had just risen from bed. "Come this way, and prove my hypothesis as you do so."

"I don't understand, sir. How can I prove anything by walking across the room?"

"All in good time," he chuckled. "Hmmm," he paused, one eye

closing and the other one darting towards the side, suggesting that his mind was awhirl with fresh thought. "In good time. Yes, well, in one time line you are already across the room and are moving back towards where you stand now. But that is not your concern. Come, come!"

Lizzie walked towards him, slowing down as she approached a foot from his position, but his fingers still beckoned her forward. "There," he said, as she came to a halt, not three inches before him. "You have empirically proven it, just as everyone else who has walked across a room towards me has proven."

"Proven what?" Lizzie asked. "That I can walk across a room? I do have feet, you know."

"No, you have proven that Zeno's Paradox is but a mad delusion. The Paradox is the ancient riddle that points out a rather peculiar impossibility in physics. Between any two points there are an infinite number of points; therefore it should be impossible for anyone to actually arrive at any destination."

"I have heard of this paradox," Lizzie said, "in my high school class work. If you halve that distance between the two points, you arrive at halfway, then if you halve this distance again, you arrive at three quarters of the way. If you halve *that* distance, you are now getting closer to your goal, but since there is an infinite number of points to cross, you will continuously be halving the remaining distance for an infinite number of times which will take forever. It is truly a paradox."

The Professor's face brightened, his cheeks flushing. "My, you have made an old man very happy. I have never had an assistant who took any sort of interest in my theories, far less knew about them before I even explained them. I think this will be a very fruitful relationship. Please sit down, and we will discuss your duties."

As Lizzie sat, she glanced around the room and began to notice its details. Over by the door was a small standing Grecian column, upon which perched a bust of Isaac Newton, his long romantic locks cascading alongside sad eyes that were, despite all the years since his death, as yet, trying to discover the secret equations that defined the universe. About the base of the column were strewn crumpled pages from notebooks alongside several scientific journals and newspapers, as if they were leaves blown across a lawn. Upon the Professor's desk, scattered amongst the countless pages of a holograph manuscript, were various objects that seemed fitting for a man of science: a broken astrolabe, a kaleidoscope, a magnifying glass, and a large leather-bound edition of

Jules Verne's *Journey To The Centre of the Earth*. The Professor noticed her specific focus on the book.

"Verne is an idealist, like me," he explained. "He believes in actually arriving at your destination." He clapped his hands. "Now, we will begin."

For the rest of the afternoon Lizzie sat enraptured by the Professor's eager sharing of his theories, elucidated with a clarity that surprised her. Although much of his discussion consisted of high mathematical principles, he spoke of them metaphorically, succeeding in painting visual pictures for her that drew out the internal logic of the equations in such a way that Lizzie, in reaching an understanding of his theses, would simply imagine arrows being shot from golden bows, stars glowing in infinite darkness, or beams of light crossing the vastness of the starry sky. As he explained more and more, Lizzie took renewed interest in his charming eyes, his generous mustache, and his gnome-like body. She began to admire him.

At the end of the day, as the sun slowly sank behind the river down the Hill, and the houses on Rock Street began to glow with the warm burning of oil lamps in their windows, he professed the need for a very early retirement, a little too early in Lizzie's estimation. He rang for Mr. Humphrey and the stone-faced man servant appeared as if he had vaporized from under the door. His well-structured and harsh mutton-chopped face bespoke many decades of dedicated service to his betters.

"Help me upstairs," the Professor told his man. "We are done for the day."

Mr. Humphrey escorted his master to the door of the study, then turned and twisted his head in Lizzie's direction, clearly indicating that she should wait for him. After several minutes, Mr. Humphrey re-appeared, a strange glint in his eye that resembled a twinkle.

"I need to discuss a delicate matter with you in private," he said.

"As you wish," Lizzie nodded.

"I am slightly embarrassed about this, but I do wish you would allow me a glance at the papers that you and the Professor are working on. I am a bit of an amateur mathematician and I can surely expand my education from seeing the progress he is making with his equations."

"I can oblige," Lizzie laughed, a bit relieved that he did not reprimand her for ill behavior towards the Professor. "I shall leave the papers on the study desk each night. Please allow yourself much freedom with them."

"I thank you," the proud man said, the glint disappearing from his eye. "And I urge you to keep the Professor in the dark about my request. He does not see me as a suitable recipient of his work, being that I am of the domestic class. If you know what I mean..."

"I certainly do," Lizzie sighed. How charming it was that a man servant was serious about advancing his education. She bowed politely and Mr. Humphrey turned to vacate the study. A moment later, Emma appeared in the doorway, her face drifting underneath a head rag, her hand holding a pail that sloshed with soapy water.

"Ready to go home?" Lizzie asked, raising a winking finger.

Emma scowled and threw the pail down to the ground, where the water splashed onto her boot. "Confound you, Lizzie Andrew!" she said, painfully. "You think I can just walk out the door like I have finished a school lesson and it is time for recess? Are you mad? They have put me up in the attic and I'm to send for the rest of my clothes in the morning."

Lizzie scratched her chin and pondered. "I did not think that Mrs. Welles would insist you play the role to the hilt."

"You make me the maid, I become the maid. You spend the entire sunlit course of the day with your midget scientist and engage in varied intellectual nonsense, while I scrub the privy and run the laundry down to the cellar. Tomorrow morning, I am to empty the slops!"

"Hmm, I will put in some inquiries to my employer."

"The employer from whom you have asked no pay but the wages of an amanuensis? How do you think that ranks against the pay of a Maggie?"

"I don't suppose they come close. Well, there is much to think upon."

A low voice, startling in its immediacy, rang out from the hallway. "The only thing to think upon, Maggie," it said, causing the two women's hearts to thump, "is that there is more ironing to be done." In the low shadows stood Mrs. Welles, an eerie displeasure across her furrowed brow. Emma withdrew with a frightened yelp into the corridor, racing towards the kitchen, dragging the pail with her.

"I am sorry to disturb Maggie's duties," Lizzie said, tipping her hat slightly forward. Mrs. Welles winked, then headed towards the front door, indicating for Lizzie to follow her. "Servants are a strange lot and it is best not to become too familiar with them. They crave attention and are often distracted from their duties."

"I will no longer pay her any mind," Lizzie said assuredly. Within moments, she was heading down Rock Street towards home, pondering

Emma's dilemma, but wondering even more about the delightful paradoxes of time and space that the dear old Professor had put into her mind.

THE DARK CONCLUSION

Lizzie's session with the Professor on the second day commenced on
a curious note. Upon her arrival, Mrs. Welles, whose face was flushed
red with frustration, met her at the front door. "He claims he's been
waiting for you for an hour," she announced.

"I am very punctual," Lizzie said, pointing to the silver pocket
watch, which she had held in her palm during her entire walk to work.
Mrs. Welles' face remained stiff and Lizzie went immediately to the
study to find the little man was already dressed and well into shuffling
his notes.

"Where have you been?" he asked, twirling the left half of his mustache. "The day is nearly half over."

"I'm sorry, Professor," Lizzie announced, "but by my reckoning it
has just begun. It is barely past nine o'clock."

"Poor girl," the Professor said, clicking his tongue. "I shall make a
mathematician out of you yet. Remember, the arrow of time is not constant. And it shall be sundown before we know it. Let's begin!"

Lizzie sat at the desk and spread out the papers on which she
was taking dictation. She took up a stylographic fountain pen of the
improved variety that Mr. Cross of Providence, Rhode Island, had personally presented to Professor Welles as a tribute to his genius, or so the
Professor claimed. She unscrewed a nearby inkwell, and with the help
of an eyedropper, topped off the pen's interior chamber.

"Yesterday, you were quite adamant about the method of Exhaustion," she reminded him, "to eliminate the trivial infinities that bedevil
any man who tries to accurately calculate the area of a solid object or the
distance between two points."

"Not quite the precise definition," the Professor said, his crinkled
eyes indicating a smile had grown under his mustache. "But I shall
elucidate. It was the Greek Pythagorean Hippasus and his Theory of
Incommensurable Magnitudes that started the whole thing. He shook
up his community by announcing that not every value in the world
could be reduced to a common unit of measure. He proved it by using
geometry. It was said that he made this discovery while at sea, and that

his cabin mates, who were also Pythagoreans, were so disturbed by his discovery that they tossed him overboard to his doom. Admittedly, I can't help but feel a sense of empathy with Hippasus, since I was also expelled from Brown University by my community of mathematicians. Yes, that was a sad day, but it turned out to be the start of a new life for me." For a moment, the Professor stroked his mustache and stared out the window as if remembering something from a long time ago.

He turned back towards Lizzie. "The idea," he continued, "that not everything in the world can be reduced to whole numbers led to Zeno's assumption that any quantity can be halved an infinite number of times and always be in the process of approaching zero, but never quite reaching zero. This led to the split between the concept of magnitude and the concept of number, freeing numbers from their paradoxes of infinity. The reason why I am so fascinated by this proposition is that it will defeat Zeno's Paradox and show that indeed one can transfer an infinite number of points by continually halving the distance, and eventually arriving at a destination."

Lizzie tried to scribble as much as she could, then eventually gave up. "Professor, I think it would be a lot clearer to me if you demonstrate how this relates to the concept of zero. You mentioned yesterday that zero is the point to which all phenomena tends toward, but at which they never arrive."

"Yes," he said, rubbing his cheek. "Always tending towards zero, but never arriving there. It is a maddening proposition, and one that I have devoted my entire life conquering." His eyes went dim, then he looked at her with renewed interest. "Perhaps, my dear amanuensis, it is time for me to lay bare for you my master plan as put forth in my new paper "Zeno's Paradox and the Arrival at the Zero Point Through Eudoxus' Method of Exhaustion" for the *Providence Journal of Mathematical Studies*."

Lizzie smiled at such a thought: his master plan. "Oh, do you mean that you have formulated a solution to Zeno's Paradox by defeating the Theory of Incommensurable Magnitudes?"

"Even better," he said, his eyebrows flaring. "By the Method of Exhaustion, one can reduce the increasingly infinite values, the ones that never quite reach zero, and exhaust them to a state of being trivial infinitesimals. Do you understand, my girl?"

"Well, it's not quite something I do on a daily basis" Lizzie confessed, putting down her pen. "Perhaps if you explain a little more..."

From the corner of her eye, through the study windows, she saw Emma walking in the yard, holding in one hand a wooden three-legged stool and a long pole on the end of which was a limp mop. Her other hand still held the watery pail from the day before as if it had never left her fingers. She came toward the study window, glancing upwards at its tall height with a sense of exhaustion possessing her face.

The Professor glanced out the window to see what it was that had caught Lizzie's gaze. "What is that girl doing? It is nearly supper time."

"Professor," Lizzie said, authoritatively. "I have only had my breakfast a scant one hour ago. I can taste it now: coffee, oat meal, and bananas."

"Nonetheless, I must get on with my tale. At Brown University, to the frustration of the students and faculty alike, I pursued this avenue of the Theory of Exhaustion to defeat the Incommensurable Magnitudes and Zeno's Paradox. In a nutshell, they thought me to be insane. I was asked to leave."

"Clearly, they could not appreciate your advanced mind."

"Precisely. But in the last few months, I have been working arduously at this theory, and I must announce that the time—and indeed when I say 'time,' I mean 'time' in the full sense of the word—is coming soon. The answer to the riddle, as obvious as it may seem, is in my future. And the future is moving towards me at an accelerated rate."

"But Professor, the future is in the future, and we are moving towards it, not the other way around."

"Ah, you have revealed to me your precious intellect once more. Charming, for you are quite right. How can we tell if the future is moving towards us, or we are moving towards the future? And if we are both moving, then are we not accelerating the inevitable moment of collision?"

"That may be all correct, Professor. But how is this proof of your theory?"

"My dear amanuensis, when the future arrives, it will be proof that it is moving towards us. And that the moment of collision is the Zero Point in the Arrow of Time. That is when the Incommensurable Magnitudes shall be exhausted and all the past, the present, and the future will actually arrive at its destination!"

The room fell silent, broken only by the clomping noises of Emma's mop against the glass panes. Lizzie felt a lump in her throat. What the Professor just said made no sense to her, but it seemed not only plausible but also inevitable. She couldn't even visualize what it meant, or how it would physically manifest in the world—the Arrow of Time moving in both directions at once, colliding at a single point in the present and coming to a conclusion, arriving at a destination. It all gave her the same feeling of awe and fear that she often felt when she meditated upon some of the Holy Scripture's spiritual propositions, like the ones where, as in the Book of Revelations, the world shall come to an end and we shall all be called to a vast reckoning. How silly it all sounded when proposed by her Reverend; now Lizzie felt an urgency that made it feel so terribly imminent.

"Do you mean to say," Lizzie asked, "that all of the future and all of the past will collide in one moment?"

He nodded, almost religiously, as if the realization were too sacred to stain with words. "A singular moment," he said. "One that shall have no past or future. Imagine that. Our frail science and incomplete mathematics can only hint at the magnitude of such a moment."

"How much longer before this happens?" she asked daringly.

"Ah," the Professor said, tilting his eyes downwards. "That is what we are here to discover through completing my work. We must answer the question: when exactly will we reach the dark conclusion?"

Lizzie glanced once more in Emma's direction and saw her older sister struggling on the wobbly stool to keep her balance while extending her arms with the long handled mop. Emma's face was seized with a colorless desperation that bespoke only the task at hand. What innocence Emma seemed to possess now, engaged as she was in the mundane daily chores that we are burdened with, not realizing that a mere few feet away, men of science like Professor Welles were probing the very shape of time and space itself, coming to some startling and disturbing conclusions, dark indeed. How much Lizzie envied Emma now, that she did not have the burden of hearing so terrible a pronouncement. Who at the moment had less responsibility, the Amanuensis or the Maggie?

The Professor walked to the statue of Isaac Newton on its pedestal and placed a calm hand on his small shoulder. "This is a man who defined an absolute space and time. He believed that it all made sense, that one can reduce it all to formula. He didn't believe that all of history was moving towards a single moment, a singular event in which a single moment is so infinitely small no human mind would ever comprehend or even experience it. Some have announced it happened at some point in the past. Others say it will occur in the future. I say that both the past and the future are hurtling in their own respective directions towards this moment. A moment that so great a mind as Isaac Newton would find strangely impossible."

"The Dark Conclusion," Lizzie said in a whisper, her fingers trembling. "Professor," she announced. "I believe we would take our supper now."

"Excellent idea!" he said, clapping his hands and gazing at the clock on the mantle. "And just in time, I may say!"

It was only half past nine in the morning.

MAGGIE'S OBSERVATION

As the weeks proceeded, Professor Welles' schedule became more erratic and unpredictable. All evidence indicated that he was losing all sense of time, that he perceived the sun going down as the sun was coming up, and that he took his meals at increasingly shorter intervals. After a weekend break, in which Emma was surprisingly exempt (Mrs. Welles had planned a thorough cleaning of the cellar and kept the maid on through the Sabbath to execute that labor), Lizzie came back, bright and early Monday morning, to find the Professor stretching and yawning. It seemed as if he had trimmed his mustache even further, and took an inch off his scraggly white hair.

"Good evening," he said cheerfully. "I don't suppose you realize that you have missed an entire day of work. I may ask you to copy some of my notes while I get a good night's sleep."

Lizzie was about to remind the Professor that it was just a short time since the sun had risen, but she figured that he had clearly lost his reason and that he would not listen to any common sense even if she tried. So she helped the Professor up the stairs, and then came back down to the study where she found his wife, silhouetted against a window, staring at her.

"Mrs. Welles," Lizzie said. "I don't suppose you failed to notice that your husband's dementia has gone far beyond a belief in time travel. He now seems to believe that the days are getting shorter."

"An obvious ploy," Mrs. Welles said angrily. "And one I shall not suffer gladly."

"Ploy?"

"Is it not obvious that he is faking? I would have hoped that you would have seen that by now."

"Mrs. Welles, it was I who told you from the beginning that it was physically impossible for your husband to be moving backwards in time. I was the one declaring to you that he was faking. Why, you merely have to notice that he recognizes me every morning, that he remembers our conversations from the day before, that I do not have to introduce myself anew with each sunrise, as would be the case if my yesterdays were his tomorrows."

"But now," the Professor's wife said smugly. "I have better proof than that. Last night I found him cutting his own hair."

Lizzie frowned. "Cutting his hair?"

"Surely you have not failed to notice that his mustache and hair are growing shorter by the day. He was in the kitchen last night with a standing mirror shearing himself with a pair of scissors. Most certainly, he is trying to give the impression that his hair is growing shorter by the day, thereby keeping up the illusion that he is aging backwards. I've never seen a man so desperate."

"Desperate for what?"

"My husband has always been furious that he was expelled from the University, so convinced that his theories are correct that he would now do anything to prove them and redeem himself in the academic community. That is why he so badly wants to show that time and space are controllable, and that one can conquer the barriers posed by infinitesimal quantities." She paused for a moment to consider her own words. "Whatever those are…"

Lizzie giggled and lifted her shoulders. "Coming from a world where the most pressing issue of the day is a dress sale down street, I would say that makes your husband most admirable."

"Yes," Mrs. Welles said sadly. "But I wish I were married to a fruit peddler. He'd live by the clock: be on Bedford Street by seven, hawk his wares, count his daily wages, and then go home. For this entire year since he was kicked out of Brown, my husband has taken refuge in his arcane equations, and he has lost my affections." She stared despondently at the sunlight that brightened the windows. "Ah, if only he had taken an interest in the arts like his brother. I can see him as a painter, sitting in the wilds of nature with his palette and his smock. Yes, that would have been quite romantic indeed."

"He has a brother, then?"

"Sydney, two years younger, and two inches shorter. The two

always argued that one wasn't younger or older than the other was. The wretched fools actually believed that they were both one year away from an ideal age that hovered somewhere in time between them. Likewise with their height: one inch off from some invisible center."

"Is Sydney also a man of science?"

Mrs. Welles laughed. "Hardly. He studied as an artist in Paris. Never have there been two brothers so unlike each other in temperament. Why, there is one of his paintings on the wall. Jonathan keeps it there as a memento, but cares not a jot for it. He took it as a birthday present, but I've never heard him say a kind word about it."

Lizzie stared at the wall where a framed painting portrayed a fog-bound seaman in cloth cap and a heavy straight-bodied jacket standing at the railing of some ship, presumably a whaler, his face pointing towards the sea, clearly contemplating the infinite, as most sailors, artists, and visionaries in any art or science will do from time to time.

"Perhaps they were not too dissimilar," came a soft voice. Both Lizzie and Mrs. Welles jumped a bit as Emma, fully garbed in her maid raiment, stood with a bucket of soapy water in the doorway. "He paints the captain with such fondness for his inner longing," she said. "You can see it in his face."

"Then my husband has never noticed," Mrs. Welles snapped. "Maggie, I was showing the painting to Miss Lizzie. You have some wood to fire on the cast iron for supper. And you must remember my peg lamp is broken and must be mended. Hop to it, girl!" She clapped her palms together, and Emma shuffled from the room, her eyes cast downward, slightly mumbling as she moved along.

"You are unnaturally harsh on her," Lizzie said, sternly. "Remember, she is only a pretend maid."

"I am paying her wages, she will do as I say," Mrs. Welles said stiffly, and walked past Lizzie towards the hallway. "I believe he is ready for bed," she concluded, and disappeared.

Lizzie stared at the painting, trying to imagine a mind unfettered by the cares of everyday drudgery, or having to make a living, or to run errands for the household. The artist-brother must be a winged soul taken alight into a realm higher than the one pursued by the Professor, a realm all the richer for its plenitude of heart and feeling. And yet the captain in the painting was staring to sea as if he were separated from some destination where he desperately needed to be, some place that, once he arrived there, would make him feel whole again.

She turned and saw the piles of paper that she had been working on with the Professor. How vain and unnecessary it all was, for the vanity of fame in the scientific community, or the God-like desire to conquer the System of the World. All men who strove for such heights were in essence divorced from their own hearts, caring little for their fellow humans and everything for abstract principles, be they university professors or simple furniture salesmen aspiring to be bank managers. They were all poor in spirit, lacking in some quality that made painters, poets, or even the lead violinist from an Academy of Music concert, more masculine, more courageous, and nobler than all the men of money and textile that populated Fall River. How petty and insignificant seemed the contributions of a Jefferson Borden now, when Lizzie stood confronted by the lonely stare of that salty whaling captain: a seafarer about to embark on his journey to bring back the precious fuel of light from the ghostly void.

There was a flutter, and a shadow appeared in the doorway. It was Emma, again, her face partly in the shadows of the room. "You have heard it from her own mouth! The man is faking. So, we are suffering here for nothing! For the petty wages she hurls at me to endure her insults and clean her show-kettles?"

"Emma, I know this is troublesome, but we are almost at a conclusion."

"The man is insane. To me, that concludes it right there." She began to remove her apron. "I am going home."

"No, stay! Emma, I need you to trust me. Something is happening that we don't understand yet. I was hired to prevent the man from killing himself, and the attempt has not yet happened."

"According to him, it has. That's good enough for me. I want to get out of here before she orders me to bang out the horse blankets."

Lizzie went to the desk and plied through the papers with unsettled hands. "No, that does not satisfy me. To him, the past is the future. At least it is the future for us. Oh, it is all so confusing. If only the man would walk and talk backwards, something irrefutable to show that he is truly time traveling. But this whole business about epicycles perplexes me."

"Epi..." Emma tried to repeat. "What? Aren't those having to do with the planets?"

"Yes, from our position upon the earth, the planets seem to move in retrograde motion, against their natural direction." Lizzie paused and saw the confused look on Emma's face as if she were trying to remember some astronomy lesson from several years before. "Perhaps it is easier to understand like this: In the old times, we would see the planets make strange patterns in the sky. They would slow down, reverse direction, and then speed up, before reversing direction again. This was all the stranger because we believed that the earth was at the center of the universe, and all the planets and the sun itself moved about us. But putting the sun at the center changed everything, and explained the motion of the planets perfectly. Now we know that epicycles are not the planets moving backwards, but merely an optical illusion as they turn within their own elliptical orbits, unlike the perfectly circular orbits that dominated in the Ptolemaic system."

Emma's eyebrows came together at the center of her forehead. "I have no idea what you just said," she sighed.

"Oh, Emma. The lesson is very simple. When we thought we were at the center of the universe, we saw the planets as moving backwards. But when we placed the sun at the center, we suddenly realized..." She came to a sudden stop and glared down savagely at the papers clutched in her hands. They were covered with numbers, formulas, equations, all sorts of non-sensible abstractions that only a man trapped in his own head would believe, a man who thought that he was at the center of the universe.

"I think I know what's happening, Emma. Perhaps in a strange way, the universe just flipped around."

"Perhaps, but I only have a few moments before Mrs. Welles screams at me for not cleaning the grease pit."

Lizzie sat down at the Professor's desk and frantically looked for blank paper. She grabbed a sheet and then steadied an inkwell before her. "Emma, how many days have we been here? Five days on duty and two days off..."

"Seven days," Emma said in a huff, "with no days off."

"Yes, but the Professor was here the first day at nine o'clock, refreshed from a good night's sleep and ready for work. Then, as the days went on his schedule began to slip and he started to have delusions that he was several hours ahead of us, which would make sense if his own future were contracting backwards."

"I did notice such strange behavior. Why, only on Thursday did he believe that it was nine at night at only three in the afternoon."

Lizzie scribbled some notes, and then thought again. Emma stood paralyzed, knowing that there was something momentous going on in her sister's head, something that couldn't be interrupted, not even for Mrs. Welles' horse blankets.

After more calculations upon the paper, Lizzie drew an X-axis and a Y-axis and began to plot some points. They seemed to follow an exponential curve up the side of the graph. She hurriedly connected them, her drawing increasing in momentum as more of the shape of the line made itself evident. Finally, she thumped the paper and hurled the pen onto the table top, sprinkling the wood with ink.

"Emma!" she shouted. "On the morning that we had arrived, the Professor had completed an epicycle and was beginning to slow down to move back into retrograde motion."

"Which he is now doing?"

"Yes, he slowed down, then began his motion backwards again. He will kill himself in three days' time."

"Yet he is a faker. He cut his own hair to give the illusion of time travel. You heard Mrs. Welles."

"Emma, it is not important that the time travel is not happening, what is important is that he believes it. We merely have to follow the strange inner logic that he thinks to be true in order to determine what he is actually doing."

"He is moving backwards to the point where he is going to kill himself."

"Not kill himself," Lizzie said smiling. "Not suicide. He is going to confront himself and murder his double. That would not be suicide; that would be merely a metaphysical conundrum."

Emma shook her head, trying to dispel the thought. "When we find Professor Welles lying on the floor with a knife sticking in his chest, I would see that as a little more than a metaphysical conundrum."

Lizzie picked up the pen again and strained to puzzle out some numbers. "If only we can determine the exact moment where he will accelerate into that Zero Point that he talks so much about. He truly believes that he is destined to arrive at the end of time and he indicates that it is three days in his past. But three days in his past is three days in his future." She glanced up at her sister as if registering a forgotten thought. "Oh, dear Emma. Forgive me, you can go about your Maggie duties, I must work at this problem."

Emma snarled and reached for her skirts and turned to go. "It is all pig squat, Lizzie! I'm going to go home right now. And I'm going to move so fast, that it would seem as if our little house on Second Street were running towards me!"

A sharp jab stung Lizzie's mind when she heard Emma's words. She bolted to her feet, darted across the room and whirled her sister about, letting her see the excitement in her eyes. "Emma! You have given me the final piece of the puzzle! The Professor is accelerating backwards in time, so a day in the future is not a single day by our reckoning, but a shorter period of time. It is indeed as if the future were hurtling towards him. Oh, Emma, thank you!"

"What have I done? I don't understand."

"You've helped to solve the riddle of when Time will end!" And with a dramatic flourish of her arms, Lizzie disappeared from the room, leaving Emma to ponder the profundity of her own accomplishment.

"Well," said the weary house maid, pulling at her gingham. "I have solved the riddle of when Time will end. Wait till the girls back at the seminary hear about this one!"

THE RECKONING

As the clock struck eleven, Emma felt more uncomfortable than usual in her small attic room. A child's rocking chair sat against the far corner, casting an eerie shadow on the wallpaper, and Emma kept glancing at it as if to make sure that it would not move. For several hours, she tossed and fretted, thinking of how abused she felt, of all the unfair labor she was forced to endure at the hands of Mrs. Welles and Mr. Humphrey. The indignities were of a kind that not even a maid-of-all-work should be experiencing, and when this ordeal was all over, it would be Lizzie who would have to answer for it. Why did her sister remain so silent? How could she let this happen when it was within her power, as Mrs. Welles' confidant, to petition to have it stopped?

After much tossing, Emma was alarmed to see the glow of a lamp underneath her door. It grew brighter, there was a small tap, and the door began to open inwards. With a startled yelp, Emma sat up in bed and drew her knees up to her chin, only to relax when she saw Lizzie, still dressed in her day uniform, standing in the doorway with a gloved finger pressing to her lips in the gesture of silence.

"Emma," she whispered, and came to the bed, sitting gently on the side. "I have finally finished my calculations."

"I thought you went home hours ago," Emma complained.

"No, I hid in the horse barn and came back in through the unlatched side door just before sundown. I have just spent the evening calculating the exact hour when Professor Welles will confront himself as he passes in two directions of time at once." She paused, and then added, "Taking into account his rate of acceleration, of course."

"I'm assuming," Emma said dryly, "that the hour is near."

"The hour is in twenty-three minutes," Lizzie announced. "Right now the Professor is in bed, ready to wake. He has completed almost two cycles since we arrived that first day, Monday last, but because of his acceleration, time is moving faster for him. To him, it is one hour in the future for us, but that hour will only take him twenty-three minutes to experience. Therefore, we should be on guard at that time."

"Lizzie, you do know how absurd this all is. The Professor is insane and that's all there is to it."

She was about to speak again, but Lizzie's hand fell like a clamp over her mouth. Someone was moving up the hallway, no doubt drawn by the light radiating from Lizzie's lamp. Within a few seconds, the two sisters were startled to see Mrs. Welles in her nightgown standing in the doorway, her eyes dark and sullen. "Has he killed himself yet?" she asked, with a strange lilt in her voice. She sounded slurred, almost drugged. Her body swayed and she steadied herself against the door frame. "I cannot wait," she added. "I want my husband back."

"Mrs. Welles," Lizzie said, getting to her feet. "Are you all right? You seem intoxicated."

"Something in my drink," she said. "I can't..." And then she fell suddenly and heavily to the rug, hitting the floor with a violent thud. Emma leapt out of bed, and the two women struggled to get their employer onto the mattress. When she was flat on her back, she gazed upwards, trying to keep her eyes open. "He's faking, you know," she managed to say. "He's faking everything except the mathematics. Unless... unless..."

"Unless, what?" Lizzie asked, shaking her shoulders. "Mrs. Welles, you must tell me."

The woman fluttered her eyes one last time, breathed out, "Two equals Zero," and then fell soundly unconscious.

Lizzie thumped Emma's arm and announced, "We must take our positions immediately."

"Where, Lizzie? Oh, this is too horrible."

"It is almost over. Come with me to the Professor's study. We have so little time before it all comes to an end." With a sudden dramatic gesture, she extinguished the kerosene lamp, leaving the two to fumble their way through the darkness towards the staircase.

They slowed near the bottom, and then noiselessly glided into the study. The room was very dark; the soft moonglow coming through the windows was not sufficient to light their path. Lizzie knew her way by habit, groping across the floor, until she arrived at the desk, her fingertips lightly touching the familiar inkwell. She picked it up and felt its comforting contours. It was heavy and seemed a good weapon to have in her hand in case of attack.

They stood there for what seemed like an eternity. For all the crazy talk about time speeding up, for Emma Borden it certainly seemed to be slowing down. The remaining fifteen minutes they waited in darkness and silence dragged on endlessly and offered so much fear that Emma's legs were buckling from the strain of standing.

"Emma," Lizzie whispered, her voice almost invisible. "The light, do you see it?"

A thin flicker appeared at the top of the stairs and began to work its way down. The two girls stood frozen as it grew in size, and they could just make out the quiet shuffle of slippers against the steps' carpeting.

"Here he comes," said Emma.

Almost immediately, from behind them, came a high pitched cackle, an almost insane laugh that struck the girls, as would a hammer being slammed at them from behind. Emma instinctively let out with a loud scream that ripped through the room, betraying the darkness with its volume.

"Watch out!" Lizzie cried, and there was a rushing noise, like something being swung violently through the air, cutting the space like a scythe, followed by a shattering crack on the other side of the room as glass was being hit with a violent force. There was a crazy series of screeches as the gears in the mantle clock, fractured by the projectile, came to a sudden halt.

The light that had been moving in the outer corridor suddenly burst into the room, filling it to the far corners with a yellowish glow. Just as soon as it entered, it fell rapidly downwards, clattering against the floorboards. Whoever had been holding the light had quickly placed it down to free up both his hands that now emerged out of the hallway shadows clutching what looked to be a huge bow and arrow.

"So," Lizzie said, "he is here." She pointed at Professor Welles, dressed in his frayed dressing gown, his hair sticking out at odd angles from his skull, his eyes wild with delight; he was framed by the doorway, holding aloft a composite Ibex horn bow. An arrow trimmed with blue feathers about the shaft was drawn within it. His fingers shook as they contained the tensile strength of the weapon.

"I am also here," came the voice behind them.

They whirled about to see an incredible sight, a second Professor Welles in an identical gown, down to the golden tasseled cord, holding an exact replica of the composite bow, except that his arrow had red feathers fluttering from its shaft.

Lizzie momentarily pondered the peculiar situation, but then her face was awash with amazement, as if something dark and ponderous had just been lifted from her. Her body straightened and relaxed, her eyes sparkled. She stepped forward towards the study door and said boldly, out loud, "Professor, I believe we have arrived at the Zero Point."

The man moved slightly towards her and Emma, his eyes lining up the shot. "Fear not," he said. "I am not going to harm you. The arrow can never reach anything I fire it upon! Zeno was correct when he created his paradox. I shall show you!" The bow and arrow angled directly at Lizzie as she stood proudly holding her inkwell.

Emma was paralyzed with fear. Deep within her, she felt a dread that surpassed anything that she had ever felt before. The care for her own safety fled and was replaced with the most intense desire to protect her little sister. Years before she had promised her dying mother that little Lizzie, then almost three years old, would be in her protective charge for the rest of eternity. Nothing would ever hurt little Lizzie; Emma would see to that.

"The arrow can most certainly reach her!" said the Professor Welles behind them. "I have conquered the infinitesimal quantities. I have exhausted the area under the curve of time! Watch and you shall see!"

Emma's mind was in danger of flickering out like the flame of a candle being blown by a strong wind. She wanted to disappear, to close her eyes and discover that nothing was happening at all, that she was back at home, safe within her room, feeling silly that her biggest problem in life was that her younger sister had to walk through her room to get downstairs. How trivial and base seemed all the problems of the world compared to this.

But here she was in the Professor's house, and not home, and the

Professor had split into two men, insane men at that, bent upon killing each other, or killing Lizzie, or killing Emma herself. What a paradox, and how unbelievable. The Professor moving backwards into his own future will meet himself as a traveler from the future moving backwards into the past. And it is the Zero Point at which they would meet, two infinities coming together at the exact center that was Lizzie.

But they cannot be the same, she said angrily to herself. *Something must be different. Think, Emma! Lizzie needs you.*

Something in her remembered a strange puzzle. A match, a candle, a lamp, and a log. Which do you light first? Lizzie had posed such a question not to teach her what to do when literally confronted by such a situation, but to teach her how to think, how to factor out the mystery to arrive at an obvious truth by exercising the most elegant way of thinking. It was like one of those imaginary number lines that the Professor had talked about, not traversing the X-axis or the Y-axis, but moving at a right angle to both of them, moving like an arrow outside the cycles of time.

"Yes," she thought. "Yes."

"Lizzie," she shouted, and as her sister glanced in her direction, she moved her face towards the framed portrait of the whaler on the far wall. Then she glanced down at Lizzie's hands. The Girl Detective understood immediately, and with a savage heave, hurled the inkwell into the air in the direction of the canvas. Both Professors seemed frozen in their tracks, suddenly distracted from their deadly experiment, and followed the arch of the inkwell. It hovered for a fraction of a second right before the murky canvas as if it were trying to make up its mind about crossing the remaining space towards its mark, and then, with a surprisingly light crackling noise, the glass broke and black liquid splattered across the face of the captain.

"No!" cried out the Professor with the blue-tipped arrow. "What have you done?" His bow dropped from his hand, the arrow tumbling forward after the loss of its tensile strength, and clattered onto the floorboards. "You have destroyed my masterpiece!" The ink was spreading across the canvas, dripping downward as if the captain's face was melting black wax. He raced towards it, spreading his hands across the painting as if trying to halt the progress of the defacement. With a single deft and athletic movement, quite unlike anything Lizzie or Emma had witnessed before, the second Professor from the other side of the room darted like a swift deer across the space between them, and clobbered his double across the back of the head with his composite bow. There was a strange sound, as if a mill throstle had become unwound and all the cotton threads were being spun crazily into the empty air. Then the assaulted man staggered with a groan only to fall flat on his back, his bushy mustache blowing upwards towards the ceiling as the air escaped from his lungs. He rolled on his side and fell into darkness.

"I never liked that piece of plug-ugly junk anyhow," the other Professor quipped, looking up at the defaced painting. His bow went to his side and he stepped forward to put a kindly hand on Lizzie's trembling elbow. "Now, my dear, don't be afraid. Sydney won't hurt you. If I were you, I would call for Humphrey to come and detain this man until the police can arrive."

Lizzie glared at him with startled eyes and said, "Professor John Wellington Welles?"

"At your service," he said, with a slight dip of his bald head. "Miss Lizzie Borden, I don't believe we have ever met. But I have heard about you during my long absence."

Emma marveled at the scene. "This wasn't the Professor?" she said, pointing at the body on the floor.

"No," Lizzie said, not taking her eyes off the small man with the funny mustache and the even funnier grin. "I don't think the real Professor has been here ever since he left Brown University."

"Oh," the sly Professor winked, "I spent a few days at home here and there. Of course, I did send this damned painting on at his request. What a silly vanity, and how unlike me. Well, it's a miracle that my wife ever agreed to consult with a detective, but I believe that was part of his plan, to murder me and win her over, as if she would never guess the switch. And of course, he coveted my life as a world-renowned expert on the mathematics of trivial infinitesimals. When there was talk of revoking my expulsion from the University, I suspected he figured out a way to kill me and take my place."

"This was all his doing?" Lizzie asked, still trying to comprehend the bizarre events of the evening.

"Why, of course. At first, it seemed like a way to cure his lunacy, his belief that he was moving in epicycles, that he was actually becoming me on his retrograde motion through time. I thought at first that this would be...uh...good for his mental health. Of course, we changed places just about a year ago, and I fed him the mathematics by post. Sometimes I would come into the house disguised as a handyman, and leave papers on his desk. He memorized my lectures and formulas and grew obsessed with the idea of refuting my Zero Point theory. He wanted to believe so desperately that infinity could never be crossed, and man would never, ever arrive at his destination, either on the physical plane or in the realm of the heart and the spirit. He was forever an infinitesimal distance away from his desire. Perhaps that's the painful truth of all artists."

"But how could he believe such a thing," Lizzie asked with a shudder. "He was preaching exactly the opposite to me over the last week. He believed in the Zero Point theory."

The Professor clicked his tongue and shook his head. "You really think he wanted to finish the theory?" he said, quite humored at the thought. "He was delaying the answer, ready to sabotage the entire enterprise. He knew that he had till midnight of tonight to finish since that was the point at which I would return. He didn't foresee the possibility that the detective hired to solve his murder before it happened would actually be the very person who would also complete the mathematics."

"Me?" Lizzie said. "I solved the refutation of Zeno's Paradox?"

"Of course I have to recheck all the calculations," he said, poking through some papers on the desk. "But if you were able to calculate the precise moment of my return through my brother's somewhat psychic ability to sense the future, then you have indeed puzzled out one of the most perplexing aspects of my life's work. Perhaps one day, my dear Lizzie Borden, I shall explain it to you."

"Professor, where have you been this past year?" Emma asked, feeling a bit uncomfortable and trying to change the subject.

"Ah," he said, coughing into his fist. "Yes, well, that's my little secret. But let's just say I got a lot of fresh air and I created a good deal of very bad paintings."

"Remarkable," Lizzie announced. "But before I wrap up this case, I wish to enquire about the safety of your good wife."

"She shall be fit as a fiddle, I have taken care to give her just the right amount of a tincture of laudanum to put her out for one hour."

"Your wife didn't know about any of this?" Emma asked, the magnitude of the situation gradually dawning on her. "How could she not know that another man was impersonating her husband?"

"She suspected, of course," the Professor said, cheerfully. "But Mr. Humphrey knew my secret and kept an eye on her to make sure she would not suspect. Of course, surrendering the amorous pleasures of life was a necessary step. I suppose if Sydney had tried to take advantage of poor Julia in the bedroom, then she may have realized."

"How so?" Lizzie mused. "By the touch of his hands upon her, the quality of his affections, the tender movements that only a wife can detect in a loving husband?" For a brief moment, she imagined the touch of a man's fingertips on her cheek and shuddered.

"I suppose," the Professor chuckled. "But you do know that in many ways, Sydney and I were always two inches off from each other."

"Oh!" said Emma, raising her hand to her ovaled mouth as Lizzie stared down awkwardly at her feet.

The silence was broken by the arrival of Mr. Humphrey who seemed to slide into the room between his mutton-chops, dragging his permanent frown with him. "So," he said, blankly staring at the prostrate Sydney, then raised his stiff chin at the Professor. "It is accomplished," he added, his voice trailing off to a low pitch.

"Yes, my good man," the Professor laughed. "You have played your role well. And many thanks for the telegram telling me the exact moment and location indicated in Miss Lizzie's notes. The bow and arrow turned out to be a valuable bit of advice."

"I strive to render impeccable service," Mr. Humphrey explained, then gave a low stare at Emma who shrank a bit from his presence.

"Time to leave Miss Emma alone," the Professor said, waving an assured hand at her. "We will find a new maid. In the meantime, Humphrey, be so kind as to ring round the police station and fetch an officer. Sydney here may not be long in waking."

By the time the arresting officer arrived, they had tied Sydney Welles to the chair behind the desk. Officer Bence, who knew Lizzie quite well, and so wasn't surprised to find her in so strange a circumstance, gave a perplexed look at the crazy old man holding the large hunting bow, and at the other man who looked exactly like him bound in rope and slumped in a chair.

"Lizzie Borden," Bence said quizzically, "what trouble have you gotten into this time? And at so late an hour?"

"I have solved a murder that never took place," she said proudly, and went on to summarize the events as she understood them for the benefit of the policeman.

"Yes," the officer said, shaking his head a bit as if trying to dislodge a thought that was stuck on one side of his mind. "If I can follow any of that, I suppose it is the Professor tied to the chair that I must arrest for attempted manslaughter. Let's get him up and see what he has to say."

Bence slapped the bound man a few times on the cheeks, arousing him from his unconscious state. At first, Sydney was confused, barely able to focus his eyes, and then he saw the police helmet atop the clean-shaven face glaring at him. "I suppose you are here because of the murder," he said groggily.

"Which murder?" Bence asked.

"The one I am going to commit in twenty-three minutes time. I have been planning it for a year now, methodically and to the last detail. I cannot convince you otherwise, I suppose. It is a brilliant plan, one that my brother will never suspect. I have even arranged for a girl detective to investigate afterwards, but she will find nothing. She will come into this house posing as my assistant, but she will not find a single clue, because the poor girl will be moving backwards in time. There is no way she could solve the murder because she will be here before it happens. And it will happen you know, all in twenty-three minutes time."

"He's now moving away from the Zero Point," the Professor said, pointing towards his brother's sullen face that was collapsing back into sleep. "I suspected as much. He is no longer any danger to any of us."

"Professor," Lizzie said, holding out her hand, "I must congratulate you on a clever scheme well-executed. But I must ask you a very important question."

"What's that, my child?" he asked, his hands taking hers.

"You could have stopped this at any time. Why did you take such a risk and let yourself come very close to being murdered by him?"

"Yes," said Emma, enthusiastically. "And Lizzie and I were in grave danger as well. How could you, with all clear conscience, put us at so much risk?"

"Risk?" the Professor said, genuinely puzzled. "My brother believed that the arrow could never conquer Zeno's Paradox. His arrow never would have reached any of you, or me for that matter."

Lizzie fell back a pace, suddenly feeling a bit uncomfortable. She looked at Emma who was starting to open her mouth, but who also fell silent. Finally, Lizzie nodded and mused, "I suppose it no longer makes a difference; it is all twenty-seven minutes in the past by my reckoning. As we move forward, it will be more and more a thing of the past, swiftly to be forgotten."

The Professor raised his eyebrows. "Time does fly, doesn't it?" he quipped.

AFTER THE END

The next morning, the two sisters walked back down Rock Street, down the Hill towards their own familiar neighborhood, where the smaller houses nestled against each other were separated by small lawns and modest picket fences. Emma had taken off her maid hat and side pockets, and had deposited them in a midden heap behind the police station. Lizzie kept her proper gait and straight-backed appearance, clearly proud of herself. After a few blocks, she stopped and looked pleasantly at Emma.

"I don't believe I could have done this without you," she said, tenderly.

"Do what? Solve the mysteries of time and space? Refute Zeno's Paradox? Tell me, Lizzie. How many show-kettles did you buff this week? How many chamber pots did you empty into the privy?"

"I know you feel you have gotten the proverbial short stick, but I do assure you that in the end, dear sister, I believe you did something that is so precious and so dear on this earth, that I cannot imagine it having been done by any other person," said Lizzie.

"What's that? Measure out the ox gall to brighten the bed sheets?"

"No, Emma," Lizzie said, reaching forward and touching her sister's cheek. "You saved my life. No greater love…" She stopped herself short, noticing that a slight tear had appeared in the corner of Emma's eye.

"I did," she said. "And I do ask one thing in return."

"Anything, Emma. I owe you all the world."

Emma closed her eyes and took a few breaths, then opened them to face her sister. "Only that in the future, you ask me…" She stopped and closed her eyes again. "That you ask my permission before you use my room as an office for your detective business."

By the time Emma had opened her eyes again, Lizzie was laughing. "Of course," she said. "And I shall knock on your door before leaving my room so as not to disturb or startle you."

"Fine," Emma said, shaking Lizzie's hand. "Perhaps this is a start. Let's get home and catch up on our errands. I'm sure they are quite numerous by now, and the day is still young."

Lizzie produced her pocket watch, lifting it high, startled to see that the hands were not moving; it was frozen at midnight of the night before.

"Odd," she thought. "But curiously fitting."

Arriving at the front of 92 Second Street, Lizzie and Emma found

Mrs. Borden, their stepmother, by the side of the house, holding some pails. She was surprised to see them, and couldn't stop staring at Emma's shapeless dress.

"I was the Maggie," was all Emma could say by way of explanation.

"Well, you can stay the Maggie for ten more minutes," Abby said sternly, handing her the pails. The water inside was brackish and smelled terribly. "Empty these and get me some fresh water."

"Ten more minutes won't hurt you," Lizzie said. "They will go by in an eye blink."

"And you," Abby said, poking a finger into Lizzie's shoulder. "Go fetch some more wood, we are going to make a fire. Your Father has a terrible cold and must stay warm."

Lizzie nodded and raced for the wood bin, dancing across the lawn, happy to feel her own family soil under her feet. By the edge of the stack was a hatchet, its gilt already faded, the handle threatening to splinter her hand. She stared at it for a moment; then lifted it up towards her inquiring eyes.

"Two equals zero," she thought. Like an axe moving backwards from two pieces of wood, and causing the two halves to fly into each other, merging into one. It all seemed so absurd. How could time move backwards? And how could anyone or anything travel across an infinite number of points?

She raised the hatchet over her head, feeling its heavy weight pulling backwards, the density of the metal, the earthiness of the wood. She always felt, when raising a hatchet for domestic chores, to be seized by some deep instinct that commanded her to wield the weapon with a savage justice, to look upon the target of her attack as a deadly menace that she must destroy or else all was lost for her, her family, her city. Perhaps as Fall River's pre-eminent Girl Detective, this menace was the bad men who plotted evil, who tried to control others against their will, or simply could not mind their own business without ruining the safety of their fellow citizens. Either way, Lizzie wished that in some small way, she could wield the hatchet in an act of justice against the dark and dangerous criminals who thought nothing of taking a life, or seizing another man's property. Would she ever reach that goal? Or was it ever an infinite number of steps ahead of her? She could do nothing but try her very best.

She fixed her gaze intently on one single log of wood that protruded from the stack, a solid half foot beyond the rest. It seemed so vulnerable, so open to attack by any weapon that would come flying through space, bringing a final judgment with its treacherous momentum.

But yet, she thought: Would the hatchet ever strike its goal? How will it conquer the paradoxes of infinite space? To test her burning curiosity, she swung the hatchet through the air, over her head, down towards the wooden log.

It seemed to take an eternity.

THE END

THE SCROOGE OF
SECOND STREET

CHRISTMAS, 1875. FALL RIVER, MASSACHUSETTS.

As Christmastime drew near in the Borden household, there was not a word said about a family celebration. Despite Christmas having been declared a federal holiday, Father had so many Puritan roots dangling from his trunk that he gradually came to resemble Ebenezer Scrooge, that perennial curmudgeon from Mr. Dickens' novel, as he stalked about our parlor scowling against wassail and Christmas spirit.

"There are new Bengaline dresses on sale at Hodges," Emma suggested to Father in good faith. "Buying them would do much to repair your reputation."

"Dresses!" Father railed. "What about that textile warehouse you have up in that closet?! Between the two of you, I'm surprised that the weight of your clothing doesn't cause the entire room to come crashing down into the basement!"

"But the spring fashions shall be here shortly," I argued. "You would not have us humiliated upon the street?"

Father screwed up his face as if trying to remember something distant. "What was that word that that fellow used? The one who sent his nephew packing and had all those ghosts come and visit him? Eh? Yes, that's it! Humbug!"

"But Father! It's Christmas!"

"Fools tide I call it! An egregious ritual!"

"What about the new year? Does that mean anything to you?"

"And what should it mean? The earth spins around the sun one more turn, my hair gets grayer, and Mrs. Borden gets stouter. You and Emma shall get older and still not have suitors. To me Christmas is an indulgence, a vanity! And besides, there is no scriptural justification for it! I simply won't have it!"

Emma and I were stunned by his proclamation, especially his comment that we shall not have suitors.

"Father, that was unkind! My heart is wounded!" I said.

His pale face remained locked, so we stormed off to our rooms where we broke into tears and held each other like frightened children.

"What are we to do?" Emma asked. "He is not Father any more. He has finally turned into Scrooge!"

"Then we shall treat him as such," I said, determined. "We shall make hay with Father's unhappiness and pretend a supernatural visitation, just like in the Dickens novel."

"Supernatural? How can that be achieved?"

"I know just the person to help us!" exclaimed Lizzie.

Homer Thesinger, the Boy Inventor of Pleasant Street, was delighted when we suggested a confederacy against Father. It was a chance to test his Spirit Box, as he called his newly improved lantern into which he could insert photographs. He had already refashioned his zazaphone, a tangled system of rubber hoses and crescent-shaped cups, into a Ghost Trumpet. His hobby was to simulate séances and thereby reveal to people how spiritualists accomplish their claptrap. He was already adept at the art of fake visitations.

"If you are fashioning your spectral attack on that Dickens story," he said, "may I suggest we all play a role? I have extended the Ghost Trumpet's range and multiplied the input cups. Now voices can come from different sides of the room and carry on multiple conversations simultaneously."

"You are a genius!" I said, giving him a light kiss on the cheek. "My Boy Inventor!"

"I prefer Electromachinician," he blushed.

Entry into Father's office at his furniture store was no problem since I had a copy of the key. The three of us slipped in there the night before Christmas Eve and we wired the place with the multiple tentacles of the Ghost Trumpet and rigged up a platform behind a potted rubber tree from which the magic lantern could project onto the large bare wall over Father's roll top desk. Homer could hide behind the tree, speak into his input cup and control the magic lantern slides at the same time. Emma and I would perch behind other furniture in the room with our own input cups and involve ourselves in the visitation.

Father made a habit of going to his office after supper on Christmas Eve. For all his bluster about disrespecting the holiday, he always responded to the increased sales as Fall River home owners bought more than the usual number of feather beds, sofas and sideboards. There was never a humbug on his lips as he quarantined himself in his counting house to catalog the money that the Christmas spirit had blown his way.

That is how we found him, close to midnight on December 24th, conveniently nodding off as he scrawled inside his books, adding up columns, calculating the quantities in his coffers. We crawled noiselessly into the room and took our places at our various nests, waiting for the right moment to initiate our ghostly visitation.

Father eventually put down his quill and stretched his arms over his head, yawning into slumber while reclined in his chair. At that moment, Homer lit the lantern and projected the first slide on the wall just above Father's line of sight. It was a spectacular vision of a hovering creature swathed in bandages and restrained by lengths of chain and padlocks. The face was gaunt and haunted and sparkled as if in motion.

Father let out a yelp and curled up his arms and knees tight against his torso. Homer was moaning into his input cup, creating a heart rending moan that echoed about the room, obscuring its true origin.

"Andrew Jackson Borden!" cried the spirit. "I am the ghost of your partner William Almy! I have come to save you from yourself!"

"William?" Andrew said, confused. "But you are not dead! I had supper with you two nights ago!"

"I am not dead!" the spirit responded, sounding a bit puzzled itself. "But I am such a miserable wretch that my spirit haunts my own offices prematurely! My sins are recognized before my death! I have neglected the poor, lining my pockets with coins stolen from hungry babies! I have colluded with the captains of industry to enslave the masses! To exploit the proletariats after seizing the modes of production!"

I blew into my spirit input cup and my voice filled the room in a crazed swirl, "William! To the point!"

"Oh, sorry," the spirit of Mr. Almy said shyly, then moaned pitifully. "You have been a miserable wretch, Andrew. Always thinking of yourself and not of your family. I behaved the same way, and that is why I suffer so!"

"Ah, poor ghost!" Father lamented. "What can I do to escape your fate?"

"List! List!" the ghost commanded. "Hear the voice of your Christmas past."

Upon this cue, Emma spoke into her cup, adopting a shrill childlike tone. "Andrew, is that you? Are you there?"

"Phoebe? My God, is that Phoebe?" Father was nearly in tears listening to what he believed to be my aunt who passed nearly twenty years ago. It seemed a pity to play upon his sadness this way, but his reaction told me that our devious plan could possibly succeed and the Bengaline dresses could be ours!

"Andrew, do you remember Christmas day when we were but children? Father had no care for it, he called it Fools Tide."

"Did he?" Father blinked. "What a silly name for..." then he stopped and pulled at his jaw bristle.

"But he found it amusing to give us those little toys," Emma continued. "He always made sure that we got our own personal toy. Mine was always a beautiful poppet dressed in silk Bengaline. The fabric was most enchanting. The dress was made from Bengaline silk and..."

I blew again in my cup. "Phoebe! To the point!"

"I remember," Father said wistfully. "And for me?"

"Yours was a wooden soldier with blue leggings and a bright red coat. We would play for hours, pretending that the soldier was courting the poppet."

"Ah!" he moaned. "You have touched upon a memory too deep for tears."

He was falling for the ruse, completely forgetting that he had explained to me once why he had a collection of wooden soldiers hidden in his cabinet. He had spoken of them disdainfully as if they were an embarrassment. Now his face was beaming even in the darkness.

"We loved our toys, Andrew. It made the winter nights all the more joyful. Wouldn't it be a delight if Emma and Lizzie could feel the way we felt? They would have the same joy, the same Christmas spirit."

"Perhaps," Andrew said. His face twitched with his upraised fingers as if he were calculating some sums in his mind. "Yes, just perhaps."

"Heed Phoebe well," Homer spoke in the ghost's rasping chatter. "And heed your own daughter well, as she speaks to you of Christmas present."

"Lizzie?" Father said confusedly. "Is she here?"

"Here but not here," I spoke into my cup. "I am the spirit of Christmas present taking the form of your daughter. I know her woes and her longings. She sits before the fire in the sitting room feeling forlorn, abandoned. Her father goes about his business, counting his dividends, totaling his sales, thinking only of his mill stock and election to the board of a great bank. He does not see that his own Lizzie and Emma are sorrowful, two shrouds haunting their own world.

"They are unloved because you will not bestow on them what you know in your heart to be the real spirit of Christmas."

"But there is no scripture that justifies the celebration of such a ridiculous holiday!" he snapped, as if lecturing the spirits. His words came as bold reprimands.

"Did you need scripture to justify your toy soldiers?" Emma said angrily. "You never refused them when they came out of Grandfather's pockets!"

Father was momentarily stunned into silence. Then he said slowly, "Lizzie and Emma sit weeping at home right now, William? Tell me, I cannot bear it."

"They are deprived of your holiday blessing!" Lizzie exclaimed. "They say vile things about you. They call you Ebenezer Scrooge and rue Christmas day as they would the passing of a loved one."

"No," Father moaned. "No, William. No more. Let me go home. There is much upon my head!"

"But Andrew," Homer said slyly. "There is one more spirit come to show you the error of your ways. Here is the wraith of Christmas future. He has grim tidings for you!"

Homer had by this time concealed himself in a dark cloth such as the grim reaper would wear. It was frayed burlap and hung over his brows, obscuring his face. From its sleeve he stuck one hand that he had painted white for the occasion. It radiated a small glow that traced in the air like a dancing flame. Father shrieked and nearly dove under his desk.

"Death!" he bellowed. "Come to reap my soul! No, you cannot have it yet!"

"Nor shall I!" Homer said in a guttural and horrific voice. He had snuck one of the cups into his cloak and was shouting into it for full effect. "But I tell you Andrew Jackson Borden of your fate! I see your daughters fleeing from your house! They take to living on the Hill, in a house much larger than the cheese box you provide for them now! They are happy up there! They have taken your money and bought all the amenities that you deny them!"

"Traitors!" Father growled. "They dare not take my money! That is theft!"

"No," Homer laughed sardonically. "Not theft. On this future

Christmas day, you are no longer on the earth."

"Eh? What? Dead? Am I dead?"

"It was the only way that they could escape you!"

Something unexpected then occurred. My father, typically a bedrock of stoicism, burst into uproarious tears. His whole torso convulsed as he poured tears into his upturned palms. "No, that must not happen! That will not happen!"

"List!" Homer commanded, which was our cue to come in with some prepared dialogue.

"Emma, isn't this a wonderful Christmas in our mansion on the hill," I said in my ordinary voice, cheerful and with a touch of laughter.

"Most decidedly so," Emma replied. "The tree is full of tinsel, candles, and merry ornaments. The gifts for the children are under the tree. The children will be so happy to see what we got for them."

"And what did we get for the children, Emma?" I asked.

"We bought them" Emma said, with an emphasis on the word 'bought', "their heart's content, toy soldiers, drums, toy trains, cymbals, whistles, bouquets of flowers, nuts, candies, sweet meats, sugar canes, gum drops."

"What a cornucopia of delights!" I squealed. "We must not forget that Christmas is for the children, and the children come first in everything."

"Children?" Father asked. "What children? Whose children?"

"The forgotten ones of the Taunton Orphan Asylum," Homer cried. "Those who have lost their families, those who never had families. Those who are alone. For one small moment, they will feel the gentle love of Christmas and those who obey its spirit. They will find joy in obtaining what was once unobtainable!"

Father's sobbing grew achingly and we sensed that it was time to ease his way out of the visitation that we had conjured for him. Homer withdrew behind his potted plant and began removing the image from the magic lantern.

"Do not forget the children!" we all chanted in unison as the lantern light dimmed and the room returned to silence. We held our breaths, knowing that Father would bolt from the room, leaving us to pack up our equipment and vacate the office.

He was flying by his coattails within seconds, alternatively sobbing and moaning. We heard his lamentations all the way to the front door of the shop and then he was gone.

We could not keep from laughing heartily and we stopped to convulse ourselves in merriment several times as we cleared the equipment from the office. All the way home we told each other lines that we had acted as the spirits and burst into fresh peals of laughter remembering Father's response.

It was Emma who darkened the mood. "I certainly hope we did not break his heart."

"Nonsense," I told her. "We have softened his heart. Tomorrow morning we will see the fruits of our labors. I can see those Bengaline dresses now, fresh from the shops, covering our bodies as we stroll about the streets."

Those dresses danced in our minds throughout the night. We could not hear a single sound from Father's bedroom besides some light snoring. Only once did we hear him shout in his sleep the single word, "Phoebe!" and that was enough to tell us that our little performance had moved him deeply.

In the morning, we hurried to perform our toilet and get into our pink wrappers. As soon as we were decent, we hurled ourselves down the stairs like a pair of school girls, but Father was not at home. We found Mrs. Borden and the Maggie preparing breakfast in the kitchen. It seemed to consist of wheat pancakes, pears, coffee and bananas. It was not exactly my vision of a holiday meal. There were no decorations, no wreaths of holly, no candles, no Prince Albert tree. There was only my stepmother washing her hands and pouring the breakfast batter.

"Did Mr. Borden go out for last minute shopping?" I asked her optimistically.

She chuckled at my absurd notion. "Mr. Borden," she told us, "has gone to his office to balance his books. He said he was too distracted last night to make short shrift of it so he'll probably be there most of today."

We were stunned into silence. When Mrs. Borden saw us mouth-gapped, she blinked and said almost casually, "But he left a package for both of you on the dining table. Some sort of gift I suppose."

With a burst of enthusiasm, we rushed to the dining room, practically falling over each other. But to our dismay, there was only a small little box with a card fastened to the top. It read:

My Dearest Daughters,
I wish you to have many happy moments with these joyful gifts.

Your Father,
A.J. Borden

We opened the box and found inside a small wooden soldier with a red coat and blue leggings. There was also a hand-stitched poppet wrapped in a small swatch of Bengaline silk. They were faded and fragile and we put them back into the box with care.

"I'll kill him!" Emma hissed, her eyes turning into dark pin points searching for some unobtainable justice.

"No," I told her. "Leave that to me."

And so another Christmas came and went on 92 Second Street. But we endured it, knowing that we had effected some small conversion of Father's otherwise impassive heart.

THE END

The Forlorn Maggie

1874. Fall River, Massachusetts.

The water-falls of the Quequechan once sparkled over their time-worn rocks, lording over a landscape in which the hornpout darted away their life-span in the dark recesses of the watery depths. That river is no longer visible to us: it flows beneath the churning wheels of the mighty mills. It is a cruel exercise to walk the perimeter walls of the dusky buildings, under the shadow of the smoke stacks and the grimy rows of windows, and imagine the Mother river beneath our feet. All we shall see is the modern factory bent across nature like a triumphant predatory beast over its fresh kill. The river, its soulful waters from so long ago, its cascades and the meditation of its flow, is now a buried corpse; lost, seemingly irretrievably, beneath the burnt red brick and the underground engines thus fueling the infernal machines. Indeed, men and women have been bound to these machines, ever to toil like submissive servants of some vast cavernous spirit.

This loss of nature was the price paid for the rise of commerce and a leisure class that need not waste their days away at the spindles and looms of industry, for on this bright and slightly-chilled September morning, not a few short blocks away from the mills, the downstreet area is awash with activity. Those with time enough on their hands (and more than a few dollars in their pockets) stroll the sidewalks, gazing through the shop windows, pausing briefly to discuss with each other the time of day and the conditions of the weather, not to mention the latest fashion of dress and much gossip about their neighbors.

Fall River, the City, unlike the stream that had surrendered its appellation even before being buried in the darkness of the mighty mills, is very much alive—Fall River is now the urban phoenix, vibrantly visible to all who walk freely under the sun.

TAKING HER FANCY

Amidst a sidewalk sea of bowler hats and frilled bonnets, frock coats and flounced bustles, two women walked from opposite directions along the main street. One came from the north, City Hall rising behind her, where the center of Fall River banking and government sustained itself with its imposing granite tower. This woman was quite young, full in the face, with light hair and a cheery little smile that curled at the edges as she soaked in the life about her. She walked with an upright and dignified posture, a lofty attitude of certainty.

The other woman was considerably older and came from the southwest. She was gaunt and sallow, covered in a threadbare print dress and a worn bonnet; her gait was clearly more rushed and less-directed, as if she had been seized with some nervous energy that had driven her compulsively into the streets. At each step, she seemed in danger of pitching forward upon the ground. No one around her seemed to notice her condition.

The two women, complete strangers, came together in the doorway of Hodges & Son, a fabric store near the corner of South Main and Columbia. The young girl was paying more attention to her surroundings, and so had time to avoid the imminent collision. The elderly woman stared wildly at her more youthful counterpart as if she were looking down upon a disobedient domestic. Then a stark change swept over her face, her features rapidly composing themselves, and said in a whispery Irish voice, "I am sorry for this, Miss. Please take your way and I shall follow." She raised a shaking hand, bidding the young girl to pass.

The woman's sunken eyes looked filled with sorrow and danger, the young girl thought, but she refrained from showing any overt concern. With a deft lifting of her skirt, she pranced into the store and went about her business.

As she picked through bolts of fabric looking for some choice material to bring to her dressmaker, the young girl kept an eye on the strange figure that had followed her in. The elderly woman was fidgeting about, her fingers quivering over fabric sample, but her eyes remained unfocused. The store owner, old man Hodges himself, a beefy man with large hands and an even larger set of muttonchops that expanded his head liberally in both directions, carefully walked near her, unobtrusively keeping a close eye upon his merchandise.

Feeling that the store was now safe in the competent hands of

Mr. Hodges, Lizzie Andrew Borden, the young girl in question, gave up her surveillance of this most suspicious woman and went about examining a few choice samples. She poked about on a table where some bolts and sewing materials were laid out, then sidled alongside the notions counter to admire some cards of mother of pearl buttons, when her eye rested upon a resplendent silver plate pin tray. A few common pins rested within, which must have been a convenience for the shop girl who was wearily winding up fabric on bolts at the other end of the counter. Lizzie's appraising eye noted the little repousee pansies, the unfurling ribbon bowknot, and the quality quadruple plating. Gorham—Yes, surely it was Gorham silver plate—and quality too!

Lizzie sniffed the air appreciatively and nonchalantly turned her back to the counter while holding up a card of buttons to the light for inspection. With one deft movement of her right hand, the silver tray found a snug home inside the back waistband of her skirt. The oval contours of the tray rested undetected over the accommodating shelf of her bustle.

As if the fates were conspiring to stroke Lizzie's guilty conscience, she spotted the elderly woman not two tables away at the cutting implements. Mr. Hodges, distracted by a flurry of activity at the front counter, had ceased to monitor her; and lo, she was also passing something small into the folds of her dress. There was just a brief flash of something metallic; the woman stood motionless with her arms by her sides.

"Oh, my," Lizzie thought. "If it is true that this woman has taken her Fancy as I have, I dare not raise an alarm for fear that they shall suspect me as well." She mused briefly upon her predicament. "This fabric sale will last all day," she concluded. "I shall simply come back when she is gone from the premises."

Then, as Lizzie strolled towards the front, preparing to escape into the streets, the elderly woman darted forward, running noisily to the front register behind which a young Mr. Hodges, a thin and weedy version of his father in appearance, the same beady-eyed face, but lacking the hairly establishments, stared straight at her. The woman reached over and, without any attempt to conceal her action, grabbed the cash box, removing it from the counter and headed rapidly for the door. At that moment, both Hodges the Father and Hodges the Son raised a general alarm by shouting: "Stop that woman! Oh, do not let her get away!"

The assembled customers, mostly women holding samples of cloth and bolts of fabric, looked up with startled cries. There was a scuffling and the elderly woman dropped the cashbox to the wood-slatted floor as if she were coming out of a trance. She raised a hand to her forehead and swooned downwards, landing with a pronounced crackling of her stiff bustle, directly at the feet of an increasingly nervous Lizzie Borden.

Lizzie raised her hands instinctively above her head, as if proclaiming her innocent to all about, thus proving somehow she had nothing to do with the attempted robbery. Many a time in the past when she had taken her Fancy, whether it was in fabric stores, apothecaries, or flower boutiques, being at the center of everyone's attention while the Fancy was concealed in her clothing had caused great anxiety; and often at night her dreams were turned to dread nightmares in which a thousand eyeballs stared unblinking at her while silverware, pearl mirrors, and hat pins tumbled to the ground from beneath her skirts.

As Hodges & Son ran for the street to call a policeman, Lizzie glanced around, trying to perceive where, in the confused midst of the disturbance and the large number of customers surrounding her, she could dump her silver tray. Divesting herself of any incriminating evidence was, at that moment, her chief concern. She abandoned the thought of getting rid of the item only when a young police officer entered the store and ran to the collapsed woman.

"What is this?" the officer asked, bemusedly. Hodges & Son, with arms flailing, hastily gave their perspective on the preceding events. The elder Mr. Hodges pointed at Lizzie, which caused her heart to skip a beat. "This girl can verify what I have said. She was not three feet from the crime when it happened!"

"Here, this is young Miss Borden," the young officer grinned. "Hello, Lizzie. How's the family?"

"Fine," she replied, hoping to be as monosyllabic as possible. She recognized Peter Gaskell Bence, not her favorite policeman, but a happy enough fellow.

"What did you see?" he asked. "Are Hodges & Son telling it straight?"

"Why," Lizzie said, tossing explanations about in her head, "I did see this woman up close, but from my vantage she seemed very nervous, almost starved. I would say if you examine her, you'll find evidence that she is positively malnourished. Perhaps she hasn't eaten in quite some time, two days perhaps, or an interval that you and I would find intolerable. I would say from her vestments that she is a cloth doffer at one of the mills, or even possibly a domestic on the Hill, perhaps removed from her job and failing to find a situation that would sustain her life in the meanwhile. I would say she came in here hoping to find a soul who would take pity on her, and, sensing only the indifference of commerce, she gambled away her liberties by plunging for the till, hoping beyond hope that she could steal the money and save her life."

There was a thundering silence. All eyes in the store glared at Lizzie Borden. Mr. Hodges broke the calm: "You seem too clever for your own good, young Miss. While you are seeing suffering and starvation, I'm just seeing hard earned dollars being filched from under my nose! 'Tis not my business that she was sacked from the mill!"

"Well," Officer Bence said with a broad smile, "let's arouse this lady and get her side of the story. Then we'll take her down to the station house and see if justice can be distributed one way or the other."

They made an attempt to awaken the woman. As they pinched her cheeks and slapped her chin and pulled at her shoulders, Lizzie saw a few twitches and eye movements suggesting that the woman was feigning unconsciousness. But she kept quiet about it, being mindful of the silver tray in her dress, hoping that it would not slide out over her bustle pouf and reveal her perfidy.

A few customers from the store stepped forward and offered to help haul the woman to her feet and carry her down the street to the police station. However, without warning, the fainted woman's eyes fluttered and, for the first time since her outrage, they opened.

"Oh, have pity," she said in a whispery voice. "Have pity on poor Fiona Conway. Ah! Have pity on the hungry!"

"There, there," Officer Bence said. "Justice shall pitch her scales and we shall balance the weight of the matter."

For a moment, the woman gazed perplexedly at the policeman's smiling face as if trying to untangle his curious metaphors, then she quickly fell back into a deep slumber. It took two men to support her weight and they moved her towards the door and into the street beyond.

"And you, Miss Lizzie," Officer Bence said, crooking a finger at her. "I'd like you to come along to make a statement and identify this woman before the Marshal."

Lizzie's heart sank again. With a helpless shrug, she followed the men out of the store and up the street—towards the last place on earth where she wanted to be with a pinched Fancy in her bustle.

MUTINY ON *THE DURFEE*

The Central Police Station on Purchase Street was not a building that Lizzie Borden had ever wished to visit. In her childhood imagination it had always been a place inhabited by all the monsters of society that she wanted banished from her world. Its tall tower rose over the surrounding buildings like an ominous fortress of torture and the stench from the nearby horse yard was quite wretched. As her official escort led her to the tall iron doors, she froze, pressing her feet tighter against the ground. The silver tray in her bustle suddenly felt heavier.

"Forgive me," she muttered to Officer Bence. "I have not a sense of where I am going or for what reason."

"Don't fear," he said gently. "We're only going to book Miss Fiona Conway, if that is indeed her name. We need you here as a material witness."

Summoning her strength, she advanced and entered the main hallway. All about her were policemen in their shell helmets, many of them conversing with each other, paying no attention to her presence. However, in her mind's eye, they were all staring suspiciously at her weighted bustle, looking for traces of her Fancy. Lizzie nervously paced down towards the squad room between a gauntlet of officers, and was relieved when Officer Bence offered her a seat on a bench near the Marshal's office, leaving her quite alone. Here she was able to retreat into the role of spectator, where she could simply observe people and not be compelled to take part in any action. She felt safer that way: being unseen but all-seeing.

The squad room was crowded, buzzing with activity. A sporting boy and his fancy girl were seated behind an untidy desk, being shouted at by an irate detective. A few Portuguese laborers were trying to make sense to a stupefied policeman who did not speak their language. Several other citizens of Fall River were present, apparently there to make complaints, or having been summoned to address matters of urgent police business. And a tall, long-haired man in a black frock coat sat near the filing cabinets in a gloomy solitary meditation.

Lizzie was about to turn her attention toward the open doorway of the Marshal's office, through which she had heard some muttering, but quickly snapped her gaze back at the tall man in the black frock. At that very instant, he stared back at her, and both of them bolted upright in their seats.

"Father!" Lizzie shouted, then slouched downward, pressing her lips together as if trying to prevent her blurted word from advancing too far towards anyone's ears.

Andrew Jackson Borden rose to his full height and advanced stealthily across the room. His daughter bravely stepped up to meet him, her chin rising to just below his bristly beard.

"Yes, Daughter," he said grimly. "I must confess that I have police business this afternoon. But I am shocked to see you in these premises. I don't suppose you are here because you have been taking a bit of … uh … your Fancy."

She waggled her slack face. "No, Father. You need not fear; there shall be no visits to the shops today. I have cleaned my hands of that habit."

"I am glad to hear of it."

As he spoke, Andrew was reaching towards his face as if to scratch it. He did this several times before Lizzie realized that he merely did not know what to do with his hands. "So," he said, "what exactly is your business here today?"

Lizzie fluttered her lids. "I can honestly say, Father, it is of the most perplexing nature. I am an innocent observer this time, purely a victim of circumstance. For upon my visit to Hodges & Son, a Maggie lost her reason and tried to pilfer the till. She was seized by the younger Hodges and brought here to this very station where no doubt she is being interrogated in the back rooms as we speak. They claim that I saw the offense, that it happened right before me, and are asking me to make a statement as to her guilt."

"And what would be the girl's reason to do such a rash act?" he asked. "Does she not get paid well by her employer?"

"I believe she has lost her situation. Hunger, despondency, and despair have driven her to such a gesture."

Andrew grunted. "Well, if there is justice in this town, she shall hang!" He turned from her to retreat to the bench; Lizzie followed behind, anxiously.

"Father!" Lizzie shouted, pulling at his arm. "What a brutal thing to say."

"She robbed a concern," he said casually. "There are laws for that. I pay enough tax money to put our peace-keepers into office. I'd like to see them stick to the letter of the law for once."

"But hanging! She is certainly not innocent, but I can honestly say the circumstances were quite understandable."

"How much was in the till?" Andrew asked.

"I do not know, but Hodges was doing a brisk business on a bolt sale."

Andrew snorted. "Enough for a scaffold, sounds like it."

"Father, I will not continue this debate with you. You know nothing about this crime and can't pass judgment on broad facts. I shall see that her offense be put into perspective."

"To each his own," Andrew said resolvedly. "The whole affair means nothing to me. I am here on matters that shall deserve the gallows."

"What may that be?" Lizzie asked, holding her breath.

"I am hesitant to tell you since I do not want to alarm you, Mrs. Borden, or your sister Emma." He glanced both ways to ascertain their privacy, then lowered her onto the bench, seating himself next to her. "I do not think that you know about the brigantine, the *B.M.C. Durfee*, that sailed from New Bedford upon two Aprils past?"

"I know a little, Father. The ship fell into evil times. The crew mutinied and murdered the Captain before tossing him overboard. They were captured off Barbados and brought back to New England in irons."

"Yes, they were evil men who did evil things. They did it all for money, imagine that. Captain Coffin is now resting in his watery bed, and his wife is despondent because of the nefarious deeds of Joseph Shove, Samuel Howe, and Oliver Fleet."

Lizzie screwed up her eyes. "But Father, were not Shove and Howe the two men who were hanged in New Bedford this past summer for their role in the affair?"

"Why, yes, Daughter."

"But you mentioned a third man."

"Fleet, yes. He was the third man, and, of the three, he was the most seething with devilish fire. He escaped from custody, killing two officers, and was last heard from in a taunting letter to the New Bedford police department, saying that they would sooner catch the Devil himself than catch Fleet-Footed Fleet. This angered the Governor to no end, and the entire Commonwealth of Massachusetts has been keeping a harsh vigilance for him."

Lizzie lowered her face, bewildered. "I have heard of the sorrows of Sarah Coffin. I did not know that her solitude was the result of her husband being murdered."

Andrew's already bitter stare grew darker. "It is said that in the mutiny, Fleet picked Captain Coffin up over his head and snapped his limbs like twigs, and when the Captain's cries were so pitiful that the Great Adversary himself would have wept to hear it, Oliver Fleet fiendishly laughed through his teeth."

"So they believe that he will return to Fall River?"

"Daughter, now we get to the heart of my business here. Fleet-Footed Fleet yearns for nothing but to be reunited with a fallen woman of this city who has taken up with him. Not only has he returned to Fall River, but he is in this very building!"

Lizzie felt a deep shudder and drew her arms tight about her shoulders. "Dear Lord," was all she could say. "Are we safe?"

"As safe as the City Marshal and his gallant lawmen can make us," he said assuredly. "For the man is in shackles in the lock-up. I have not seen him yet, but I shall within the hour."

"You?" Lizzie asked. "Why you?"

Once more he glanced about to certify that no one could hear. "Here is where I am most ashamed, Daughter. I must confess that four years ago I invested heavily in the *B.M.C. Durfee*. I own a hearty portion of its stock. Its success would have meant a valuable expansion of my capital. The dividends from its sugar and molasses run would have been quite handsome for me. The mutiny was a savage blow, from which, financially, a part of me has not since recovered."

"So are you here to give Mr. Fleet a part of your mind?"

"My Daughter," Andrew said sternly. "The officials merely want me to look him in the face and say Yea or Nay that it is positively him. I may be one of the few men in Fall River capable of fingering him. While others have seen his likeness, he has changed it through alteration of his whiskers. But I have heard his voice, a deep tone, which can rattle your bones when you hear it. The police believe my testimony will be binding, and they will be assured that they have their man. It is a heavy burden."

"Yes, Father. A heavy burden, indeed, which I share. For I am also here to identify a prisoner, although I am determined to prevent Fiona Conway from hanging as long as I can testify to her sorrow! Just because she is a Maggie, that doesn't mean..."

Andrew stiffened and his eyes turned to marble. "Did you say, Fiona...Conway?"

"Why, yes. We heard her name from her very lips as she swooned on the floor of the fabric store."

His face brightened. "Why, she is our woman!" He threw back his head and cackled.

"Father, is your reason unhinged? What do you find amusing?"

He got to his feet and fingered his lapels. "Why, I have found a way to lighten my burden. Fiona Conway is not a Maggie, as you put it, but Fleet-Footed Fleet's lady of the night, his fallen woman of Fall River!"

A shaft of light descended inside Lizzie's mind. "I have been such a fool," she announced. "Father, you have handed me the missing piece of the puzzle! Fiona Conway did not attempt to lift the till because she wanted to steal the money. It was an act of desperation, yes, but not one of passion. She knew that her long-lost lover, one whom she despaired of ever seeing again, was within police custody, and she deliberately broke the law in order to join him in the cells!"

"You are sure of this?" Andrew said hastily, "Perhaps it is not her but ..."

"There is only one way of finding out," Lizzie shouted, and then darted across the room to a desk where Officer Bence was taking statements from Hodges & Son.

"Violate my peaceful business, she did!" the elder Hodges was shouting. "On the day of the bolt sale, no less! Now I have a half-witted tide-waiter tending till and a bumbling Bristol man walking the floor while we waste our time here! The store will be in chaos by the time we get back!"

"Officer Bence!" Lizzie shouted in a loud and startling voice, causing Mr. Hodges to bury his rambling words inside the waggling of his side chops. "I know this is a strong cause to advance," Lizzie explained, "but the Maggie known as Fiona Conway can exonerate herself if only the truth will out."

"Are you mad?" Hodges the Son said. "You saw what she did, you were right there!"

"Yes, but I have information that you must consider." She turned and motioned for her father to advance.

Andrew crossed over nervously and stammered, "She is right, Lizzie is right. We do not believe that she intended to steal the money. We believe she intended to be caught before she left the store."

Mr. Hodges pulled at his chin. "What? Of all the preposterous monkey-dash!"

With a quivering voice, Andrew explained his story to the astonished assemblage. He paused a few times, blushing at his own public admittance that his own money had once sunk like rocks to the bottom of the ocean instead of providing him with healthy dividends. While he related his tale, Officer Bence's face grew lighter and less ponderous, while the faces of Hodges & Son grew more gloomy and despondent.

When her father had finished, Lizzie completed the picture with her interpretation of the events in the fabric store. "The Maggie's plan was to get inside the cell with her lost lover. What she plans to do, whether she plans to help him escape, or she merely wants to lay one more look upon him before she next sees him dangling from a rope, I cannot say. But it is certain that she is not what she claims to be."

The Officer was hurriedly on his feet and headed for the City Marshal's office. "He must hear this," he said bemusedly. The tall, ponderous Marshal had soon joined them, stroking his beard, while Officer Bence repeated Andrew's story.

"By Jupiter, this is fire indeed," the Marshal nodded. "The girl is a crucial part of our prosecution, we must see to this immediately. Officer Bence, please advance an invitation to all our guests here to join me in five minutes in the interrogation cell. Both Fleet-Footed Fleet and our Irish scullery maid are in for a momentous surprise."

"Aye, Marshal," Bence said, and then turned to Lizzie, Andrew, and Hodges & Son with a chuckle. "You're all coming with me to the Tower," he announced.

"Now, Daughter," Andrew said, patting the back of her hand. "We shall witness the sinking of Fleet-Footed Fleet."

"May God have Mercy on the Maggie," Lizzie intoned.

A HEART UNVEILED

They climbed the wooden stairs into the station tower where sunlight flooded the hallway, coming in over the rooftops of the smaller surrounding buildings. A short ten minutes previous, Lizzie would have been horrified beyond sensibility to walk this far into the station, no matter how secure the locks. From the street, she had always glanced up at this tower as if it were Fall River's dark castle, deeper and more haunted than the currents of the hidden river below the mills.

But now, as she entered flanked by her father and the City Marshal, accompanied by Officer Bence and Hodges & Son, she swaggered with a sense of excitement, experiencing a desire not only to be a spectator, but also a direct participant in the drama that was unfolding about her. Her mind no longer lingered on her bustled Fancy.

Entering the lock-up, Lizzie immediately was overpowered by a harsh odor. To the far right was a barred cell, inhabited by a few drunken vagrants. Their strange aromas, mixtures of various scents typically absent from Lizzie's comfortable and reasonably clean surroundings, mingled with those wafting from the horse-yard below, and filled the whole interior of the tower with an almost palpable wave of unbearable air.

To the left was a solitary lock-up inside of which an indistinct form was silhouetted against the light flooding through the back window. An officer was already on guard nearby, and he stood to attention as the Marshal gave a barked command. Lizzie's eyes were adjusting to the contrasting shadows and now she could make out, within the confines of the cell, an imprisoned man perched on a cot like a braced animal; she could discern two angry eyes and a savage mouth surrounded by thick black hair.

"Stand to attention," the officer-on-duty said harshly. "The Marshal will address you."

"You can tell the Marshal," a deep voice sounded from the darkness, "that he can kiss my bottom's beard!"

"Do you see?" Andrew asked excitedly. "How brutal! For that alone he must hang!"

"Hang?" barked the man. "And who are you that you shall judge me?"

"Andrew Jackson Borden," said Lizzie's father. As he puffed up his chest and thrust out his whiskers in a mild attempt at confidence, his voice crackled and his trousers trembled.

"Never heard of you," the man said with a dismissive sneer. "How can I be judged by a complete stranger?"

"I am not a complete stranger. I personally recruited you from the Iron Works to be first mate on the schooner. Do you not remember? I came to your apartment..."

"Nope," the man said lightly.

"I brought you round to the shipping office. I was there when you signed your lay commission."

"I am not the man! But wait, I have heard of you, Andrew Borden. You're a furniture maker. You made my cabinet. Perhaps I recognize you from the day you carried it up my back stairs like the servant you are!"

"God's wounds!" Andrew shouted, and curled his fists.

The Marshal stepped forward. "Fleet, be still. We shall corroborate with one more witness. If two people positively identify you, then we shall ignore your claims that you are Horatio Phelps of Boston."

"Then you shall be a poor policeman, for I am Horatio Phelps. My business is real estate. I have witnesses!"

"A drunken card sharp and two prostitutes," shouted the Marshal. "And the only real estate you own is currently being used as a brothel."

"Stuff your witnesses," Officer Bence added. "We have your girlfriend."

The man, full of swagger and boisterousness, went strangely silent. Then his voice returned with a disoriented scatter in its rhythm. "What are you talking about?" he asked. "I don't have a girlfriend. Perhaps you are mistaken..."

The metal door to the prison opened with an ominous squeak, and two officers entered guiding Fiona Conway between them. She was dull in her senses, her eyes barely open, her face slack and pale. She moved forward like a senseless thing, stepping where the two officers urged her to step. They stood her before the lock-up.

"Fiona Conway of County Galway," the Marshall explained. "I believe that you know this man?"

Fleet muttered the name, "Fiona...", then choked and broke out into a coughing fit. "You had me over for a bit! I know not this woman."

The woman calmly lifted her face and peered into the dimness of the cell. "But I may know this man," she said in a bitter voice. "Let me a little closer..."

Lizzie came forward and took the woman's hand in hers. She held it gingerly and stroked it with her other, while saying gently into the woman's ear, "I know what you did in the store, Miss Conway, and I know why. I beseech you, help us to bring a bad man to justice today. If anything, for the sake of Captain Coffin's widow."

The Maggie turned her head and looked at Lizzie with a strange light in her eyes.

"Let go of this man," Lizzie continued, "and live the rest of your life in peace. He shall be sent to the gallows by a jury of his peers."

"He shall go to the gallows?" The light sparkling in her gaze seemed almost like hope.

"Yes," said Lizzie still holding her hand. "You need not lie and let him free. For then he would forever rule tyrannically over your life, and you shall always be his slave. Do what is best for yourself. My father shall take care of you."

"I shall?" Andrew asked.

"Yes, and I shall make sure you are housed and fed and the rest of your days shall be lived in peaceful happiness. Why, you can even come and work for us! We are looking for a Maggie!"

"We are?" Andrew asked.

The woman smiled with a curious twist in her lips, and then said to Lizzie, "Have no fear. All shall be as it shall be. My love lies deep." Then she turned to the Marshal and said with a renewed sense of vigor, "Let me in to examine him at a closer range. I shall tell you if this is your man or nay."

The Marshal nodded to the police guard, who produced the key to the cell and opened the iron gate. Conway's hand slipped from Lizzie's fingers, and as they did, Lizzie sensed something odd. There was something about her hands. Something...

My love lies deep, Lizzie repeated in the privacy of her head.

As the door swung open, the river of reason that flew through Lizzie's buried mind burst free and in a split second she understood what was happening. With a hair's breadth of time as the interval, Lizzie and the Maggie leapt forward, both women flying as if they had been hurled off their feet by some demonic energy. Someone was yelling, and Lizzie was certain it was herself. Perhaps she was raising an alarm, making an inhuman inarticulate noise, because to explain in rational words would have taken too much time. One split second delay and Fleet-Footed Fleet would be dead.

What Lizzie had seen, or rather felt, all in a flash, were the smooth, white, soft hands of the Maggie, hands that were accustomed to no heavy housework, but instead had enjoyed a lifetime of silk gloves and rose water and glycerin cream. She did not feel the chapped, work-worn calluses of a Maggie, or see the red splotches that would have been impossible to disguise. These were the hands of a lady, not of a servant. These were the hands of a Captain's wife.

My love lies deep.

Before anyone else in the jail cell could move or breathe, Lizzie Borden was tossing her body through the dark air towards the disoriented Fleet, closing the distance between them. As she fell across his body, she saw a flash of light glisten on a pair of scissors: the same scissors that Lizzie had seen disappear that very morning off a cutting table at Hodges & Son and into the bustle of Sarah Coffin when she was disguised as an Irish scullery maid. It was only as the teeth of the scissors plunged with deadly accuracy towards Lizzie's back, when they were about to penetrate into her body with a speed and ferocity that nothing but Providence seemed capable of aborting, that she did recall that Coffin had been standing at the sewing table. In that brief flicker of memory, Lizzie recalled the flash of light off the hard steel disappearing into Sarah Coffin's clothing for concealment.

"For my Captain!" screamed the forlorn widow.

Then the scissors struck home and Lizzie felt as if she had been punched hard in her kidney. For a brief moment, she screamed, hearing loudly the cries of a dying woman, perhaps herself acting as observer to her own murder.

Within the briefest of intervals, Fleet-Footed Fleet had sprung to his feet and tossed Lizzie to the ground like he was dumping his slops onto a midden heap. He roared with a voice filled with fire and savagely grabbed Sarah Coffin about the throat with a massive, knuckled hand. The scissors scattered to the floor and the couple stood silhouetted against the dark light. No one could move, such was the paralysis of fear within the cell. The only sound that could be heard was Sarah Coffin choking as she struggled for her life.

Andrew Jackson Borden broke the tension by stepping forward into the cell. He walked up to Fleet, who barely paid attention to him; such was his intensity upon strangling the Captain's widow. With a strangely casual gesture, Andrew lifted his index finger and pointed it towards Fleet's head.

"Sink my investment, you will!" he shouted, and then, as Fleet's face turned to face Andrew, the finger shot forward and jabbed full force into his eye.

"Gee-yah!" the man screamed, letting go instantly of Coffin's throat. The girl slid down senseless to join Lizzie on the ground.

Fleet danced about with both his hands to his eye, his feet tapping along the stone floor, his movement much like the convulsions of a dying chicken. Then Andrew kicked him in the shins and sent him crashing back down on the prison cot.

Police officers darted forward and all became a chaotic blur. Hodges & Son ran about screaming, raising an alarm. The vagrants in the common lock-up were laughing and hooting, shaking their toothless faces. Somewhere in the middle of a dimly lit dust, the blue pewter-buttoned coats of the officers and the heavy boots of the City Marshal were rolling upon the ground, clashing with the dark patched jacket and wild black hair of the screaming maniac.

"A pestilence upon you all!" he was shouting.

In the midst of the melee, Andrew slid to the floor and found Lizzie. She was shaking her head as if trying to remove cobwebs that blurred her vision.

"Father," she said.

"Lizzie," he said gently, and pressed a palm against her face. "You are unharmed."

"No, Father," she said, amidst the tumult of the police officers, frenzied mutineer, and fabric store owners, "I feel a pain, as if the moments of my life are numbered. Ah! The darkness descends!"

She paused and glanced down at her torso, and then furrowed her brow. Reaching back behind her bustle, she pulled out the silver pin tray that she had completely forgotten since she had entered the police station. There was a hefty ding in its surface as if something hard and metallic had attempted to penetrate it.

"Lizzie!" Andrew said, pointing at the tray. "You have been taking your Fancy, I knew it!"

She held the item up to the light where it shone with an almost-spiritual air.

Then Mr. Hodges, snatching it from her hand, turned it over and examined it with a distended eye. "Young lady," he said, his face reddening. "You'll have to pay for this!"

Lizzie reached up and snatched it back. "Monkey-dash!" she spat. "Just put it on my Father's account!"

New Dawn for the Maggie

Lizzie Borden woke the next morning in her own bed in her tiny room on Second Street. The northern light came down on her, drawing her up towards a new day. As she dressed, she felt the bruise on her backside, a cold reminder of the events of the previous afternoon.

She left her room, alighting directly into the spacious bedroom of her sister Emma. The older sister was standing by the bed staring at Lizzie, her long face betraying no inner thoughts.

"Why, Emma," Lizzie said with a flutter of her lids. "Out and about so early?"

"There are visitors," her sister said, plainly.

Lizzie looked about the comfortable room with its quaint rose wallpaper, generous sunlight and fainting sofa. *Perhaps one day*, Lizzie thought to herself. "I shall have it," she completed the thought out loud.

Emma stared puzzled, opened her mouth as if about to speak, then glided out into the hallway, retreating down the stairs without another word.

Lizzie went down to the sitting room, where, to her surprise, she found Mr. Hodges & Son sitting with her father and smoking cigars. There was an affable and cheery disposition to all, and Lizzie was warmed to see her father so jovial. When he spotted her, he slapped the empty side of the couch on which he sat.

"Come Lizzie! Come sit!" he bellowed, and she slid into place beside him.

"The girl of the hour," Mr. Hodges said and his on nodded, almost reluctantly. "Why, if it wasn't for your fast action we would have been in quite a barrel of spindles, eh, Andrew? Yes, it was fortunate indeed that you are such a keen observer. I never would have guessed that Sarah Coffin was attempting to enact her higher purpose."

"If you mean murdering a man in cold blood," Lizzie said, "then I would consider another phrase besides 'higher purpose.'"

The younger Hodges waved a finger. "The man was a devil. He deserves death regardless of how it comes. I say it would have been best to let him be killed by someone who held a passion for it."

"Her hands are clean of blood," Lizzie said. "If I…if we…had not stopped her, she would have been as tainted as the man she hunted."

"Now, Lizzie," Andrew said, blowing a healthy cloud of smoke into the air. "We need not engage in any philosophical niggling. We are all alive and healthy and happy. Are we not?"

The room was exploding with a round of head nodding and hearty calls of "Yes, 'tis true," when there was a knock upon the front door. As the men conversed, Lizzie went to answer it, and, to her surprise, she saw two women standing on her front stoop. One was Sarah Coffin, now dressed in her blue satin finery and her Lady's cap, and the other, to Lizzie's even greater astonishment, was a young woman dressed in the plain dress of an Irish scullery maid with threadbare bonnet.

"Miss Borden," Sarah said gracefully, holding up a gloved hand for Lizzie to touch. "Forgive me any trespassing on your privacy, but I thought it best to come to your home and thank you personally for the great good you have done for me."

"I am honored," Lizzie said, her lips touching upon a smile.

"I have talked at great length with the City Marshal and I am pleased to say that he is satisfied with my disposition. Yesterday, I was not in my right mind. I was driven by an inner madness that I can barely identify as having come from myself. In my rage and clouded passion, I fear I could have committed murder."

"I am glad that I was instrumental in stopping you," Lizzie said.

"I don't believe anyone can understand a loss such as mine, and what an unhealthy state of mind into which it can put one. I am truly sorry if I have caused any inconvenience in your health, either physical or mental."

"I am doing alright," Lizzie said, with a slight nod.

There was a moment of awkward silence while Sarah Coffin struggled to maintain eye contact with Lizzie, then she stepped back a pace and raised a hand towards the girl behind her. Her small mouth was pressed tight, her eyes cast downwards, her hands thrust into her side pockets.

"May I introduce Fiona Conway, late of County Galway."

The Maggie dipped her knees in a slight bow. "Ma'am," she said.

"I have sought her out," Sarah Coffin said, "to explain to her my role in the affair, and to beg her forgiveness."

"There is nothing you need to apologize for," the Maggie said in an explosive, unexpected burst. "I have told you that in my youth I was glamorized by the man, but now in my clear sight I see him as much the devil as you do. I am glad to see him hang."

"That makes things easier," Sarah Coffin said with a weak smile, then turned back to Lizzie. "I have taken Miss Conway on as my domestic. I will provide for her a bed and a job. She shall not be wanting."

"That is very kind of you," Lizzie said. She reached over and pulled the Maggie's hand and looked her in the eyes. "The very best of luck to you!" she said.

"Thank you, Ma'am," the Maggie said, blushing a faint red, and pulled her hand back.

"Well," Sarah Coffin said, staring up at the sky. "It is a beautiful day, and I do believe I have some fabric shopping to do!"

"Good day to you both," Lizzie said smiling. "And if there is anything I can ever do for either of you, please let me know."

"I shall," Sarah said, and turned to leave. At the bottom of the steps, she paused and turned and looked up at Lizzie. "Miss Lizzie," she said. "If I had done the deed, and become a murderer, would you have judged me?"

Lizzie thought for a moment, a bit distracted by the open-eyed stare of the Maggie, then said carefully, "We all do what we must do…at the exact time that we do it."

Sarah nodded and stared into space as if digesting the words. "Yes," she said finally. "That is a good philosophy of life. I must remember that. Good day to you, Miss Lizzie."

They turned and headed upstreet. Lizzie watched them as they receded into the crowd, crossing through the bustle of the horse-drawn carts and vegetable peddlers. In the distance, a factory yard bell was tolling and the sky overhead was clear blue without any clouds.

All is well in the world, thought Lizzie Borden. *And I have made that happen. All I needed to do was to pay attention to the details. How easy it was to stop evil from happening. Perhaps if I apply these powers to other situations, other people in trouble, I shall stop more bad things from occurring.*

All was indeed well, for due to the mental and physical actions of Lizzie Borden, two tormented women of Fall River have just found their peace. Perhaps three, she added.

"I must think further upon this," she concluded, then closed the door and walked back towards the smoke-filled room of loud, laughing men.

THE END

THE SCULLING BOAT

1868. FERRY STREET, FALL RIVER, MASSACHUSETTS.

ANDREW AND CROOKED JEFFERSON

The small patch of floor behind the sofa arm was always where Little Lizzie played her imaginary games. in that corner of the sitting room, she imagined herself either an explorer pitching a tent on a virgin landscape or a wealthy adventuress rolling away the stone before a great Pharaoh's tomb. In the darkening evenings, the fireplace cast a crackling brilliance on the wall above her and the generous glow from an oil lamp perfected the light she needed to populate the space with a parade of pirates and knights. She called their kingdom Cloudland because it only existed in the fog of her mind.

Little Lizzie's favorite noble to conjure was Sir Andrew who could build anything from a castle to a coffin. He had his charmed adze and hammer and belt of nails and rulers. He was proud, courageous, and willing to take on any job—to build any house, any shop, even a cathedral that, she decided, he could raise to the sky with his own hands. Think of all the money he could save not having to hire any carpenters to help him!

Sir Andrew met with the King of Cloudland every day to bring His Majesty up to date on all the construction happening in the kingdom. He came home every afternoon to his two daughters, whom he loved so well, beyond his own life even. Sir Andrew was the model knight, wise and practical, reasonable, and faithful.

But Cloudland was plagued by the evil pirate Crooked Jefferson, a mutton-chopped monster whose naughtiness knew no limits. What Sir Andrew built up, Crooked Jefferson burned down. What Sir Andrew created, Crooked Jefferson destroyed. Sir Andrew's mills would always burn up in flames, entire blocks of the city laid to waste, and all of   Sir Andrew's beautiful work would be reduced to blackened ash.

Crooked Jefferson lived in a splendid manse that had been financed by the banks on Main Street. And a vast army of workers crawled all over the halls and rooms, maintaining, cleaning, even serving food for Crooked Jefferson's pleasure. You could not get as different a man from Andrew. The two were like day and night, like the glorious sun and the haunted moon.

Lizzie pleaded time and oft with Sir Andrew to raise his hammers in anger and to rid the land of Crooked Jefferson. But Sir Andrew continued to build his city blocks, knowing that at any moment, Crooked Jefferson could release fire from his furnace and consume the city in a great conflagration.

In the lamp-lit space behind the sofa arm, Little Lizzie batted about two iron soldiers that had been given to her by her Uncle John. They had no faces, and their uniforms were tattered, but they had the sturdy fortitude befitting knights of Cloudland.

She shook one and spoke for Sir Andrew: "I refrain from violence against you, Crooked Jefferson, obeying my oath to follow the Lord's principle of turning the other cheek when you slap mine." Then she shook the other soldier: "Then I shall slap the other cheek as well!"

The man who builds and the man who destroys, these two clashed within Lizzie's mind. She often imagined a terrible end, one that she hoped would never happen: Crooked Jefferson takes up a battle-axe from the trophy room of his manse and swings it brutally against the skull of Sir Andrew as he sleeps in his bower. Then Cloudland shall be at his mercy and not even the King and his court advisors would be able to stop his enslavement of the land.

One autumn evening as the night descended on Ferry Street, the entire family gone to bed, including her father and her sister Emma and the woman Abby that her father had married, Little Lizzie got out of bed, crept downstairs, and hid behind the sofa arm where she was able to drift without limit into Cloudland for a special peace conference she had arranged between the Knight and the Pirate. She had encouraged them to talk sensibly to each other, negotiating a treaty that would stop the burning of the mills and put Crooked Jefferson in service to his countryman as a form of penance for his crimes. No one knew exactly what Crooked Jefferson would agree to, but Lizzie Borden knew she could persuade him to act sensibly.

"I would rather put back out to sea and drown myself in a squall than sign a treaty of friendship with Sir Andrew," Crooked Jefferson announced, much to Little Lizzie's surprise.

"Then do so," Sir Andrew said proudly. "We have your brigantine ship-shape and ready for launch. All you need is to lock up the manse and take to the seas. Seek plunder in the lands of the Antipodes and leave your own countryman in peace."

"Argh! I shall not abide!"

"Ayeh! You shall!"

Just as the two were about to clash, a broad, crusted and hairy face shot over the sofa arm, its eyes crinkled and sparkling in the light, its bristly chin stubbled with endless gray hair, and ten fat fingers waggling by the ear.

"Whee!" It said. "Pah!" Then it blew a flappy wind with its tongue.

Little Lizzie screamed and tossed her solders into the air. They clattered to the ground as she crouched down to the floor and threw her arms over her head.

"Please, Grandpa!" she said, her voice muffled. "You scared me!"

"Hey aha!" came the warm and glorious laugh, that mad large laugh that only Grandpa Abraham could summon. He came over the sofa arm like a mountain climbing from its earthen home. *How unusual that he would be here so late*, Little Lizzie thought. *Why was he not back home across the street sitting by the fire and drinking from the big pewter mug that Uncle Hiram had given him last Christmas?*

Her took her in his calming hands and hooked his thumbs under her arms, lifting her over the sofa and settling her down by his side. Overcoming her fright, she carefully opened her eyes and saw his endlessly joyful face, his cherry red cheeks and his wide teeth exposed by his open lips. His cutaway-coat smelled faintly of trout and sported oversized clanky buttons that Lizzie knew all too well. They tapped against her cheek as he hugged her close.

"Playing with your regiment, I see," he said, elbowing her side. "What is it this time? Waterloo? Agincourt? The Bordens were at all those battles, don't you know? I think your father doesn't admit that much, being that he's a moneyman and not a sporting fellow. How are you this twilight, Lizzie? It's a bright, starry evening, isn't it?"

"Grandpa," Lizzie said, calmed by his quips, "I was just contemplating good and evil."

His lips flapped with a surprising gust of wind. "Now what are you bothering your pretty head with that business for?" he asked, perturbed but still smiling. "Such thoughts for a seven-year-old."

Lizzie crossed her arms and pouted. "I'm almost eight!" she insisted.

"Ah, yes. I forgot your party is soon coming. There is much to celebrate; you should be thinking of floral arrangements and gardening tips. Perhaps a bit of interior decorating, cheer the place up a bit. What do you think?"

"No, I want to understand, Grandpa. I don't want to go through my entire life and not understand why bad people exist."

"Well, that's quite a task you've set for yourself. But you know the universities are chock full of scholarly minds that are trying to figure that out. And the libraries are bursting with books by those very folks trying to explain it all to the rest of us folks."

"What about the church?" Lizzie said. "We go to congregation on Sunday and Dr. Adams talks about people who are good and other people who are bad."

"Yes, that's another way to approach the subject, I suppose," Grandpa said, "but I don't reckon Dr. Adams has come to any great conclusion any more than the university scholars I told you about. I guess it's all still a mystery."

"Well, why can't we solve the mystery? Someone must have some clues."

He settled her on his knee. "You know, Lizzie, mysteries aren't that easy to solve, you have to have a unique combination of talents and I'm afraid the Bordens are a more practical family. We build things, start a bank, or a boat line, or a cotton mill. That's what we do; we don't tackle the big questions."

"But I can solve mysteries," Lizzie said, impatiently. "I solved one the other day."

"You did, didn't you?" He rubbed his chin with a stubby hand.

"Yes, for my sister Emma. She was in quite a dodgy situation."

"Emma? But she's so much older than you!"

"Yes, Emma's ever so clever. But I'm..." Lizzie's eyes blinked as she searched for the word, "...cleverer," she concluded.

"Can you tell me how you did it? I'd be delighted to hear it." His eyebrows shortened and his ragged teeth peered out from his lips.

THE SCULLING BOAT

Lizzie began. "I saw Emma posting some envelopes, and she looked quite sad. She was trembling and could hardly hold the wrappers. I asked her if everything was alright, and she said, 'Oh Lizzie, I am afraid that I am bewitched.' And I said, 'Dear Emma, you can't be bewitched; you are a darling girl and will do great things in your life.'

"'No, Lizzie,' she said. 'I can prove that I am touched with evil. Remember last month when I went to Marion to visit with the Stoves? I had a very grand time there and I learned ever so much, including how to hook bait and choose a sinker and I even caught a trout! But on the afternoon that Josephine Barclay and her family were going to return to Fall River, she asked me to row out on the bay with her where we could spend some time and talk about all the things that we daren't discuss in front of her parents. So after dinner, we went to the dock and got into the sculling boat and bailed out the water so we could have some dry feet, then we cast it off into the water. We had a dear time, just the two of us, rowing and watching the clouds float over Marion, and commenting on all the little homes at the edges of the bay and how each little house was filled with a funny little captain who was going to go off and get whale oil or carry some load of coal off to some foreign war. It was ever so exciting, and then we started talking about that book by Mr. Melville about the captain who had one leg and was so angry at the whale.'

"'By that time and hour had passed since we left the house and the clouds were turning to dark, like they were meaning to rain, so we went back to shore and kicked our feet up on the pilings at the water edge. Then I began to get very drowsy and tranquil and full of wonderful thoughts, and I wanted to go to sleep. But Josephine was talking and I wished that she weren't there. I wished that I were completely alone. Then, before I can blink my eyelashes one more time, she was gone. Vanished, almost before my eyes, and so was the sculling boat. It just vanished.'

"And I said, 'Emma that's impossible.'"

"'Perhaps,' she replied, 'but it happened. One moment I was watching Josephine standing by the water, the sculling boat bobbing in the waves, and the next I was completely alone, no Josephine, not even the boat. I went to the water and looked about but the boat was nowhere to be seen. It had vanished as quickly as my friend. I went back to the house and found that the Barclays had already packed up and left Marion.

Their buggy wasn't in the carriage house and the front door was locked. It was ever so disturbing. And the sun being behind the clouds made everything very haunted.'"

"'Did the sun ever come out again?' I asked"

"'Why no,' she told me. 'It never did. I went back to the Stove's house on a dirt road shadowed by trees and it was as if it where night. I arrived just in time for supper and told them I had made a whole family disappear. No one believed me and said I was telling nonsense. I didn't even see them the day after, or the day after that. I guess Josephine and her parents are wandering in some sort of limbo, sent there by my own wicked thoughts. Maybe Josephine's taken the sculling boat so she will have something to sit in because I don't think they have floors in limbo. You kind of float there. Poor Josephine. I willed her into nothing, and her entire family as well. Oh, Lizzie I didn't mean to do that, I just wanted to be alone on the dock so I could sleep.' And she began to cry."

"I asked her to repeat a few small details of her story and then it occurred to me. It suddenly seemed so simple that I began to laugh, and Emma thought I was laughing at her. 'No, my dear sister, I think there's a perfectly common-sense explanation. Didn't you say you had set out for the docks right after dinner and that you had to bail some water out of the boat before you could cast it off into the water?'"

"'Why, yes,' Emma replied."

"'And didn't you say that you were only with Josephine for an hour and then you went to the Stove's and arrived just as they were starting supper?'"

"'Why, yes,' Emma said"

"'How did all that time elapse between the time you finished dinner and the time the Stove's had their supper? That must have been about four hours, at least. How do you account for all that time? The answer is quite simple: when you were on the dock wishing for Josephine to leave you alone, you were drowsy, watching the clouds drift, and tired from rowing the sculling boat. So you feel asleep, dear Emma. Josephine didn't vanish, you did, or at least the part of you that's in your head while you are awake. Josephine, not wanting to disturb your slumber, must have slipped away and found her family preparing for their journey back to Plymouth. You slept for two hours, perhaps three; there is no way of telling. Your friend was just being polite.'"

"Emma sat for a long time and said to me, 'I am suffering embarrassment, Lizzie. Your explanation is quite simple, indeed, and I'm afraid it has made me blush. The distance in time between dinner and supper did not occur to me; I shall be more observant next time.' Then her eyes brightened and she said, 'However, you still have not explained the disappearance of the sculling boat. The Barclays certainly couldn't have taken it with them. Where do you suppose it went?'"

"I said to her, 'Considering how the boat had to be bailed before you could take her out, I merely speculate that the sculling boat was taking on water and simply sank to the bottom of the Bay while you slept. Perhaps if one were to dive down off the dock into those waters, one would find it scuttled on the rocks below.'"

"Emma didn't say much to me after that, but quickly left the room."

"And did anyone in Marion check your theory?" Abraham said with a grin on his florid face.

Lizzie nodded. "The very next day, father sent a boy over to the town to check the dock. Sure as punch, Grandpa, the sculling boat was found below the water line, just where I had said it would be."

"My Lord," Abraham squawked, punching her upper arm, "that was a marvelous bit of investigation. And you did it all from your bedroom in Fall River, didn't even have to go visit the scene. Lizzie, there is something remarkable about you. In future years, we'll have to put those talents of yours to good use."

"Thank you, Grandpa. Maybe you can get Emma to speak to me again. She whimpers and runs away every time she sees me."

"Ah, I shall see what I can do. Now tell me, what do you have there? Iron men? And with their colors on no less! My how toys have grown. My father gave me a wood block and said, 'Do your best, you silly twit!'"

"This is Sir Andrew the Knight," Lizzie said proudly. Then her face darkened. "And this is Crooked Jefferson. He burns down Sir Andrew's mills."

Abraham's face brightened. "Then we'll just have to get an army and protect your father's mills!"

"My father?" Lizzie replied. "He doesn't have any mills. He builds furniture."

"Yes, Lizzie," Abraham replied. "That he does. But don't you think it's any less noble than Sir Andrew's works? Your father has done great things in his time. You see that City Hall building up the street? His hands helped to build that. And when you go to Jefferson Borden's house on fancy Canal Street and sit at his dining table, who do you think built the chair you're sitting on? Don't for one moment make your father any less than what he is."

Lizzie's voice shriveled. "I don't want to go to Jefferson Borden's house," she said. "I'm scared of him." And she threw one of the iron soldiers down to the floor where it lay crooked against the sofa.

"I see," Abraham said. "Well, remember what you were saying a few moments back about good and evil? Well, sometimes they're not divided between two little men like you have in those iron soldiers. Sometimes there's a little bit of a Jefferson in an Andrew. You may not see it now, my dear, but one day...yes, one day."

"I don't like it!" she said, pursing her lips and holding Sir Andrew tightly against her chest. "I'm going to find out all of Crooked Jefferson's crimes and punish him for every last one!"

"Just like you found the sculling boat?" Abraham laughed and kissed her forehead. "Ah, there's a great woman inside you, Lizzie Borden. Your grandfather's very proud of you!"

Little Lizzie rested plaintively against his coat and took refuge in his odor, which was like oak leaves in the rain. His pockmarked face had weathered many years and Lizzie could only imagine living as long as he. His confidence in her brilliance warmed her greatly, but the unsettled fear of the iron man on the floor still gripped her and made it harder for her to breathe.

Despite the simple solution to Emma's problem on the Marion dock, Lizzie knew that there was another possible explanation: the notion that Crooked Jefferson, with his twisted shoulder, ugly mouth, and odorous breath, had been to Marion that day, and seeing two innocent girls enjoying themselves on the placid waters, decided to introduce some mischief. And then he separated the girls, sank the boat, and placed the idea in Emma's impressionable head that she was possessed, that whereso'ere she now roams, she will carry with her the shadow of black magic, like darkening rain clouds that obscure the presence of the sun. Now her sister, who often blamed herself for everything bad that had occurred, was forever shrouded in a robe of self-doubt, even fear, of her own evil.

Little Lizzie's brilliant solution to the Mystery of the Sculling Boat had made Emma even more afraid. Emma, who had promised Lizzie's mother on her deathbed to protect her baby sister from all the harms of the world, now needed protection from herself, and only Lizzie Borden, Girl Detective, could solve the mystery and make the world a better and safer place.

THE END

THE SINGLE HATCHET THEORY

BY ARLEN SPECTOR BORDEN

FALL RIVER HERALD, APRIL 23, 1893

The faculty of Reason is all that separates the snarling beast in the field that rolls in his own excrement from the cultured gentleman in his Parlor Room who smokes his tobacco and reads his Longfellow. Reason is a gift that has been bestowed upon our species as a tool that enables us to master the Elements and defeat dark ignorance. Reason fits hand in glove with Wisdom, which we can define as that which is derived from the lessons of experience that have been revealed to us by Reason.

Having said all this, I must declare that it is with the hammer of Reason that I shall shatter all myths about the recent Fall River Tragedy that has been bandied about so much in our press. Many people who have turned their amateur microscopes at the brutal slayings of Andrew Jackson Borden and his wife Abby Durfee Borden seem to have abandoned the faculty of Reason and fallen into the crucible of delusory thinking. The end result of this has been a multiplicity of theories, some of which have yielded some piddling fruit, others of which has been festooned with laughable conclusions and misguided perceptions. It is only with Reason that we shall arrive at a solution that satisfies all known facts, as well as destroys into dust all false theories.

For the benefit of my cultured audience, and I do presume the readers of the *Herald* are men of esteemed education and civilized accomplishment, I must explain that my primary source for much of the material you will see is not one that can be explained through Reason. This is the one failing of which I plead *mea culpa*. However, it is my esteemed opinion that the introduction of spiritual agents into this tale of rational detection does not in any aspect take away from the positive materialistic stance of the theory or the evidence.

It was upon a dreary night in December that I, in my shirt sleeves, climbed in bed, all gussied up for a perfectly calm and peaceful sleep on the barge that will carry me towards dawn. But before my heavy lids could come together into that death-like repose that we welcome each and every evening, there was a whispery moan and a muddied white figure floated across the room near the foot of my bed. I shivered and asked it, "What do you want of me?" and it said very plainly, "Revenge!"

After some discourse, I discovered that the apparition was from the future, and that it was stuck between worlds, occluded from ordinary time. It seems to have come from Texas, where it had suffered some horrific disruption of its spiritual journey and was now wandering, lusting in its heart for retribution.

"What can I do?" I asked. "How may I help in alleviating your suffering?"

"Tell the truth!" it said in a voice I shall carry to my chilled grave. "Let it be known there was only one bullet!"

It then proceeded to tell me a tale that seemed to come from the pages of H.G. Welles or Jules Verne more so than from ordinary human history. It told of a very wealthy politician who was traveling in an engine propelled carriage that had no horse, and he was struck down by an assassin, a grisly anarchist who had hidden himself in the upper story of a warehouse. From that gunman's perch, armed with a musket of uncanny range, the assassin fires three bullets, one of which missed the politician, the third of which struck him in the head, thereby effecting his death, but the second which passed through his throat and went on to strike another politician who sat in the carriage before him.

It is hard to discuss this in the past tense, since the apparition claims that the event will not happen for at least another 70 years. In Texas, he said, and I made a small reminder to myself to write to the Texas governor at the next possible opportunity to give him advanced warning!

THE END

ABOUT THE AUTHOR

Richard was born and spent most of his boyhood in the garden Bay neighborhood of Queens, NY. In his teen years Richard and his family moved into the Forest Hills neighborhood of Queens, and then in his early adulthood, Richard's work brought him to suburban New Jersey, although he was always a New Yorker in his heart and soul. While living in New Jersey, Richard met and married his wife Anna, and soon afterward they moved to New England. It was in this, the happiest period of his life, that Richard was able to focus on his writing, filmmaking, and podcasting.

Richard and Anna co-founded Nine Muses Books so they could personally publish his writings, including his *Lizzie Borden, Girl Detective* series of mysteries, for which he is best known. Richard wrote easily in many genres, in both fiction and non-fiction. His fiction short stories and non-fiction essays have been published in a variety of journals. He was also a lecturer on historic Victorian women and on silent film comedy. Richard also was a budding actor and appeared in several local plays. His GardenBayFilms Channel on YouTube contains a variety of short films Richard made, mostly centered on Lizzie Borden. Richard's *Lizzie Borden Podcast*, available on iTunes, examines the Lizzie Borden case with various historians, as well as contains a radio play of *The Agitated Elocutionist*, one of his Girl Detective short stories.

Richard had plans to continue to create films, write stories, deliver more lecture series, and to interview more historians for his podcast, but his ill health caused him to put his plans on hold. When he learned that he did not have much time left, he said, "But I am not finished yet!" After it became tragically clear that Richard would not recover, he indicated to his wife that he wished his writing to be published posthumously.

Anna, with the help of Richard's sister Susan, gathered Richard's writings and sorted the finished pieces into three different books: Richard's personal writings, which would be part of his Garden Bay Stories; his non-fiction essays, which would be part of the *Of Moons and Monoliths* essay collection; and his Lizzie Borden, Girl Detective stories collected into one complete volume, *The Audible Amnesiac and other Lizzie Borden Girl Detective Mysteries.*

Richard is sorely missed, but he leaves us a legacy of fine work in a variety of media and genres.

AN INTERVIEW WITH AUTHOR RICHARD BEHRENS ABOUT LIZZIE BORDEN, GIRL DETECTIVE

How did you first come up with the concept of Lizzie Borden being a girl detective?

I happened to order a few old Nancy Drew books over EBay. My intention was to read them for fun since my sister had all of them when I was growing up and I had read several when I was in grade school. Reading as an adult, I now find them so breezy and a lot of fun, but I was surprised how much sinister stuff was in them. The older 1930s Nancy Drew smoked and actually carried a gun. This opened up the possibilities of an alternative vision of a girl detective, one drawing on the Nancy Drew model but with larger dimensions. So I decided to sketch out a spoof of the genre, just for fun. I made up a girl detective living in the 1930s. Her father is a big attorney in town and she has a kooky house maid and sidekick pal from school, etc. But when I wrote a few pages and read it back, it seemed too much like the original, like I couldn't spoof it because it already had that comic edge to it. The only thing I could do to make it funnier was to place it in another century. I toyed around with a few time periods. For a while I wanted to do London during the time of Queen Elizabeth, so the girl detective could be the illegitimate daughter of the Earl of Southampton and have access to people like Shakespeare and solve the death of Christopher Marlowe. But I admit I got lazy and felt it would involve too much research. I had already been reading about Lizzie Borden and visiting the Bed & Breakfast and all that Fall River stuff was fresh in my mind. So I sketched out a girl detective in New England during the 1890s. She can solve the Borden murders, I joked. Then it hit me like a thunderbolt. Why not make her Lizzie Borden? After writing a few pages I had myself in stitches and I knew I had hit upon something with great entertainment value. The Borden Family turned out to be a better source of satire and drama than an Elizabethan theater company.

Did you have any hope at that point of getting it published?

I felt it had great commercial potential. The title alone made everyone crack up. But it was still a few years before books like Abraham Lincoln, Vampire Hunter and all those Jane Austen monster mash-ups so I wasn't quite sure. Besides I had to write the stories first and see how they turned out. Fortunately, I had an offer from The Hatchet magazine, the journal of Lizzie Borden studies, to pursue this and had help from a few people who knew a lot about the historical Bordens. Talking to them and visiting Fall River gave me a lot of inspiration. With the great encouragement of Stefani Koorey, I began publishing the stories in *The Hatchet* and its sister magazine *The Literary Hatchet* and felt content with that for a few years. The concept was still taking shape. What did you have to do to prepare for writing about Lizzie Borden? I chatted up everyone I knew who had connections with Fall River or the historic house. I visited the Fall River Historical Society, studied as much Fall River history as I could, and read thousands of pages of primary source material including the murder hearings, the trial transcripts and the few books that could be historically trusted. Two of the best references are *Lizzie Borden: Past and Present* by Len Rebello and *Parallel Lives* by Michael Martins and Dennis Binette of the Fall River Historical Society. So many books out there are junk, especially the true crime paperbacks. The best book for an introductory experience is actually a graphic novel called *The Borden Tragedy* by Rick Geary. It's accurate, extremely well drawn and scripted. The challenge was that I wasn't writing about the murders, but about a time period nearly twenty years earlier. I had to really get to know the 1870s as Lizzie and her family would have known it.

You eventually progressed from short stories to novels?

Yes, the first five short stories, two of them novellas really, were published by PearTree Press in 2010 and it brought to the end the first stage of my effort. The second stage, now that I had established the characters, the setting, and had hit upon an appropriate tone, was to enlarge the fictional universe. *The Minuscule Monk* was a sixth short story that had grown in scope to a full-length novel. I had been reading a lot about the Kansas-Missouri border wars and it seemed as if an extended flashback to another time and place was appropriate. Arthur Conan Doyle wrote two Sherlock Holmes stories that had extended flashbacks to the old West and Pennsylvania mining towns. For half of those novels, Holmes doesn't' even show up. I liked the idea of having all that back story.

Why did you start Nine Muses Books?

The scope of the project had grown to the point where I needed to dedicate myself entirely to the Girl Detective. The e-book market has grown exponentially in the past few years and the traditional relationship between writers, readers and publishers has completely changed. Putting out all this material in such a short time period is an experiment, one that I hope will reach new readers and keep them amused. It also encourages me to work harder on new material.

After The Minuscule Monk, what can we expect?

There's more short stories coming. The next novel is called *The Wilmarth Immovables* and it has a lot to do with Shakespeare, patent medicine, and the origins of vaudeville. (Editor's Note: Sadly, this story remains incomplete so it will not be published.)

The last question I have is the obvious one. Did Lizzie do it?

Well, that's a question for the sixth novel! I do plan to cover that. (Editor's Note: Sadly, this story remains incomplete so it will not be published.)

OK, fair enough. What about the real Lizzie Borden?

I have no idea. The more I studied the crime, the less obvious it seemed. Everyone has to make up their own minds.

www.ingramcontent.com/pod-product-compliance
Lightning Source LLC
Chambersburg PA
CBHW070155260626
47160CB00002B/347